HEART OF NIGHT

BOOKS BY ANGELINA J. STEFFORT

THE WINGS OF INK SERIES
Wings of Ink
Heart of Night

THE QUARTER MAGE SERIES
The Quarter Mage
The Hour Mage
The Never Mage
The Ever Mage

THE SHATTERED KINGDOM SERIES
Shattered Kingdom
Wicked Crown
Shadow Rule
Lost Towers
Secret Court
Dark Refuge
Reborn Throne
Fatespun

THE TWO WORLDS SERIES
Blood of Two Worlds
Heir of Oblivion
Knight of Redemption
Rule of Dominion

THE BREATH OF FATE SERIES
Torn
Unraveled
Unforgiven
Tethered

THE WINGS SERIES
White
Black
Gray
Spark
Fire
Ashes
Crash

HEART OF NIGHT

OF

ANGELINA J. STEFFORT

HEART OF NIGHT

THIS BOOK IS PART OF THE

First published 2024

Ebook: ISBN 9783903357747
Print: ISBN 9783903357839

Cover by Fantastical Ink.

www.ajsteffort.com

"To live without hope is to cease to live."
—Fyodor Dostoyevsky

Cliffs of Ansoli

Ansoli

A R E A

Seeing Forest

Plithian Plains

Fort Perenis

Meer

T A V R A S

Gulf of
Tears

Dunai

Horn of
Eroth

Quiet Sea

SOUTHERN CONTINENT

ONE

AYNA

Lentil soup is something I'll never get used to. I hated it back in prison, and I'm certainly hating it now when it comes with a side of gloating evil.

It's been three days since I woke in this suffocating space of russet, cream, and too many ornamentations, and my body still doesn't feel right. Where strength and determination once were moving my limbs and my magic, shaky weakness is all that's left. The constant nausea hasn't ebbed either. Quite the opposite—whenever I think of what happened in the Seeing Forest, it's like I'm spiraling into a nightmare because, when I come back to reality, I'm in this luxurious room where my wounds don't hurt and the air tastes of lilies so much it turns my stomach with every breath. Whereas, in my nightmares, I see endless oceans of fire consuming everything and everyone I love. I see them die one by one.

I'm not surprised to watch my father and the pirate captain I once loved go up in flames; the guilt for their deaths has been hovering over me for too long. What's new is the handsome pale face of the Crow King, motionless like a marble statue before me as I cry tears of despair and fury.

Those tears can never escape when Ephegos is in the room with me, though, for he can never know how close to breaking I am.

As if summoning his attention with my thoughts, the traitor Crow glances up from the piece of parchment he's reading, training his malicious focus on me with all the ice I'd never believed could show in such warm brown eyes. Although I've been here for a few days, it still comes as a surprise how someone whom I once called *friend* can have betrayed us so deeply. It's a wound entirely different from my splintered heart where Myron's death has left an irreparable mark.

I'll never be the same, and both Ephegos and I know it. Ever since I woke in the mockery of comfort that is this room, I've been holding on by a thread—and that is without the pain in my limbs and spine where the traces of battle are still showing.

Myron might have healed the stab wound in my side, but he didn't have enough energy left to heal me completely before he exhaled his last breath and left me behind in this world where nothing but pain and heartache is waiting for me. And fury. Endless fury at the thought of what Myron did. He fucking sacrificed himself for me.

Biting back the tears building behind my eyes, I take another spoonful of lentil soup and focus on the blandness of the taste. It's all I can do not to scream my rage at the Guardians. It should have been me, not him. He should have lived to see the curse broken, and I should have died for my own blindness, for my failure to understand sooner that only love could break a curse like the one the Neredynian gods placed on the Crows.

"You should eat more than a few spoons, Ayna," Ephegos says in that soothing voice I know is as fake as the smiles he used to give me. When I still believed he was a friend … while in secret, he'd been out for my blood.

I spit the soup in his general direction, watching it land on the plush carpet beside the bed where I'm sitting propped up against thick pillows.

In response, Ephegos clicks his tongue in a vivid reminder of the days he used to have a beak to click at me, and I suppress the impulse to shrink into the silken softness behind me.

"Not very becoming of a queen, that behavior," he scolds, smoothing back his rye blond hair in a practiced manner that tells me nothing he does is coincidental. From his smile to when and how he laces his fingers in his lap in a gesture so casual he could merely be a male feeling comfortable enough to lean back in his chair and keep his hands far from the knives strapped to his belt.

But Ephegos is a spymaster. He used to be the one bringing information from the borders of the Seeing Forest to the Crow King, but I know now that Myron wasn't the only one to whom he delivered information.

"As betraying one's best friend isn't becoming of ... well, anyone." I give him a grin of gritted teeth, which I intend to be scarier than I actually achieve since Ephegos laughs one of those warm laughs I had once considered affectionate. Now I know it's as fake as the crease of concern between his brows when I catch him studying me from afar sometimes. As if he is indeed worried.

Which he probably is, just not about me—my health or my mental well-being—but about how long it will take until Royad or Clio will find us and make quick work of him—or slow work by torturing him until his blood dyes the fucking plush carpets the color of his suffering. I just hope they are alive to get to me before he can execute whatever evil plan he's harboring in that traitor's mind of his.

"Can you truly call it *betrayal* if I haven't considered Myron my friend in a long time? Longer than you've walked this realm, Ayna."

I hate the sound of my name on his lips, hate how smoothly he delivers a truth, managing to cut all the way to the center of my chest all over again.

"If you intend to insult me by implying I'm young and naive, by all means, try." There is no way he can do any worse than what he's already done. He can't kill Myron all over again, and if he intends to watch me wallow in my own misery, he's welcome to take a first-row seat. I don't have any fight left in me other than proving the bastard wrong. I'm not going to break after everything.

"Not insult you, Ayna. I wouldn't dream of it. You're still the same delightful creature you were the day I first met you. It's nothing against you—"

"Then why? Why bring me here, wherever here is?" I haven't managed to get that piece of information out of him, and I'm not ready to beg him to tell me. Not yet. "Why not kill me like you did with your *king*?" Treason is the word I don't need to speak because it's in every glare I give him, in every breath I take in his presence.

Ephegos straightens out of his chair, revealing the russet brocade upholstery, and paces to the arched window overlooking a small, forest-framed garden. It's the only window in this Guardiansforsaken room, and it reveals nothing of value that might tell me where I am—other than that it has to be a noble residence for all the comforts the room offers like the spacious bathing room furnished in porcelain and brass.

"That is for me to know and for you to never find out," he answers with one of those looks allowing me to glimpse the full evil behind the polished facade of the Crow Courtier and spy.

"Never, because I'll be dead soon enough?" I square my shoulders, debating leaping out of bed and using my spoon as a weapon the moment he turns his back. At least, it would be something better than my teeth and nails—which I would gladly use if they ensured me any chance at freedom—when I can't get my hands on a blade. But where strength hummed before, I can barely sit up, let alone wield a weapon of any sort.

My magic hasn't responded since the battle at the palace. Whether it's because I depleted myself and it will take time for it to return or because it died when my heart splintered at the sight of Myron dead, I can't tell. I can't even think about it without falling into despair. All I know is that I'd have used the soup to boil Ephegos's eyes had I had a thread of my power left to hurl it at him.

But I've become useless, a means to exact a personal vendetta on a male who no longer is around to witness it.

I bite back a tear.

No tears. *No* tears. It's the thought I cling to so I don't fall into despair. As long as I don't shed those tears in front of my captor, I can keep at least the semblance of strength when I try not to imagine the brands of torture he has in store for me.

"Not dead, Ayna. I have something better planned for you."

I clasp the spoon harder, suppressing my shudder at his words.

Let's see how Myron's ghost will like it when I watch his bride wither away just like he watched my sister fade and die. That's what he'd said when I'd woken to this nightmare of comfort and luxury. Something I don't deserve after everything, after failing yet again to save someone I loved.

"Something *better*?" I challenge. "You mean something *worse*."

Ephegos doesn't even have the decency to hide his amusement at my remark. "Depends on who you refer to."

I refuse to ask the question he's set me up to ask, staring him down with cold determination. Icy and hard like my heart when I manage to shove down those painful memories of Myron's beautiful face, lifeless and dead, and…

I'm not going there or the tears will spill.

"And I assume you aren't inclined to let me out of this room today either." It's not a question when he made it clear the first time I woke that I'm a prisoner. That I won't see more of this place than the obnoxiously comfortable room I'm being kept in and the slice of sky and garden outside the window.

"I'm glad you're such a quick learner. It will come in handy in the future." The look he gives me informs me that, whatever this future is, I won't like it.

I'm trying not to dwell on the fact that he's using the word *future* as if referring to a longer timespan rather than a few painful weeks leading to my eventual death, so whatever torture he has in mind will be slow. I try not to quake with fear at the mere thought of what he must be capable of if he so easily sold out his best friend and his entire people to take revenge for a death Myron had no hand in.

"You're insane," I tell him instead of begging him to let me go, instead of reasoning with him. I've tried appealing to his kinder side before, and it didn't end well. A purple bruise is still blooming on my jaw where he struck to shut me up, to show me that he wasn't kind at all and I should never attempt to appeal to that supposed softer side of him, which he doesn't have.

It's easier to show him hatred; he knows what to do with that, and there is no reasoning with the mad.

"Finally something you got right, Ayna." The smirk he gives me makes a chill creep through my bones. "Now get out of bed and clean up. We have visitors coming over." Before I can ask him who, he's on his feet and heading for the door. "Don't disappoint me, Ayna."

I'm too weak to throw the half-empty bowl of soup after him, but I flip my middle finger at his back, tears shooting into my eyes at the realization that it's the only thing I can really do. There's no escaping this place without my strength or my magic, and Ephegos is doing all he can to keep me weak. He doesn't even need chains to keep me shackled to the bed, and no matter how hard I try to believe that things will turn for the better, there's a part of me that has given up since the moment I laid eyes on Myron's lifeless form.

This is my new prison.

And I'm never getting out of here.

TWO

AYNA

When I make my way to the bathing room, a set of clothes has already been laid out for me. For a moment, I stare at the elaborate blue and eggshell silk and the myriads of golden and russet blossoms embroidered into the fabric of the bodice. My feet are unstable, as are my hands, but I lock the door behind me and strip out of the plain linen shirt and pants I've been wearing the past days, focusing on the task at hand. The bruise on my jaw has turned a shade lighter since I last looked at it, but it hurts like the wrath of the Guardians when I run my fingers along the tender spot. It will be a challenge to bathe myself with the hundred ways my body is inclined to fail me, but my strength of will is the best weapon I have—against Ephegos and against my own weakness.

So, I take a stabilizing breath and untie my hair, running my fingers through the long, ash-blonde tresses while I brace one hand on the edge of the clawfoot tub to stabilize myself.

If Ephegos is dead set on my being presentable, it must be someone important coming to take a look at me, or he wouldn't have placed a dress fit for a queen in here. A silent part of me wonders when he did it, if he sometimes sneaks into my room when I sleep. The thought alone makes me want to scream in horror. I'll have nightmares of a different sort for sure now.

Getting into the filling tub is an exercise in self-control, but I manage. Since Ephegos didn't give me a time limit, I don't rush as I submerge myself in the hot water. I haven't felt clean since the moment I woke in this place, and I'm reluctant now to wash away the last of the battle stuck under my nails and in my hair, but if there is one thing I've learned during my time at the Crow Palace, it's that appearance impacts greatly how strong or weak one is perceived. Whomever Ephegos is bringing to visit, I'm inclined to look my best, to wear whatever clothes he provided like armor and my smile like a shield. As long as I can keep that up, Ephegos hasn't won. As long as I don't break, I haven't let Myron down.

For a heartbeat, I imagine his deep voice rumbling his agreement, that I can take whatever comes my way. Then I remember that I'll never hear that voice again, and my heart splinters all over again, a million pieces that not even my steel will can hold together.

It takes me three rounds of soap to get all the grime and suds out of my hair, but when I get out of the tub, I smell of lilies and rosewood, and I'm clean in a way that makes me want to check if the bath washed away my memories as well.

They are right there, striking with a vengeance as I conjure Myron's death-pale features, the strong, featherless arms I got to see only once. The blood smeared on his chest where Clio tried to close his wound with her healing magic.

Tears fall onto the white marble of the floor, mingling with the water dripping from my hair, and I pretend I'm not crying. I pretend that I can put on that dress and be fine long enough to convince Ephegos that torturing me will not do anything to Myron's ghost. That there is no such thing as anyone's ghost, and if there were, Myron's would certainly not care what happened to me.

Ghosts don't need to exist for Myron's memory to haunt me. It will until the end of my days, and whatever Ephegos has in store for me can't be half as bad as watching Myron die in my sleep over and over again, knowing he chose my life over his.

With a shaky breath, I comb out my hair and pull it up into a tight bun—there is no way I'll make a shred of effort for Ephegos and whatever mysterious visitor he's expecting—before I pick up the heap of silk and blossoms on the carved wooden stool.

In another life, I might have appreciated the dress. The bodice is tight and covers my breasts in a sweetheart neckline before it continues in a nude fabric ending in an ice-blue silk high collar. The long, sheer sleeves are wide enough to slip in easily, but when I turn before the mirror to take in the pattern of flowers embroidered all over my torso and arms, it's something else that catches my attention.

On my right shoulder blade, stretching to my neck and spreading on the back of my upper arm, a large black form covers my skin. Instead of buttoning the high collar at the back of my neck, I pull the shoulder of the dress down to take a closer look and gasp as I recognize what I'm looking at.

A crow is inked into my skin, its outline a swirl of black and its shading like blotches of ink spreading on wet paper.

How it got there, I can't even begin to understand, unless Ephegos took the liberty to tattoo me while I was knocked out after the battle. But if this was a fresh tattoo, I'd know. The skin would have been raw and painful in the hot water, and sleeping on it would have been painful. I remember from when the guards at Fort Perenis inked the slender chain that is a sign of all inmates around my right wrist. I was in pain for days.

Whatever this is, it's not new. It can't be old either. I'd remember if I'd gotten a tattoo at the Crow Palace.

Before I can panic, someone knocks, and Ephegos's voice sounds through the heavy wooden door. "Time to get ready, Ayna. Your visitor is approaching."

Jerking into motion, I almost rip off the sleeve of my dress, and it's all I can do to hold onto the edge of the cupboard as the world starts swaying before my eyes like a nutshell on the ocean.

"Are you still in there?" There isn't a hint of concern in his tone, only smooth coldness. "I don't like to let people wait."

Different from the bathing room I tried to escape from on my first day in Myron's palace, this one doesn't have a window. "There is nowhere I could go, is there?" I snap with more strength than I expected to muster. "I'll be done in a moment."

Smoothing out the eggshell-hued silk layers of my skirts, I straighten then close the two buttons of the collar behind my neck. When I open the door, I try not to let my hatred show—or my despair. Keeping my face devoid of all emotion is the best I can do to give Ephegos as little as possible to work with. But he's known me for too long to understand how to land a hit, and so he does when he looks me over with a grin laced with malice. "Myron never deserved you, Wolayna. You were always too beautiful for a monster like him."

I bite back that he's the monster because, if I start down that path now, I might end up with another bruise on my face. I also don't think of the tattoo on my shoulder. Ephegos hasn't been known for giving answers. At least, not since the day he tried to tell me the Crows couldn't fully shift. That was right before the first Fire Fairy attack. The attack where he faked his death and joined his new allies.

"Too bad he's dead…" Clicking his tongue, he holds out his arm as if expecting I'd even consider touching him. "It would have been the best of entertainment seeing him study you with that starved hunger of his. You know, the way he always looked at you when you turned your back."

I cringe at the implication of his words. Before Myron and I had gotten close, all he ever showed me was his cold indifference, a cruel Crow King who cares for nothing and no one. Then we made the pact about him setting me free at the next Ret Relah if I managed to survive until then. Knowing how long he'd been waiting for me burned like a white-hot iron in my chest. We could have had more time together had I not been so blind. Had I been able to admit to myself how I felt, I might have broken the curse sooner and saved them all before the Fire Fairy attack.

"It doesn't matter now, does it? There can always be some-one else to admire you." The way he says it sends a shiver of wrongness down my spine, and there is something about the way my legs are unsteady that tells me falling and pretending to faint might be a good idea. Then, I wouldn't put it past Ephegos to slap me awake or dump a bucket of ice water over my head just to watch my terror and pain.

"It doesn't," I confirm. "And I don't need any admirers."

At that, Ephegos whirls on me, his warm brown eyes sparking with amusement, the expression so much the court-ier I got to know at the Crow Palace that my heart aches for a beat. But I catch myself before I can return the smile he gives me.

"Good. Because I most definitely don't admire you, Ayna. You're a pathetic creature. Not magical, yet not hu-man enough anymore to just die like you were supposed to."

"What do you mean *not human enough*?" My heart picks up pace at what could have been a slip-up or a deliberately dropped comment.

"Ah … wouldn't you like to know…" He paces ahead, gesturing at the small sitting area of russet brocade chairs and a carved table that could be of any origin in Eherea, but the wood is dark enough to remind me of the furniture in my father's old merchant office.

I try not to allow it to distract me from the obvious bait Ephegos laid out for me. Another truth he owns and that he can now dangle before me like a tool of torture of its own.

"What do you mean *not human enough*?" I repeat, tone so sharp it could cut through ice. I grip the bedpost with one hand, placing the other one on my stomach to stabilize the nausea churning in my belly.

Ephegos considers me with those eyes that betray nothing if he doesn't want them to, and what they are saying right now is that he is enjoying seeing me fight retching all over the floor. He's enjoying seeing me like this—weak, defenseless, behind on information, and wondering until my head spins. "Maybe another time." He dismisses my question with a wave of his hand, but I could swear his fingertips flicker into claws for a heartbeat before he tucks it behind his back and strides for the door. "Why don't you sit down, Ayna? We don't want our guest to make a wrong assessment of your state."

"And what state is that?" I spit, wishing I had more lentil soup to throw after him as he gives me a pitying smile.

"The obvious one." With those words, his magic creeps around my shoulders, dragging me to the chair and pushing me down like a doll, and tying me to the backrest with invisible bonds.

It doesn't matter that I try to kick out with my feet; his magic circles my ankles, securing them to the legs of the chair. I don't give him the satisfaction of screaming and claw-

15

ing at his magic. After what I've seen during my time at the Crow Palace, there is no mistaking this for a situation I could get myself out of on my own, even if I had my full strength and magic. I know, and so does Ephegos because he shoots me a wide, satisfied grin.

"Time to play the sad little widow, Ayna."

His words are another slash to my heart, but I swallow the pain as I swallow the need to scream and cry. Instead, I lift my chin, willing the nausea to settle as I focus on the embroidered blossoms on the ice-blue corset of my dress. "Don't widows usually wear black?"

Ephegos halts, hand on the brass doorknob and eyes narrowed as if finally I've landed a blow of my own, though I have no idea what I said that would upset him so much. I don't have time to celebrate my tiny win before his magic slaps across my face, right on the already bruised side, and I wince, teeth cutting into my cheek at the shock of the searing pain.

If the smirk on Ephegos's features is anything to go by, he doesn't care how many hits I might manage. He already won the battle.

THREE

AYNA

My heart is thumping in my throat as the bonds around my body tighten to a point where they feel more like knives cutting into my skin than invisible ropes, but I pin a bored expression on my aching face and stare Ephegos down as he turns the doorknob, his gaze lingering on mine as he relishes the sight of me incapacitated.

"Smile, Ayna." It's the last thing he says before he pulls the door open, revealing the view of an ornately decorated hallway. I spot curls and whorls of brass and marble curving along the walls, a set of stairs leading down not far from my room, and on the threshold—

I blink at the sight of the familiar blue and black of the Tavrasian military.

Tavrasian. All sorts of fears flood my system, making remaining still in my seat easy as petrification sets in. How Ephegos knows Tavrasian soldiers, I can't even begin to understand, but it's definitely what the man is. A soldier, unless the uniform is stolen, which would be a mystery of its own.

Forcing down a breath, I count the stars on the Tavrasian soldier's shoulder and swallow a fresh assault of nausea as I realize he's high up in rank.

"Adrian!" Turning his back to me, Ephegos spreads his arms wide to embrace the man entering the room with two clipped paces.

"It's good to see you, Ephegos." Adrian meets the Crow's embrace as if it's nothing to fear, and perhaps I would have felt the same mere days ago, before I'd known of Ephegos's betrayal.

The greeting is brief and clinical despite the warm words of welcome, a habit rather than genuine excitement, though I can tell from the way Ephegos's movements become more springy and his features brighten that he is happy to see the man.

It's only when they both turn toward me that I get a good look at the visitor's face. His head is shaved, and the mustache is gone, but those pale eyes I'd recognize anywhere.

"You weren't lying when you said that the months in the Crow King's care were good for her complexion," the man says with a smirk that makes me want to tear at my bonds all over again, but I refuse to give any inclination I'm not seated here out of anything but my free will. I won't give any sign of weakness. Not to the man who captured the Wild Ray and ordered the death of the family I used to know, who ordered Ludelle's death and put me in prison for almost a year before he sold me off to the Crow King. I don't flinch as his gaze roams down my chest. "Though I have to admit, her face isn't the only thing that has benefitted from a few months of proper feeding."

Ephegos's responding laugh sends a chill through my bones. "Yes, she's quite something to look at. A real prize."

The general nods his agreement while he turns to scan my room with the gaze of a military analyst. "What a gracious host you are to grant the widow of your enemy such comforts." His eyes snag on the gardens outside the window. "And such a lovely view. Not comparable to Fort Perenis, is it?" It's the first time he is speaking to me directly. The expression on his face gives the impression he might as well have been conversing with a piece of furniture, that this is a nuisance for him, but a necessary one, a duty.

I don't deign to respond. I don't seethe at him either. The best I can do is keep up the bland facade so I won't break. Because of all the people he could have brought to me, this is probably the worst. From the first time I met the general, he's only been bringing pain and destruction to my life. There is nothing indicating this time will be any different.

His uniform has polished gold buttons lining his chest in two parallel rows from his collarbones to his waist where the jacket parts beneath a belt to give his legs space. It's a dashing cut, designed to impress and to function in combat, but when I look at him, all I see is a monster. One of the real sort, without wings or beaks or claws. The Tavrasian general is a nightmare come to life. And side by side with Ephegos, I can't even imagine what horrors they've dreamed up for me.

"No words for me today?" he provokes. "No fists either?" His eyes wander to my right hand, the one the soldiers injured during the capture of the Wild Ray and that had never been properly set and healed, tracing the chain tattoo identifying me as a former inmate of Fort Perenis.

Oh, I remember the cracking of his nose under my fist when I hit him the day he sold me to the Crow King. I remember the fear, the fury, the lack of any sense of self-preservation I'd felt back then.

I shake my head. "Not today." Today is different. Today I have a heart so splintered I barely feel anything other than the all-consuming pain of Myron's sacrifice. And the need to hide it at all costs.

I've been at my lowest in front of this man. He's made sure I break over and over again. And I can't allow him to glean this truth in my eyes. I can't allow him to see the monster he sold me to might have been my salvation had I not fucked up and failed to save him first.

All I know is that I need to be strong. I need to be strong so Myron's sacrifice wasn't in vain.

"You've met before, good." Ephegos finally inserts himself into the conversation.

Both the general and I nod, but it's Adrian who inclines his head with an icy gaze. "Wolayna Milevishja. I didn't think

Ephegos was telling the truth when he sent word you out-lived King Myron's care." His lips curl in a way that makes the skin around them wrinkle, giving away his age when his hair no longer can. "Quite unexpected."

"Indeed," Ephegos confirms as if this conversation is the most normal in the world and not one about the likelihood of my survival, a situation one happily put me in and the other had an active part in seeing to my end. "The first bride to survive the marriage to the infamous Crow King in thou-sands of years."

"The hundredth bride of King Myron of Winghaven." Adrian gives me a knowing look, and I nearly fail to register what he'd called Myron. Myron of Winghaven.

I've never heard that name before.

"Yes, your husband kept a lot of secrets, Wolayna," Ephegos sprinkles in, just to land another one of those blows to my chest, the pain of which I'm determined to ignore. "Damning secrets."

The general measures me with those calculating eyes, probably figuring out where to hit so it hurts the most, even though I still don't know what his quarrel with me is apart from, you know, treason. If looting the Tavrasian royal fleet can be called that. But the answer is there in his face as he takes a step closer, leaning down and bracing his hands on the table at my side.

"Milevishja… a name so common in Tavras I didn't think at first you could be the daughter of Ivan Milevishja. Yes… I remember him." He reads the question right from my eyes. "I remember how he betrayed the late King of Tavras."

"My father's crimes, not mine." It comes out as a whisper because, no matter how much I try to be strong, I falter at the mention of my father's treason. At the way things fall into place.

"Traitor by blood." It's all the general says as he straightens again.

Ephegos throws me a grin over the general's shoulder, the Crow still taller than the man even when he is comparatively short for a Crow male. "Oh, the many ways one can commit treason," he chimes as if we weren't talking about my family's crimes, about mine, and my right to live.

"You know that the punishment for treason hasn't changed, Wolayna." The general lifts a brown-gray brow as he surveys me. "While your father paid with his life, your punishment turned out a bit less permanent, I fear."

There is no sign of that supposed fear in his eyes. All they speak of is the countless ways of punishment he can come up with.

"Luckily, my friend here"—he lays a hand on Ephegos's black-clad shoulder, and it's the first time I notice the fine making of his jacket—"alerted me that you survived your sentence, which I'm here to remedy."

Everything inside me goes still as the meaning of his words hits. Death. He's come to execute me after all. The punishment for treason is death.

The warm sound of Ephegos's laugh fills the room, and I want to cry as it wraps around me with such familiarity just before I catch myself and remember that he is a traitor of his own. That the warmth isn't real. That he doesn't care about my suffering other than that it happens. He wants me to pay for Myron's hand in his sister's death.

Sariell, I remember. A half-breed of Crow and Fire Fairy blood. One of Myron's countless brides who died because of the curse, not because Myron willed it so.

"You're too kind, General Katrijanov." He turns to the man he'd called Adrian before, and the ice in my veins solidifies. Adrian Katrijanov. General Adrian Katrijanov. King Erina's general and the youngest general in Tavrasian history under Erina's father's rule. I didn't care much for Tavrasian politics during my time as a pirate, but some news made it out to even the remotest ports where the Wild Ray laid anchor. Adrian Katrijanov's promotion before the late king's death is one of them.

I'm trying to hide the thoughts clanging through my mind behind a mask of boredom and calm as one piece after the other falls into place like a tapestry-sized puzzle I am merely getting the edges of.

Apparently, I fail miserably because Katrijanov gives me a smirk. "Don't worry. I'm not going to execute you on the spot." He runs his fingers over the pommel of the sword at his hip. "Your punishment was always meant to be something worse than death."

It's not the first time I've heard that line. *A punishment worse than death.*

And it's not the first time I crumble at the multiple ways life can be worse than death. I'm living my personal nightmare right now, even without Katrijanov's interference. Losing Myron is bad enough for a lifetime of heartbreak.

But the Guardians must be in a horrible mood today since they paired up the traitor Crow and the man determined to punish me for both my father's crimes and my own. Two men determined to see me suffer and both with a track record of the lengths they are willing to go to make it happen.

"Why don't you simply tell me what will happen to me." I hold Katrijanov's gaze, meeting that pale stare with what I hope is more fire than I feel. Anything is better than being locked away for a year again without knowing what fate awaits me.

"That, dear Wolayna," Ephegos cuts in before the general can open his mouth to answer, "is not for today. For today, our task is done." The last words are for Katrijanov, and the man gives a brief nod, snapping his heels together as he turns on the spot, marching for the door.

On the threshold, he pauses, glancing at me over his shoulder. "Don't die anytime soon, Wolayna. We have great plans for you."

FOUR

AYNA

An hour after the general and Ephegos leave, my hands haven't stopped shaking, and I can't move from the chair the Crow tied me to, even when he removed the invisible bonds upon his exit.

It doesn't seem to matter how far I sail or run, the past always catches up with me. Even in the fairylands, the reach of the Tavrasian king extends deeply enough to put a sling around my neck.

Then there is the little detail of Katrijanov and Ephegos working together. It doesn't add up in my mind. Not yet. But if Ephegos meant what he said, that I'll be here for a while, I'm ready to put my efforts into finding out so I can prepare myself. Anything is better than being pushed into dire situations blindly. It was hard enough with the prison in Fort Perenis and then being dragged across the lands by Royad. No matter how he became my friend later, at that point, he was a monster to me, and I nearly shat myself at the sight of him. Not to mention what the news of being a tribute for the Crow King did to me.

How fate twisted to gift me a friend and a lover out of that terror, I am yet to come to terms with. Perhaps losing both of them is the price I'm paying for stealing hope from darkness. Perhaps it's the rage of the gods the Crows pray to, the same ones who cursed them for their ancestors' wrongdoings.

So much I yet have to learn… So much to wonder and guess and break over if I'm not careful.

My hand absently wanders to my shoulder, tracing where I now know a crow tattoo graces my skin. Yet another mystery to add to the pile, and the pile is already sky-high.

I take small comfort in the fact that Ephegos isn't here to watch me fall apart, in the fact that I'm not chained to a dungeon wall with moldy bread and stale water as my daily meal. It's not anything I trust to remain, though. I've seen what Ephegos is capable of, how he doesn't shy away from spearing his friends with blades for self-righteous reasons, have been on the receiving end of his blade. There is no way I'll live in silk and luxury forever. This is a temporary reprieve, and the more I think about it, the more I wonder if it's preparation for something more, something worse than the dungeons of Fort Perenis. If darkness hits worse in bright and cozy places like this, where it can hide behind polished corners and between shiny ornamentations, and you'd never see it coming when it finally sneaks up on you.

A knock on the door tears me from my thoughts. With a quick hand, I wipe away the tears threatening to fall and take a stabilizing breath before getting to my feet, fingers gripping the backrest of the chair to keep my balance as I stand as straight as a silk-and-blossoms-covered pillar.

Before I can say a word for whoever knocked to come in or stay out, the lock on the door clicks, and a woman strides in, her long brown braid bouncing on her shoulder as she carries a tray to the table in front of me. Her linen pants are as brown as her hair, and the leather vest covering her torso is that of a fighter or hunter rather than of a household servant—as are the knives strapped to her thighs and the sword peeking above her shoulder as she sets the tray down.

"Order of Ephegos," she chirps while dishes clink against each other as she jostles them, not paying attention to her task and taking in my appearance instead. "Nice choice."

Whether she means the dress, my still-drying hairstyle, or just *me*, I can't tell. I'm too flabbergasted that Ephegos would let any other being near me without supervision. And more than that: the woman is human. Her ears are rounded, and her face is gloriously … normal. Pretty, but not fairy beautiful. No sign of immortal grace or other magical attributes to give away that she's anything more than an average human.

"Who are you?" The words slip out so fast I can make a conscious choice to ask.

The woman gives me a clipped smile. "Kaira." Abandoning her grip on the tray, she picks up an elaborate teapot and pours steaming liquid into a cream and brass cup the size of a doll dish.

"Kaira," I repeat, leaving the word hanging in the air with the expectation of an explanation.

When she's done pouring, Kaira sets down the teapot, gesturing for me to settle in the chair I just made an effort to get out of. "You should drink and eat while you can. Who knows when Ephegos will feel another surge of kindness and allow such luxury?"

I smother the impulse to gesture at the obvious luxury of the room I'm being held in and do as she bids, especially since I notice her hand drifting to the knife where it casually hovers within range to draw the weapon effortlessly.

"You are human." I don't know why I'm surprised. Katrijanov just left, and he was human. It's only logical there would be another human around.

"Mostly." A grin splits her lips.

"And the other part? The non-human one?" Whatever loosens my tongue, it can't be the tea she poured, for that is still sitting in its cup, untouched while Kaira steps back, surveying me with alert brown eyes the approximate color of her hair and clothes.

"Flame." She adds a little shrug as if it's something to accept rather than to be proud of.

"You're part Fire Fairy?"

Her fingers curl beside the hilt of her dagger. "We prefer the term *Flame*. You know, since most of us are no longer all fully fairy-blooded."

It takes me a moment to digest the information and the fact that she's so willingly given it.

"So, this is the residence of the Flames?" It's a long shot, and I don't expect her to answer since Ephegos has so expertly kept our whereabouts a secret. But now that I have a talking Flame in front of me, I need to at least try.

"One of the many." Again, her tone is nonchalant as if this is common knowledge and I'm not a prisoner.

"Are you saying the Flames have a lot of…" I glance at the ornamentations on the walls, searching for words. "Palaces?"

Kaira's laugh bubbles through the room like I've said something hilarious and she can't help herself, but her hand is on her knife, quite in contrast to the smile on her face.

"We don't have palaces," she finally says, face colder than I've seen since the moment she entered the room. "Not anymore. The last one was taken over by the Crow Fairies thousands of years ago and was destroyed in our final attempt to take it back a few days ago."

My heart stutters.

"Destroyed?"

"Let's put it this way." She holds up a hand as if weighing her words on her palm. "Flame fire doesn't do well when combined with certain traits of Crow magic."

Images of that fateful battle come back to me: Myron's power holding off the assaults of flames, my water magic lashing out fires in the entrance hall. The Crow magic hadn't caused explosions then.

"What do you mean, *combined?*"

Kaira grimaces, and this time, there is no tell that her face is telling another story than her hands. The knife is tucked back to her side and she looses a slow breath. "The Crows fighting on our side fueled our fire with their invisible powers. It didn't end well."

I remember the explosions from the throne room, the debris. I remember being hit by something before I blacked out over Myron's body.

"You were there? Did you see what happened to the others?" Again, I'm quicker speaking than thinking, but this Flame is *talking,* and I so desperately need answers. I still have no idea what happened to Clio and Royad or whatever Crows remained after the battle.

"I was here. Nobody wants a *mostly* human warrior on a magical battlefield. At least, not on the side of the Flames." The appraising look she gives me makes my skin crawl, even when she hasn't made any declaration she's here to hurt me. I can't tell if she's my enemy, but she's not my friend either. "As opposed to your side. I heard King Myron let you fight at his side. A human wielding magic… Fascinating."

It's not an answer to my question, but it's information I tuck away for later. Any puzzle piece I can come by, I'll take.

"So, you don't know what happened to the … survivors?" My stomach tightens at the thought of Royad and Clio not having made it out. Guardians. If the Fire Fairies— the Flames—collapsed the entire palace, they might have been ended then and there among the rubble. And Myron's body ... buried in the ashes of a home he never truly owned.

I hide the tremor in my hand by sitting down and tucking my fingers into the folds of my skirts.

"The Flames tended to their wounded, and most of them returned to their settlements. Of course, our warriors are still hunting leftover Crows." The glint of menace in her gaze tells me exactly what she thinks of the Crows, and this time, I can't hide the shudder raking through my body.

This woman is a warrior as well. One carrying trays and making conversation with prisoners, but a warrior anyway, and there is no doubt she isn't happy that again she has been left behind.

Another piece of information I tuck away for later.

"So, there are still some Crows left?" I can't help the rapid rising and falling of my chest as my heart kicks into a gallop. They might be alive. Royad might be alive. And Clio... Not a Crow, but she fought at our side anyway. If I ever see her again, I will ask her what got her to work with her enemies instead of against them, when letting the Crows die would have rid the lands of Askarea of one more breed of monsters.

"Some." Kaira's hand twitches back toward her knife, ready to draw it and slay one of said Crows should they decide to step out of a pretty corner of my room.

For a moment, I wait for her to continue, but she remains quiet, eyes distant as if in her mind she's already gone on a hunt.

"Can you tell me what Ephegos wants with me, Kaira?"

ANGELINA J. STEFFORT

FIVE

AYNA

For the first time since the warrior Flame entered the room, her expression becomes guarded, and she is fidgeting, almost like she is anxious she might spill secrets that aren't hers to tell. Not that I'm surprised Ephegos would have put a lock on all that information he's been unwilling to share with me himself, and his vengeance is nothing I'd want anyone exposed to, so I shake my head at Kaira, pretending my curiosity and fear aren't eating me up. "It's all right. I'll find out in good time." If I never find out, it's soon enough.

Kaira's shoulders relax, and she heaves an obvious breath of relief.

I might not get the information I want, but if there's one thing I've learned at the Crow Palace, it is that there's always something else to learn that might come in handy later, so I brace myself for all the possible answers to my next question. "Where is this residence located? Are we still in Askarea?" Not that I'm in any condition to attempt an escape, but if I ever get a chance, I'd better know what to expect if I make it past the pink and yellow blossoms in the gardens outside my window.

Kaira shakes her head, then nods. "Kind of. We're right at the border."

My heart beats wildly enough to make me wonder if the full-blooded fairies in the estate can hear it through walls and floors. "Which border?"

There are only two borders with Askarea, and both of them are human territories. Cezux and Tavras.

"The Plithian Plains." She gestures at the window as if the forest and flowers would explain everything, and my stomach sags to my knees.

"Tavras." The word leaves me in a gust, hollowing out my chest until I have no breath in me. I haven't seen the Plithian Plains in the north of Tavras since my childhood when my mother dragged me across the land to find a new home for us. The flatland sits nestled between the lush grain fields in the northeast of the capital Meer and the Askarean border. It's a region of harsh winds and wet storms that hosts only a few settlements. Merchant outposts mostly, where goods for trade with the fairylands are being temporarily stored, inns and blacksmiths provide for travelers, and then there are the horses.

I've never seen as many horses as on the Plithian Plains where they graze in vast stretches of flat lands with sheds built against copses of trees as shelters and waterholes scattered between the occasional fence for keeping them from meandering into the fairylands.

When I was a child, I thought galloping through the Plithian Plains on one of those slender horses would equal freedom. Then I grew up and became a pirate. Riding is nothing compared to the winds whipping across the ocean and the sense of flying they induce when the ship cuts through storms and waters.

"Not quite. We're technically still on Askarean soil. It's the only way to make sure Tavras can't interfere—" Eyes widening, she slaps her hand over her mouth, stopping herself, but I've soaked up every last syllable, and there is no unhearing what she said.

"Interfere with what?" I prompt, hoping she'll slip up again.

Kaira takes a step back, gesturing at the tea. "Drink. I've already said too much."

"Not enough," I correct her, and I notice that guarded expression again that tells me something is going on behind those brown eyes that could make a difference in my escape.

That makes the woman chuckle before her gaze darkens. "I always say too much. It's a Guardiansdamned miracle they let me do anything at all."

"Who are *they*? The Flames? The Crows working with the Flames? General Katrijanov?" I have to at least try. After seeing the Crows bleed when answering questions the curse forbade, there is nothing that can happen to Kaira if no one ever learns she spilled secrets. "I won't tell anyone you said anything," I promise, wondering if Flames—or even part-Flames—make bargains like other fairies.

Kaira only shakes her head at me. "I value my life too much to tell you. But know that, even if this seems to be a dire situation, not all Flames are happy with Ephegos's leadership." She doesn't say if she agrees, but the fact that she mentioned Ephegos as a leader confirms the impression I got at the battle when the Flames seemed to flank him and protect him like a king of their own.

Inclining my head, I reach for the cup still waiting on the table. "I won't forget your kindness, Kaira."

She's already stalking toward the door, knife back at her hip and shoulders tight as she reaches for the brass knob and hesitates. "I'll try to come back tomorrow. Just don't upset anyone in the meantime. Flames are a fiery people and their tempers almost as bad as that of the Crows."

I accept her warning with a tentative smile. "A perfect match, those two people then. If only they wouldn't try to rip each other apart."

Kaira returns my smile before she leaves the room.

I'm wearing the same eggshell-and-blue dress with blossom embroidery when I wake in my bed, what could be minutes or hours later. An ache in my shoulder makes me roll to the side and reach up to rub it, but my arm is stuck between the mattress and my body, and the sensation vanishes as I try to remember how I ended up here. The last thing I know is sipping the aromatic brew Kaira poured for me; everything after is a haze of jostling and nausea.

A glance at the table confirms the tea set is gone, and I wonder what sort of poison they gave me that makes my stomach feel like I have a ton of sawdust to hurl.

When I roll out of bed and hurtle for the bathing room, I barely make it to the porcelain toilet. But all that comes up is bile and memories of a beautiful pale male lying lifeless in a puddle of blood and water.

"Myron," I whisper as if somehow that would summon him from behind Eroth's Veil. His name bounces off the marble tiles and brass accents in the room, but in my chest, all it does is sink into the darkness I'm harboring there like a rock into ink.

By the time I'm done dry heaving, I'm shaking from exhaustion, and sweat beads my neck and forehead, but my head is clear, and where I had little to no idea of where I am and why I am here a day ago, I now have an estimated location of my whereabouts and the knowledge that the Flames and Crows working together might not be as happy with their alliance as they seemed when acting against Myron.

The thought should give me hope. Instead, it's like another downward spiral in a growing assortment of downward spirals. If only I understood how Tavras fit into the equation, if this is merely about a failed punishment that needs to be re-exacted, or if it's something more. Something personal.

Before I can come to a conclusion, the door opens with a bang, and two males in leather armor stride in, lifting me from where I kneel by the toilet, and dragging me back to the bedroom. No, not the bedroom. They hook their arms under my shoulders and pull me into the hallway while I protest with weak kicks and wriggles.

There is no getting rid of a Flame I learn as I'm being hauled down the set of stairs where windows are black as the night outside, the only thing illuminating the tall hallway is the bright fire flickering in brass sconces lining the walls. A distant part of me notices how similar they look to the torches at the Crow place, and it's suddenly very clear that I'm at a Fire Fairy residence and these are everlasting flames.

Sharp pain runs through my arms and sides as the males tear at my shoulders to pull me into a more upright position. The hem of my skirt catches on a heavy boot, the fabric ripping somewhere at the height of my ankle. The male on my right curses, but the one on my left growls for him to shut up. I don't get a proper look at either of them, other than that they are tall and powerfully built, before I'm being shoved through a hidden side door down a narrow set of stairs. I barely catch myself on the wooden handrail attached to the wall and slither to a halt on my knees at the bottom of the stairs, heart pounding as I take inventory of my bones. All are intact.

It's not the fall I should have feared, though, but the creature awaiting me in the small, dim room, towering over a plain wooden chair. He turns to face me, a cruel curl to his lips, and cracks his knuckles.

"Welcome, Wolayna." He gestures at the chair with his leather-clad arm, golden blond hair shifting into his harsh face as he nods in clear dismissal at the door behind me where I know the two guards must still be standing.

I don't dare turn around to watch them close it. A heartbeat later, the sound of a lock clicking shut confirms they locked me in, and the terror in my veins won't allow for me to tear my gaze away from the hulk of a fairy in front of me.

"I've been looking forward to this moment for quite a while." He gestures at the chair as if I had a choice whether I sit or turn and run. "Take a seat."

Trying not to acknowledge the petrifying panic surging through my body, I push myself up instead and stand on shaky legs with my hand braced on the wall. How I wish I had my dagger—or any weapon for that matter—even when I doubt any fighting trick I have up my brass and gold embroidered sleeves might help me defeat the male in front of me.

"I said *sit*," he growls, the only warning I'll get before he uses his brute strength on me; I can see by the gleam of violence in his eyes.

My legs barely carry me, but they march on to the chair anyway, the traitors.

"Good girl." He pushes me down by the shoulder, the touch like fire, right over the tattoo I discovered before Katrijanov's visit.

"I'm not a girl." My voice is as weak as my legs, but I grit my teeth and hold the male's stare as I face him from my position in the uncomfortable piece of furniture.

That merely costs him a rough laugh. "I don't care *what* you are, Wolayna. Only *who* you are."

"What's that supposed to mean?" Call it bravery or sheer stupidity—or the missing energy to reflect on my words before speaking them—but I speak unfiltered as I defy him with all I have. Which isn't much, considering I've barely eaten and have been poisoned or drugged—who knows with Ephegos; I wouldn't put it past him to kill me slowly with poison—since I almost died three days ago. Four, perhaps, if I count the time I was passed out after the gloriously sedating tea Kaira served. I make a mental note to tell her all about how little the taste of the brew was worth the pain I went through after.

"Just that we have things to talk about, you and I." He turns to the shelf against the wall where a set of tools is waiting to be used. Sharp metal and tough wood. Leather slings and various thicknesses of ropes.

"Are you going to torture me?" It's a stupid question to ask a male who seems to be ready to exact violence and pain on any soul stepping into his path, but I need to know. I need to know if I have to brace myself for more pain or if I can take a breath.

"What makes you think I'd revert to such primal methods when I have the perfect ability to lead a conversation that's not dictated by pliers to pull your teeth and hammers to shatter your bones?" His stark, gray gaze slides to my stiff wrist as if he knows exactly where I'm most vulnerable.

He's wrong, though. The most vulnerable part of me is the splintered lump I used to call my heart. And that can be hurt most with words. So, I brace myself for a storm rather than the stabbing pain of a blade and study his scar-flecked face, his sharp, stubbled jaw. He seems older than most fairies I've seen, who are all timelessly beautiful, frozen in the prime of their years. But this male looks more like he's in his late thirties. Handsome still, the pointed ears slightly out of place.

"Since you already seem to know who I am, how about you tell me who *you* are?" I pray to the Guardians that he will opt for words rather than the instruments of torture he's turning toward again and fold my hands in my lap in aspiration of indifferent calm.

The male barks a laugh, his leather armor creaking as he lifts his arms over his head to reach for an item high up on the shelf. "Herinor."

I wait for more as he rummages above my line of sight for something, I'm not sure I even want to know what, but he leaves it at that one name.

"Herinor," I repeat.

He hums his confirmation.

"Are you a Flame?" I know better than to call him a Fire Fairy. While Kaira's anger seemed manageable, I don't want to be on the receiving end of this male's fury.

"Do I look like a Flame?" He glances at me over his shoulder, brushing back his hair with his free hand while he tucks a small, longish item into the side of his belt. I'm too busy squirming under his brutal stare to notice what exactly it is.

"Is there a right answer to this question? Because I have only seen so many Flames from up close, and I have no idea what other fairies live in this estate." It's not exactly the smartest response, but it's one that leaves room for him to pick up the conversation if that's what he's set on doing.

He measures me with a sharp look before cutting his gaze back to the shelf and arranging a few tools.

"I'm almost disappointed you don't remember me, Wolayna. It's been less than a week since I last saw you, and you have already forgotten."

I rack my brain for a memory of this male, of his tall and broad frame, his scarred face and unique eyes, but come up blank.

"Nothing, Ayna? Really?" He raises a light brown brow, shooting me a gaze that somehow feels familiar, yet his features are as unfamiliar as they were two minutes ago.

When I don't respond, the male turns and leans against the shelf, one hand braced on the worn wood, and pins me with those gray eyes. "I must say, I'm a bit disappointed. I guarded your sleep for the past months after all."

His words clang through me, taking with them all my resolve to remain unbothered, strong, and my mouth opens wordlessly.

"I do look a bit different now, I'll give you that. You probably remember a winged monster with beak and black eyes."

And feathers on his features, I add in my mind, but when I study him, I see the similarity of his build. The Crow who stood guard the first day I woke at the Crow Palace. I never paid much attention to who guarded the door to Myron's chambers, too occupied with either Royad or the Crow King himself at my side whenever I left the room.

He's one of the Crows who used to glare at me when I walked the hallways, one of those who believed I didn't have a place there and that his people were better off without a broken curse—at least, that's what I assume from his appearance in the Flame residence.

"Are you a traitor Crow or just an opportunist?" Clutching my fingers in my lap, I scan his features, memorizing the straight nose and light stubble, the pointed ears, and the waves of his hair. In his leather armor, he looks every bit as menacing as he did in his half-Crow form, but I refuse to balk, refuse to panic. If anything, this male is another source of information. Finding enough of those, may help me piece together what's going on here. Because, no matter how much Ephegos hates Myron for the death of his sister, that cannot be the only reason I'm here. If revenge was all he wanted, he'd torture me himself until I beg for death. But he hasn't even hinted that's what he has in mind. Not yet.

"Neither." Herinor gives me a grim glance that makes me wonder if he is all that dangerous or merely a male stuck in a position he hates. When I measure him, he shakes his head. "Don't look at me like you wonder if I'm better than them because I'm not." He gestures at the ceiling in the general direction of where I assume the other inhabitants of this residence must be located. "I'm not upset the curse is broken, even when I didn't believe it necessary. There was power in the way our bodies were locked in claws and feathers. It gave us an entirely different way of perceiving the world, made us strong, resilient."

I don't interrupt, despite the millions of questions about how he knows the difference, if he is one of the ancient Crows responsible for the curse or if he is just like Myron and Royad, who were infants when the curse hit.

"Do I mourn our king?" He shrugs. "More than I mourned Carius. I hated that male, thought there was something inherently cruel about Myron's father that made it impossible not to follow his lead. Something charismatic, almost like a song of violence our Crow nature answers to. Of course, our people turned into what we are today. Of course, the gods would—" He stops himself, hand wandering to his mouth where he wipes as if expecting blood to spill from his lips. But the curse is broken, and nothing is keeping him from speaking the truth of his people, the curse, and whatever gods placed it on them.

"Who cursed the Crows?" I half expect the Neredynian gods to rain vengeance down on me for the mere question, expect anything other than an actual answer.

All the more surprised I am when Herinor holds my gaze and says, "Vala, the Goddess of Life and Water."

My breath catches in my throat. I haven't the slightest clue about that goddess, but if she cursed a people to be stuck in their monster form, to become unlovable and cruel, she can't be a deity I want to pray to.

"You probably haven't heard of Vala. Neredynian deities aren't commonly known in Eherea, let alone Neredyn, our—"

"Home," I finish for him, eager to get on with the conversation now that I'm finally getting information. "How did she curse you? What happened exactly that justifies taking away all females of a people and damning them to slowly go extinct?" Taking away a species's females so they can no longer bear offspring and spread across the lands to cause more destruction is an effective punishment—a cruel, brutal punishment. The curse merely missed that Crows bred with humans and, apparently, Fire Fairies whenever they could get their claws on them. I shudder at the mere thought of the horrors the Crows symbolize.

All those conversations with Myron and Royad come back to mind, how the Crows had taken from the lands of Neredyn whatever they pleased—resources, women—that they'd wreaked havoc wherever they went. And after the curse hit the Crows, Carius brought them to Eherea where he eradicated the people living at the palace in the Seeing Forest. He didn't care to ask for land. He took. He killed for it.

Maybe Vala was right.

I was, I hear a non-distinct voice in my mind, the sound familiar, an echo of the moments I'd begged the murderous lake of brides' tears to help me save Myron.

Everything goes still inside of me, listening for another sound from what I now understand can only be the voice of the goddess herself.

Why? she'd asked me. Why I wanted to save the Crow King.

And I'd answered I was the only chance he had. Back then, I didn't realize that the lake from the sacred chamber was more than just the former brides' tears but a medium for the Goddess of Water.

Guardians save me.

Had I not been sitting, my knees would have gone weak now.

"You were there when it all happened, weren't you? You were with Carius from the beginning."

Herinor nods, folding his arms over his broad chest, leathers creaking. "I was just as bad as Carius. I killed and raped and looted. And where we went, a trail of death and destruction followed. The human race was very new to Neredyn back then, and the gods had already left the realm of the mortals, and our creator with them."

"Shaelak." It's a wild guess, but Shaelak is the god the Crows kept referencing.

"You are quite observant, Wolayna." Herinor measures me with a glance that's almost civil. I try not to think how many ways this situation can go wrong with his track record of crimes. "No wonder Myron risked everything to make you fall for him."

"He didn't *make* me fall for him," I correct. "Quite the opposite. He tried to warn me away countless times."

"That kid has always been too soft for a Crow." The expression on Herinor's features isn't unkind, yet not fond either. But something changed the moment I walked in. He isn't trying to scare me or threaten me. Herinor, the hulk of a Crow guard, is doing exactly what he said he would. He is leading a conversation, and I'm getting surprisingly much information out of it. So much, in fact, that my head is swimming.

"Only the God of Darkness can create a species such as ours. I believe he considers us Crows his *one mistake*." There is regret in that voice, a darkness deeper than the one in the half-shifted Crows' all-black eyes when they'd been stuck through the curse. Darkness and remorse.

SIX

AYNA

Herinor reaches for his belt, draws a small, simple knife with an efficient blade and smooth, leather-wrapped hilt, and points it at me. His gaze locks on mine, that menace back that has softened over our conversation, and with it, my panic returns in full force.

He's going to hurt me after all. He's going to slice me open, torture me so Ephegos doesn't need to dirty his hands.

"Are you scared, Ayna?" His voice is a rumble echoing off the walls, and by the Guardians, I am. I'm scared out of my wits. I'm not strong enough to fight, let alone a Crow. I can barely stand on my own feet. "You should be. You should be afraid for more than your life."

Don't break, I tell myself. *Don't show weakness. Don't believe for one second that anyone here will help you. Don't trust a soul.*

Herinor's mouth splits in a feral grin that has my breath catching as terror floods me, making my resolution to keep strong fly out the non-existent window.

He pulls the knife up to my chin, placing it at my throat, ready to slit it and end me then and there.

A part of me is ready for it to be over, for this life where I have lost everything I ever loved to end. But something inside of me refuses to break. I can't give up. Not when Myron gave himself up to make sure I lived. I cannot throw that gift away—that curse. It's my curse to bear now.

I steel my spine, balling my hands into fists to stop them from shaking.

"I'm a fool, Ayna. I should have known the day you woke in Myron's palace that you'd be the one to save us. But I was blinded by centuries of failure. I was blinded by the desire for freedom and Ephegos's vision. I gave up when I should have had faith—in my king, in his queen. In the gods themselves."

I try to make sense of his words, but the knife scraping along my skin is distracting me from grasping a clear thought. If he moves a fraction of an inch, the blade will nick my artery, and that will be the end of it. So, I don't even swallow the lump in my throat. All I do is breathe, panting through my nose as I hold Herinor's steely gaze.

"I made a bargain with Ephegos that, if the curse wasn't broken by the time of the Flame attack, I'd join his ranks. And you know how fairy bargains are very specific." His hand quivers the slightest bit, the tip of the knife jerking away from my skin, allowing me to take a moment of reprieve. "The curse was broken—but not before the attack. It doesn't matter how I regret ever agreeing, doesn't matter that you loved Myron in the end. The curse hadn't been broken when Ephegos and his allies attacked. And I'm bound to do his bidding now. The new King of Crows—of all Crows who remain," he adds quietly, the veil of menace lifting, and all that's left is a broken male as he lifts his hand yet again, setting the knife to the side of my neck as if ready to stab me, but doesn't move from there.

His words register, and my entire system floods with horror all over again. "What do you mean, all who remain?"

Royad...

"It means there is no one left except for the Crows who joined Ephegos. Or there won't be once the Flames find them and end them." The warning in his eyes doesn't leave room for questions or even desperate pleas to stop the hunt for survivors. "I'm bound by the bargain I made, and Ephegos told me to hurt you, Ayna."

I shrink back in my chair, but there is nowhere I can go. He's right in front of me, blade scraping along my skin as his magic wraps around my arms and ankles to pin me in place.

"Please don't." I'm not beyond begging. Not when I see the time for conversation is over. This is real.

Herinor shakes his head. "I don't want to, Ayna, but the magic of my bargain demands it, or I'll pay with my own life."

He doesn't want to. The expression on his features doesn't betray if he's telling the truth, but the slight drop of his shoulders tells me this isn't his choice. There's no reason for him to lie. He told me about the gods and the curse, answered my questions. If anything, this male has been more forthcoming with information than any of the Crows I've encountered before. What irony that the one most inclined to help me now is the one obliged to torture me.

"Don't worry, Ayna." He shakes his head at me as if forbidding me to panic when my mind has long checked out of any rational thought. All I can do is try to detach myself from my body as best I can as I prepare for the pain that's coming without question. "I have a plan. One where I don't need to break my bargain and where the pain will benefit you."

Readying myself, I grit my teeth. "And what plan would that be?

Stepping around me so I can no longer see his face, Herinor tightens the bonds of his magic and slides the blade to the back of my neck. "I cannot tell you, Ayna. The bargain with Ephegos forbids it. But if there has ever been a time in your life when you needed to trust someone unconditionally, now is the moment."

There is no warning before the blade slides through the fabric of my dress, slicing into the skin next to my spine, and drawing a slow, curved line all the way to my bicep. My cry of pain isn't enough to express the breath-arresting agony. No matter how hard I try, his bonds hold tight, his hand on top of my shoulder unyielding as he pins me in place while he carves me open.

By Eroth—

"Please—" I gasp between screams.

Herinor leans in close to my ear, whispering as he drives his blade down the side of my arm. "Be brave for *him*, Ayna. He gave everything for you. Don't let him down." I don't know if I imagine the remorse in his tone or if it's wishful thinking that there is any meaning to his words, that he might actually have a plan that doesn't include the mere destruction of whatever is left of my sanity.

By the time he lifts the knife from my skin, my face is tear-streaked, and all I can feel is the throbbing wound on my shoulder. Herinor's bonds are the only thing holding me in my chair, and had I not heaved up my guts earlier, I'd empty myself out right here, on the silken folds of my skirt. At least he's no longer cutting into me, but as he steps around me, bloodied blade in his hand, I can tell he's not done with me.

"Hate me if you must, Ayna," he whispers as he leans in to grab the fabric covering my other shoulder and tears it off with one harsh tug. "But this is the best I can do."

He lifts the knife to my bare arm, and I fight with all I have to get out of his reach. If I can tip over the chair, perhaps I can free myself from his magic. Maybe I can kick out and catch him by surprise…

I don't get as far as to try it, for he has my arm in his grasp within a heartbeat, lowering the knife to my skin. But when it connects, it's not the sharp edge biting into my flesh, it's the flat of the blade he slides along my biceps, tracing the same line as on my other shoulder.

"I'll make it look like I cut both sides, he explains as he traces his fingers along the tender area beneath the gashing wound on my other side with surprising gentleness. "If I smear enough blood and etch a thin line on your skin—nothing as deep as on the other side," he throws in when I flinch under his touch, "I can make it look like I partly healed you, and no one will question why I carved the line on your other shoulder."

"Why?" It seems it's the only question that ever matters with all those Crows. It was the question Myron wanted me to ask; it was the question I should have asked when General Katrijanov first let me live instead of killing me off like the rest of the Wild Ray's crew. "Why are you doing this to me?"

The bargain, he said. Hurt me or show mercy for me, a nobody to the Crows now that Myron is dead, and pay with his own life for breaking the bargain with Ephegos. But there has to be more. There is a meaning to his words I can't fully grasp with pain clouding my thoughts.

"Because I did wrong by Myron. I didn't trust him enough to believe when he said he knew what he was doing, bargaining away the right for new brides in exchange for the fairy princess's help with your magic." He shakes his head, gesturing at my forearm. "I need more blood." He doesn't ask, simply slices into my wrist.

The new pain shocks me into silence, and he makes quick work of smearing the welling blood along my arm and neck, letting it spill over my skirts, before he places his hand over the wound. Warmth spreads where his magic knits the tissues back together, and before I can comprehend what's happening, he's done, stepping back, and assessing me like a particularly difficult piece of craft he's been working on. A frown is etched between his brows, giving him an expression of strain as he takes in the sight of pain and devastation.

The bonds of his magic fall away, and I almost tumble out of my chair. He catches me with a strong, efficient arm.

"I'm sorry, Ayna. It's the best I can do for you." His hand smooths back the hair that's fallen into my face, and I'm certain I have a trace of blood along my hairline as well. "I'm your ally. Probably the only one you have in this place, so play along. Pretend to hate me and curse me to your Guardians and back, to Eroth and Shaelak and even Vala. Just don't be stupid enough to tell a soul I spared you."

A pained chuckle escapes my lips as I try to comprehend what just happened. "I wouldn't call carving me open *sparing me.*"

"It doesn't matter what you'd call it. If I did everything right, you'll understand soon enough." He doesn't look at me as he turns and gently leans me back into the chair, careful not to rest my weight against the injured shoulder. "Just trust me. Trust me like you trusted Myron."

With those words, he strides to the door, knocking his large, bloodied fist against it, and his expression turns back into that cold and menacing one he wore when I first entered the room.

It promptly swings open, the Flame guards' curious faces appearing on the threshold as they peer inside to make out the mess Herinor left on my skin.

"Take her back to her room." It's an order, and judging by the way the Flame guards flinch under Herinor's stare, they don't want to upset him and end up on the receiving end of his particular skills.

Wordlessly, they scramble down the small flight of stairs and grab me by the arms. My scream of pain isn't an act when they lift me out of the chair, dragging me across the dusty floor past Herinor, who gives me a warning glance. But his eyes are soft when they track the smear of blood along my forearm right above where he cut into my wrist.

Before the pair of guards shove me over the threshold into the hallway ahead, I dare a last glance over my shoulder.

Herinor simply places a finger over his lips as he watches them drag me away.

SEVEN

MYRON

The landscape I'm glancing down at is the same one I've been staring at for the past centuries and centuries, yet flying feels different when I know I can land and make my wings disappear at any time. Where a palace used to stand, rubble and debris cover the large circular clearing. The gardens are devoid of life as is the scorched ground where the explosion hit. What I've called my home for longer than I care to remember has become a wasteland at the center of magical greenery.

Turning my eyes from the site of destruction, I lead the flock across the thicket of the Seeing Forest, letting my mind drift to the lands I cannot reach—the ones that lay beyond what my bargain with the King of Askarea allows. I no longer care for that bargain. The wards on the borders have long been unwoven by the unique magic of my people, and the ancient magic working such bargains hasn't fried the Crows who left, or we'd long have been rid of Ephegos and his treacherous ass. All I care about is finding a trail, anything that will tell me where they took Ayna.

My chest aches at the thought of her name, right where my friend's blade pierced it, and I try not to allow myself to think of the sensation washing through me when she told me she loves me.

Of course, I fail miserably. The pain intensifies one hundredfold at the mere memory of her voice, desperate and full of the redemption I'd been craving for longer than I can think. I'm a marked child of an era of wars and destruction wreaked by my own people. There is no such thing as peace in my heart. But with Ayna, I had a glimpse of what it could be like to finally let go, to forgive the ones who made us unworthy of Vala's absolution or Shaelak's forgiveness.

Below, movements catch my attention, and I bank right, into the treetops, my cousin following suit, as do the five other Crows who came on this trip to scout the location where the era of Vala's curse was ended by the only creature in this world who will ever have my heart.

A fissure runs through said organ at the thought of Ayna in Ephegos's claws, and the pain is no easier to bear in my crow form than in my fae one.

Royad flutters ahead with a few powerful wingbeats, his focus honed on where mine should lay, but I've been a shadow of myself since my death and resurrection. Like there is a hole in my body that's dripping energy into the nexus between realms. Royad darts through the branches before he lands on one high up in a nearby tree, head cocked and beak pointing down to where two males in brown leathers are sneaking through the forest. It's the third time we've seen this particular pair. Like all Fire Fairies, they wear slender blades at their hips. What's new are the crossbows they carry in their gloved hands, ready to shoot something from the sky within a heartbeat. I assume I'm not wrong in guessing that they are on a hunt. A hunt for large, black-feathered birds. Shifter ones in particular.

Nodding at Royad, I land beside him while the others settle a few branches up. In our bird forms, we are small enough to blend in with the trees, still difficult enough to kill with our magic and smaller targets, but we've come across dead crows—the real birds, not shifter ones like us—lately. Looking at the sharp bolts poised on the crossbows, the holes puncturing the bird carcasses make more sense. They've been systematically shooting crows from the skies, and it's only a matter of time before they'll catch us instead of some poor unaware creature who has no fault in the decline of the Fire Fairies or their residence.

While the previous times, we've simply followed them around, observing whether they'd drop any words of Ephegos or Ayna, this time, I'm too restless to simply wait and see. Giving a flutter of my wings, I signal the others I'm about to shift. Then, I let the magic wash through my body, let it eat up all the feathers but those of my wings. My weight pulls me out of the treetops, but I beat my feathered arms enough to break the fall while I send bonds of invisible power at both Fire Fairies, ripping their crossbows from their hands and shoving them to the forest ground where they wrestle the strength of my magic with an onslaught of flames.

I break the first one's neck with a tug on my power before I even set foot on the rock-scattered moss of the forest ground. The second, however, I pin to the ground with a boot to his throat, menace raging within me at the mere thought that he is one of those creatures who took Ayna from me. My self-control hangs on a thin thread threatening to snap at one wrong word, one too-deep breath of the Fire Fairy.

"Where is she?" I shove the flames he sends my way back into his face, watching his deep brown eyes flare with terror as he realizes who is upon him.

"Myron," Royad's baritone sounds from a few steps ahead, a warning not to forget myself.

We've talked about that, since the land won't give away which direction they hauled Ayna off to, it's time to find a different source of information. I guess the Flame male writhing beneath my power is the lucky one.

Well... not really. The one I killed on the spot was. For there is nothing worse than the wrath of a Crow King who's been robbed of the woman who saved him.

"I don't ... know ... who you're ... talking ... about," the fairy stammers, gasping for air in between words.

I lean down, blocking his attempts at singeing me with his fire with half a thought now that my fae powers have been freed. By Shaelak, I still marvel at what I'm capable of. Had I thought I was powerful before, now that the curse is broken, it's like someone lifted a veil on everything I am and everything I'm capable of.

My senses are sharper, my instincts more pronounced, my thinking quicker, and I'm not even starting on the physical strength. It took me a solid day to gain full control over that, and I'm still struggling with keeping my magic on a tight leash lest I hurt what few are left of my people.

"Don't play stupid." Royad is at my side, his steady presence calming as always. But the face he shows the Flame is that of the beaked monster he wore so bravely for all our lives. He crouches a few feet away from the fairy who's still trying to free himself, and graces us all with a display of his violent side. "You heard my king. Where. Is. She." He doesn't even phrase it like a question, just a series of growls that could belong to a beast. Perhaps some of the monster is still left in all of us. Even when we're free of the curse and redeemed of our ancestors' wrongdoings, it doesn't mean we aren't ready to commit our own.

In this case, none of it is wrong. There is nothing I wouldn't do to get Ayna back, so I don't think as my magic curls tighter around the fairy's neck. I merely pull back my foot and stand over him, watching his face turn blue while his flames snuff out at his fingers without any of them having touched Royad or me.

"I'll spell it out for you because I'm having a gracious day." Not exactly a lie. I was gracious this morning to let Royad have half of my breakfast, but the Flame doesn't need to know I'm anything but gracious when it comes to my Ayna. "Where is my queen?"

The fairy moves his head an inch to the left, then to the right. That's how far my power will allow it, but it's a clear shake of his head.

"You don't know? Or you don't care to share your knowledge?"

The fairy shakes his head again.

"So, you don't want to talk?" I loosen my hold just enough to give him a chance to prove me wrong.

It's enough for him to grasp his blade and stab for my thigh. The tip collides with my leathers, right above my knee. A sharp pain runs through my flesh, and I tighten my magic around his throat before I yank him off the ground and throw him against the nearest tree trunk.

I don't know who is more shocked, Royad or me, when the male slides to the ground, head lolling to the side at an odd angle and chest no longer heaving for breath.

"You killed him," my cousin notes, and I can't tell if there's accusation in his tone or simply surprise.

"I didn't mean to." It's the truth. I meant to force those words out of the Fire Fairy before I sent him straight for Eroth's Veil, but my power is overwhelming, and it seems I have no control when it comes to Ayna. Finding her is the priority, and I've just destroyed our chances by accidentally killing a potential source.

Royad doesn't say anything else, neither do the others as they land around us, shifting into their fae forms as they touch the ground. The sight of all of them bare-chested and bare-armed, no feathers, no beaks, no sign of bird other than the few tattoos some of them bear is something I yet need to get used to. I haven't gotten used to how naked I feel without a layer of feathers protecting my arms and shoulders either, the sensation of wind and sun so much more intense on my skin than on my feathers, but it's a good feeling. Proof that this is real. That the curse is broken.

Now, all I need is to find my wife, and I'll never look back on the torment that my life has been.

If only I knew where to find her.

When we sit by the fire that night in the cave near the Silver Stream that marks the western border of the Seeing Forest, the twenty Crows still left of my people chew silently on their roast meat. We brought back a few hares from our scouting trip, and some of the Crows helped prepare them. With our magic fully returned, it's easy work, and with our Crow urges lifted by the breaking of the curse, raw meat is no longer a craving any of us possess. My mind drifts back to my last wedding banquet, to the horror in Ayna's gray eyes as she'd observed the way my people hacked away on bloody meat with their beaks. It's a miracle she sat through that dinner without throwing up.

"Thinking of her again?" Royad nudges my leg with his knee where the thin cut is still visible in my leathers. The small injury beneath has long healed, but I didn't bother to wash off the dried blood.

"We need to change our strategy," I tell him instead of confirming my mind lingers on Ayna. Because we both know it always does. "It's only a matter of time before the Fire Fairies find us here, and if they come in numbers, we might not be able to defeat them." Even at our full strength. I don't need to add that. We all know twenty normal Crow Fairies and two royal Crows don't necessarily make an army. We are deadlier than ever, but we aren't invincible, I'm fully aware of that.

"Glad you still have your thinking straight," Royad jokes, giving me a wary smile that makes his scar tug awkwardly at the corner of his mouth. We try not to talk about how my father sliced his face open to punish him for being kind to a bride. Even when Crows heal fast, that wound had been too deep and brutal to seal without a scar.

He notices the stare, and a silent understanding passes between us. We've gone through all of it together, his scars and mine, but the curse was never his to shoulder. It was always my burden, even when he treated me like we were in it together, too. Under different circumstances, many of the brides might have preferred his humorous personality and warrior's body. But my deal with King Recienne had left me the only Crow allowed to marry even when I truly didn't want to damn any female to being bound to a monster like me—and by that, sentence them to die.

A shudder rakes through my body, the chill from the cave walls creeping along my naked back even when the fire warms my front.

"We'll find her," Royad reassures me the way he's always reassured me that things will work out for the best.

Why is it that I have trouble believing him when he's always proven to be right? He's the one who told me to keep trying, to show Ayna some of my more charming character traits so she'd at least get the chance to see the real me.

The real me meaning bottomless darkness where countless deaths coat my hands with blood.

"We need to get out of this fucking forest to find her." Silas inserts himself from a few feet away. The male is one of the oldest among us, having only a few decades on Royad and me. So, he had been still considered a child when the curse hit. He remembers more than all of us others as well. More of the violence from the first years after the curse, the way my people had sought a new home after Vala took everything from us to protect her humans.

The irony that it's a human who saved us doesn't fail to conjure the dark grin on my lips, which I've perfected to scare away my brides.

"He's not wrong." Royad gestures at the male chewing on a piece of meat, studying the harsh lines of his face visible behind a curtain of black hair.

That earns us the attention of the rest of the Crows. We've gotten used to the lack of privacy with twenty-two of us in the cave and all of us equipped with fae senses, but rarely do we pry on each other's conversations.

I have to admit, I spent too much time, in those first few days after coming back from the dead, on sleeping off the exhaustion overcoming me on occasion and the rest of my time searching the forest for traces of my wife to know much of anything else.

"She's obviously not in the forest, or we'd already have found her?" I snap, fully aware that those are the few loyal Crows left and that I shouldn't get on their bad side, or they might abandon me like the rest—the ones who didn't die in battle. But I don't have enough air to breathe, knowing that Ayna is in Ephegos's grasp. Time is running, and I need to act before that traitorous shit kills her.

Forcing my breathing to calm, I turn to Royad, intending to tell him that I'm ready to leave this place and turn over every pebble in Eherea until I find her, but a sharp pain sears my shoulder where the tattoo of a crow mid-flight spreads across my shoulder blade all the way to my biceps, and I release a hiss instead.

The look Royad gives me is a clear indicator he knows something's up.

When I found the tattoo shortly upon my waking in the clearing, I thought little of it. Many Crows are inked in various ways, and I wondered if it might be a mark I'd been given as a baby and which had been hidden beneath a layer of feathers. But when Royad spied it, he made it clear that this was something different. One wing of the crow would have peeked out from under my feathers where it spreads up toward my neck, and there had been smooth skin before the curse was lifted.

Perhaps that's what it is, a reminder of Vala's punishment. But the way pain is lashing through my shoulder right now, I doubt it's a mere image on my skin serving to never let me forget. Right now, this thing feels alive, like it's clawing at me with sharp talons.

I exhale with my eyes closed, shutting out the murmurs and crackling of the fire, the shuffling feet of deer and rabbits out in the forest, and the occasional caw of a real crow, until the pain is fading and I can think again.

If losing Ayna won't kill me, this thing on my shoulder just might.

"You all right?" Royad leans in, pretending to reach for his knife, which he dumped on the floor behind us earlier, and subtly checks on my shoulder.

When I give him a nod, he frowns. "You don't look all right."

Gritting my teeth, I breathe through the fading sensation in my shoulder and direct my mind into the shine of the fire in front of me. For a while, all I can do is count my heartbeats, convincing myself that not everything is lost, that I still have time to find my wife.

It's when I decide that I'll set out first thing tomorrow that the pain turns into something else, a tug directing me toward the cave wall that has my full attention. I stand, ignoring Royad's stare as I pad to place my hands on the rough, moss-overgrown stone standing between me and the place the tug is pulling me.

It's weak, but there is no mistaking whose magic is calling to me from what has to be miles and miles and miles away.

"Drop everything," I tell what's left of my people as Royad comes to stand beside me, his hand on my shoulder as if in comfort—or to caution me from clawing my path through the hard stone. "We're leaving now."

EIGHT

AYNA

When I wake, I'm not alone in the room. My head is pounding, and my stomach is roiling in a sensation not so different from when I woke up after Kaira poisoned me, but I sense the presence in the corner of the room, looming and dangerous.

Keeping my eyes shut, I take inventory of my body. The pain has faded from my shoulder and arm where Herinor cut me, and I can no longer feel the bruises where the guards dragged me through the palace to dump me unceremoniously in my assigned bedroom—my luxurious cell is more like it.

"I can hear your heart pick up pace, Ayna," Ephegos says, accompanied by light footsteps I only hear because he wants me to. I've spent enough time in the presence of Crows to know they don't make a sound if they don't intend to alert people to their approach. "Open your eyes."

I do because the only thing more terrifying than facing the male who put me in this new prison is not seeing him coming.

He's at the side of my bed—the very same bed I crawled to and curled up on top of, crying my eyes out after the guards had left.

There are no tears in my eyes now, only steel determination as I sit up and measure him head to toe like he's vermin even when his fine black pants and russet jacket suggest otherwise. Even his hair is smoothed back into a perfect ponytail today.

"What's the occasion?" I let my gaze drift over the brass buttons at the front of his jacket, wondering if they would make a good weapon if I managed to tear them off. If I had a slingshot, they might.

The self-satisfied grin on Ephegos's face is every bit as warm as the ones he used to give me at the palace in the Seeing Forest and nothing like the monster he actually is. "I took the liberty to heal what was left of your wounds while you were sleeping." His gaze follows the frayed fabric of my sleeve where Herinor tore it off. "Must have been quite an encounter if it left you that exhausted."

I don't know what is worse, that he's been in this room and laid a hand on me without my noticing or that it seems to give him pleasure that Herinor's torture knocked me out cold eventually.

All I give him is a bland expression as I swing my legs from the bed and stalk for the bathing room. The fact that I sway the moment I start walking doesn't escape his attention, and he's sending a too-warm laugh after me that could have fooled anyone had I not known what sort of cruelty he's hiding behind that courtier's facade.

"Yes, Ayna. Go clean up. Today is the day you'll finally leave this place."

I freeze on the threshold, using the wood to stabilize myself as I glance back at him over my shoulder. "What do you mean I'll leave this place? Where are we going?"

His grin only becomes wider. "How nice of you to assume I'll be accompanying you on your travels. And closer to that ocean you love so much."

It takes me a heartbeat to understand he actually answered my question—sort of.

"We're going to the Quiet Sea?" The ocean in the east of Eherea where I spent years on board the Wild Ray, soaking up the sun and relishing the wind on my skin. Freedom. And a crew of misfits I'd come to love.

"Not quite, my dear." Ephegos tilts his head, assessing me head to toe while his expression changes as if he's looking at something offensive. "But you can't go to King Erina's court in a bloodied dress, can you now? Wash up, and get dressed. Your things have been packed, and the carriage is waiting."

He turns on his polished boots and heads for the door while I scramble for anything to say. I haven't been speechless like this since the moment I woke in this Guardiansforsaken room, but this... This does it.

By the time I find my voice again, the door has closed, lock clicking into place, and I'm alone, staring at the carvings blocking the view of the hallway.

Erina—

Ephegos wants to take me to Erina's court. Lead spreads in my stomach, keeping down the bile threatening to rise in my throat.

That's why General Katrijanov visited. He's taking me to the very king I offended with my crimes—and this time, Erina himself will make sure I'll pay for them.

"No—" The word breaks out in a panicked whisper while my heart speeds in my chest. I can't go to Meer, the city where my father was executed for treason. I can't go back to a place I escaped as the child of a shunned family. I can't show my face in a court having become the same traitor to the crown as my father was.

A whole different sort of fear grasps me as I stand in the doorway like a frozen pillar of blood and silk.

Being taken from Fort Perenis to the Crow Palace was terrifying, but this is on a whole new level. I ran away as a youth to live with outlaws far from society, making a choice never to return to my birth home again to escape my shame and guilt for being the one who sold my father out to Tavras's soldiers.

"I can't go back there." I don't know who I'm speaking to or why, but when a voice answers from behind the bathing room door, I hit my shoulder hard on the doorframe, stumbling back into the bedroom.

"I'll help you."

Kaira appears in front of me, her leathers slightly askew as if she dressed in a hurry. Her knives are sheathed at her belt, and a bow is slung over her shoulder.

My legs are trembling, and I find myself reaching once more for the well of magic inside me that used to respond and has become as silent as a pile of rocks, but on the sideboard, a small brass candelabra sits within reach. I grab for it and wield it in front of me like a dagger.

The expression on Kaira's face is one of part amusement, part annoyance, with a portion of pity thrown into the blend.

"Oh, don't look at me like that. I'm not here to assassinate you."

The way her hand flicks to her knife makes me seriously question the truth of her words, but the smile on her face seems genuine as she waves me into the bathing room, latching onto my blood-caked wrist when I'm not moving, and simply pulls me over the threshold before I have a chance to object.

Damn fairies—Fire or Crow or otherwise. Being the only human here sucks harder than I could have ever imagined.

Shaking off the panic, I rip my arm back, bringing some distance between the woman and me, but she's already closed the door and herds me to the bathtub where tendrils of steam are rising from hot, lavender-scented water.

"Maybe not with a knife." I glance pointedly at the bathtub.

That costs Kaira a small laugh. "I'm not going to hurt you, silly. I'm here to help you get ready for your big journey."

There is something about the way she says the word *journey* that makes me wonder what exactly she knows about Ephegos's plans.

Debating whether I'll live longer if I confront her with words or if I try to fight my way out with my bare hands, I look her over. She's not aggressive, and no hint of malice mars her features. Then again, Ephegos never had any tells he was about to sell us all out to our enemy while he took revenge on Myron for his sister's death.

I also debate screaming, having the guards rush to my aid. The woman has spiked my tea before after all.

"Please don't alert the guards," she pleads as if reading my mind—perhaps she merely read my glance to the door. "I promise I'm not here to hurt you. I'm here because I overheard a conversation Ephegos had with one of the Flame leaders. They want to sell you to King Erina of Tavras."

There is no logic for me to trust a word she says.

"Old news," I quip, and choosing to hold off my attack a while longer, I brace my hands on my hips and give her an expectant glare. "You came to see me shipped off?"

Kaira shakes her head. "I want to come with you."

Air leaves me in a rush. "Why? Not that I'm intending to go…"

"Ephegos is bound to send a lady's maid with you if you are to join Erina's court," she explains as if that's all the reason she needs to participate in a journey of doom.

I need to sit on the edge of the bathtub before my knees give out. "What makes you even think I would want to take you with me? You poisoned me last time we met."

Kaira's brown eyes widen then narrow as if she's pondering her response. Her hand glides over her leathers, smoothing out some of the awkward angles where they aren't properly secured. She appears harmless, yet the steel on her body tells me she can strike fast if she wants to.

"I merely brought the tea."

I blow out a breath, letting both my fear and anger dissipate on the wafts of steam.

"All I wanted was to meet you, and the tea gave me a perfect opportunity." She twists her mouth as if realizing she just said too much, but the words are out, and I'm like a bloodhound now that I have someone in front of me who might have answers.

"So, why did you want to meet me so badly?" I fumble with my torn sleeve, pretending curiosity isn't burning a hole into my belly. And definitely ignoring the sense of dread that every passing moment conjures in my chest at the thought of going back to Tavras.

Kaira gestures at me as if that's answer enough before she explains. "You're a legend already. You broke a millennia-old curse on a mythical people. Crows are fairytale creatures in Eherea. Even in Askarea, hardly anyone has seen them in over a hundred years. You are a human turned Crow Queen. And—" She lowers her gaze, blushing to her hairline as she fidgets on the spot like a little girl.

"And what?" I don't let her out of my sight even for a heartbeat. I've learned my fair share of trusting fairies, Herinor being the latest addition to the list of creatures who hurt me despite what they speak in words. His warning floats to my mind.

I'm your ally. Probably the only one you have in this place, so play along

If Herinor is to be trusted, Kaira might be just another enemy. But something about the way she glances up at me tells me there is more to her than just the part-Flame.

"Spit it out, Kaira."

The woman nods, shoulders lifting with an inaudible sigh. "You found love strong enough to break a god's curse." Her eyes lock on mine as if searching for answers there.

I'm almost certain all she can find is a mirror of the pain crashing through my chest at the mention of said love. A love strong enough to break a god's curse. But also a love that has destroyed me.

"It doesn't matter now how I feel for him, does it? He's dead."

Kaira flinches at my words, but she recovers quickly, straightening her spine and gesturing at the water behind me. "Why don't you take a bath while we talk? I promise not to poison you." She adds the last words with a little smile, and I almost want to smile back, but it hurts too much, the memory of the male who brought my heart back to life only to leave me behind in this realm of the living where suffering has no end.

"Tell me what the poison was for, and I'll think about it." It's the least I can do. She snuck into the bathing room behind Ephegos's back after all and came to tell me about what his plans are.

She picks up a washcloth from the stack on the shelf beside the tub and holds it out to me. "I already said I merely brought the tea. I didn't add any poison."

"How do I know you're telling the truth?" I've been burnt too many times trusting the wrong people. If I open up to anyone, trust anyone, and it proves to be a mistake, I don't know if I'll survive it.

Clio and Royad are the only people left who I can call friends, and I have no idea if Royad is still alive with the Flames hunting for survivors, and Clio… I wish I had any indication she survived the explosion. A heaviness settles in my chest at the thought of how truly alone I am in this mess.

"How many Crows are left in the Seeing Forest?" I ask Kaira, eyeing the russet cloth in her hand warily. "Did the hunters return successful?"

Kaira gives me a long look. "The hunters came back two men short."

Hope surges in my chest. If two Flames died on the hunt for the Crows, they might still be out there, fighting. Maybe Royad is among them, taking his place as Myron's heir and the Crow's rightful king.

It takes me a moment to notice the sadness in Kaira's words, but when I do, I lock eyes with her, finding the inconspicuous brown of her irises full of worry.

"Was one of them a friend of yours?" It's not exactly a question I should be asking a fairy I don't trust and who has no reason to trust me, but I'm curious about the dynamics of the Flames' community, their hierarchy. The more I learn about the enemy, the better.

At least, for a heartbeat, I think so. Then I remember I'm about to be taken back to Tavras, far from the fairylands.

"I wouldn't consider anyone here a true friend." Kaira's voice is hushed to a near whisper, and she glances over her shoulder, hand at her weapon as if expecting to find Ephegos in the doorway—or one of the other Flames she doesn't consider a friend. Only when she's convinced herself the door is still closed and we're alone in here does she relax and her features turn less guarded.

"Look, I know you don't trust me or anyone in this house, but you can believe me you're not alone in that. I don't trust anyone who considers Ephegos a friend. Our Matrone does, and so do our warriors. They followed him blindly into a quest to regain our old seat of power. For thousands of years, the Flames have been scattered across the lands of Askarea, the borderlands to Tavras, and some have even moved on farther south in hopes of making a new home. But there's a core of Flames who aren't willing to let go. Matrone Jeseida is a direct descendant from the line of Flame leaders who fled the palace in the Seeing Forest. Her ancestors never gave up plotting to take back their home, but there were never enough Flames ready to aid her cause. It's only since Ephegos joined our ranks that my people have been rallying for a final strike."

My blood is pounding in my veins as she lays out Flame history in front of me like a peace offering, and it costs me all I have not to attack her with hundreds of questions. There is only one I need to ask since Flames are actual fairies and I have no knowledge of their workings. "When you say *line of Flame leaders,* do you mean Flames are mortal? Like humans?" Because if they are, it might give me an advantage when I try to make my escape the moment they put me into a carriage to Meer.

To my surprise, Kaira bobs her head. "If by *mortal* you mean that Flames die a natural death at some point, then yes, we are." Her features twist. "At least, the full-blooded ones among us are. Not many Flames survived Carius's attack on our palace, so it's not like there were many pure-blooded Flames to carry on our people."

Before I can ask specifics, she shakes her head. "That's how halflings like me happened. Though human blood was bred into my ancestors' line generations before I was born. If anything, I'm human with an affinity for fire." She manages a self-deprecating laugh.

"And the others?" I think of the male with pointed ears who attacked me when the Flames first breached the Crow Palace. I wasn't able to pay attention to the shape of the Flames' ears during the last battle, but the one who nearly killed me in the first attack definitely had pointed ears.

"Some lines believed it better to strengthen our people by breeding with other fairies." She gives me a meaningful look that I can only interpret as her finding it an abhorrent idea. "Those are the strongest fighters among us now. But Jeseida is a full-blooded Flame. She'll die after her natural lifespan ends, which is approximately two hundred years. She's in her hundred and twenties now. At the prime of her Flame years."

It still boggles my mind how something like that is possible, but I am not quick enough to ask Kaira how long she will live before she gestures at the water once more and gives me an expectant glance.

"It was Herinor who put the poison into the tea," she offers, not giving me a moment to process. "Now get into the tub. The sooner we get you ready, the sooner we can get out of here."

I open my mouth to ask what she means by *we,* but again, she has an answer ready.

"You didn't think I'd let you leave alone."

NINE

AYNA

It's not even an hour later when I sit at the table in my room, fully clothed in an entirely too pretty and uncomfortable traveling dress with long, ice-blue silken sleeves and skirts and a russet bodice that could as well have been part of the brocade wallpaper stretching along the wall around the window.

After informing me that she intends to join me on the journey to King Erina's court, Kaira braided my hair into a coronet at the crown of my head and added pearl-tipped pins until it looked like a tiara. I'm still processing everything she shared, but one piece of information is particularly bothersome: Herinor put the poison in my tea.

The same male who told me he might be my only ally tried to poison me before he tortured me.

I wish I had a moment to confront him, but the odds are that Ephegos will put me in a carriage and have me shipped off to Tavras before I get a chance to even see the rest of this estate.

Maybe it's for the best. The sooner I'm out of here, the sooner I'll get a chance to escape.

I've scoured the room for anything resembling a weapon, but the pins in my hair are the closest thing to something sharp I could find, so here I am, waiting for my captors to take me outside and send me off where I'll hopefully be able to sneak away during the night with my driver none the wiser.

Suppressing a sigh of frustration, I reach deep into the depths of my being where my magic once sang to me, but all I find is a sputter of cool energy that might as well have been the beginning stroke of resignation.

I have so many questions, and every time I gain information, all it does is bring up more questions until I'm buried beneath a pile of them. If Herinor told the truth, Vala was the one aiding me at the Crow Palace. The murderous lake was infused with her power. Maybe that's all it was—a brief helping hand of a goddess who saw someone worthy of breaking her curse.

My head is a mess, and my limbs aren't any better. I'm still weak, but the bath at least rinsed away the evidence of that weakness. I'm now clean and presentable again, an image of nobility and grace—if I manage to keep my spine straight. When Ephegos comes for me, I'll hold my head high and pretend not to care. I'll pretend for Myron and the memories we created. For the warmth of his touch I'll never feel again and his sacrifice, I'll be the unbreakable Ayna who once boarded a pirate ship to see the world and leave behind all the chains of guilt and sorrow.

I'll be more than that. I'll be the queen he made me, even when I don't have a kingdom to rule or a people. I'll bide my time until I see an opening, and then I'll run like the wind blowing into the Wild Ray's sails.

And then, I'll find Royad and Clio.

I swallow the lump in my throat at the thought that I might find neither of my friends even if they still live. They are magic-wielding fairies. And I'm... I no longer know what I am. Ephegos said I'm no longer all human, but it doesn't answer what that makes me. I'm not a Crow or a Flame. And I'm most definitely not high fae.

A knock on the door tears me from my thoughts, and I leap to my feet, determined not to show an ounce of weakness to whoever enters this room.

The door swings open, revealing the view of Ephegos in brown leathers, silver sword attached to his belt and an unbothered smile on his lips. "Ah, good, you're ready."

He strides right for me, holding out his hand like a courtier even when there is no invitation in his gaze, only command.

For a moment, I debate not taking it. Then my attention drifts to the scars along his skin. He gave up his wings to betray his best friend. He blames Myron for Sariell's death. He is acting like he rules the Flames even when Kaira mentioned a Matrone. Then there's the fact that he's working with General Katrijanov. Too many loose threads are running together in his mangled hands.

The irony doesn't slip my attention when I place my bad hand into his. "How do you know the Tavrasian king?" I give him a pointed look that I hope will take him by surprise.

The good thing about Ephegos is that he is not only smart, vengeful, and stealthy, but he is also a self-adoring asshole who wants to rub his superiority in my face. So I'm only half surprised when he chuckles and reels me closer to him like a rope on a ship and says, "There is a reason I gained so much power among the Flames, Ayna." He turns, pulling me along as he heads for the door. "I've been coming and going from this place since I learned of Sariell's existence. A halfling fathered by a Crow and carried in the womb of the Flame Matrone. A princess, so to say."

My stomach drops like I missed a step even when we're still on the even, polished floor of the hallway.

"If there is anyone who hates the Crows more than me, it's Jeseida." His smirk is manic, and so are his eyes, and when he runs his free hand along his forearm where his Flame armor covers the featherless flesh, I understand that perhaps he is glad that the final evidence of his Crow heritage was burned off his skin.

"And now you're their prince." It's a long shot, but I've learned that prompting Ephegos works better than asking questions. His one weakness might be that he feels the need to justify his actions, and I'm ready to take full advantage of that.

"Something like it. An adopted son of sorts. But don't get me wrong. I haven't escaped Myron's rule of terror only to become second choice over another dwindling people." He leaves it at that since we reach the stairs, and a pair of guards join us on our way down. This time, I pay attention—round ears. So they must have human blood. I'll only know if the original Flames have pointed ears once I meet the Matrone, which I'm not positive will ever happen since Ephegos tows me through a brass and cream entrance hall, straight for the open wing of a set of heavy double doors.

Outside, a black carriage big enough to hold four people is waiting, the four brown horses harnessed to it stomping impatient hooves. On the bench in front of the cabin, a driver sits, his tall, broad form clad in brown Flame leathers, but he wears a hooded cloak on top, hiding his face in shadows.

My legs turn weak at the mere thought that I'll have to trick a soldier of his build in order to flee, and I grab onto the doorframe so I won't stumble down the three granite steps leading down to the gravel path from the lush estate grounds into the forest.

"Get inside." The door opens on a phantom wind at Ephegos's flick of fingers, revealing comfortable russet and brass cushioned benches.

With a glance around the walls framing the grounds, I climb into the cabin, ignoring the sinking sensation in my stomach that I might have been better off staying here. It gets only stronger when Ephegos follows me and sits on the bench across, wearing a grin on his face that would have made me believe we're going on an exciting adventure had I not known the real him.

"You are coming?" The question bursts from my lips even when I'd rather pretend this can't be happening.

"You didn't think I'd risk you slipping away on the journey, did you?" He waves his hand, and the door closes so loudly the sound echoes in my mind the way the clicking lock of the prison door used to when I was locked up at Fort Perenis. "I know how good you are at sneaking around. You even managed to escape in the Seeing Forest." He considers the horror on my face then adds, "Once."

"And I was caught before I made it far." It's not my fondest memory, but the hours with Myron that followed contain some of the turning points of my relationship with the Crow King, so I find myself replaying those quite often.

"Of course, you were. It's not like a human girl could ever outrun a fairy." As he pauses, his gaze travels the length of my body, and I cringe under his scrutiny. "But you are no longer all human, so I'd rather keep a close eye on you. Myron already made all the mistakes of letting you out of his sight."

The way every mention of Myron makes my heart throb anew isn't even the worst part of the pain. It's the hatred in Ephegos's eyes when he speaks of his former friend and king.

I shake it off, focusing on the only thing that should matter right now. "What do you mean, *not all human*? What changed? I haven't turned fairy, or I'd have my magic." Perhaps, it's not a smart move to ask him about my magic, but I have to know.

Ephegos pulls his lips into a wide smile and shrugs. "You didn't think breaking a goddess's curse wouldn't leave a mark on you."

It's not an answer, more of a hint, but I'll take it. He doesn't know Herinor shared the story of Vala's curse with me, so he doesn't know he gave me more information than he intended to.

Before I can sort my thoughts, a whip cracks, the horses whinny, and the carriage sets into motion. I catch a glance of the tall, white and russet building that was my prison these past days, not failing to notice the intricate details carved into the facade. But it's the lean, leather-clad form dashing from bush to bush that catches my attention. Kaira.

I don't need to see her face to recognize the long brown braid bouncing with movement. A small pack is strapped to her shoulders, and in her hand, she holds a bundle I can't identify.

The path bends away from the estate, and I lose sight of the Flame as tall hedges frame our path all the way to the iron gates opening for the carriage.

.

TEN

AYNA

We roll through the forest for hours before the first break. All that time, I try to keep a casual eye on the trees outside, but there are no landmarks that would help me orient, and it doesn't matter where we are. I know where we're going, and I can't go there.

"Don't get any ideas," Ephegos warns as he opens the door and gestures at a nearby bush where I'm supposed to see to my needs. "King Erina didn't specify in what condition he wants you, but I assume you don't need both your feet to be a guest at his court."

Ice slides down my spine as the male who drove the carriage leaps off the bench at the front and steps to my side, obviously intending to accompany me to the bushes.

"I won't run." It's not a promise I intend to keep, but how else am I to get the guard off my back?

"Don't worry, Wolayna." Ephegos tosses over his shoulder as he flexes his arms and stretches his legs in a few long strides in the other direction. "Herinor will make sure you won't."

My heart stops in my chest then picks up at double pace. Herinor towers over me, his scar-flecked skin and stubbled jaw the only recognizable parts of him under the hood he's been wearing, but as he slides it down, his full features are illuminated by the soft sunlight piercing through the cover of leaves above. Eyes of fir green stare back at me with a warning, and for a beat, all I can think is that I couldn't make out their color in his torture chamber with the dim torch light.

"Move." He shoves me by the shoulder until I stumble into the thicket, legs sluggish with paralyzing fear. A glance at his belt confirms that the knife with the leather-wrapped hilt that inflicted all those cuts on my skin is traveling with him, but there is a sword attached at each hip as well, and a small hatchet.

When I meet his gaze, all I find is the same warning from when I glanced at him before the guards took me back to my room. I don't speak a word, merely take a deliberate step back into the bushes where I hope he won't follow.

Of course, there is no way for me to escape with both Ephegos and Herinor paying close attention to my every move, but that doesn't keep me from hoping to find a window of opportunity later. Later, before we make it to Meer.

I don't even know how many days of travel lay ahead, how long we'll remain in the merciful cover of trees that might allow me to hide if I ever manage to make my escape. The moment we're out in the open, the vastness of the Plithian Plains will make it practically impossible to sneak away. Ephegos and Herinor's fairy senses will spot me across the flatlands even if I crawl on my belly.

"Isn't there supposed to be a lady's maid traveling with me?" I make conversation more to distract myself from having to pee within earshot of a male who recently cut me with his knife—or any male. "Or did Ephegos bring you for the job?" It's not a smart move on my part. All the more, I'm surprised when Herinor laughs.

"I'd make a fine lady's maid. It would be a very different type of task for once. Not that I don't enjoy torturing, but I've heard Tavrasian fashion is almost as good as a knife to the throat with its fishbones and tight lacings." His eyes travel my torso, stopping at my waist. "Go see to your needs. I'll be right here."

It's all he says before he turns around so his back is to me, but I hear words unspoken that do not match his grumbling tone or the menace of his appearance. *If you need me.*

I decide not to listen to the silent add-on. I can't trust him. Herinor put poison in my tea. And I sure as the Guardians are Eroth's children can't confront him about that with Ephegos this close by.

A few awkward minutes later, I step out of the bushes past the male's shoulder. He follows at a few paces distance back to the carriage where Ephegos is waiting with a basket of food in his hand and a smile on his lips as if all he wants is to have a sweet picnic with the master of torture and me right here on the forest ground.

The horses stomp at the scent of apple and sugar filling the air, and I pause as I realize that I can actually smell the pie sitting in the basket from a few steps away.

"Here, Ayna." Ephegos holds out a piece to me. I don't wonder where he conjured the porcelain plate from or the silver fork but simply take it from his hands and start eating. Being rattled to the bones inside the carriage while my stomach has been clenching with trepidation hasn't helped my already shaky condition. It's a miracle I'm not swaying on my feet as I march to a fallen tree trunk and sit down, already shoveling the pie into my mouth. Herinor follows me like a prison guard.

"So, what about that lady's maid?" I ask between bites.

Herinor's jaw feathers as he turns those fir-green eyes on me, and I squirm at the promise of more knife-cutting if I don't shut up.

By the carriage, Ephegos observes us with a raised brow. "Interesting you should ask. I already sent someone ahead for you. I don't know if you'll be happy with her, though. She's quite a wreck."

Something deep down in my chest turns to ice, and at the back of my mind, a small voice is screaming a warning. Ephegos is planning something. I don't know what it is, but it includes the entirety of his wicked cunning.

"Now eat up. We've got somewhere to be." He watches me finish my pie before he waves me back to the carriage. I don't even try to resist, knowing that Herinor's strength unquestionably outmatches mine even if Ephegos wouldn't get involved in dragging me back.

At the door, he holds out a small canteen. "You haven't had anything to drink in a while, Ayna." Again, it's not an invitation; it's an order. So I take the canteen from his hand and take a sip before handing it back to him.

The familiar taste of herbs spreads on my tongue, and I know I've been poisoned again. Before my senses fail me, I shoot an accusatory glance at Herinor, whose eyes are already on me, conflicted, yet he doesn't make a move to help me as I drop to the forest ground, uncaught by protecting arms.

The ground beneath me sways, making it difficult to keep my balance. I haven't been in a storm like this since the night before the Wild Ray was captured by Tavrasian soldiers—by General Katrijanov to be precise. The ship aboard which I am standing isn't the Wild Ray, though. This is a simple sailing yacht, big enough to hold a small crew, but nothing as formidable as the pirate ship I once called my home.

Gripping the railing harder, I glance over my shoulder, trying to figure out how I got here, if I'm a prisoner, or if I miraculously escaped Ephegos and made it to the ocean. Perhaps I'm on my way to freedom and the storm is the only obstacle standing between me and the Eastern waters of Eherea bridging the way to Neredyn.

"Ayna." Myron's voice pierces right through my heart. I don't see him, but his scent drafts into my nose as I whip my head around to locate him… Wind and pine and something reminding me of freedom. My chest clenches at the possibility of him being here, of all of the horrors from the Seeing Forest being nothing more than a horrific figment of my imagination.

"I'm here!" The gusts of air whipping around me swallow up my voice, tearing at my long, heavy dress, at my loose hair, until my view is blocked by strands of ash blonde.

From within the haze, Myron's powerful outline appears, black-feathered arms hanging loosely at his sides as he takes me in, head to toe—the tight leather pants, linen shirt, and vest that are my pirate uniform, the daggers sheathed at my hips.

My heart stops as his all-black eyes lock onto mine, and he closes the distance between us in a few long strides, wind ruffling his feathers and tousling his hair. He's just like I remember him: the lean muscle rippling along his torso with every step he takes toward me, the darkness of his mood mirroring on his face. I still haven't taken a breath when his talon-tipped hands wrap around my waist, pulling me against him, and I crash against his chest like in free fall. I'm still free-falling as he lowers his face, aligning his mouth with mine. A rush of heat brushes my lips, and I remember to breathe, remember that he shouldn't be here, that he's dead. But he's kissing me in a symphony of all the memories he and I made during my time at the Crow Palace.

My stomach flutters as he nudges his tongue against my lower lip, requesting access … and I give it to him. I give him all of me because this might be the last time I'll get to see him.

Tingling warmth turns into liquid heat as he slides his tongue into my mouth, at the taste of him, his fingers splaying on the small of my back as I tilt my head to give him better access. The wind relentlessly beats against our silhouette, trying to cool down the fire Myron ignited in me, but his touch is a million times hotter as it finds its way up my spine until he's cupping my neck, fingers tangling with my hair, and I sink my hands into the soft feathers of his arms.

Guardians—

I moan as he presses his hips against mine, trapping me between the railing and the hard planes of his body, lining them up with my curves—until I forget where we are and that this can't possibly be real. Until all I can think of is how to get him out of his leather pants and have him take me right here, right now on deck of this ship—

A ship...

This isn't real. I carefully pull back my right hand, bending and rolling the wrist. It moves like it's never been shattered, like it used to when I was still able to wield a dagger with it.

As reality settles in that this is a dream—a dream I don't want to let go of—Myron is tugged away by the ruthless storm, his wings flaring as he fights the relentless forces that are the weathers at sea. He doesn't stand a chance. Neither do I when I push my path after him through the fog hiding his beautiful face from view once more.

"Don't leave me." Panic grasps me as the last of him is swallowed up by a barrier of dense white, and I have to hold onto the railing so my strength won't leave me.

"Where are you, Ayna?" He sounds close enough to touch, but I can't find his outline in the haze spreading along the planks of simple wood I stand on, eating up every inch of clear sight until I'm trapped in smoke and mist and my own thundering heartbeat.

I try to grapple my way through the haze, pierce it with my gaze, but it doesn't yield. "Myron…" I pant his name, another gust of wind stealing my breath.

"I will find you. And if it takes a lifetime, I will find you."

The promise still echoes in my head when I claw at the barrier pushing toward the source of his voice, then something hard hits my face.

Pain explodes along my cheek, blooming like a spring meadow of torment as I shoot to my feet but am jostled back into a sitting position immediately. The haze has lifted—or I blinked the dream away when Herinor slapped me with his brutal hand.

The ground *is* swaying, but it's not a boat. It's the carriage, and Herinor is riding in the cabin with me, face grim and eyes hard as a frozen lake.

"Pay attention." His hiss is almost as harsh as the wind in my dream—a dream where Myron's voice called out to me. Biting my lower lip is all I can do to fight the tears pricking behind my eyes.

Herinor gestures at the window, and I finally focus on something other than the gaping hole that the thought of Myron being alive—and waking to it having been a dream—left in my chest. Swallowing all signs of the spreading agony, I follow his gaze to find we've cleared the forest, and all I can see are the grassy plains outside the windows. Herds of horses should be grazing here and there, but the pulsing pain trapped inside my skull doesn't allow for me to focus enough to make out those brown and black dots in the distance. I must have hit my head when I fainted.

"Drink this." A canteen of water dangles from Herinor's hand on a leather strap. "You've been out for a while."

He doesn't need to say it when it's written all over his face: I missed my opportunity to escape in the forest. From here on, it will only become harder to avoid the keen eyes of my company—if I ever manage to slip away.

Ignoring the canteen as well as all the reasons I should spit in Herinor's face, I pin him with a gaze. "Where is he?"

For a heartbeat, the massive male sitting on the bench across from me squirms. Then, his features smooth over, turning into the mask of the male who sliced me open in the basement of the Flame estate. He stashes the canteen under the bench he's sitting on and faces me, shoulders squared and scar-flecked jaw feathering as he scans my features. "You mean Ephegos." I can't tell if I imagine the relief in his tone when he realizes I'm asking for the Crow traitor.

"Who else would I be asking about?" For there are only two males I want to see, and one of them is dead. Wherever Royad is, I hope he's still breathing and fighting. I can't bear losing another person, no matter how far away and how unlikely I'll ever see him again. If he's smart, he'll take whatever remains of his people and flee Eherea.

Herinor shakes his head. "He's driving the carriage." The look he gives me is all I need to know that Ephegos hasn't cleared the field to give me space. Someone needs to drive the carriage, and since Herinor is in here with me, I assume the pain in my chest and head won't be the only ones for much longer.

It takes the blink of an eye for him to reach for his simple knife and set it to the side of my arm. "I'm bound by my bargain with Ephegos," he reminds me as he slices through my sleeve, making me cringe back into the cushions of the bench.

Panic grasps my voice, and I can't get a scream out. Even if I did, no one would come to my aid. No one would care if Herinor reduced me to a bundle of bloody ribbons—as long as I was still breathing so Ephegos could deliver me to Erina.

"*Please.*" I mouth the word, not daring to speak out loud when Ephegos is within earshot. "*You said you were my ally.*"

Herinor understands and nods, but his blade bites into my upper arm anyway, right where my tattoo wraps to the side of my biceps. A brief, stinging pain tears through my arm before Herinor pulls back his knife and sheaths it without wiping off my blood.

"I'm not supposed to make a mess in the carriage. Just do enough to keep you in line and occupied on an otherwise boring journey." The bitterness in his voice doesn't match the cruelty of his actions or the remorse in his eyes as he scans my arm, the streaks of blood running down my sleeve, then my face. "*I'm sorry,*" he mouths, too, before he opens his mouth as if to say something more.

I shake my head at him. He hurt me, poisoned me. Hurt me again. I don't want his apologies or his pity. I want nothing to do with this fairy at all.

Fighting all the anger, the pain, the fear, and frustration, I clasp my wounded arm with my free hand and pray to the Guardians that this journey will be over soon. If I want a chance to make my escape, I can't eat or drink to avoid another dose of poison, and I can't sleep because I won't miss another opportunity.

At least, the pain keeps me alert when my body is exhausted from the aftereffects of the poison. I yet need to learn what it does besides putting me to sleep for extended periods of time, how long it will take for it to finish me off for good, though I'm not ready to ask Herinor anything. I'll bide my time until an opening arises. And then, I'll run.

ELEVEN

MYRON

The lack of pain in my shoulder is a small reprieve while my panic hasn't eased for even a moment. It's the second time the tattoo felt like someone was trying to cut it off with a burning knife, and I have yet to learn what exactly that pain means. The only thing I know is that it's somehow connected to my Ayna.

We've combed over every last inch of ground on our way out of the Seeing Forest—not one trace of her. She isn't here, and the uncomfortable sensation lingering in the intricate tattoo covering where feathers once met the skin of my shoulder blade keeps calling me forward.

The decision to bring Royad and Silas along was the right one. The rest of my people— not even twenty now— will have to hold out in the Seeing Forest while we run for their queen's rescue.

"How much farther before we rest?" Royad wants to know.

I cut him a glance suggesting, if he even considers resting before we've found her, I'll shift into my bird form and bite off his head. I am about to voice that thought when the air ripples a few paces in front of us, and the tall, broad form of the Fairy King's general appears, auburn hair bound at the back of his head and eyes of a similar shade finding mine across the small distance.

Beside me, Royad and Silas draw their weapons while I merely stand, calling upon my fae magic and summoning it to my fingertips. The last time I saw Astorian in leathers and fully armed like this was on the battlefield over a hundred years ago when he fought alongside his king and Princess Cliophera. For a heartbeat, I wonder if the female made it out of the Flame attack alive. Royad said Ephegos took Ayna, but no one saw what happened to the fairy who helped train her.

Guilt stirs in the pit of my stomach. I asked for her aid, made that bargain with her to make sure Ayna would be adept enough with her magic to survive a Flame attack.

"Lord Astorian." I address him by the social title he holds in the fairy ranks, not his position at the fairy court. "To what do I owe the honor?"

To my left, Royad grunts his disapproval of my manners while Silas draws a second blade from his belt.

The fairy general doesn't lift a finger toward his weapons. He doesn't need to. Even with all fae powers having returned to the Crows with the breaking of the curse, the Askarean fairies are still strong and skilled. His magic is nothing I care to test the limits of my own powers against.

The male tilts his head, studying my unruly state, the ripped and dirty leather pants, my bare chest and wind-torn hair. "You are about to leave Askarean soil." It's an observation and a warning. "You left the Seeing Forest a while ago."

"I haven't forgotten my bargain with Recienne." Whether he believes it or not.

Astorian waves away my reassurance, gesturing at our surroundings. "Yet, here you are, ready to risk everything for a human." I'm not sure I imagine the approval in his tone, but his eyes light up with a challenge I'm more than willing to meet if it means speeding this up and continuing on my quest. The tug in my shoulder has become nearly unbearable, and if I don't follow it, I fear Ephegos will have damaged Ayna beyond repair by the time I find her. I can't let that happen, no matter how many fairies stand in my way.

"If Recienne has a problem with my leaving, he can come after me himself." The bite in my voice gets Astorian's attention, and he studies me—really studies me—those vigilant eyes wandering my feather-less arms, my shoulders, until they land on my eyes.

"So, it's true." He gestures at where the last time I saw him feathers were sprouting. "The curse is broken."

I don't need to ask how he knows about the curse. Of course, Princess Cliophera told her king and his general

101

about the weakness of their enemies. But I don't see them as enemies anymore. Cliophera helped save Ayna. I'll be forever in her debt.

A simple nod is all I give him. "Lower your weapons." I glance left and right at my cousin and Silas, who both give me incredulous looks. "Our quarrel is no longer with the fairies of Askarea—at least not with the high fae." Meeting Astorian's eyes takes more courage than I expected, but when I do, a wealth of understanding is brimming there. He knows. He knows what happened at the palace in the Seeing Forest. Knows that the breaking of the curse means the Crows no longer require brides—all our bargains are moot.

"There is no more need for brides, and whoever of my people are remaining in the Seeing Forest won't harm anyone." It's a promise I can easily give since these few Crows are all loyal to me. The traitors have all gone with the Flames and Ephegos to wherever cowards run off to. And they've taken *my* Ayna. I exhale a controlled breath to prevent my fury from clouding my judgement. It's a futile effort.

Astorian gives me a nod of appreciation, his powerful arms folding over his chest. I've seen him fight with those arms and have no desire to be on the receiving end of that menace. And that's just his physical prowess. I've also seen him use his unique magic—melting stone. Besides the Fairy King, he's one of the most dangerous creatures in Askarea.

"Recienne is happy to see you leave his lands. Don't come back. I'll relay the same message to the Crows remaining in the Seeing Forest." He turns on his heels, ready to march away, but before he takes a step, Royad raises his voice.

"Have you heard all of what happened in the Seeing Forest?"

Astorian spins around to face my cousin, murder in his auburn eyes. With two long strides, he's in front of Royad, one of his countless blades in his hand and pointed at Royad's throat.

"I don't care what happened between you feathery lot and the ones who can't keep their fire under control. All I care about is that my mate hasn't come back since she returned to the Seeing Forest to help your human bride." He throws me a sideways glance, cataloguing the way I've raised my hand to direct my magic at him if he moves the knife at Royad's throat even a fraction. Beside me, Silas has drawn his sword once more, ready to take on the fairy general who shakes his head an inch.

"Where is she?" The earth shudders beneath me.

Silas swipes at him with his sword, but a string of liquid rock rips from the ground, slinging around the blade and ripping it from the Crow's grasp.

By Shaelak—

The fairy princess is missing. She either never made it out of the explosion or she ended up in the Flames' claws. I can't tell which option is more terrifying—not because I care excessively about the female who helped save Ayna but because the male before me does. His mate—Cliophera is his mate. And we all know what that means.

He won't rest until he finds her. He won't spare anyone standing in his way. If the fairies of Askarea are anything as relentless when it comes to their mates as my kind, it doesn't matter that he's facing three powerful Crows. He will eviscerate us with strength fueled by his need for vengeance.

"I don't know." The truth isn't what Astorian wants to hear, but he recognizes it as such anyway. At least, he doesn't suspect us for holding his mate captive. "If you got your information from the right sources, you'll know that your mate isn't the only one who's gone missing. My wife is gone as well. Taken by the traitors working with the Flames."

There is no logical reason to give him this additional information other than the anguish, the terror, the panic I recognize in his eyes as they snap to mine. We might have been enemies for longer than either of us can remember, but when it comes to this sort of loss, he and I are the same. We both won't rest until we get back the females who were taken from us.

As this small moment of recognition passes between us, Astorian lowers his blade from Royad's throat. Heaving a deep breath, my cousin staggers back, leaving Silas the only one at my side, trapped by the solidified rock Astorian wove around his sword. It melts away, setting the older male free as well. Astorian releases my wrist and vanishes into thin air the way his kind like to do before popping up a few paces away, blade sheathed and conflict written on his features.

What a convenient and utterly annoying skill.

"I know what you gave up to save your queen, Myron. And so do Cliophera and Recienne, or they wouldn't have agreed to aid you." He turns his head to scan the bushes and trees at the seam of the forest, unbothered by the three deadly Crows he just attacked, and grinds his teeth as if fighting a whole flood of words he isn't supposed to speak but needs to get out anyway.

It's enough to trigger the sort of compassion in me kings are supposed to show, even if Astorian isn't part of my people. Not even an ally. And most definitely not a friend.

"I'm sorry." The words slip out so fast I can't even think them through, what they might entail if the fairy male interprets them as an apology for my involvement in the disappearance of his mate.

His gaze snaps back to mine, and the rage brimming there is more than I can handle.

Bracing myself against the onslaught of his anger, I reach into my magic and draw it to my fingertips, the vast power buzzing and sizzling as it aches to break free. I haven't used the full extent of my abilities since I woke from the dead, so there is no way of telling what I'm actually capable of. I'm not sure if now is a good moment to find out either.

Royad and Silas don't seem to have any such reservations as their magic flickers through the air, weaving together in a shield protecting the three of us from one wildly upset fairy male. A shield. I haven't thought of creating one of those since I died. It didn't stop me from being stabbed last time. It didn't stop Ayna from getting hurt.

The guilt washing over me has nothing to do with my apology toward Astorian and everything with the part I've played in Ayna's sacrifice.

"Don't be." Astorian's words surprise me more than another attack would have as he folds his arms over his chest in a clear gesture that the time for weapons and fighting is over—for now. "My mate is as stubborn as she's brilliant. No measure of warning could have stopped her from returning to the Seeing Forest to help save the human in your claws. *From* you, preferably, not *for* you," he adds with a grim expression on his features. There is no mistaking the despise, the centuries of enmity and hatred between our peoples. Clio, however, had taken on the harrowing presence of the Crows to help a human. That's more than any of my people could have said for themselves. My people preferred to let people die.

A shiver as the wrongness of everything the Crows stand for crawls through my system.

Astorian gives me a glance that tells in all detail what horrors he would have in store for me had I been the one to harm or abduct his mate. "For once, you're not to blame for the disappearance of a fairy female."

Beside me, Silas gives a humorless chuckle, his curtain of black hair swishing over his shoulders as he slowly shakes his head. "You say you don't hold us responsible, yet you're ready to rip our throats out." He speaks out of turn, and we all know it, yet nobody reprimands him since he's addressing an obvious truth.

"Oh, I'd be happy to rip *your* throat out," Astorian hisses, the sound reminding me of the half-human forms we used to be trapped in so much I can't suppress a shudder.

Vala lifted her curse from us and allowed us to return to our normal forms. She even gave us back our ability to shift into our bird forms.

"Silas, don't." I lock a band of invisible steel around his arms as he twitches for an attack once more. The grunt of anger is nothing compared to the horror in Royad's eyes as they meet mine.

It takes me a moment to understand why he shakes his head at me. Drops of crimson fall from Silas's fingers as if I've sliced open his skin with my magic. I reel it in so fast it lashes back at me like a whip.

"Seems like your abilities have improved since that last battle," Astorian notes with the cool assessing tone of a general. I can't place the expression in his eyes, but it's something more than hatred. It's something more than the centuries we've been fighting each other. "Perhaps you could be useful to the Fairy King, Myron."

"I want nothing to do with the Fairy King." The words are out too fast again. I need to learn to control myself better, or they'll one day be the end of me.

I know Royad and Silas agree, even when Silas is currently sneering at me despite my lifting the magic binding him in place. The hidden wounds stop bleeding immediately

"All I want is to find Wolayna." Another truth, one that I am not ashamed to speak when Astorian feels the same about his mate.

Astorian takes a step closer, leaning in as if sharing a secret. Beside me, Silas and Royad tense for battle. "Get your fucking people out of Askarea. Recienne has had enough of you." A breeze stirs loose strands of auburn hair framing his face. "Get them out today if you can. And then, for fuck's sake, we'll need each other's help to find our females."

Much as I loathe to admit it, he's right. The Crows shouldn't remain in the Seeing Forest where Flames are hunting for them. They should flee to the coast and take the next best ship they can find to sail East. Homeward to Neredyn where the gods no longer despise us.

If the heaviness of my heart is any indication, this would be a bad decision. Yes, the Crows are in danger from the Flames if they remain in the Seeing Forest much longer, but they can also take out those bastards little by little with every hunting party they eviscerate. However, if they're gone, I won't have a people to support me in a fight against the Flames if we ever come to face them again in battle.

Apparently, Royad knows exactly where my mind has wandered because he plants himself closer to me and grabs his sword like a guard rather than the next in line for the Crow throne. "I'm not leaving you." His own guilt resonates in every word as does his determination.

Part of me battles to tell the fairy general I'm not taking orders from him while the other part wants to tell him the aid of one of the most skilled fairy warriors I've ever seen is exactly the help I need.

So, I heave a breath of unease at the decision I have to make.

The air smells of remorse and defiance, and a fair lot of clematis, as I pin Royad with a gaze only he could understand then turn to Silas, who seems as ready to march into battle with me as my cousin. They both nod, and I know I have their support, no matter what I decide.

"How about a bargain, Astorian."

The male cocks his head, his predatory focus turning lethal. "What do you propose?"

Swallowing my pride, I pour my own magic into a shield around Royad and Silas just in case Astorian is unhappy with my suggestion. "Odds are that, if Clio didn't come back to you after the battle, she was taken captive by the Flames." The general cringes at the thought of his mate in the Flames' hands, and right he is, but I continue. "She certainly hasn't crossed behind Eroth's Veil, or you'd feel it in your bones that she's no longer breathing."

A quick dip of his head is all the confirmation I need.

"So, here's what I believe."

He goes so still I could swear he is nothing more than a handsome pillar carved, colorful stone as he listens.

"Wherever they took my queen, they must have taken your princess. Find one, find both." It's a wild theory but the one making the most sense. If Ephegos wanted Clio dead, he'd long have killed her and, as her mate, Astorian would have known. The traitor must have plans for both of them, and I'm not eager to find out what they are. I'd very much prefer to see both of them alive and safe instead.

"Those are mere suspicions, Crow." Astorian's hands have wandered to his hips, fingers grazing the hilts of two daggers I truly don't have the patience to knock out of his hands. We have more important matters to deal with. "No bargain."

"If you work with me to find them both, I'll take my people and leave Eherea."

The fairy general tilts his head as if measuring each of us for the worth of his own mission as he contemplates my offer. His brows slant, eyes narrowing, and I think he's going to turn on his heels and disappear into thin air as he sets out to find his mate on his own. But his expression smooths over, and all three of us startle with surprise when Astorian claps his hands, spinning toward the edge of the forest. "Let's go, Crow King. And you better be right. I'd hate for Recienne to tear my head off for agreeing to a foolish bargain that won't guarantee to get you off his lands in case you're wrong."

TWELVE

AYNA

I was wrong. There won't be another opening to run. If I wasn't certain when Ephegos forced the poisoned water down my throat, I'm sure now. It's become impossible to tell the number of hours or days passing between my poison-induced periods of sleep and the time I spend vomiting and fighting a pounding headache when I wake up again.

This is the third time they've poisoned me on the journey to Meer, and every time I open my eyes, it's night, so I can't make out more than the immediate surroundings when Herinor marches me to a thicket where I can take care of my needs.

With nothing staying in my stomach for long, I've become weak and incapable of even thinking about running.

"Over there." Herinor points at a low hedge that seems all too domesticated for us to still be in the Plithian Plains.

I follow where he's pointing and double over, retching until the nausea ebbs and I'm able to breathe again.

The male hasn't spoken about his oath to Ephegos again, or about how he intends on breaking it to help me the way an actual ally wouldn't. Then, I've given up hope that anyone is my ally in this world. The only person willing to save me died to actually do so, and his death still haunts me in the nightmares of my poison-sleep.

I'm about to gather myself up and stagger back to the carriage when movement in the nearby bushes catches my attention. Before I can make out what sort of animal snuck up on us, Herinor darts over and reaches into the twigs, extracting a human shape clad in leathers. A bow and arrow are slipping from the person's hands as Herinor slams her down on the ground where he pins her with his steel grasp.

Not any person, I realize.

"Kaira—" My voice is weak and my legs shaky as I stumble toward her, pulling on Herinor's shoulder to get him off her. "Get off her. She's not an enemy."

Herinor doesn't seem convinced, for he grabs the woman by the throat as he pulls her back to her feet, skillfully evading my attempts to shove him off her.

"Is something wrong with your eyes?" He jerks his chin at the bow and arrow. "She was pointing that at you."

Kaira's brown gaze meets mine through the pale, moonlit night, and she tries to shake her head. She's wearing the exact same clothes she was when I saw her sneak along the hedges at the Flame estate.

"Did you follow us all the way here?"

"Apparently, or she wouldn't be hiding in second-rate bushes to fire arrows at you." Herinor drags a struggling Kaira toward the carriage, his free hand herding me along. "Only thieves and assassins sneak through the night like this."

Under different circumstances, I might have raised a brow at him, asked him if he was serious, but with my head spinning from lack of nourishment and the aftereffects of the poison, I am in no condition to challenge him about anything.

"Don't hurt her," I ask instead, hating how helpless I've become. If only I had my magic—

It's a topic I try not to think on too much anymore when all it does is give me flashes of the day when even magic wasn't enough to save Myron.

Herinor's chuckle rolls through the field, bouncing off the polished walls of the carriage as he marches us up toward Ephegos's elegant form. "I'm not the one who decides what's to happen with her." I can't help noticing the disdain in his voice. "He is."

"And *he* will make sure the lower Flame is properly punished for an attempt on my prisoner's life." Ephegos pushes away from the carriage, prowling toward me as if cataloguing any injuries. Of course, all he is doing is making sure I'm not visibly damaged when he delivers me to Erina.

113

My stomach sinks despite the excitement and adrenaline coursing through my blood. If Kaira truly meant to kill me… Perhaps Herinor was right that I have no allies.

He releases her, shoving her to the ground in front of the Crow traitor, her whimpering as her knees hit the hard earth making me shrink an inch. "Followed us all the way from the estate," he notes, stepping back so he's standing beside me—probably to make sure I won't bolt.

The thought brings a dark laugh to my lips. As if I could run in this state. As if I could do anything other than exist.

Holding my breath, I scan the Crow from the side, searching for any indication he's going to push me to my knees next, but Herinor stands like a statue as he waits for his master to exact justice on the would-be assassin.

Something in the way Kaira quivers under his stare tells me she's been in this position before and knows exactly what's going to happen next.

Since I woke in the Flame estate, I haven't seen Ephegos lay a hand on anyone other than me, friend or foe, but when he strikes Kaira's face with the back of his hand in a wide swing, it's obvious he has more practice beating up his prisoner than he'd let on.

At the gasp of agony from Kaira's lips, something tries to rise inside me like a memory of the power I once held, but there's no water around us. No stream. Not even a puddle … if I don't count the spiked liquid in the canteen that's sitting under the bench inside the carriage.

"I tolerate a lot of things." Ephegos stalks away from the cowering part-Flame, folding his arms as if he hadn't just struck her in the face and musing at the stars above is the only concern he has. "But I don't tolerate insubordination, Kaira. You were worth nothing in Jeseida's service, and if you're stupid enough to sneak up on two full-blooded Crows in the middle of the night and try to kill their charge, you're even more useless than I initially thought."

He stops to eye Kaira, who is shaking with suppressed sobs. Sobs of fury, I realize as she turns to watch Ephegos, and I can make out the ire written on her features. Her bow and arrow have dropped to the ground in the process of Herinor dragging her to the carriage, lying in the dirt and leaves right at Ephegos's feet. He swipes them up with a swift hand and snaps them in half.

I could swear a part of Kaira's defiance withers at the sight of her weapon being destroyed.

"I should end you for your disobedience." His hiss is the closest I've experienced him to his Crow self since the breaking of the curse, and it's enough to remind me what sort of creature I deal with.

Fear flashes through me, drawing upon what little energy I have left, making my knees buckle. Before I can hit the ground, Herinor catches me with a massive arm, and I wish I could jerk away from his touch.

The forest and Ephegos's hissing disappear in a dark void as my consciousness leaves me for what feels like the hundredth time.

My hip hits something hard, and I jerk out of oblivion. I don't get far, though, with the hard grip restraining my legs and the way I'm slung over someone's shoulder. The scent of leather and sweat climbs into my nose, making me want to weasel out of that iron hold.

"Stop moving," Herinor orders. "You'll only hurt yourself more."

I want to ask him since when does he care whether I get hurt, but all I get out is a dry, raspy sound that could have been a complaint or a grumbling whine.

"We're almost there. Ephegos ordered you cleaned up before we meet the King of Tavras."

I force my eyes to stay open and focus on the tall, colorful buildings, the countless arches and carvings lining their roofs, windows, and countless little towers. The morning sun gleams from the small spheres sitting atop each roof tipped with needle-sharp spires pointing toward the perfect clouds above. A wave of childhood memories rushes through me at the sight of narrow streets weaving between ornate fences painted in fir green and azure and butter yellow. For over a decade, this part of Tavras's capital was my home. I walked each of those alleys when my mother took me to luncheons and parties hosted by Meer's society, knocked on too many of the carved, painted doors when I accompanied my father on his visits with clients.

It doesn't feel like home, though, when I glance around to take in the otherwise empty streets. It's too early in the day for the noble quarters to come to life with artfully dressed Tavrasians and too late in the day for the servants to fill the streets on their early errand runs.

All color blurs, and the evenly spaced cobblestones are the only things I see as my head slumps against Herinor's back, cheek resting against his leathers.

Fuck—

We've arrived in Meer … and I'm hung upside down over Herinor's broad shoulder.

The scent from days' worth of travel climbs deeper into my nose, the intensity making me cough.

"Maybe *you* should clean up," I murmur, responding to his earlier statement.

Of course, the male hears it with his damned Crow ears. His laugh rumbles beneath me as he turns into an alley and marches up a set of blue-painted, wooden stairs. "Don't worry. I will. But first, we've got to get you presentable."

"And by *we*, you mean?"

"If you're worried I'll lay a hand on you, you can stop right here, Ayna." Herinor's laugh has faded, leaving behind the same serious tone he used in his torture chamber when he tried to explain that he's my ally.

The fact he even says something like this tells me that Ephegos has to be out of earshot.

Wiggling myself into a more comfortable position that won't make my stomach empty itself all over again, I heave a breath to convince myself it's a good idea to even bring it up.

By the time I work up the nerves, we're inside a small, dim entrance hall. Herinor sets me on my feet, his hand remaining locked around my arm to stabilize me, not to hurt. I notice that detail, too.

"Are you still my ally?" My eyes lock on his, and I refuse to bleat with fear at the way the morning light makes his countless scars stand out even more.

With a shrug, he leads me past walls hung with portraits of Tavrasian kings and queens. From the corner of my eye, I spy one of Erina's father in his uniform rather than ceremonial dress. He's still young in the painting, the way I remember him from his visits to my father's warehouse.

"More than you'd think and less than you'd hope." He shoves me inside the next room, closing the door behind us before he follows me into the corridor leading to what must be sitting rooms, dining rooms, and reception rooms. All houses in this part of Meer have a similar layout when it comes to the ground level where nobility likes to impress their guests. This home is no exception.

"What do you mean, *less than I'd hope*?" I turn, my arm brushing the wood-paneled wall and almost swiping a small painting down. After Myron and Royad, I've become accustomed to fairies speaking in riddles, but I need to know who I can trust, or I'll slowly lose my mind—perhaps that's already happening.

"It means exactly what I've told you before, Ayna. My bargain with Ephegos prevents me from helping you the way I want to. Nothing has changed."

The way he says it, flat and matter-of-fact… A shiver rakes through me, and my legs go weak all over again. He's going to hurt me again, to poison me again. Even if he doesn't want to.

"In there." He reaches around me to open another door, this one leading to a large bathing room with a tall milky window. The scent of lavender and berries floats in clouds of steam from the porcelain tub. "Your lady's maid will be there soon."

Herinor turns to leave, but my hand latches onto his forearm in an impulse that might have been stupidity or desperation.

"Please tell me I'll get out of here. Please tell me there is a different life for me than being Ephegos's toy. His to sell to whomever he chooses." I hate that I'm begging him—especially when he's done nothing to aid me since the moment he carved me open in the torture chamber. He hasn't proven that he's on my side. Has poisoned me over and over again.

He's also the only one I have left to talk to. The Guardians know where Kaira ended up. I wouldn't put it past Ephegos or Herinor to have made her their supper, and I don't dare ask.

The look Herinor gives is all I need to know there is no other future—and that he wishes there was.

"If I can promise you nothing else, I can promise you that I'll be the one guarding you at the palace. I might have failed Myron, but I won't fail my queen." His words are a murmur, his hair bouncing into his face as he leans closer to share this secret. "And before you ask, I will continue to drug you. It's the best way I can protect you for now. I can't torture you when you're out cold. Even Ephegos has to acknowledge that."

Blood rushes to my head with the new understanding of what a slim line he's walking in fulfilling his bargain with Ephegos and actually trying to do the right thing, and I am tempted to thank him. But there is more. More words he is about to say, more truths swirling in his green eyes. He's murdered and raped and tortured. He used to believe Myron's father's path was the right one—until he started to see there was a different way. Myron's way.

"Have you had any dreams?"

The question takes me by such surprise that I forget to be afraid of him. Heat flushes my cheeks as the dream about Myron on the Wild Ray comes back to me. I can almost feel the wind on my face, almost smell the ocean, feel his lips on mine and his fingers on my skin. And his voice echoes in my head like he's standing next to me.

I will find you. And if it takes a lifetime, I will find you.

Smothering all evidence of the pain filling my chest at the mere thought of the hope flaring when I'd heard him in my dream, I let go of his arm and step back until my shoes hit the rose and creme granite tiles of the bathing room.

"About what?

Herinor's gaze flickers to my shoulder, and for a heartbeat, I believe he's going to tear off my sleeve again and cut my skin all the way to the crow tattoo gracing my shoulder.

All he does is shake his head. "When I was little, my father used to say some dreams are real. Not all but some. And you'll know when they are."

Before I can ask what he means by that, he closes the door in my face, and his footsteps disappear down the hallway.

THIRTEEN

AYNA

I'm not even trying to figure out what he meant. The moment silence enters the bathing room, I yank on the door, hoping to open it, but of course, Herinor locked it—with magic, I suppose, since I didn't hear a lock. It doesn't even rattle.

"Shit." I curse the Guardians and Eroth and even the few Neredynian gods I've heard about when my legs go weak again and I need to grab for the oval sink beneath the arched mirror to my left. So I'm not getting out through the door.

The window then.

The glass is milky white, preventing me from seeing more than dark blotches, which I suspect to be bushes. Hopefully. Bushes are a good hiding place … if I ever make it through the window.

The last time I tried to escape from a bathing room, it was high up in the wall, and I broke a shelf, probably alerting half the Crow Palace with my noise. But this window is easy to reach and big enough to climb through.

Bracing myself on the sink, I reach for the handle and pull.

The window doesn't open.

Fuck the Guardians if they won't help me…

I pull again, harder this time. The window doesn't move a fraction of an inch.

All right. If it won't open, I'll have to break the glass. I grab the largest bottle I can find on the sideboard and hurl it at the window.

The bottle is all that breaks. Big surprise.

I need something larger. Something strong enough to shatter the thin layer standing between me and freedom.

The plain stool by the bathtub seems like it's up to the task, but my strength isn't. Just when I start picking it up, my head spins, and I need to lean against the wall to stay upright. Damn Herinor and his poison. Damn the Flames and the Crows and everything magical. I need to get out of here.

The scent of rosewater spreads from the shards of the bottle scattered beneath the window, oil dripping from the dark wooden windowsill into the mess on the floor.

A few deep breaths later, the dizzy spell is over, and I turn to pick up the stool once more when the door opens again and

Kaira walks in clad in a plain blue cotton dress that complements her eyes, and drops into a curtsey. Her gaze finds my hands on the stool then the mess beneath the window, and realization flickers across her features. "Don't even try to break it. He put a magical barrier around the entire room. You're not getting out. *We're* not getting out unless he wants us to."

The relief washing over me resembles an ocean wave near the Horn of Eroth. "Of course he has." Only now that she's standing before me, I realize how much I'd feared Ephegos killed her after all.

When I keep staring at her, she smothers the grin spreading on her face and drops into another curtsey. "At your service, Wolayna."

"You…" A glance up and down her body tells me she's wearing not just any dress; she's wearing a servant uniform. "You're my lady's maid?"

"Ephegos wasn't joking when he said he has a better punishment for me than death." She smooths her skirts with an efficient hand.

"He said that?" The last thing I remember from before I blacked out is that he told her he should end her.

"And that I'll loathe serving the human I intended to murder. Which means you, by the way." The expression on her face tells me she finds it funny. "Of course, he took all my weapons first, and just like Jeseida, he believes I'm not a threat—especially with Herinor standing guard." She glances at the door.

I'm not convinced I find any humor in the situation. "And?"

"*And* what?" She raises a brow at me, closing the door behind her and marching across the room to the bathtub, graceful like the warrior she is.

"And were you trying to kill me?" I can't be certain with anyone…

"No." Dipping one hand in the water, she rummages through the shelves filled with soaps and oils until she finds what she's looking for.

"*No?*" I glower at her back. "That's all?"

"No, I wasn't trying to kill you, Your Majesty." She winks at me over her shoulder in an impressive display of defiance and nonchalance for the topic at hand … and the bruise blooming on her cheekbone where Ephegos struck her. The light filtering in through the window emphasizes her injury by casting shadows. It can't be more than a day or two since it happened.

How long was I unconscious, asleep, or in whatever state the poison puts me in?

"You don't need to call me—"

"Your Majesty? I know." She opens the purple flask in her hand and sets it on the edge of the tub. "But there is something about your love story with the Crow King that makes me want to acknowledge you as the Crow Queen." Humor shimmers in her eyes when they meet mine, but something more lingers beneath. Something I can't name. "And before you ask: No, I don't have plans to kill you anytime soon either. I wanted Ephegos to believe I did so he'd take me along."

Digesting the news takes a moment, but when I finally do, things fall into place.

"You knew he'd make you a lady's maid?"

Kaira shrugs. "Suspected. Since I overheard him speaking about the lady's maid he already sent ahead to King Erina's court, I assumed he wouldn't bring me if I offered. He'd be suspicious of my reasons, and I'd be stuck at the estate forever. Not good enough, in Jeseida's eyes, to do anything worthy of a Flame..." Her voice trails away as I sway on my feet, and she's next to me in a heartbeat, arm wrapping around my shoulders as she guides me back to the stool I've abandoned. "Here, sit." She shoves me down and starts undoing my braid. "I keep forgetting you just woke from another forced sleep. You must feel horrible." Her fingers brush my forehead in a motherly gesture. "Let's get you something to drink."

"No." The stool almost topples over as I shrink away from her touch, but Kaira just catches me by the shoulder, stabilizing both me and the chair, and smiles.

"No poison. Promise." She gives me a nod, inviting me to mimic the movement, and damn my head, it bobs once. "Good." Her fingers slide off my shoulder, and she turns to the sink but stops mid-motion. "No attacking the window again. Even if you managed to break it, you wouldn't get out. And we'd be left with more shards to work around in here."

She grabs a cup from the shelf beside the mirror and fills it with water before returning to my side. "Here. You must be parched."

Now that she mentions it... I drain the cup in a few greedy gulps, yet my throat remains dry. After days of drinking only a few sips of that poison water, I can't even remember how much fluid I should be having in my body. The returning dizziness tells me *not enough.*

"So, what's the poison for? Other than making me miserable," I wonder, grateful that this time I am not vomiting my guts up. It's a small mercy.

Kaira shrugs again. "Do you really think Ephegos tells me anything? He barely tolerated me at the estate, let alone now that he believes I wanted to kill his leverage…" She stops herself, realizing she said more than she intended to.

Naturally, the sentence she didn't finish is the only thing my brain can focus on. "Leverage? Leverage for what?"

Kaira shakes her head. "I haven't figured that one out yet." The way her brows lower into a line of determination tells me she is ready to dig up all the secrets.

"And he's willing to let you near me if he believes you want to kill me? Doesn't sound logical to me." Unless he found a way to force her hands to stay well away from anything capable of ending me.

The haunted look entering Kaira's eyes tells me that's exactly what happened. "He's powerful—even more so since you broke the curse. All Crows are. But he's particularly dangerous since he believes himself to be a Flame now."

"A Flame without fire," I amend, and in response, Kaira's grin returns.

"Despicable bastard, isn't he?"

"The worst." I'm not surprised at the conspiratorial look she gives me, like we're two friends planning our escape from a cursed fortress rather than … enemies? Unlikely allies? I'm no longer sure what we are, but we're definitely not

126

on opposite sides of a war here. We're more of right in the middle of a war we never signed up for. It's nice not to feel alone for once.

"I told you I wouldn't let you go alone."

I don't fight her when she gestures for me to get into the tub but strip out of my dirty clothes and slide into the luxurious heat. A sigh falls from my lips as the water swallows me up. I haven't washed since we left the estate, and I reek of vomit and sweat and dirt from the journey. The fact that I stank up the carriage cabin while either Herinor or Ephegos were riding with me gives me astounding satisfaction.

Kaira doesn't speak while I scrub at my hair with the lavender soap she hands me, busying herself with plucking at a heap of fabric I hadn't noticed in a basket in the corner. She could shove my head underwater easily. Ephegos must truly trust Herinor to leave me alone with anyone on the male's guard—whether they intend to hurt me or help me. Only, when I emerge from the water, I'm reluctant to leave the soothing warmth of the element that once wrapped me in armor to protect me from fire and sword. My shoulders slump, the revitalizing effect of the bath draining in an instant.

"What do you think will happen at court?"

Kaira glances up from the blood-red satin skirt she's smoothing out over her arm. "All I know is that I am to dress you in these." Setting down the skirt, she lifts a cream top with detailed flower embroidery in the same hues. "And then you'll go to the palace. I'm not sure what else will happen, other than meeting the king, of course."

"Of course." My empty stomach folds itself over. I'll be returned as a traitor's daughter, a traitor myself. A widowed queen of a mythical menace.

Steeling myself, I dry off in a surprisingly soft towel and take the plain undergarments Kaira hands me, then the skirt, and put them on. The top is scratchy, made from a type of flax native to the north of Tavras. Elbow-length sleeves complement the loose cut of the piece, the embroidered blossoms giving it structure and adding detail the average Tavrasian woman couldn't afford. It's a sort of fashion I haven't worn since I left Meer with my mother, and I can't help it, nostalgia takes me over as I try to push back all the memories beloved and hated.

With a few efficient moves, Kaira has my hair swept into her hands, and before I can tell her not to do anything elaborate with it, a wave of heat rushes along my scalp, making me shrink toward the sink and the mirror to check if the Flame has set my hair on fire.

It falls neat and dry over my shoulders in a waterfall of ash blonde like someone spent hours combing it out as it dries on its own.

"The perks of having at least a spark of Flame magic in me." She shrugs at me through the mirror before I find my voice. "Let's get it all nice and tidy so the King of Tavras doesn't notice Ephegos brought a warrior queen into his home."

A laugh bubbles to my throat, and I want to tell her I'm far from a warrior. I have fought but one battle. The expression in her eyes tells me she's serious, though, and I take it as a compliment.

"We wouldn't want him to make a mistake." It's been over a decade since I've last seen Erina. I don't even know what he looks like now. If the deep-set eyes of his father or the lovely mouth of his mother made it into his adult features. All I know is that he wasn't bad as a child, just entitled, unaware of the sorrows tormenting the lesser in his kingdom—a kingdom of wealth where a shortage of food has never been a problem—or the threat of magical creatures taking his lands, his people, his everything.

Except for that one woman every three years, of course, when it used to be Tavras's turn to supply a bride for the Crow King. He was aware of those.

My stomach tightens painfully. That Crow King no longer exists. His final bride has returned to Tavras.

And Erina was the one to sanction my imprisonment, my being made into a tribute to a mystical people known for their brutality and bloodlust.

Perhaps the kindness of child-Erina has ceased entirely.

"Do you know anything about him?" Kaira prompts, probably reading from my absent gaze that I must have wandered into my memories.

"Nothing that would help me now." Truth. After what he did, I no longer know what to expect.

Kaira's fingers tug my hair into a tight braid starting at the crown of my head and pulling new strands in with every time she weaves another layer. It's a more elaborate version of the braid she's wearing, and with my ash-blonde tresses, the effect is startling. I don't think I've worn my hair like this since my childhood years when my mother dressed me up for social events. All of a sudden, I'm eight years old again, and I'm sitting beneath a banquet table, listening to the voices of noblemen and women, to the society of Meer, their laughter and chitchat.

I wish I was small enough to hide under a table now.

There's nowhere for me to go, though, as the door swings open after a single knock announcing someone is about to let themselves in.

In his black and russet uniform, Herinor looks like a brutal half-god. He's washed, trimmed his beard, and tied his hair at the nape of his neck. Had it not been for the scars on his face and the grim line of his mouth, I might have been fooled that he isn't the torturing Crow who's poisoned me over and over again.

"Ephegos insisted." He shifts on his feet, surprisingly uncomfortable in the well-fitted clothes.

"They look good," Kaira reassures him before I can tell him I don't care one bit what Ephegos insists on.

Am I imagining Herinor's cheeks turning a shade darker? Might be the light.

Kaira clears her throat then gestures at me. "All done and ready."

I don't feel ready as Herinor walks me down the same hallway we took on our way to the bathing room, Kaira a step behind us.

"I'll see you later tonight," she whispers, her hand brushing my arm in a gesture that could mean to comfort me. A moment later, she turns to the narrow staircase we're passing and disappears with near-soundless footsteps.

Herinor stops in the entrance hall, flashing his teeth in an attempt at what I suppose should be a grin. "Ephegos is already at the palace," he announces, reaching for his belt where only three blades are attached in matching sheaths—and one is stuck in the waistband of his pants like it won't slash open his skin at one wrong movement.

That's the one he draws and holds out for me.

I blink, more out of shock that he isn't offering me the pointy end to cut myself on but the hilt.

"Take it. Hide it under your skirts. There should be a leather pocket sewn into the folds." He draws his brows into a tight line, urgency defining his features as he waits for me to pick it from his fingers.

It takes me a moment to understand he's serious, but when I do, I don't hesitate a heartbeat. With careful fingers, I pull it from his grasp, my other hand already reaching my skirts for a sign of that secret compartment for even more secret weapons.

Herinor studies me with more impatience than makes me feel comfortable, and when I don't find what he told me to look for fast enough, he darts for my skirts and pulls at them so fast I don't even get to scream before his arm is half-way up my calf. My heart races with fear. He's a Crow. One of the earlier creatures of his people who were the reason for Vala to place a curse on them.

No matter how much I want to, I don't shrink away when he catches a slip of fabric inside the masses of satin and tugs it to the outside by shoving up the crimson layers.

"Here." He doesn't explain, simply grabs the wrist of my hand holding the knife and guides it to the leather attached to the underskirt. "It might bounce against your thigh while walking, but no one will notice it."

I'm still a pillar of shock and horror when Herinor drops the skirts and my wrist and steps back so we're face to face, features turning into a grimace as he finds my gaze. "Don't believe everything you hear in the palace. Listen for everything, though. You will know what's the truth and what's a lie by listening to that annoying moral compass of yours."

"You're talking to a pirate," I remind him, just in case he forgets who I was before I became his queen. "A traitor to the kingdom you brought me to, a prisoner sentenced to a fate worse than death."

His lips tug up at the side. "Turns out *worse than death* was actually pretty good." The little smirk he gives me reminds *me* of who *he* used to be before he turned over to my side—which, after he's handed me an actual weapon before sending me into enemy territory, is where I believe he stands. In my corner.

If it weren't for that Guardiansforsaken bargain he made with Ephegos, he might have gotten me out of here.

"Don't die, Ayna." It's all he says before he opens the door with a wave of his hand and gestures for me to walk to the carriage waiting for us at the bottom of the granite stairs.

FOURTEEN

MYRON

The world is a kaleidoscope of colors in this part of Askarea. Rolling hills smooth out toward the coastline in the distance. Emerald trees and lush bushes scatter along the landscape in clusters like someone splattered blotches of paint. The air tastes of magic and wildlife; a herd of deer jumbles toward a patch of trees, attuned to the dangerous creatures walking these lands. As a Crow Fairy, I'm not the regular creature walking their territory, but the leather-clad, auburn-haired fairy male next to me is.

As if sensing me measuring him, Astorian lifts his gaze, a crease forming between his brows while he studies me without the slightest sign of deterrence. I might be a king—one without a people—but he is a general in the mighty fairy realm. He has the support of King Recienne of Askarea, and Recienne is not amused that his sister hasn't returned to court.

Now that I'm thinking about it, I'm almost certain it would have been a matter of time until Recienne showed up on my—no longer existent—doorstep and demanded the whereabouts of his sister. The commander of the Askarean armies going on a search in his stead speaks for itself in a very different way.

"Beautiful, isn't it?" Astorian earns a growl from Silas and a sideways glance from Royad, who both haven't left my side—like the fairy I made a bargain with, who might stab me in the back any moment.

"Your hair?" Silas asks with his signature dry tone that makes me thirsty immediately. "It's a sight to behold. If you're into redheads."

Royad laughs quietly, his hand on his weapon and his gaze on the road ahead. Without the fairy general, we could have shifted and crossed the lands high up in the air—wings sure have their advantages. But with Astorian on our asses, I'm nowhere near in a mood to expose my cousin and the Crow I've come to call *friend*. Wings have their disadvantages, too. Shifting into our smaller bird form makes us agile, yes. It also makes us more vulnerable. A small arrow can tear through our bird bodies and shred us to pieces while our humanoid forms have no problem surviving a stab in the heart—as long as our magic works, we survive almost anything.

Astorian grumbles what could have been a bitten-back chuckle, I can't be certain. "Oh, I *love* redheads." His grin is so broad it turns his features into a mask of threats.

"I'm sure you do. Since you're mated to one." Using what I think could be my diplomat tone—I can't be sure, I've never had the need to play the diplomat—I turn my gaze to the sheep-shaped clouds hiking the skies. "Cliophera is a lovely female, by the way." Before he can growl at me to let me know he'll gladly tear off my head if I ever imply that *loveliness* is something I'd do more than admire from afar, I add, "I never really thought about my own preferences, you know, not having a choice in who I marry and all. Somewhere within the whole process of losing one bride after another, I lost the ability to get attached to a female."

Royad clears his throat while Astorian shakes his head, loose auburn strands sliding over the metal bits on his shoulders. "Liar."

It's my turn to shake my head. "I can't lie the way Eherean fairies lie, Astorian. I'm not an Eherean creature. We function differently."

"You sure got attached to Wolayna," Silas throws in for nobody's benefit, saving me from immediate questions about our origin and the exact nature of our species. I'm not ready to spread more than the need-to-knows of Crow history at an Eherean fairy's feet. We might be allies, but I sure as Hel won't share all the gory details of my people's past just because we've joined forces for what might be a moot rescue mission. My stomach flops uncomfortably.

"He said he *lost the ability to get attached*. Not that he never regained it," Royad rushes to my defense, ever the loyal cousin. "And of course he got attached to her. She is an incredible female. *I'm* attached to her—not in the same way," he quickly amends when I tense at the mere thought of anyone developing feelings for *my* Ayna. Royad gives me a pitiful smile. "Myron fucking fell in love with her. That's what broke the curse."

"That and the unlikely whim of fate that allowed her to fall for me, too. Or we'd be still walking around with permanent wings and uncontrollable beaks and claws."

It takes a few hours to fill Astorian in about the basics of our existence—not a detailed history, of course—that's for people I trust, but I manage to give him the bare bones of the curse and how Ayna broke it. It's a small relief that his face draws into lines of distress when he learns what my people used to be capable of—still are. Enough Crows have chosen to follow Ephegos's traitorous ass into battle against me and my own. If anything, the hatred he holds for my species must be growing while we make it through the thinning bushes and trees into the Plithian Plains.

The mostly flat lands defining the Tavrasian north are everything I remember from those early days of my life in Eherea when the Crows weren't confined to the Seeing Forest yet. I've flown my rounds over the fields of grain and lush meadows often enough to know each hill, each stream cutting through them. Yet, it's an entirely different world from the last time I've been here. It's mid-summer, neither harvesting season nor sowing season, so the humans working these lands are safely tucked away in their farmhouses and scattered villages, staying among themselves. A part of me wonders how many of them still know the tales of the winged fairies who will steal their women—only, it's not a tale.

I follow Astorian's glance to the only well-kept fence along the path we're walking.

"What is this place?" Silas is the first to comment on the tall estate mostly hidden behind a manicured hedge and rows of trees as if to keep it from prying eyes.

A gravel path leads up to a set of stairs I recognize to be of south Tavrasian granite—the russet and cream shimmering in the afternoon light are unmistakable. Memories of my father sending me out with some of his trusted Crows to bring home a few women for Ret Relah push to the front of my thoughts, and my stomach twists as echoes of their screams fill my head.

Too many humans have died because of him, because of all of us.

"Just another human home," Royad answers, taking the burden off my shoulders when I have trouble speaking from the guilt piling up inside of me.

To my right, Astorian is oddly quiet, his gaze trained on the segments of windows visible between heavy branches. I wish I knew what he was seeing there with his fairy eyes. My fae senses pick up the scents of blossoms, horse sweat, and freshly cut grass, but I can't make out a human scent.

"There's no human in there," Astorian says without turning toward me—

And my heart plummets to my knees. Did he just—

Royad and Silas exchange a glance of concern as they both reach for their weapons while I merely shoot more of my power into the provisional shield I've built around myself. I probe it to make sure it's woven tightly around my thoughts as much as my skin. Rumors of Askarean fairies plucking thoughts from people's heads reached the Seeing Forest long before the last Crow War, and I can't help but feel nervousness at the mere thought of becoming transparent for the enemy.

"It's not abandoned, though." Royad leans toward the fence where obvious traces of recent repairments betray the otherwise silent appearance of the premises.

"So, who's hiding in there?" It's Silas's undiplomatic tone that challenges us all, reminding me that I'm no longer a cursed Crow but a fae capable of shifting into my bird form at will, a fae with senses and powers beyond what I'm used to employing from centuries and centuries of disuse. From never properly learning how they work and understanding how to use them to my advantage. Royad is the same. He was as young as I was when the curse fell upon us. We need to learn how to be proper fae while, for Silas, it's like coming home—he's said it himself.

In reflex, my gaze shoots toward him, studying his features as his focus seems to drift ahead of us to where his trained ability to use his Shaelak-given senses and uncover truths I yet need to learn.

Gods, I wish I had time to become the predator he is, to become comfortable in my own skin the way Astorian is. I wish the sun on my face wouldn't constantly remind me that I've failed at saving the woman who saved me.

"You won't like what's in there," Silas says, giving me a brief glance that I have come to interpret as a harbinger of mayhem.

"What's in there?" Astorian is brave enough to ask a heartbeat before he goes still like a rock, nostrils flaring. "Fuck the Guardians."

I'm about to demand what's going on when her scent drifts into my nose. A growl rips from my throat, so unlike the hisses and caws I'm used to. It's pure animalistic rage welling up inside of me as I taste Ayna on my tongue—wild-flowers and summer heat. And blood.

"I'm going to rip his throat out."

Royad's and Silas's aren't the only hands landing on my shoulders and arms, restraining me as I strain to charge through the fence and hedges, straight to the source of the scent. Astorian's magic locks around my ankles, holding my feet in place while his hand lands on my chest with the force of solid stone.

"Don't." It's all he says while Royad is doing his best to calm me with about a hundred reasons why it is foolish to barge into the enemy's home and demand for my bride. My queen. My—everything. She's my *everything*.

I loose a cry of frustration, and it turns into a hiss, then a caw as I shift into my bird form under their fingers and flutter out of their grasp, wings beating like I'm fighting a flood threatening to drown me.

Royad's curses follow me as I take off across the trees, and even Astorian's fairy magic isn't enough to keep me from finding the missing piece of my heart.

By the time I make it to the front of the building, Royad and Silas are both at my tail, and I have the distinct feeling Astorian isn't far behind. Perhaps he can't shift into a bird, but if he has the same ability as his mate, he can site-hop through the world like it's a spiderweb of magical gridlines taking him wherever he pleases. I don't care. Ayna's scent is like a hook in my chest, drawing me closer and closer and closer. My pulse pounds in my veins, fueling my wingbeats as I make quick work of the last feet of open ground before I circle above the roof. She is there. She has to be in this house. The entire fucking building radiates her scent. No matter how many times I've buried my nose in her hair or scented her skin, this is different. More potent than anything I've ever experienced.

Like a silver thread, the tang of blood mixed into her scent pulls me in. If she is hurt. If Ephegos harmed a hair on her head. If he laid even a finger on her body—

My wings are shaking, feathers dissipating into inky mist as I land beside one of the many chimneys, hands braced on the age-worn roof tiles. I don't care that they seem brittle in places. It's not my fucking problem if their roof collapses under my weight. They *stole* her from me. They took my life and my heart. Vala returned the first to me. I'll take back the second in the name of all that I've suffered. That *she* has suffered. "Ayna!" My voice rips from my throat in blind panic as the smell of her blood begins to overpower the notes of wildflowers.

I'm vaguely aware of Royad landing at my side, his muscled form unfolding as he shifts back. Silas follows suit, his sword drawn and ire tearing at his features.

"Wait," Royad urges. "Let's think this through."

"She's in there." I don't bother waiting for a response as I blast through the roof with the vast power collecting beneath my skin. Like a detonation, it radiates in all directions, shoving Royad and Silas toward the edge, almost pushing them off. Royad catches himself on the elevated tiles above a roof window, his gaze locking on mine in warning.

A part of me knows I should be concerned, should be careful, but Ayna is all I can think of. Like a primal need, her name pounds in my blood, driving me on and on into a frenzy I know will only stop once I lay eyes on her and I know she's all right.

It's too late for second thoughts anyway. My magic has torn a crater into the structure carrying our weights, and from below, a woman with a warm, brown, lined face and a braid of fire-red hair is staring up at me, the smirk on her mouth telling me that I've made a fundamental mistake.

"It could be—"

"A trap." Royad finishes for Astorian as the male appears at my side, his arms locked around my chest from behind as he keeps me from tumbling over the frayed edge of the hole gaping at my feet. I'm surprised I haven't tumbled into it.

Silas shifts into his bird form to prevent himself from falling off the roof and flutters closer. Once back at my side, he shifts into his fae form, his sword in hand, and glances at the sight beneath. "Fuck."

It's all there truly is to say.

At the woman's feet lies a heap of blue and cream fabric smeared with blood—Ayna's blood.

"We need to get out of here." Royad is the voice of reason, and he's right. But my body won't move, and it has nothing to do with Astorian locking me in place. It's something more. It's like every cell in my body is determined to stay here where there is at least hope of finding her. Where I have people to *interrogate*. People who have Ayna's blood on their hands.

"Looking for this?" The woman's voice is husky like she is partly made of black smoke and crackling fire. The little flames dancing at her fingertips inform me that it just might be the truth.

This is a Fire Fairy female. A powerful one, judging by the air of magic and suppressed heat swirling around her.

"Shift," Royad orders. My cousin never orders me, but he is right to do it now. He is right; we need to get out of here.

"We can take her on," Silas says from my other side, bloodlust in his tone. He's eager to sink his blade into someone, be it not in revenge for what the Fire Fairies did to us or for Ayna.

"Perhaps we—" Astorian is cut off by a blast of fire shooting up at us. Our shields take the brunt of the impact, but the roof isn't stable, and four massive males are too much to support for the singed beams crumbling away under our boots. I don't have time to shift before I fall. The fire would only take my feathers like it did Ephegos's, so I choose to take the impact on the hardwood floor with my shoulder instead.

Astorian is the only one not to groan at the impact, his site-hopping abilities keeping him from falling alongside us. When he hits the floor beside me, it's by choice and on his feet. In his hands, he holds two fistfuls of rocks, and they are already melting at the touch of his power.

"Seize them," the female shouts at the doorway behind the fading fire.

Before I can wonder how the room remains untouched by the fading flames, at least ten Fire Fairies charge the room. Ignoring the throbbing pain in my shoulder, I'm on my feet in a heartbeat, ready to meet an attack with my shield or with my magic while I fumble for my sword.

Silas is the first to attack. He leaps at the nearest Fire Fairy with a battle cry, slicing clean into the male's shoulder. He was right. There are over ten of them, but we're fighting in closed quarters, and the four of us have magic of our own. One fairy and three Neredynian *fae*. Power surges in my chest like a thunderstorm, straining for release. I hold it until I find a target close enough. The female has moved toward me as if expecting to grab me and restrain me herself. In her hand, she holds the fabric with Ayna's blood. It's fucking *burning.*

Everything inside me revolts as if it were Ayna burning between her fingers, and my blood boils with all-consuming rage.

"I will end you," I growl. "With my claws and beak, I will break you apart." It's a promise.

The female merely smirks at me as she halts just out of reach. "I'd like to see you try. I have something you want, and you won't risk *her*, will you?"

It's torment to fight the need to eviscerate her with that storm of magic brewing inside my chest. She's right, and she knows it. I will never risk Ayna. Never again.

A glance at Royad tells me he knows it, too. He's locked in battle with a Fire Fairy, his shortsword driving back the elegant silver blade of the male he's facing. He's holding the male off but not going for the kill, making himself vulnerable as he waits for my order.

Astorian's liquid rock has melted a hole in a Fire Fairy's chest, leaving the female splayed uselessly on the ground, and it is aiming for the next enemy. His mind is clearer than mine with Cliophera's scent missing in the equation. For a heartbeat, I wonder if he'd act the same if it was her blood instead of Ayna's. If the seemingly stoic fairy general would lose control the way I just did.

My gaze lands on the smirking Fire Fairy again. "What did you do to the Crow Queen?"

The female has the nerve to smile—wide like Ephegos would. My stomach turns.

"What. Did. You. Do. To her?" Menace laces my tone. The pain and fear and anger of millennia accumulating at the thought of being too late.

"Your *queen* is fine, Myron. Don't worry." She knows me. And she isn't surprised in the slightest that I'm alive. I tuck that thought away for later.

Royad has disengaged himself from battle by knocking out the Fire Fairy at the tip of his sword and has stepped to my side, while Astorian is wielding liquified rock from my other side.

"If I were you, I'd hand over the woman he's ready to destroy the world for or he might let you live just long enough to see the rest of it crumble to pieces before he takes you out slowly and painfully." By Shaelak, Royad is a master at being visual when it comes to threats; I've always known that. But he isn't being visual right now; he's being literal. I am ready to do just that.

"Wolayna is safely on the way to Meer." The female waves her hand in the general direction of the door, and I think she means Ayna is just across the threshold. The storm of magic strains to break loose.

Not yet. I need to know where to find my queen first.

When I take a step forward, drawn by that same blind need to find her, something wet hits my back, and I gasp as all strength leaves me. Astorian's curse is the last thing I hear before two Fire Fairies grasp me with brutal hands and kick my legs out from under me.

At least, the floor isn't marble. My kneecaps scream at the impact anyway.

"What's goin' on?" Silas is the first to ask from beside me where he's being forced to his knees as well. "Why can't I—"

"Use your magic?" The female stalks toward us, lowering her dark brown eyes to meet mine even when she's speaking to Silas. She reads the questions on my face as well as I try to pull up the unrelenting power that threatened to burst me open at the seams a moment ago.

There's nothing left. Not one ounce of magic roiling or coiling or even slumbering.

"What did you do to us?" Even my growl is less threatening without the reassurance of that power at my disposal. It's like someone took all air from my lungs and all that's left is a wilted leaf in the Fire Fairy's wind.

She gestures at the liquid soaking my shirt, dripping from my hair. "You mean this?" Her smile broadens as she watches me strain against the Fire Fairies' hold, watching all four of us tear and thrash for freedom. "It's a little invention Ephegos and I have been working on for a while. Quite useful."

"I hate to break it to you," Astorian murmurs from behind me, "but nothing good ever comes from things the Crows touch—or the Fire Fairies," he adds before I can take offense. "And worst of all if they touch something *together*."

The way he says it… Like it's a joke. But when I listen more closely, there's fear in his tone. The Askarean general is afraid.

If nothing else, that's a reason for me to know that we're in serious trouble.

I'm not certain it is smart to admit to what extent that *little invention* worked and reveal that I've lost access to all of my magic. It's obvious I'm weakened enough for the Fire Fairies to bring me to my knees, for them to restrain me as sweat beads my skin from my efforts to break free. I haven't felt this helpless since Ayna was dying next to me. At least then, I had the choice to give myself up to save her. Now, there is nothing I can do. Nothing I have to give that could satisfy the Fire Fairies. So, I hold my tongue.

"We've been working on it for a while, and it seems it has the best effect if administered orally, but it's hard to force something down your throats if you're all magically shielding, so our best guess was to dump the drug over your heads and see what it does." The female leans in closer, and I still as realization hits me.

This is a trap. Ayna isn't here. She might have been at some point, but this—the blood-soaked fabric holding her scent—is the honey laid out to trap a bear. They must have been anticipating I'd eventually come across this estate on my search for my queen. All they needed was a little patience—and some drug that could smother magic.

Gods, if Ayna was treated with the same drug, she might not be able to use her own powers either. She's as helpless as I am.

There is truly only one question for me to ask—the same question I kept urging Ayna to ask over and over again. The only question that ever matters. "Why?"

The female glances at the Fire Fairies holding the four of us in place. Even Astorian and Silas have followed my lead and stopped fighting a battle they cannot win—for now. Behind Royad's eyes, I can see the wheels turning. Instead of drawing attention to him by getting involved in the discussion, he's assessing the brass and cream wallpapers decorating the room, the carved chairs tossed over the polished floors. We're in a sitting room, not that it makes any difference. Royad is already calculating how to best get out of here, freeing my focus to negotiate if there is anything to negotiate with.

"Oh, Myron," the female says, too excited for a dire situation like this, except, for her, it must feel like a win to have the Crow King kneeling before her. She's a Flame after all. "Haven't you heard? The King of Tavras is eager to announce his engagement to a recently recovered Tavrasian noblewoman, and Ephegos and I helped him retrieve his bride for him—in return for our own conditions, of course."

Everything crumples inside of me. She can't mean—

"What conditions?" Astorian demands in that cold general's tone I am familiar with, and now that I've seen a different side of him, it's hard to consolidate those two versions of him in my mind.

The sound of a fist hitting flesh comes from his general direction, followed by a groan, and a Flame hisses, "You only speak when spoken to, fairy scum."

I manage to turn my head enough to spot the blood trickling from the corner of Astorian's mouth.

"You are mighty curious for an all-knowing fairy," the female taunts as she steps past me to take a closer look at him. "Not so powerful without the King of Askarea and his armies at your disposal, are you?"

I don't know if they've met before, but the enmity is one to last for eons if the hatred in Astorian's eyes is anything to go by. He spits out the blood to the side, nearly hitting one of his captors.

"The conditions are between Ephegos, King Erina, and me." She turns on the spot, pivoting toward me and shoving the fabric with Ayna's blood in my face without warning. My fae reflexes are still there, allowing me to avoid the full impact as I turn my head to the side. There is no escaping the devastation spreading in my stomach as I realize there is only one reason they would lure me here: Ephegos knows I'm alive, and he isn't done with his revenge.

FIFTEEN

AYNA

The palace of Meer is larger than I remembered with its towers tipped with roofs shaped like onions and vast hallways where too many golden doors lead to reception rooms, sitting rooms, banquet halls, and rooms I don't know the use for. I haven't set foot in the palace since my childhood, and I could have done without it for the rest of my life. I don't have a choice, though, as Herinor walks me up the stairs leading from the roof-high entrance hall to the first floor where I remember the throne room to be.

Guards in black and blue stand along the walls, their uniforms plain compared to the colorful tapestries lining the space between doors and columns. The knife brushing my thigh every other step is a reassuring weight even when I can't grab for it without exposing my leg. For now, it'll have to do. I don't wear armor, but I hold my chin high the way I used to at the Crow Palace. Herinor is a few strides behind me, his presence as much a comfort as it is a threat. If Ephegos orders him to hurt me, he'll have to do it. There is no way around it for him other than the choice of how to hurt me. Not so comforting now that I think of it.

At our approach, a man in an entirely black uniform hurries toward us, bowing low at the waist as he stutters, "Wolayna Milevishja. His Majesty is awaiting your arrival." He straightens, already walking as he turns his balding head to glance at me with light blue eyes. "Follow me."

There is no sign of excitement or fear in his middle-aged face as he looks over Herinor. Whatever position he holds at court exempts him from ever picking up a weapon, I assume. I've seen such people in noble households before. Men and women who deliver messages for their lords and ladies, whose weapons are manners and knowledge.

Something about him reminds me of Ephegos, and my stomach churns beneath the intricate shirt.

"Don't forget to smile," Herinor reminds me as we do as the man said and make our way into a wide hallway leading toward a set of open double doors covered in golden filigree. I instantly miss the dark plainness of Myron's palace in the Seeing Forest.

Myron—

"And don't show him your emotions. Keep a cool head. It's the only weapon you can use in here without drawing attention." Herinor spent the entire carriage ride briefing me on the current state of Erina's court. The nobles in charge and the etiquette required. My head is full near bursting, and I'd prefer taking a long, peaceful nap over setting foot anywhere near the man Ephegos is selling me to. No matter that we shared croissants under banquet tables as children.

I discreetly tap my skirts. "I remember."

In this palace, at least, I don't need to worry about being overheard by fairies of any sort. This is human territory, and Herinor and Ephegos are the only immortal creatures with superior hearing. Erina and his guards must rely on their human senses to protect their king. Not that I'd get anywhere near Erina with the small knife before someone would intercept and execute me on the spot.

This might be a human court, but that doesn't mean it's any less cruel. Just in a different way.

The guards' gazes follow us, and while the man leading the way doesn't recognize Herinor for the threat he is, the guards very well do. Their hands inch closer to the swords at their hips as we approach, and they don't relax even when we've long passed.

"Your Majesty," the man in black says with a bow as he stops on the gold-framed threshold. "Wolayna Milevishja is here to see you."

The answering voice is warm and welcoming even if it swims with reflections in the enormous room. The guard blocking our path steps aside, and we step into a sunlight-bathed hall of sepia and gold. Swirls of light dance across the walnut floor as the breeze falling through the open balcony doors stirs the air, and my chest tightens at the sight of the man sitting on a carved throne finished with golden, onion-shaped ornamentations at the top of the backrest, just like the towers of the palace.

"Welcome to my home, Wolayna." Erina straightens, a hint of respect while he doesn't bother to stand up and meet me across the hall, not that I expected any kindness or heart-felt welcome. We were kids back then anyway, and he probably doesn't even remember those few times we talked and what he offered.

"Curtsey," Herinor hisses a reminder that sounds a lot like a warning, so I drop into a Tavrasian curtsey, the very one my mother drilled into me as a child.

"Come closer, Wolayna." Erina stares down at me with dark eyes matching the sepia of his uniform. The gold high-lights on the shoulders and the belt and sash only make his short-cropped, light brown hair stand out more. His face has matured into that of a handsome young man, forming sharper angles accentuated by high cheekbones and thick eyebrows. Details become more apparent as I approach. The straight line of his mouth as he keeps his face as expressionless as only a monarch needs to. I'd seen him do that as a child when he sat his time through festivities. Something about it is deeply upsetting, but I'm not certain yet if it's because the lack of emotion makes it difficult for me to read him or because I'd secretly harbored hopes this is all a misunderstanding and I'm not being sold, but he brought me here because he remembers the little girl he shared pastries with.

"It's a pleasure to see you again after ... such a long time." The brief hesitation in his words reminds me that the last time I'd seen him was before my father's execution.

Forcing myself to hold his gaze, I take a final step until I'm at the bottom of the small dais elevating his throne, and manage a bland smile that doesn't represent the resentment swirling in my stomach.

"I'm afraid Ephegos won't be able to join us before the banquet later today, but I'm sure we have a lot to catch up on in the meantime. My general told me you have quite the journey behind you." The expectation in his eyes makes it clear he will hear all of it, whether I'm willing to tell or not.

Tension tightens my shoulders as he finally stands from his throne and walks down the three polished steps to meet me at the bottom of the dais, and nerves make my knees wobble.

Thankfully, he doesn't notice my struggle as I steel my spine to keep upright since his attention flickers to the side where the man in a black uniform is waiting like a dog for an order. Disgusting.

"Arrange for refreshments." Erina waves his hand in dismissal, and the man dashes from the room through a small door blending into the tapestry of sepia and gold in a way that made me miss it until it opened.

The momentary relief immediately vanishes as Erina's head whips back toward me, and he features a polite smile that is so much like that of the prince I used to know.

"Tell me, Wolayna. Is it true that your new status matches my own?" His eyes remain unreadable as he waits for me to speak.

"I'm afraid I don't know what you mean, Your Majesty." I lower my gaze, ready to step back as he leans forward as if intending to take another pace closer. There are only a few feet between us now, and it's close enough.

Behind me, Herinor clears his throat; whether it's a warning for me or for Erina, I can't tell. He's on my side, but in these halls, he's playing a role—and is reminding me to play mine.

"Please, call me Erina. You are part of my court now, and I'm inclined to start on friendlier terms than our fathers ended up." The blatant reminder of what he sees when he looks at me makes me squirm.

A traitor. I'm a traitor to this kingdom. I looted his ships after my father was executed for treason. I am vermin in the eyes of this king. A chill so icy I can't suppress a shiver marches down my back, and I wonder if the summer gardens visible through the balcony doors are an illusion.

"Right." I clear my throat. "I'm afraid I don't know what you mean, Erina." His name is vinegar on my tongue, but apparently, it's good enough for him since his smile becomes slightly more sincere at the sound of it.

"The story of how you ended up at my friend Ephegos's doorstep." Whether he believes what he's saying or is spinning the truth while already knowing how I was mutilated and kept prisoner before being forced to marry a man I believed to be a monster, I can't tell. I can't tell anything at all from the refined mask of the king he's become.

My left hand finds my stiff wrist, protectively wrapping around it as if I could hide any part of my past, anything at all. Naturally, his attention drifts right there. Great.

"That will be a long, *long* story. It's been years since I left Meer," I try. If I'm lucky, he'll allow me to push back the retelling of my failures until we aren't framed by guards whose ears seem to grow longer in hopes of catching a piece of our conversation.

"I reserved the whole day for you, Wolayna. I'd love to hear what detours you had to take to return to me."

It sounds off. Entirely off and practiced. And the tone gives me the creeps. I never left *him*. Just Tavras—

"Leaving my kingdom equals leaving me, Wolayna." He studies me, smile fading, and for a heartbeat, I spot something bending the facade of the king, but before I can identify what it is, he continues, "You left Tavras. And I've heard you spent quite some time making the seas along its coast a place to be feared by the most seasoned and cunning captains."

A pang of nostalgia creeps through my chest as I think of Ludelle and the Wild Ray. The entire crew of friends I lost in the capture of the pirate ship. Then a smile tugs at the corner of my lips. "Captains feared us?" It probably isn't what he was going for, but it gives me satisfaction to hear that word of the Wild Ray has spread all the way to his throne room even if she was just one single pirate ship.

"It's a capital offense to loot the king's ships," he whispers, leaning into my space as he eventually takes that step closer, and my smile slips.

Shit.

His breath hits the side of my cheek, his woodsy scent climbing into my nose. He smells like this throne room—like too much pomp and power.

"Don't worry, Wolayna. I know you've paid dearly for your offenses. No one here knows you were part of the Wild Ray's crew, except for General Katrijanov, of course."

As if on cue, Katrijanov strides into the room, bowing briefly before he marches toward us. Herinor tenses as he moves a few inches closer in what seems to be an instinct.

"The crew is dead for all that the public knows, and *you* have been miraculously recovered from the fairylands of Askarea by our brave general after narrowly escaping the menace that was the Crow King. Oh yes…" he adds as I flinch at the mention of my dead husband. "I know all about him. People might believe they are fairy tales, but I know better. I've been sending a woman to die every three years after all. How pleased do you think I was to see your name on the list when it was time to make the choice last year? Another traitor down."

Katrijanov reaches us, standing at attention as Erina continues to speak so softly, not even Herinor should be able to pick it up. "But don't worry. I've forgiven you. It takes some tenacity to survive all of that. That's the material true queens are cut from."

I'm not sure it's a compliment, and I don't want to know. All I want is to run from the room and let the tears pricking at the back of my eyes flow freely.

But Erina isn't the only one standing in my way. When I turn around, Herinor is blocking my path, a grimace of menace on his features that makes the scars on his skin stand out like a warning of what he's capable of—and what he's capable of surviving.

"I wouldn't try if I were you." His tone is that of the torture master once more, and what little confidence I'd gained since the moment he handed me the knife tucked between the folds of my skirts is swept away by a man-high wave of fear.

ANGELINA J. STEFFORT

SIXTEEN

AYNA

My heart beats out of my throat as I struggle to keep my feet in place when Erina's hand slides down my arm until it rests on the side of my elbow. Herinor doesn't blink. He doesn't save me. He *can't* save me from anything. I wonder why a part of me believed he might try.

"Welcome, Wolayna," Katrijanov says in that cold, assessing tone of a commanding officer. His uniform is impeccably clean, and the only wrinkles are those around his eyes and the slight lines around his mouth where his mustache was drawing attention the first time I met him.

My stomach is mercifully empty, or I'd throw up on his polished boots. "I didn't expect to see you so … alive," he finishes with a cruel smirk.

"Must be the climate," Herinor says in the same icy tone he used on me a moment ago, and my heart dares to beat. "Early summer in Askarea becomes humans." I'm almost certain there is a flicker of sarcasm in his voice—or a lot of sarcasm… All right, it's dripping with sarcasm, but I doubt either Erina or Katrijanov pick up on it. They are too busy staring at me as I refuse to fidget under their scrutiny.

"I must say, when you told me you found out she was alive, I was wondering what you'd bring me, General Katrijanov." Erina's eyes crawl along my form, lingering on the loose hem of my shirt where the skirt pulls in at my waist, revealing more than enough of my shape even when the shirt is covering up enough of my torso with its straight cut.

"Last time I saw her, she didn't look quite as … vibrant."

What's with all those deliberately picked descriptors Katrijanov chooses when talking to me, about me, or talking in general? It gives me the distinct feeling I'm missing something—again. I've had a whole few months of missing too much and ending up almost dead. Of losing the male I love because I was too ignorant to realize what it takes to break a curse.

Not again. I can't do this all over again.

Herinor shifts his weight, the sound of leather scraping over metal disrupting my downward spiral long enough for me to force a breath down my lungs and blink a few times to clear all emotions off my face. It was his advice, and even if he wasn't on my side, it's good advice. They already have enough ammunition against me. Anything else I give them could be disastrous.

"Ah, perfect." Erina's gaze swings to the man in black uniform returning through the hidden side door followed by a row of servants in sepia and skirts and white aprons, each of them carrying a tray with tiny dishes as they keep their eyes on the floor in front of them on their way to the small table and four chairs a handful of men are carrying into the room. They curtsey and bow when they pass their king before hurtling on to set up our meal. Erina watches in silence, his attention undoubtedly making the servants uneasy. A young woman with bronze curls pinned to the back of her head under the white maid's cap stumbles as she accidentally meets the king's gaze, and I can almost feel her shame as she drops into a low curtsey before she scurries from the room, almost forgetting to set down her tray. One of the older women intercepts her, picking the silver piece from the younger one's hands and sending her on her way before passing us in a perfect maneuver.

I don't know if I pity the bronze-haired one or am impressed by the older one who doesn't even seem tempted to glance in our direction. She must have seen a lot in her years to be able to ignore the massive Crow Fairy standing in the middle of the throne room. The other servants have more issues pretending not to notice him—or me. However, none of them dares make eye contact with Erina. They know the court rules, and so do I.

When they are done, a perfect small meal is prepared by the columns separating the balcony doors, a place with a perfect view of the gardens behind the palace. And a perfect place to shift into a bird and fly away—if only I could.

The way Herinor eyes the clouds lets me believe his thoughts don't differ much either.

We wait until Erina picks a chair and sits down before I dare follow him to the table.

"Tavrasian specialties from the coast," he announces with a gesture at the colorful foods. "I had them brought in solely for this occasion." He turns to me, gesturing at the chair next to his. "Sit, Wolayna. I'm sure you could do with some food that brings forth childhood memories."

I don't trust the smile on his lips or the reason he wants me to remember my childhood. I don't trust him at all. The fact that he's working with Ephegos is enough to make him a red flag.

Katrijanov follows suit, seating himself across from Erina, which leaves one chair for Herinor, who looks like he isn't sure he is supposed to sit down at all.

"Please," Katrijanov invites him with a cold smile. "Ephegos would want you to eat with us. It's been a long journey for you from the … estate." His sideways glance at me informs me that he remembers the day he came to the Flame residence to appraise me like a chest of goods for shipping.

It's more than fresh in my mind, his words echoing as if he were speaking them all over again.

Don't die anytime soon, Wolayna. We have great plans for you.

Now I know what these *great plans* are: I've been sold to the King of Tavras to continue the punishment for my treason—for my *father's* treason in part, I'm sure. The way Katrijanov keeps exchanging looks with the king speaks volumes about the hidden layers of these plans.

Herinor steps behind me, his hulking shape alarmingly close to my shoulder as he shakes his head at the general. My blood stills, my entire body tensing for an assault with one of his blades the way he'd carved me open in the Flames' torture chamber, but he won't hurt me unless he's openly commanded to—by the male he so thoughtlessly pledged his loyalty to. "I believe Lord Ephegos would have objections if his guards ate with a king and a high-ranking general."

The corner of Erina's mouth lifts as if he realized the insult Herinor delivered with his words. Not only the refusal but the fact that Adrian Katrijanov is *the* general of the Tavrasian troops. No one stands above him but the very king facing him across the table.

"Very well." Katrijanov brushes the insult off, reaching for his crystal goblet of Tavrasian wine the servants poured before scurrying from the room like ants from a focused beam of light. "To the recently recovered Wolayna Milevishja." His pale blue eyes chill the warmth of nervousness from my body as they meet mine. They are like the death he ordered delivered on my friends from the Wild Ray, like a hand of pure ice as they slide along my features as if in reassurance that I'm truly me, that he wasn't tricked by a wicked fairy. He lifts the goblet, waiting for Erina to do the same and drink first.

Something about the gesture feels off—orchestrated in a way that I have started to develop a sixth sense for. I only wish I had my magic so I could pull the wine from the goblet and whip it into his face. The power that saved my life in the Seeing Forest hasn't stirred since the last time I'd woken from the poison-sleep.

In reflex, my gaze slides to my own goblet filled to the middle of the Tavrasian shield crest etched into the crystal on one side. My stomach tells me I need fluids and food, but I don't trust anyone in this room enough to believe the wine isn't spiked with the same substance that kept me sedated half of the journey here.

Both Erina and Katrijanov take a deep drink, ignoring me as they help themselves to the meat pastries stacked on gold-rimmed plates. For a while, I watch them eat—Katrijanov across the table, and Erina from the side with secret glances that anyone not knowing my situation might have mistaken for the interest almost any young woman might hold for a bachelor king. At least, I think he doesn't have any attachments. On instinct, my gaze drops to Erina's left hand, to his middle finger, where a wedding band would sit in old Tavrasian fashion.

All I find is a sepia gemstone the size of a kidney bean framed in gold attached on his index finger. The same ring his father used to wear.

Right when I come to the conclusion that there is no current Tavrasian queen, my stomach growls loud enough to draw attention, and Erina catches me staring. His brow rises before he smooths his expression and picks up the pastry platter to offer me a piece. "You should eat, Wolayna. We've got a long day ahead of us."

His words remind me so much of Myron's that first morning after our wedding that my hunger turns into nausea, and I swallow the bile in my throat, shaking my head.

One breath, and another, and my heart rate slows enough for me to form a clear thought. "Why am I here?" I ask the one question I maybe should have asked the moment I laid eyes on the King of Tavras, should have demanded an answer to.

Katrijanov's mouth tightens while Erina smiles at me freely. "Why, to be part of my court, of course."

The lie is blatant and obvious, and I want to spit at him. Herinor's forearm brushes my shoulder in warning as my emotions bubble up, threatening to boil over. *Keep calm. Knowledge is your friend. Play their game.*

I get the message, but I also need to know. I need to understand what is coming for me, if I'm to be thrown in the dungeons eventually and tortured to death—

"King Erina is turning twenty-five this summer," Katrijanov explains with so much honey in his tone he almost doesn't sound like the general at all. "He needs to think about the future of his kingdom."

Twenty-five. A bit young to think about a legacy when you already have a kingdom at your disposal.

I'm still trying to decipher the merits of my role in said *thinking* when the man with the black uniform enters the throne room once more, bowing low before stepping over the threshold.

"Your Majesty," he starts, his gaze darting between Erina, Katrijanov, and Herinor before they land on me.

"What is it, Odja?" Erina doesn't turn away from me, plate still in hand and a hint of annoyance showing on his features. I try not to look too closely at his perfectly shaved chin or the way his lashes curve around his eyes. He is attractive by objective standards, but nothing stirs inside of me at the sight of him. Nothing other than a deep-seated sadness.

Before I can examine the sensation, Odja crosses the room to lower his head next to the king's ear.

Herinor's Crow hearing isn't the only one to pick up the words when Odja whispers, "The prisoners have arrived, Your Majesty."

SEVENTEEN

AYNA

Herinor ushers me out of the throne room at Erina's command so fast I almost stumble over the hem of my skirts as we make our way from the room and up a wide set of stairs leading to what must be the residential quarters of the palace. I've never been up far enough to know the entire layout of the royal home. A few minutes later, Odja points at a tall, walnut door, and Herinor stops, facing down the guard beside it. The man almost shits himself at the sight of the menacing male. His pointed ears are a dead giveaway of what he is—not human.

Nobody appeared surprised though, from the servants in the throne room to the king, and now this guard. If anything, he knows exactly what Herinor is capable of, or he wouldn't clutch the hilt of his sword in a death grip.

"He's under orders not to attack His Majesty's staff," Odja reassures the guard whose chest rises in a breath of obvious relief as he stands aside to let us pass.

When Odja shows us into the room, I can't help but blink, multiple times, at the devastating beauty of the space. Lush golden wallpapers cover the areas between dark wooden panels along the walls. The windows are framed in the same dark wood, their arches high enough to allow me to study the gardens I missed taking a closer look at when seated next to the Tavrasian king. Rows of pink wisteria rain down along pathways crisscrossing through the neatly arranged greenery, sheltering courtiers marching slowly and locked in conversations the content of which isn't meant for other ears. Stone benches in secluded corners offer refuge to those tired of walking along the gravel paths, and multiple fountains offer reprieve from the heat streaming in through the open windows.

I've forgotten how far south Meer is. And how close to the ocean.

A hint of salt lingers in the air that I hadn't noticed before, all of my capacity focused on the fear eating me up, the anger that has been building in my chest. But… Ocean air. Something comes to life inside, and my legs can almost feel the swaying deck of the Wild Ray beneath my feet like a phantom limb.

"I hope your accommodations are to your liking, Wolayna," Odja says as he retreats from the room. "His Majesty will have someone sent to help you prepare for the banquet. Fresh clothes will be provided. For you, too." His gaze darts to Herinor, and his already pale skin turns chalk white. "Not that you need to if you don't feel like it..." His words trail away at the single step Herinor takes in his direction.

"Leave." His tone is darker than the dim lights of the Flame estate's torture chamber, and the shiver running down my spine is enough to ease the heat of late summer.

The expression on his face changes the moment Odja closes the door behind him, leaving Herinor and me to ourselves. I don't know what to think about any of it—the strange way Erina talked to me, kind on the one hand, almost threatening on the other. Apparently, Herinor does, though, since he marches to the walnut sitting arrangement by the far wall, gesturing for me to sit.

"So, you don't sit in the Tavrasian king's presence, but you do in mine?" I'm a queen after all. *His* queen. Not that I feel like one.

His shoulders rise in a slow shrug, leathers sliding across his muscles. "We have a lot ahead of us, so we best both rest."

His tone is so at odds with the way he just kicked out Odja that it startles me all over again.

"You know exactly why I'm here, don't you? Not just that I'm to be part of his court. There is more." I pin him with a glare as I settle into the chair across from him. "Spit it out."

"I am not allowed to tell you, but you're a smart woman, Ayna. You can put two and two together. Why would a twenty-five-year-old king invite you to his palace?"

Katrijanov said that Erina needs to think of the future of his kingdom.

"By the Guardians—" Things click into place. "No. No way." I'm out of my chair, pacing the gold-threaded carpet before the wide bed by the far wall. I'm exhausted from travels and being poisoned again and again, slightly surprised I'm still on my feet after all of it, but *this* keeps me wide awake. "I'm *not* marrying the King of Tavras." Because a legacy—progeny—would be the only reason he'd invite a young woman to his realm. Not invite—*buy.*

"Couldn't agree more." My head whips around at the familiar wind chime voice announcing the new arrival from the threshold, and my knees finally give out.

Herinor catches me by the shoulders a moment before my head hits the edge of the bed.

"Ayna." Her copper braid swings toward my face as Princess Cliophera of Askarea leans over me, shoving the Crow aside with her small shoulder and cupping my face with one hand while the other wipes across my forehead. "Are you all right?"

No. "What are you doing here?" It's the only thing I can think of asking. Not how she's alive after being in the explosion that took me out after the battle in the Seeing Forest.

Clio sighs, and it might have been the heaviest sound I've heard in my life, and I've heard my fair share of burdened sighs—Guardians, I've sighed them myself.

"Long story." She turns to Herinor, a frown etched into her features. "Is this one trustworthy?"

"Depends." I struggle into a sitting position, allowing both Herinor and Clio to stabilize me. Guardians, it's good to see her. Even when she looks different. Very different, now that I take a closer look.

The copper of her hair isn't as vibrant as I remember, and her movements are slower, less edged and honed. And her eyes... The usually bright jade has dulled to a nearly human hue. Above her face rests a white maid's cap that directs my eyes toward the sepia uniform with the same white apron I've seen on the servants in the throne room. "What happened to you?"

"First, I need to know what happened to *you*?" Her tone doesn't leave room for discussion, so I give her the brief version of the Flames capturing me and my time at the estate. I don't leave out how many times I've been given poisoned water or how frequently I've vomited my guts up. When I try to explain Herinor's role in all of it, her eyes narrow on the male who has returned to his chair and is watching like an eagle as I paint his character in the shades of gray I can find. To his credit, he doesn't object when I accuse him of hurting me multiple times, he doesn't defend his position or try to make himself look any more honorable than he is—which isn't very much at all.

"You can be glad I don't have access to my magic at the moment, or I'd freeze you and shatter you with a good punch to your sternum," Clio throws over her shoulder with enough venom to make Herinor visibly shudder.

"I'm not going to hurt her if I can help it," he merely says. "And before you start, I've learned my lesson. I am fully aware how bad an idea it was to bind myself to Ephegos."

"Truth? Or a convenient lie so you can shove a knife into her back the moment she starts trusting you?" Clio is on her feet in a fighting stance, and even in her servant's uniform and without a weapon, she is a sight to behold. Fierce and ready to defend me to the death, I can feel it in my bones.

Wiping his hand over his scar-flecked features, Herinor shakes his head. "You forget I'm not an Eherean creature. While you Eherean fairies can lie until your throats bleed, Neredynian fae can't. Shaelak likes his creatures truthful."

At that, Clio straightens. Something passes between them like a silent communication only ancient creatures have access to. "You can still bend the truth to your advantage," Clio claims, and I want to chime right in with my agreement, but Herinor beats me to it.

"I could, and I have. But not on this. I made a mistake. I pledged my loyalty to a power-hungry male in false hopes of freedom. Instead, I ended up in an even worse sort of prison. Look at me." He gestures at his chest, his weapons. "I'm a warrior. And Ephegos made me into a babysitter for a queen he wants taken care of so he can follow his own aspirations." His mouth closes as if he's said too much and is expecting blood to pour from his lips.

This isn't the curse Vala placed on them, though. The curse is broken, and he can tell me whatever he wants—except for whatever his bargain with Ephegos prevents him from saying.

Guardians—could things be any more complicated?

"Now what's *your* story," he bounces the question back to Clio, who has relaxed her posture if only slightly. She still appears ready to kill on my behalf if Herinor as much as breathes wrong.

"I was knocked out by the explosion the combined Crow magic and Flame fire caused. Ephegos used the opportunity to haul me to Tavras and drug me so I can't use my magic." Her gaze wanders to me as if expecting for me to remember.

"What do you mean ... *drugged?*" The emptiness in my chest and palms where my magic once flowed tingles as if in response before Clio can answer, and my head whips to Herinor. "The water?"

He dips his chin but doesn't speak.

"Whatever unholy brew it is, Ephegos has found a way to sedate magical abilities."

Fuck—

Not poison. They weren't trying to slowly kill me so it would be a longer suffering than a swift execution. It's a fucking *drug*.

"You sent my magic to sleep?" I don't know why I'm surprised after everything I've been through in the fairylands.

Relief as sweet as a poison of its own rushes my veins at the thought that my powers aren't gone, merely dormant. Gently, I reach into my body, searching for hints of the cool liquid magic running through my veins—hidden but still there, somewhere beneath the layers of sedation.

"Ephegos demanded it at first, but I chose to continue on my own. I already told you, he'd never order me to hurt you while you are sleeping. He'd want you fully awake and alert for torture." The fact that I now know whatever Herinor says is the truth is as unsettling as the thought that, without the drug, I might be strong enough to free myself from this new prison.

"Yes, yes, you're a selfless hero." Clio turns her back on the fairy as she looks me over. "We need to get you ready for the banquet. And before you ask, yes, I'm your lady's maid."

I don't ask. Her outfit is proof even when a tiny part of me had hoped she was here to get me out rather than dress me to meet the man who intends to marry me.

Instead of screaming at the top of my lungs at the thought of having ended up in another arranged engagement, I turn to the only person who's been around this court long enough to perhaps have a clue what the Tavrasian king wants with a traitor. "I thought he'd execute me to make a statement, not put me in a wedding gown. Why does he want to marry me?"

Both Herinor's and Clio's gazes whip to mine, Herinor shaking his head and Clio's face filling with pity. "If there is one thing I've learned about things involving the King of Tavras, it's that whatever it is he wants, it can't be good.

"His court doesn't know who you are, Ayna." Herinor's voice is so quiet I can't believe he's spoken, but when I meet his gaze again, he's nodding with encouragement. "King Erina, General Katrijanov, and Ephegos are the only ones who know, and they won't lift a finger to advertise the King of Tavras intends to marry a convicted criminal and foreign queen." It feels like those are the most words Herinor has ever spoken to me, their meaning sliding over me like poisonous honey.

I left Meer so long ago that no one here will remember my face even when I remember too many of them. I left as a traitor's daughter, and I've returned as a nobody. So far, I haven't decided if my anonymity is a blessing or a curse. If I had someone … only one person who remembers my family, I might have another ally—or another enemy.

Before I can choose to be strong, I slump over my knees, and tears fall from my eyes.

Clio's arms wrap around me so fast I gasp as she pulls me against her chest, sitting down beside me and rocking me back and forth like a child. "It's all right, Ayna. Cry those tears now so Erina will never see them. He can't know how close to breaking you are, or he'll make it a public spectacle to watch you come apart."

I don't question her. She's been in this palace longer than I have. As a fucking servant. The horror of one of the most powerful creatures I know ending up in a human king's service… It nearly breaks my heart.

If Myron could see me now, he'd be ashamed of the woman he entrusted his heart to, and his people.

On instinct, my fingers wander to my biceps where the edge of the crow tattoo curls around my arm. *Myron.* If he were still alive, he'd bring down this palace with his vengeance and pick me from the rubble. He'd break apart Ephegos and Erina like twigs until their blood tinted the ground the color of nightmares, and even Herinor for the role he played in my pain.

It's not much but enough to shock my tears into submission. As I trace my fingers over the fabric covering the corner of my tattoo, a current courses along my skin all the way to my spine where the tattoo ends. It's stronger than a caress, near painful.

"What's wrong, Ayna?" Clio's voice is pushed to the background at the flicker of darkness running through me like an echo of Myron's touch, and I jolt out of her arms, heart racing and breathless.

EIGHTEEN

MYRON

I'm used to utter and complete darkness. Being a creature of Shaelak comes with lots of experience in that department. What I'm not prepared for is the stench of rot and mold greeting me as I wake to a hint of starlight and lots of pain—and weakness. My limbs are like the tentacles of starfish, trying to stack themselves under my body as I pant at the stinging sensation in my shoulder that woke me mere heartbeats ago.

I've seen the dungeons in the palace in the Seeing Forest, have used them for one or the other prisoner, but *this* is worse than even those forgotten cells flecked with blood.

My legs are trembling from the effort to push myself up, and my hands keep slipping on the wet sheen on the ground. I don't bother wondering if it's blood or vomit or my own urine as I roll over to my back, forcing in slow, deep breaths.

"Myron," someone whisper-shouts from not far away.

In reflex, I shoot to my side, managing to get into a kneeling position. Gods, whatever they did to us, it knocked me out so thoroughly I can't tell what time has passed or if I am alive or burning in the pits of Hel's realm.

Again, that voice pierces through the throb in my head, in my shoulder, in my entire body.

"Are you awake, Myron?" *Royad.*

Of course, my cousin would be here. He'd follow me even to Hel's realm if it would ensure I'm fine.

I'm not fine.

I respond with a groan.

"Oh, thank Shaelak you're awake. I was beginning to think they knocked you out for good."

"Perhaps they should have." Every word hurts.

"They gave you an extra dose of the drug." I try to make out Royad's form in the darkness, but my eyes won't work the same way. They are weak the same way the rest of my body is. All I pick up is the glint of steel bars in the summer of starlight falling in through a tiny window far up in the wall. In fact, the window is the only reason I know it's an actual wall. "They drugged Silas and Astorian again, too. They will curse the day they were born soon enough when they wake."

"Why does it sound like you mean *if* they wake?" My voice scrapes through my throat like I've swallowed gravel.

Royad shifts, the leathers scraping over the stone floor as he comes closer. At least, my ears still work well enough to distinguish directions and haven't given up on me the way my eyes have.

"Because who knows with the Fire Fairies and Ephegos." The movement stops, and I know he must have reached the bars separating our cells or he'd already be at my side, helping me up. "They forced the drug down your throat in your sleep without regard for whether you kept breathing or not." The panic in his tone tells me he hasn't quite gotten over the memory, no matter that I'm awake and breathing now.

"Are you all right?" It's more important than worrying whether Ephegos would have let me die that easily—again.

A long silence lingers in the stinking air of the dungeon—because that's obviously what this is—before he speaks again. "As all right as anyone could be under these circumstances."

A breath of relief leaves my lungs. "And what are the circumstances?" I remember the Fire Fairies capturing us with some substance they sprayed on us to annihilate our magic. The conversation with the female... And eventually—

"Where are we?"

"Tavras."

"Where in Tavras? Are we still at the Flame estate?" I wouldn't put it past the Fire Fairies to have dungeons like these ready beneath their residence, just in case.

"Meer. We're at the royal palace in Meer. In the dungeons of the royal palace in Meer, to be specific." I almost laugh at the irony in his tone. "It's where they brought Ayna."

Everything stills inside me, and my hand finds my shoulder on instinct at the mention of her name. *Ayna is here.*

The breath stuck in my throat doesn't move until Royad continues. "Apparently, that was Ephegos's plan all along, seeing her to the King of Tavras. You know, with her history of looting the Tavrasian royal fleet, King Erina has an interest in getting his hands on her to exact justice."

"For treason," I repeat so pain doesn't wipe my ability to think rationally. It's one of the things I've perfected over centuries of living as a cursed king with one bride after the other dying under my fingers like withering flowers. Her becoming my bride was supposed to be her punishment even when it might have saved her.

The panic is insistent as it eats away at my forced calm.

But I *died,* and she was taken away from me. Now she's in the enemy's hands and—

I pause. "How do you know all of this?"

"The guards checking in every other hour to make sure we're still in our cells. Humans become surprisingly reckless around fairies when they believe we are powerless."

"Which we are." I flex my fingers, trying to summon my magic. Even a fraction of what I used to be capable of would be enough to blast a hole in the wall and set us free.

Nothing happens. Not even the slightest tingle. My powers are under lock and key behind the effects of the drug.

This time, Royad continues without my prompt. "What they want with us specifically, I can't tell you. Can't be anything good though if they need to drug us and throw us in the dungeons."

I nod my agreement, wondering if he can see in the dark. "How long have we been here?" Gathering facts. That's what I need to do until the rest of my body answers to me again. Gods, I feel like someone cut off a limb where my magic used to rush like an untamable beast.

"They put us in here a few hours ago. I don't know how long the carriage ride was, but it must have been a few days. I only woke once, and they knocked me out with a fist to the face rather than the drugged water the way they did with you." A familiar sense of anger rises in my chest, giving me more strength than my body can handle, and I stumble back to my knees as I attempt to rise to make my way to the bars to check if he's all right. No matter if he's told me that he is, I need to assure myself that there aren't any other injuries he hasn't told me about. He's my only family, blood. If I can't keep him safe, how can I rule a kingdom—

A kingdom that no longer exists. What few Crows we left behind in the Seeing Forest are less than a usual court, and the Crow traitors who joined Ephegos I no longer consider part of my people.

"Can't you two shut your mouths for a moment?" Astorian groans from a few feet away. "I have a massive headache."

"As long as it's only *your* head," Silas retorts from somewhere behind Royad, and my cousin whirls around, judging by the suddenty of it, and rushes toward Silas's voice. "My entire body feels like I've been dragged through the rubble of the Crow Palace."

"I'm afraid it's worse than that," Astorian comments as he scrambles closer until he appears near the shimmer of bars on my other side. Apparently, my eyes have adjusted enough to make out the outline of the fairy general. "Someone took away our powers."

"Fuck." Silas again. This time, it's in clear agreement with Astorian's assessment.

"That, and I'm going to tear someone limb from limb for letting me sleep in my own piss," Astorian says as he holds onto the steel bars, eyes glinting with fury that makes them shimmer auburn in the near darkness even when the rest of the space is tinted in grayscale. It's an eerie sight, and had I not been convinced Astorian is one of the strongest fairies in existence, I'd be now without a doubt.

I try again, harnessing the general air of vengeance filling the dungeon to push myself to my feet. This time, I make it all the five paces to Royad's cell where I lean against the bars, panting as weakness threatens to take out my legs all over again. My cousin's hand lands on my shoulder, a familiar touch that has helped me through a century of misery. He doesn't deserve to be in this hole of disgrace with me. No one does. Not even the fairy general, whose alliance might be as fleeting as his interest in my wellbeing on the roof of the Fire Fairy estate.

"How exactly does one take a fae's magic away?" Silas grumbles from his cell, his outline coming into view another few paces behind Royad. Those aren't cells, they're cages.

Above our heads, the bars bend inward to form a slanted roof following the angle of the low stone ceiling beyond before they blend into the wall with the window out of my reach. Whether they believe we could break through the stone ceiling even without our magic or because it was built this way to begin with, I don't care. I'm in a cage like the animal I am—I used to be.

For long, long centuries, my Crow nature dictated my actions, my entire being, while the curse kept me from shifting out of my bird form entirely. Not anymore. Ayna freed me, and if I deserve this cage, it's not because of the monster I am but because of how I've failed her.

"Stop wallowing over there, and participate in some strategizing, King, or we'll rot down here while your precious woman is being handled by the King of Tavras." Astorian's remark brings me right back to the present where the stench is near-overwhelming.

My head is gradually clearing as I pace along the bars, grabbing onto them for support. Royad follows me on the other side of the steel fence, worry furrowing his brow.

"I'm not wallowing. I'm making a self-assessment. As a warrior, you, if anyone, should know how important it is to understand your physical and mental state before thinking about breaking prison—without access to a weapon."

Free hand gliding over the belt on my hips, I confirm that I was stripped of all blades I brought on this journey. This will make things even more difficult.

"I self-assessed during the time it took you to get over yourself to stand up," Astorian retorts, obviously grumpier than even Silas when he's woken early from a bad night's rest. "My head is hurting. My balance is shit. My magic is a song in the wind above the Quiet Sea. I haven't eaten in days, and the aftereffects of the drug they gave us make me wish I hadn't drunk in days either. My left ankle is bruised—no idea what they did to it, probably pinched it in the carriage door—and someone cut open my forearm—probably to taste the sweetness of fairy blood." His growl makes me wonder if he is serious about that last part. I don't know about Eherea, but stories about ancient Neredyn suggest that a lot of out-of-hand situations with the Crows occurred because they let humans taste their blood.

"Just kidding, Myron. No one will drink us dry in this shit hole." Astorian's teeth flash like moon-cast pearls in the darkness. "So, any ideas on how to get out of here?"

"And by out of here you mean wait until we have our powers back before we blast the entire palace to rubble?" Silas supplies so drily I barely realize he's being sarcastic.

"Odds are we won't have our powers at our disposal by the time we need to face the Tavrasian guards," Royad argues, pragmatic as always. "There are no loose rocks or other items we could employ as weapons."

"So hand-to-hand it is." Astorian folds his arms over his chest, swaying slightly on his feet before bracing his shoulder on the bars as if to mask his imbalance.

Silas snorts. "You don't look like you could do shit with hand-to-hand right now."

The glare the fairy general throws him is anything but. "That's because I can't *do shit* right now. You're not any better off, by the way."

I slide down the bars into a sitting position, resting my head against the cold barrier cutting me off from Royad's cell. "This is worse than presiding over the Crow assemblies," I groan, wiping my face with the back of my hand.

"What's that supposed to mean?" Both Silas and Astorian ask at the same time, and I can't help but grit my teeth at an involuntary grin.

"Focus on that strategy of yours, General. I need to wallow some more."

Astorian is smart enough not to push me. We are all weak and drained of our powers from the drug the humans gave us. Right now, it hardly matters how the substance works, only that we need to work around our limitations. Without food or water to recover our strength, it will be difficult to break free from our confinements. The alternative is to wait until someone comes for us and surprise them with an attack. For that, they'd have to open all four cells at once so we could fight together to overpower them. And again—without our strength, we might not be a match for armed human guards.

"We're fucked, aren't we?"

Royad sighs in response, and Astorian kicks at a pebble which his magic could have turned into a liquid projectile with half a thought.

"From all directions." Silas sits back against the wall, grimy black hair falling into his face as he shakes his head. "From all directions, my king."

NINETEEN

AYNA

The palace is tinted in light like liquid gold as Herinor escorts me down the stairs to the throne room. In front of me, Odja sets a pace that keeps me thinking he's not satisfied with the limited speed my ridiculous heels allow.

The pain in my shoulder nearly pushed me to black out, had it not been for Clio who helped me breathe through it like she's done that a hundred times. She examined the tattoo with much curiosity but few words, merely wanting to know if I've always had that and if it was the first time it hurt. The skeptical expression on her face, as she traced the inked bird's outline, didn't help with my confidence, but eventually, she smoothed the frown off her face and helped me into a dress made of a lighter shade of red satin for the flowing A-line skirts and silk blossoms patched together to make up the bust. The neckline is too low for my liking, and the large hoop earrings keep tangling with the loose strands of my hair falling from the bun she coiled to the back of my head. Not a lady's maid, the warrior princess, but she did an incredible job hiding the red blotches from the tears I'd spilled when we discussed the future Ephegos and Erina have agreed upon for me.

Maybe this is a different sort of torture Erina has come up with—let me go through the horror of believing he wants to marry me, let me believe I will live rather than die a painful death, just so he can strike with even more cruelty when the time for my execution comes.

How far will he take it? How long will he let me hope there is a chance at survival? Does he have his henchmen ready in the throne room? This might be my final walk, and there is only one thought swirling in my mind:

I'd rather die than marry the King of Tavras. Even if I'd never fallen in love with Myron—and lost him—I couldn't marry a man who despises my family, let alone someone I don't know or don't have feelings for. So perhaps it's the more merciful option if Erina is awaiting me with a blade to run me through and bleed me out because my heart couldn't take betraying Myron's memory even in name only.

Vala help me, my hands are shaking as we reach the bottom of the stairs and the golden double doors of the throne room come into view. The formerly empty hallways are filled with courtiers and guests—nobles residing in and around the city, I assume—their conversations forming an atmosphere of amusement and too much wine by the end of the night. I experienced such events from the sidelines as a child.

This time, however, I'm the main attraction. Groups of chatting ladies and lords part to let us pass, their eyes greedily falling upon me like on a chest of treasure. If Erina intends to kill me today, he sure has summoned an audience to witness my passing.

My shoes click along the polished floor as I take a slow step forward, the court's eyes following me with rapt attention … until they notice Herinor, and a healthy flash of fear crosses their features. A few of them hide their gasps behind their hands, tucking their heads together as they whisper about the *fairy* in their midst. I wonder how many of them see one for the first time and how frequently Ephegos walks these halls.

The moment I think his name, the male steps out front between the spectators, bows at the waist as if in respectful greeting, then holds out his arm for me. "I've been looking forward to seeing you, Wolayna." He closes the gap between us when I stop, ignoring Odja's murmured complaint that the king is waiting, and picks up my hand to place it in the crook of his elbow.

Herinor shoots me an unnecessary glance of warning to play along. There is no escaping this, and the last thing I want is for Ephegos to realize how close to breaking I am. He can't know, or he'll push even harder. Seeing me shatter is what he lives for these days.

That and whatever benefits selling me off to Erina gets him.

My bland smile is the only thing protecting me from the scrutiny of hundreds of eyes as Ephegos leads me into the throne room, past a long banquet table, and straight to the dais where Erina is presiding in his sepia uniform. While earlier today, he seemed more casual, he is now wearing the ornate crown I'd last seen on his father's head. The jewels set into the band and spikes shimmer just like his dark eyes.

"Good evening, Wolayna." He inclines his head as I curtsey.

Herinor stands at my side, one hand braced on the pommel of his sword while we all know only Ephegos could outmatch him in these halls. The rest of them are human like me.

Not like you, a voice whispers in my mind. I recognize the goddess of water and try not to shiver.

It's not a kind voice, more like a reminder of my guilt, the role I've played in the deaths of everyone I ever loved. No surprise that guilt manifests in the voice of the creature granting me power.

Then, perhaps the voice is right. If the drug Ephegos and Herinor have been giving me is truly subduing my powers, that means I still have magic. And humans don't have magic—at least not since the last Mages of Eherea.

Ephegos has hinted at it before, that I'm not entirely human.

Before I can elaborate on the thought, Ephegos pulls me forward, and I need to hold onto his arm to keep my balance. I hate the way my fingers dig into his russet finery, the way the bronze buttons of his jacket shimmer as he twists the slightest bit to watch me gather my balance with a smile that could be mistaken for kindness, concern even.

I know him better than that. He's betrayed Myron and Royad, the two people he's been friends with his entire life—because his half-sister died from the effects of the curse. It wasn't Myron's fault, or Royad's. Neither of them could have changed a thing about it. Even if she might have fallen for him, Myron didn't fall for her, or the curse would have been lifted back then.

He fell for me. And now he's dead.

"King Erina will be pleased with you," Ephegos murmurs, his mouth brushing against the ash blonde tresses shifting from the bun to my shoulders. "You have something wild about you tonight, and the king has been known to tame wild women."

I don't even want to know what he means by that. Instead of telling him as much, I give him my best indifferent smile and train my eyes on Erina, who has gotten to his feet and is meeting us halfway at the bottom of the stairs to the dais.

I have to admit, he looks like a real king in his attire. His regal posture adds to the image as does his refined manners.

"You are a sight to behold." He picks my hand from Ephegos's arm, entirely ignoring the Crow bowing at his waist, and indicates a kiss to the back of my palm. So very Tavrasian. So very unwelcome.

I smile through it, keeping my revulsion to myself while Herinor stands an inch closer to my side. At least, the other guests have resigned to observing from a distance, and I'm positive I have the menacing Crow to my right to thank for it. Ephegos gets a few glances, but he doesn't have a cruel air about him the way Herinor does.

"Thank you, Your Majesty." Keeping to court protocol seems to be the safest option for now. Who knows what will happen if I call him by his first name in front of everyone? Familiarity is my enemy here. It breaks down natural barriers protecting me from unwanted touches and words I intend to never hear. There are no blades ready to cut me down, no torture masters. Only Erina and his appraising eyes that tell me I'm not here to die, and a shiver of revulsion runs down my back.

If Erina wants to make me his bride, he'll have to drag me to the altar. Not even Myron did that when I still believed he was a monster.

Erina is the opposite of the Crow King, though, with his politeness and clear display of social status. He is nothing if not a king, and the whole room knows it. His rule isn't a brooding, dark, and desperate one the way Myron's was. In this palace, pomp and glamor rule as much as the House Jelnedyn.

The jewels on his hand gleam as he holds out his hand in invitation, gesturing at the banquet table with the other. "Please, sit with me."

Refusing isn't an option; I don't need Ephegos's and Herinor's confirming glances to know, so I place my hand in Erina's warm palm, thinking of the wind on my skin when I stood on the Wild Ray's deck, looking out over the turquoise waves of the Quiet Sea.

One day, I'll sail again.

The knife Clio transferred from my earlier skirts into the pocket of this dress is a reassuring weight against my thigh.

I won't hesitate to use it should it come to it—away from prying eyes, of course.

Memories of my last wedding night press to the front of my thoughts, how Myron pressed a knife into my hand, equipping me with a tool to save myself from him should he lose control over his Crow temper. He didn't call it for what it was back then, but I know now. I know he would have never hurt me, even when he hadn't developed feelings for me yet.

Erina is a whole different story, though. I was sent to the Seeing Forest on his order, sentenced to a fate worse than death. It seems Ephegos got the missive and is following in his footsteps by placing me in that very same position.

Sold as a bride.

"She will make for a beautiful bride," Ephegos says to Erina, the two men tall enough to talk over my head in the literal sense.

It costs me everything not to scoff or scream or try to pull away from Erina's hand, which is clutching mine so hard now I remember what shackles feel like. The pressure puts my stiff wrist at an awkward angle, making pain throb there for the first time since the battle against the Flames. I swallow the hiss when the pain shoots all the way to my shoulder until the tattoo stings like it's been set on fire. Good the dress has short sleeves covering the general area of the inked bird mid-flight. I'd hate having to explain anything to Erina or his court. It's enough that Herinor, Kaira, and now Clio—and apparently Ephegos—have seen it. The rest of the world can remain oblivious for all that I care.

Clio's odd silence at the sight of it creeps back into my mind, and I fight the urge to reach for my shoulder and touch the bird hovering there like a real presence.

At my carefully blank expression, Ephegos raises a groomed brow. "Have you informed her, Your Majesty?"

Erina shakes his head, his grip pulling me outward and forward, guiding me into a chair one of the servants is pulling out for me. The sepia upholstery is repulsive, as is the golden paint covering the wooden frames of the chairs.

"I thought the honor would fall upon you, my friend." That Erina is calling Ephegos *friend*… My stomach reminds me how little it can handle food with the constant nausea from the news being sprung upon me every other minute.

"Well, Wolayna." Ephegos waits for Erina to sit to my right at the head of the table before he takes a seat across from me, bracing his scarred hands on the meticulous white tablecloth as he captures my gaze with a fake friendly one of his. "Since you lost your former husband, I'd hate for you to fall back into a life of poverty and stealing." He clears his throat when his already soft voice breaks into a whisper. No one pays attention to our conversation since they are all whispering and murmuring their own speculations over the seating arrangement at the end of the long table. "So, instead of tempting you to loot King Erina's ships again, we made an agreement. You become his bride."

His words hang in the air as if unfinished, and my brain is working overtime to fill in the blanks while keeping myself from reacting to the obvious insults in his statement. "What do *you* get out of the bargain?" I ask in my sweetest courtier tone, remembering every painful moment of my mother dragging me to noble receptions throughout Meer. I can do this. I can be strong, unbreakable. I can be the Ayna who defies all odds—for Myron, who defied all odds for me.

Erina braces his elbows on the table, leaning into my space as he whispers the answers I'm demanding from Ephegos. "My friend came to my general with an offer I believe everyone in the human realms will benefit from. You are the price, Wolayna. But since you should be already dead, sacrificing you doesn't feel like too much of a price, does it?"

The gasp escapes my lips—I can't help it—and I could swear Herinor tenses behind me. I don't know how far away he is, but I know he won't leave me alone in here—even when it's not for my benefit. It's his orders that keep him glued to me. And perhaps a little bit his honor.

A sour taste rises in my throat, and it has nothing to do with the odor of the colorful, fish-topped salad a servant is placing in front of me. My stomach dips at the thought of potentially more magic-subduing substance in my food.

If only I could feel the power slumbering in my system… It's been silent for too long, and I wonder if they'll let me go without the drug long enough at some point for me to recover at least a fraction of it. A fraction would be enough to overpower a human guard and fight my way out.

Absently, my hand makes it to the side of my thigh where it comes to rest upon the outline of the knife, fingers itching to draw it and stab Ephegos in the eyes he's blinking at me like he can't quite believe I am finally showing a reaction to the news.

Erina's mouth is still too close, his breath hot on my cheek and his nose grazing the shell of my ear. I can feel all eyes in the room on us as the courtiers observe what they believe could be a scandal—or their next romantic sensation.

"I will not marry you." My voice is toneless, so soft I can barely hear myself speak, but determination rings true in it anyway. With all the strength I can muster, I turn my head so my face is lined up with the king's, put on my sweetest smile as I draw back an inch, and repeat, "I *will not* marry you."

Across from me, Ephegos shifts in his chair as if he wants to respond to a comment he obviously isn't supposed to hear while Erina's face turns unreadable as he studies me with dark brown eyes glinting with resolution. "I'm afraid you don't have a choice, Wolayna. Try to refuse, and I'll destroy the one thing you hold dear."

"There is nothing I hold dear anymore." The words are out so fast I can't believe I spoke them. But I did, and their meaning makes my life appear even bleaker than it already is.

"Are you so certain? Would you bet your life on it?" His finger comes to rest beneath my chin, tilting my head up an inch so I can't look away, no matter how much I want to. "Or, let's say … the life of the male you love, perhaps?"

My heart stops—literally stops. I can't breathe, can't think, can't remember to keep my expression blank and my emotions locked away. In my shoulder, a light tingle spreads as if something is fighting for my attention.

"Everyone I love is dead. You and your *friend*"—my eyes dart to Ephegos, who's doing his best at pretending he isn't listening in on the conversation, fingers interlaced at the edge of the table—"made sure of that. And your general of course. Everyone I love is *dead*."

How Erina remains unfazed is beyond me. He merely twists his mouth into a regal smile, leaning back in his chair, releasing my chin. "Are they now?"

The air is thick, the pressure on my chest making it impossible for me to take the deep breath I so desperately need.

"You will marry me, Wolayna. If you refuse, I will destroy him." Reaching into his pocket, Erina retrieves a shiny black feather, twirling it between his fingers like he is musing about the meaning of it.

It could be any bird's feather. Any Crow's. Ephegos could have forced Herinor to give up one of his.

The panicked pounding at the center of my heart tells me, though, that it belongs to Myron. And that I'm about to lose him all over again.

ANGELINA J. STEFFORT

TWENTY

AYNA

Odja is the only one from Erina's court I see for the next week. No matter how many times I beg him to let me talk to Myron, or to ask the king to let me see my husband, he remains adamant about executing his orders of keeping me secluded in my room. At least, I have Clio who visits twice per day with the task of getting me dressed in the morning and dressed for bed as if she weren't a princess. Today is no different.

When she steps into the room, her sepia maid's uniform clashing with her copper hair and jade eyes like it's actively trying to, I sit up where I've curled into myself on the broad bed to forget the world and the impossibility of escaping my fate.

I tried to sneak out of the room three times the first night without success. The palace guard caught me the first two times, and when I opted for the window and climbed down the ropes of Tavrasian wisteria along the palace wall, Herinor was waiting at the bottom, a frown on his features and an apology on his lips as he marched me back to my room. He doesn't have a choice. His life depends on keeping me in line.

After everything I've learned about him, I no longer know if I even want him to consider giving up his life to save me. Myron did that.

Yet, he's alive somehow. I haven't laid eyes on him. Haven't gotten the confirmation I've begged of everyone who'd listen for seven days in a row, to no avail, that he's truly alive. That he is here in this palace. They have been drugging me at every chance, making certain my magic remains dormant and me compliant through weakness.

I can't remember how many full meals I've eaten—and how many I've vomited into the porcelain toilet in the adjacent bathing chamber. Clio says that if I eject one more meal, I might no longer be much of a bride to marry.

Her good humor is the only thing I'm looking forward to when I wake in the same pompous prison as every morning for the past week. And Herinor… He spends his days outside my door as a backup for the human guards who failed to contain me the first two times.

It's the eighth day when I finally wake without the usual headache and nausea. A tingle in my shoulder reminds me of the tattoo, and I roll out of bed, bracing my hand on the edge of the table as I stand in front of the mirror in the corner. The fact that my head is a little clearer today is enough to make me question everything Erina said. Myron can't be alive. I watched him die. I fucking cried onto his still chest. His heart wasn't beating.

The flicker of hope having come to life inside of me won't go away. And hope is worse than fear or hatred or even anger. Once it takes root, it can destroy the strongest armor established around a shattered heart. It creeps between the pieces like poison, tugging and pulling on them so when the final blow hits to destroy, whatever protection kept it safe will no longer stop anything from eviscerating.

I can't allow for that to happen.

Yet, my heart is lighter than it has been in weeks. It doesn't matter what Erina wants from me as long as Myron is alive—as long as the guilt of being responsible for another loved one's death is lifted from my shoulders and I can *breathe* again.

"Good morning." Clio enters on silent fairy feet, startling me as I take a step toward the mirror. Naturally, she is there before I can fall to my knees, my balance still disturbed from the drug.

"Why do you look like a goddess even after being drugged every day?" I ask her with the same disgruntled tone I have ready for Erina should he ever show his face again. "And why haven't you bolted from this place? You're apparently still fast enough to outrun any human."

Clio heaves me onto the sepia sofa, sitting next to me as she places my hands in my lap and brushes back my hair like a mother does with a child.

"The drug affects fairies differently. We recover faster from the side effects. But trust me, I've hurled up my guts more than once since I was brought here." Her sympathetic expression is more than disconcerting. It's nothing like the fierce warrior princess I remember. What has this place done to her?

"Does your magic return faster, too?" Again with that hope. The drug is doing its best to destroy me before Erina can deliver the final blow.

She bobs her head, copper braid sliding over her shoulder and covering the wooden button of her apron. "They have resorted to injecting me with the drug." A grimace distorts her beautiful features as she pulls up her sleeve to expose the cluster of red dots in the crook of her elbow. "Apparently, King Erina is all for innovation and progress. He has a group of people working on new drugs to use in war. I overheard the guards when they brought me in for my daily dosage."

"Why haven't you tried to run?" By the way her shoulders cave, I know I shouldn't have asked. "I'm sorry..."

"No... It's all right." Straightening her spine, she sits back a few inches, facing me fully. "I was half dead when they brought me in. I can't even remember what happened and how I got here. It was Ephegos who told me about the explosion and that I got caught in the rubble of the destroyed palace and a rain of magic."

Half dead. I hate the way I want to thank Ephegos for saving her even when he made her a prisoner—a slave.

"Then he locked me in a cell to test variations of the drug on me until he was sure it had the right effect to take out the strongest fairies at mere skin contact."

I hate where this is going. "They used you…"

"To create a weapon. Something that will take out fairies the way a punch to the nose can take out humans." Fear crosses her features, but she masks it with the face of the sassy female I met back at Myron's palace. "A weapon against Askarea."

"Guardians—" If this is really what Erina is doing… "He wants to attack the fairylands."

"He's far from finding a solution. Producing the drug takes too long to create large amounts. But eventually, yes. I believe he wants to attack Askarea."

And with a weapon like that, the fairies would lose their advantage. How I can feel sympathetic toward a people I feared mere months ago, I don't even want to understand. Myron, Royad, and Clio made a difference in the way I view the fairylands. They might be dangerous and powerful and cruel if need be, but they are also my friends. My family.

"Is Erina telling the truth? Is Myron alive?"

Clio shakes her head. "I don't know. I haven't been in the dungeons since those initial days. I tried to escape too many times for them to let me go anywhere on my own. The only reason they allow me into this room without supervision is because Herinor is standing guard outside, and his fairy ears pick up every word we're speaking." Her hand finds mine in a comforting squeeze. "I can't fathom even trying to run again now that you're here. I won't leave you behind. If we escape, it will need to be together. And I know you're listening, Herinor," she adds a little louder. "If you say one word to Ephegos, Erina, or anyone, I will cut your tongue out, magic or no."

I believe every word she says, and oddly enough, for once, my rage isn't on my behalf but on that of the female who has suffered because she stepped in to help in the Seeing Forest. She suffered because of me. It's my responsibility to get her out of here.

We talk more as she helps me dress for the day—not that I can't do it on my own, but there is comfort in the silent companionship of this task. My thoughts circle around the extent of cruelty both Ephegos and Erina are capable of and around the probability of Myron being held in those same dungeons.

If he's alive, truly alive—

Erina could have simply let me believe it so he has leverage over me. It could be all there is to it, I try to smother the flame of hope growing inside my chest with each passing day.

If I could talk to Herinor in quiet, perhaps he could give me the answers I seek, but he only ever escorts me places, and the night I tried to escape, he only shook his head in denial of my request. I'm not getting anything from him because Ephegos doesn't allow it. Herinor's life depends on his silence the same as it did with the drug.

A drug—at least, I'm not slowly dying with every time I drink the laced water. My magic isn't coming back to life either, though, so the situation doesn't improve.

If Kaira would visit, maybe she could shed some light on the mystery of Erina's words. She was there, at the Flame estate. Perhaps she knows something.

I'll ask Odja about her the next time he drops by my room to deliver a message from the king or Ephegos about the daily schedule—sit around and wait—or bring in a seamstress to measure me for my wedding gown.

I hate that man for his blind compliance to a king who's forcing a woman to marry.

And I'm one hundred percent certain Erina is not a cursed king. He's merely a man who places his own needs above those of all others. He needs a bride, a queen, to continue his bloodline.

Clio nearly pulls my hair out when Odja knocks on the door an hour later and lets himself in. I'm wearing the shimmering brown gown Clio brought in for this morning, and I can't help but gasp when the corset keeps me from properly breathing.

"Apologies, Lady Wolayna." He bows at the waist in the same manner he bowed to Erina. Now that the engagement has become common knowledge, everyone who enters the room does. Except for Clio and Herinor—I refuse to let them even try. "The King is ready to see you."

I'm so perplexed that I barely notice Herinor's tight features as he glimpses over Odja's shoulder.

Something is up, and it can't be good. Why that surprises me is beyond me. I should be prepared that nothing good ever comes my way anymore.

We leave Clio behind as Odja leads the familiar way to the throne room. Instead of entering the pompous space, he turns into a side corridor where the sunlight doesn't reach and shadows hide the ornate details of the tapestries covering the walls. I spy a portrait of the late king and queen woven into the cloth and do a double take at the similarity between Erina and his father.

At the end of the hallway, a small round table is carrying a vase of Tavrasian wisteria, the blossoms hanging over the edge in a waterfall of pink. The image would be stunning were it not for the man standing in the doorway beside it.

"Wolayna." Erina holds out a hand in invitation as he steps back into the room.

I'm tempted to spit in his face as Odja leads me past him, inside, before retreating with a bow.

I'm alone with Erina. Not even Herinor is here to witness whatever the king has to say to me. The male was the one to close the door after Odja, probably taking up post outside with his Crow ears listening to every breath I take.

"You wanted to speak with me?" It should be my question to ask, but Erina beats me to it.

I bob my head.

"So Odja told me. You've been asking for an audience all week."

He knows damn well I have been wanting details on Myron, confirmation of some sort that he's alive and well, but he must humiliate me by making me repeat myself.

Too bad I no longer care about my dignity. If Myron is indeed alive, I'll do whatever it takes to make sure he's all right. "I need to see Myron."

Erina cocks his head. "Interesting how deeply in love you are with a man who forced you to marry him. Do you believe this is something you might be able to repeat?"

The audacity… And he doesn't even mean it as an offense; I can tell by the way his features remain open, no hint of cruelty. Only curiosity. Similar to when we were children eating

206

croissants under banquet tables and he offered for me to get one every day.

"Myron was different." I keep the fury out of my tone, the hurt and the pain. "Take me to him."

"I will."

My heart leaps.

"If"—there's that cruel smile—"you put on my engagement ring."

"And why would I do that?" I glare at the golden band he pulls from the sepia velvet box he picks from the desk by the wide window. It's an office of sorts, small enough to feel only cozy if it wasn't for the hard and straight furniture and the assortment of sabers and rapiers displayed along the left wall. I swallow hard. One of those blades could save my life. If I could make it to the wall and get one short saber into my fingers, I could injure Erina and climb out the window. This is only one level above the ground floor. I might survive a jump. And then I could hide in the corners of the gardens until nightfall and I can sneak off the premises. I just need to keep him distracted long enough to make a move. "There is no logical reason for you to want to marry a traitor daughter, a traitor herself."

"But you're wrong." Erina weighs the jewelry in his palm. "You might be a traitor, but you know nothing about the current state of Tavras, do you?" Lifting his gaze for a moment, he perches on the edge of his desk, shoving a stack of documents aside so he can brace his free hand behind him. "Tavras needs stability. And stability demands for a clear line of succession."

"Succession," I repeat like a parrot because that's the only thing I can do at what his words imply.

"Succession," he confirms. "Your mother was a firm believer of the union of our two houses, you know. She was the reason my father contracted yours for business—to get to know the ... competition."

"Competition." Again with the repeating. I can't help it, my brain is in overload. "What are you talking about?"

"Wolayna Milevishja, daughter of Ivan Milevishja and Elenja Milevishja." The way he states my name and heritage like it's something to wonder about—or something to fear. "Haven't you ever wondered why a king would be so close with a merchant? My father didn't pay this much attention to all of his business partners. Your father was a very special case."

"He traded for the Crown," I blubber. "Special acquisitions..."

"Special tasks for a special man," Erina agrees, but disdain is all I find in his eyes rather than the sort of admiration one would expect connected to a man deserving of a king's attention. "My father needed to keep an eye on the last surviving male Milevishja."

"What do you mean?" I'm trying to piece his words together into something that fits my memories of Tavras. "There are thousands of Milevishja's in Tavras. The name is as common as the average street merchant."

"And for good reason." Erina picks up the top paper from the stack behind him, putting the ring back in the box he placed beside him on the desk. "There was a time when Tavras needed to forget how special the name truly is."

I come up blank. There is nothing special about the name… Only, there is. "*Remember who your father was, Ayna,*" my mother used to say. She said it even after he'd been executed and we'd moved away from the capital and prying eyes. But I was too young then to understand the meaning of her words.

By the Guardians…

"There was a line of Milevishja kings, Wolayna. You remember that, don't you? Long before the House Jelnedyn came into power. It was a time when all Milevishja were executed until they found that hunting the heirs down caused more hatred toward House Jelnedyn. So my ancestors used a trick to make the importance of the Milevishja line disappear. Over a hundred years ago, my great-grandfather had random families in Tavras renamed to the name of the former ruling house. Merchants, farmers, nobles, even whores. The families were paid off for their silence, of course, and over the years, people stopped asking about whether someone belongs to the royal Milevishja line because, at times, every third person in the room carried that name."

By everything that's holy and unholy. After killing most of the royal Milevishja line, Erina's family took away their importance by making their name common. No one thinks of the early Milevishja kings anymore when hearing the name on the streets. Not even in the palace. All traces of their rule have been erased.

"There are no royal Milevishja left when it comes to public knowledge." Erina rolls on, and I wish I wasn't alone with him in this room. Hopefully, Herinor is hearing all of this. I need a witness, someone who knows what's going on, what the House Jelnedyn is capable of. "But there is one left if you know where to look. *One* last royal Milevishja."

I don't dare think for fear I already know where this is going. It can't be.

"Your father agreed to never expose his true heritage and claim the throne of Tavras, Wolayna. That's the reason my father allowed him to carry on his business. It's also the reason he kept such a close eye on him."

My father wasn't a merchant. He was the last male royal Milevishja. I need a moment to breathe, or I'll black out. My body is already showing me the limits after a week of barely keeping down food and constantly being drugged. This could very well be one huge hallucination, and I'll wake with a massive headache and regrets over the last meal I've eaten.

"He made a mistake, though. He didn't stick to his promise to keep his hands off the throne." He holds out the paper for me to read, and I take it with shaky hands.

Numbers are scribbled in a table similar to the shipment papers my father used to write in his office.

No—this *is* one of those papers. I recognize his handwriting, the dark green ink on yellowed parchment. It's one of the shipments for the Tavrasian King.

"Read it." I don't need Erina's order. I'm already halfway through it, the blades on the wall forgotten.

One thousand Tavrasian gold in coins. Seventeen thousand silver pieces. A cerulean vase from the neighboring human province of Cezux, derived from a chest of carved oak.

I remember the shipment. Not the list or this exact paper but the contents. That's what I witnessed him loading into the carriage. Gold, silver, and a large cerulean vase of Cezuxian making. Cerulean vases are rare, even in Cezux.

Guardians—

"Sound familiar?"

I don't react, too busy piecing everything together. There is nothing odd about the shipment. Just usual items and money. Lots of money.

"Who was it for?"

My mind wanders back to the day the Tavrasian soldier bullied me into admitting I'd seen my father load exactly that shipment. It's the reason he was executed for treason.

"What was in that shipment that made my father a traitor?" I don't care if my emotions are plain on my features. This is a whole new level of intrigue. If what he's saying is true, my father was royalty. A rightful king of Tavras. The Jelnedyn line murdered their path to the throne.

Erina's smile is handsome and painful because the blow will land so much harder now that I understand everything might have been a lie—my entire childhood, my life, my family.

"The shipment was for an assassin to murder my father, my mother, my uncle, and … me." The smile slips.

I grasp for the single chair next to the door, sitting without permission before I faint.

"You're lying." It's the only way he can be saying this. It can't possibly be the truth. My father would have never—

"I'm afraid not, Wolayna, last living royal Milevishja." Pushing away from the desk, he picks the paper from my hands and reads out loud. "To be delivered to Harian Aleji upon completion of his assignment."

I glimpse my father's signature at the bottom of the paper as he turns it over one last time before placing it back on the desk.

"Harian Aleji was executed the same day as your father upon questioning. This was found days later in Aleji's home. He was one of the most feared assassins of my father's era, running errands even for His Majesty himself."

I don't have words even to comment on the fact of Erina admitting that his father employed an assassin—the same assassin *my* father hired to kill the King of Tavras.

The lump in my throat grows larger and larger with every detail coming back to my mind.

"My father wasn't a tyrant, Wolayna, you know that. You met him several times." Erina's expression softens as if the memory of his father is dear to him. "He offered your father a fair deal long before he became a traitor. You."

"Me?" I don't care that I stare at the current King of Tavras like a fool. He caught me off guard, and this is eradicating all capacities to remain composed.

"Consolidating the Milevishja line into the Jelnedyn line by marrying the Prince of Tavras to the … would-be-Princess of Tavras." The awkwardness is heavy in the air as if there was a time when a younger version of him considered the merits of marrying me on a romantic level.

"Our parents agreed to a secret engagement. I was told at a young age you'd be the girl I'd marry. I have the contract right here." He picks up another piece of paper, holding it up for me, and I recognize my father's signature at the bottom. "You should have been mine, Ayna. But your father made a mistake…"

His words fade as I remember that day we shared a marzipan croissant under the table when we were kids and he invited me to the palace.

"I could show you around. Menia could tailor a dress for you, and we could walk the hallways like we're the pair destined to ascend the throne one day." A smile plays on his lips, his roundish cheeks forming dimples. He's pretty for his age, not overly tall or stretched in awkward proportions like some boys his age. Like from a picture from fairytale books. Even his sepia and gold jacket looks like he stepped right off a miniature version of a throne, no matter if he's hiding under a table with a merchant daughter.

"Wouldn't that be considered treason?" I whisper, the fingers of my free hand half-covering my mouth.

The smile on Erina's face slips. "For you, not me."

He'd known. Guardians, he'd known back then. And my parents had left me oblivious to a duty they expected of me. My heart breaks for a whole new reason, cracking in places I didn't even know it could shatter. I'd always believed in the wrongness of his execution, in some sort of ploy that had put him at the king's mercy. And now… now I don't know what to think, except for: I was supposed to marry this man all along. My father intended to have him killed. To clear the throne of the Jelnedyn line.

And I have royal blood.

"I want to see Myron." Because if he's alive, I know that this is all a dream and I won't need to deal with the truth of it.

Erina purses his lips, picking up the ring again and shoving it onto my finger in a not-so-gentle motion. "Don't worry, Wolayna. Everything is as it was meant to be. Even if you love your Crow King, you'll be mine. I'll make sure of it." His gaze hardens as he holds my hand like in a vise. "The Jelnedyn line will not be challenged ever again."

I breathe in through my nose, forcing down air as the room closes in on me. "Why not kill me? You already sent me off to die in the fairylands. Why not kill me now and save yourself the trouble?"

Erina cocks his head, pulling me close to his side so I stand beside him like a bride marching for an altar. "Trust me, I've considered it. I was considering it the day you were brought to my palace. But when I saw you"—his gaze creeps over my face, lingering on my mouth—"I decided you'd be more valuable by my side than forgotten in a grave. By marrying you, there will be no heirs of your line that won't be of mine as well. No heirs of the House Milevishja who could one day question my claim to the throne, even if the Guardians have been hiding another unlikely heir of your line in the pockets of this realm. The Milevishja royal line will disappear, assimilated into the House Jelnedyn, and when I'm done with you, there will be nothing left for your Crow to mourn."

There are no such things as fairy tales. Life simply delivers one blow after the other.

Until even hope is smothered and the only thing living inside your chest is a wasteland.

HEART OF NIGHT

The ring feels like a shackle, and I can't muster the courage to look at Erina as he pulls me to my feet and leads me from the office.

ANGELINA J. STEFFORT

TWENTY-ONE

AYNA

The path down the winding stairs makes me dizzy, the hem of my gown catching on the sharp edges of the stone steps and my hand slithering along the wooden handrail that is now the only thing keeping me upright. Erina is taking me somewhere, but it's not a cheerful engagement party the way a normal king would do. Whether his court knows or not that he intends to marry the last living Milevishja royal, I can't tell. There is little I can be certain about with everything that has happened in the past twenty-four hours.

I'm no longer a merchant's daughter or that of a traitor. I'm the daughter of a king who was ready to put blood on his hands to take back what should have been his birthright. Treason of a very different sort. The question remains: On which side? Was Erina's father's order to execute my father treason or are my father's attempts to hire an assassin? Is a traitor on the throne now?

My gaze snags on the glinting gold band resting atop Erina's short hair. This man knows exactly what he wants and has no problem sacrificing others' happiness for it. Their lives as well if his decision to send me to the Crow Court can be taken as a measure of his character. Had I died in the Seeing Forest, the Milevishja royal blood would have disappeared with me, and no one would have been any wiser.

But I didn't die. Myron didn't let me. And if the thick, moldy stench of the air greeting us as we reach the torch-lit bottom of the stairs is anything to go by, it's safe to say that he just brought me to the dungeons. Whether he'll lock me up here or Myron is actually down here, I don't dare think about, or that relentless spark of hope will come to life all over again just to be stomped out by Erina's boots with a finality I won't recover from.

"Not far, Wolayna," Erina narrates, his shoulders straight and posture regal as ever, even down here where the mere sight of bars and cells combined with the odor makes me cave in on myself. I've spent too many months in a dark hole like this, and if the shaking of my body is anything to go by, the trauma still roots deep. "At the end of the corridor."

He gestures ahead where two men in leathers stand guard by a narrow, steel-reinforced door. They dip their chins but don't fold into a full bow, their attention on the hulking form behind me.

Herinor has been as silent as only fairies can be, but his presence is a constant. Since Erina pulled me from the office, he's followed us like a shadow, and I could swear the tension in his body has only increased.

Had it not been for him, I might have withdrawn the knife that now wanders from dress to dress, a fixture in my inventory, and stabbed Erina in the back. Herinor might even stand by and watch—unless Ephegos gave him orders to protect the King of Tavras from me. Maybe I'll try on the way back—if there *is* a way back up for me. Erina might as well lock me in one of these cells.

But first, I need to see if he told the truth and Myron is alive. If I attack Erina, he won't ever tell me, and I'll be left to fight my way through the entire palace in hopes Myron is stored somewhere in these halls—or dungeons.

The guards unlock the door and step aside, making way for their king as their eyes swipe across my form quickly before returning to Herinor. *He's* the threat, not me. I'm a puny human without magic.

The room we enter is even darker than the stairwell and the corridor. Not one single torch lines the rough stone walls. A tiny window allows a lone ray of cloud-diffused sunlight to sneak into the space, revealing enough of it to make my stomach clench with a fresh wave of nausea. I grab onto the nearest steel bar for support … and pull back my hand as the metal bites like poison.

"What was that?"

Erina smirks at me over his shoulder, the torch light falling in through the doorway illuminating his features. "This, my dear Wolayna, is my latest invention." The pride in his gaze would have been adorable had he been a child and his *invention* not something enforcing the bars of a dungeon cell.

"A magic-neutralizing substance," Herinor supplies, reaching a finger along the bar next to my shoulder, but before it can make contact, he pulls it back so fast the motion blurs before my slow, human eyes.

Of course. This blends right into what I already know about his experiments. Whether Clio was held in one of these cells, I try not to think about. Too much pain comes with the thought of her suffering because she returned to the Crow Palace to protect me.

"Ingenious." With the energy draining from my system fast, it is no challenge to keep my voice so low Erina doesn't hear it. He can lock in his magically gifted enemies even as a human king. Between the drug he keeps administering on Clio and me, the weapon to suck magic from fairies that he needs to spray on his opponents, and this, the playing field of an Eherean war is leveled.

"So … do you hold magical prisoners down here?" The bravado I muster comes as a true surprise as I hold Erina's gaze.

He shrugs. "I needed to take precautions. Just in case, you know…" His words trail away as he turns and continues into the near darkness.

About halfway into the room, more bars come into view, more cells. My heart beats like a drum as images of Fort Perenis flash through my mind. The darkness, the dirt beneath my bloodied fingernails from etching lines into the wall for each day I spent in that shit hole. The walls are closing in. Tighter. Tighter. I can't breathe. Can't—

Searching for anything that would allow me to ground myself, my eyes land on a still, human form at the back of the room.

My heart stops for the second time this morning, and I take a step closer to the bars, trying to get a better view of the prisoner.

"Myron—" Knees shaking, I stumble past Erina, uncaring of the little shocks running through my body every time I touch the bars.

Erina doesn't hold me back. Neither does Herinor. They merely follow me as I push myself along the rows of cells until an iron fence blocks my path, and I can see the long, brown hair covering Royad's scarred cheek. His chest rises and falls with slow, shallow breaths like in a restless slumber. Not dead. He's not dead.

"Royad." My gasp dies as I scan the cell for more prisoners. If he is here…

It takes half a heartbeat for me to spot the tall, muscled form with a black curtain of hair sprawled on the floor in the cell next to Royad's.

Tears shoot to my eyes, spilling without permission. I don't care.

My knees crash to the hard ground, screaming at the impact, hands sliding down the bars as I hold onto them like a lifeline. "Myron." It's less than a whisper, but my heart is flying.

He's here. He's alive.

"Myron." This time, my voice doesn't fail me. "Myron, can you hear me?"

A groan sounds through the dungeon as the male lifts his head, gazing at me with dark eyes.

Like a meteor, my moment of relief plummets behind Eroth's Veil as the unfamiliar face twists and contorts with pain.

"I'm afraid … not," the male croaks, pushing up to his hands and knees on the rough stone ground of his cell. His pointed ears peek through the straight lengths of his hair like beacons, as does the brutal tattoo inked to his arm. "Good. To." He coughs and spits to the side. "See you, Ayna." The smile he flashes me is more of a grimace, but I recognize it as genuine relief to see me. "Myron will be … pleased you're alive." Each word seems harder for him than the last, but he pushes out every last syllable, determined to speak what he has to say. "Don't trust the … bastard of a king behind you."

Myron. Myron is here. Myron is *alive.*

The bars rattle as Erina slams his hand against them, and the male cringes, almost slumping back to the ground.

"You didn't have enough last time, did you?" Erina steps to my one side, Herinor to the other, framing me like I'm about to explode the way the fairy magic did at the battle. "I can send in General Katrijanov again, now that you're awake. I'm sure he has more … questions for you."

"What do you mean, *questions?*" The sour taste returns to my mouth at the meaning implied even when Erina ignores my demand.

I can't keep my eyes from pivoting to scan the rest of the cells, though, until I spot two more sleeping forms to the right of Royad's cell. It's hard to tell if either of them is Myron. After guessing wrong two times already, I am cautious not to allow myself to hope before I'm sure it's him. There could be more Crows trapped in more cells, and it could take all day for me to find him—if Erina doesn't drag me away before I succeed. Or he might hold Myron isolated somewhere—

Before horror scenarios can unfold in my mind, my gaze catches on the bare, pale back of the prisoner in the first cell to Royad's right. It isn't the muscled form or the black hair touching the neck and shoulder that hold my attention but the distinct black shape curling between streaks of blood and grime from his biceps to his neck.

My blood stills. My skin prickles. My breath catches as I recognize the crow mid-flight inked onto the male's skin.

"Myron." This time, I don't need to see his face to be certain. The tattoo on my own shoulder stings as I scramble to kneel in front of Myron's cell as close as the bars will allow. The steel no longer stings, probably having leeched all remaining magic from me for now, so I stick my arm between the barrier as far as I can reach, praying to the Guardians that it's enough.

The bars bruise my shoulder, my neck, where I push farther and farther until my fingertips are mere inches from his elbow sticking out to the side, but I can't quite reach him. Frustration creases my features as I strain against the unmovable barrier while Erina and Herinor watch on.

"Wake up," I sob. "Please wake up, Myron." *I love you. I love you more than words can express.*

He doesn't as much as twitch.

"He'll be out for another few hours if we can trust his usual pattern." Erina crouches beside me, studying my face from up close with morbid interest. "If I'd known how much of a motivator he'd be, I'd have taken you down here the moment they brought them in.

The prisoners have arrived, Your Majesty. Odja's words as he entered the throne room the first day come back to me.

That was them. Myron, Royad, and the male who's awake. My gaze darts to the fourth fairy locked in the cell behind Myron's.

"Who's that?"

The question is directed at Erina, but it is Herinor who answers, speaking to Erina rather than to me. "Your Majesty has gotten hold of King Recienne of Askarea's general. However did you capture him?"

All color leeches from my face as I realize two things at once: There aren't only Crows in there but Crows and a fairy belonging to the royal Askarean court like Clio. And if Erina is truly holding an Askarean general prisoner, war with the fairy realm might be more imminent than I could have ever believed.

TWENTY-TWO

MYRON

S ilas is awake when I open my eyes, his dark gaze piercing and full of an emotion I haven't seen on him ever. Emotions aren't necessarily his strong suit—except for the menacing kind pushing him into action and violence.

I roll my head from side to side to take the strain out of my neck before sitting up and taking inventory of my body. A few new bruises bloom along my abdomen and jaw where they used me as a punching bag, but apart from that, it's mostly older aches from the first few days in this dungeon.

My head clears a little faster this time, a small mercy I thank Shaelak for.

"Are you coherent?" Silas asks without delay. None of us asks if we're *all right* anymore because none of us ever is. Ten days of torture will do that to a fairy. Especially one lacking their usual ability to heal fast. It's the first time I understand Ayna's frustration with her human body. Only, while she used to see herself as weak, for me it has always been a special sort of strength, putting yourself in harm's way fullknowingly that one good blow could cause pain for weeks or even months if bones are broken.

"Enough to tell it's the middle of the day." I glance around to find Royad asleep and Astorian sitting in the corner of his cell, a tray of food beside him, which he hasn't touched. "Royad?"

"Been out for a full day. Astorian was the first to wake this time." Silas gestures at the male with the stringy auburn hair. Gods, even the formidable warrior doesn't appear as intimidating with hunched shoulders and gaze lowered to the ground. If it weren't for the constant glint of vengeance in his eyes, I'd be inclined to believe he's broken under the pain they expose us to on a regular basis. He even has a fresh burn mark on his forearm, something they'd done only to me so far.

I absently trace my fingers over the angry skin where they planted a white-hot iron poker the other day.

When I woke last, Silas wasn't in his cell, and when they brought him back, he was far from coherent, blood trickling down his chin from a split lip, and curling over himself as he tried to walk into his cell on his own two feet. A fresh knife wound graces his side as well.

Those human bastards. If they'd at least tell us what they want from us, but they basically simply enjoy hurting fairies is what it seems like.

Royad is the only one not sporting any fresh injuries, and I thank the gods for that in particular if there's nothing else to thank them for.

"Shall I eat, or shall I refuse?" Astorian picks at the stale bread on his tray, lifting his head as he studies me getting to my feet with a wince. "Got you bad last time, didn't they?"

I don't bother confirming. The way my body has turned into one big bruise speaks for itself.

"Stop pitying yourselves and listen." Silas's voice is more animated than I've heard him use since the day he swore to break King Erina's neck if he ever gets his hands on him.

Stepping up to the bars to check on Royad, who lies close by the fence separating our cells, I nod at Silas.

"I saw her, Myron. Ayna is here."

The world turns silent as I hold my breath.

"What do you mean, *here*?" Astorian beats me to it. "What is the Queen of Crows doing down in the dungeon? Did they lock her up, too?"

Whatever hope came to life a moment ago leeches from my chest where fear is spreading like a plague.

"Shut up, Astorian," I snap at the fairy general. "Let him speak." *Before I lose my mind.*

"While you all were mercifully napping in your own filth, Erina brought Ayna down here to see you if I understood correctly." He purses his lips for a heart-stilling moment before continuing. "And fuck me, she shattered when she knelt in front of my cell and realized I wasn't you."

Every cell in my body revolts at the thought of Ayna in pain—any sort of pain.

"Did you talk to her? What did she say?" My pulse is pounding in my throat, my entire system on alert as if that would bring her back so I could hear her voice rather than Silas's retelling of it.

"Not much. Mainly, she was searching for you. She begged you to wake up." He shrugs awkwardly.

And I failed her again. I didn't sense her, didn't react to her the way I used to with my full fae senses at my disposal.

"Was she all right? Any injuries? Was she in shackles?" Because it doesn't matter that I am in this dungeon as long as she is all right.

"She looked better than the last time I saw her. All dressed in finery. No injuries that I'm aware of."

Thank Shaelak. I sit down against the wall with the window and stare at the bars in front of me, forcing one calming breath after the other through my nose until I can think clearly, then turn to face Astorian, who's still toying with the piece of bread in his fingers.

The male inclines his head with recognition as if to say that we found her. That if Ayna is here, his mate should be, too.

"Was Ephegos with them?" he asks, pouring the cup of water on his tray into the drain at the edge of his cell. He's made his choice. No more drugged water.

"No sign of the traitor Crow. But Herinor was with her."

"Herinor?" Royad joins the conversation as he wakes from his drug-induced rest. He seems more alert than any of us after waking up, but the bruise covering his eye where it's swelling shut tells me he was in for a treat as well.

"Apparently, he is loyal to Ephegos now," is Astorian's conclusion. "Not that I know who this Herinor is." He places the cup back on the tray, plopping a piece of bread into it like it was a game.

"One of the oldest Crows who crossed the ocean with us," Silas responds, unaware of how little I want Astorian to know everything about my people.

"You mean one of the murdering, raping, looting monsters who were the cause of the curse?" Royad adds as he sits against the wall in a mirror of my own position. "Exactly that."

Astorian's brow rises as his gaze bounces between the three of us. "Do I need to understand what that means?"

I shake my head. "The only thing you need to understand is that I thought he was on my side. He helped guard Ayna at the palace in the Seeing Forest." He betrayed me like Ephegos and half of my people is what I don't say. Astorian is a smart fairy; he can read between the lines.

Before we can deepen the topic, the door flies open, and in marches General Katrijanov, his blue and black uniform perfectly pressed and his boots as polished as his shaved head. His gaze finds us in the half-light like a shark scenting blood, and he stops a few paces away from my cell.

"Your presence is requested."

Before I can ask where and for what, the two guards who usually handle us when pulling us from the cells step up and unlock my door. The clicking of the lock comes with the same ambivalence of fear and relief as every time.

"Where are you taking him?" Royad demands as they grab my arms and lift me to my feet while I let myself slip as much as possible to make it harder for them, to mislead them a little so they don't realize I'm relatively stable and strong today.

"There's something His Majesty needs his help with," Katrijanov says with that sneer and a glint of anticipation in his cold blue eyes I've become familiar with. It's the same expression he has before landing an especially brutal blow whenever we're strapped to the table in the chamber at the back of the dungeon. The shouts of agony of Silas and Astorian when it's their turn will haunt my dreams for all eternity, but it's Royad's screams that break me. If I could trade places with him when they pick him up for *questioning* as they call it, I'd happily trade places every single time just to spare the one person who has never stopped believing in me.

"It will be all right," I call at him over my shoulder as they drag me away.

Even if I can't technically lie, this lie I can tell, as long as I don't amend that by *all right* I mean anything but us.

I can tell by the look on Royad's face that he sees right through it.

TWENTY-THREE

AYNA

I didn't eat breakfast today, or lunch. I refused the tea and the water, too. At least, with my own bathing chamber, I have access to un-spiked water whenever I want. It's the food I need to be wary of, I've learned. My stomach grumbles uncontrollably as the door opens and Clio enters with a bag draped over her arm.

"Good day, Ayna." She marches up to the sofa where she sets down the bag then drops onto the sepia cushions right beside it.

"Is it a good day?" I cross the room from where I've been staring out the window, following the unusually dense activity along the gravel pathways of the gardens. More courtiers seem to be arriving as the day progresses, their dresses and suits more elaborate than even at the banquet on my initial day.

We've discussed what happened with Erina a few days ago in length and multiple times, and much as I hate to admit it, Clio looks happier since I told her who is with Myron in the dungeon.

"Good if we're both alive."

She isn't wrong. My chest has been lighter since I've seen Myron for myself, alive and breathing, even behind bars. I'm not naive enough to believe they aren't hurting him. The condition I found him in speaks for itself. If anything, now I have confirmation that Erina is willing to capture, incapacitate, and torture magical creatures in order to get what he wants. And what he wants?

I wish I knew.

Annihilating the royal Milevishja bloodline by marrying it into his own line is one goal. No competition when it comes to the throne of Tavras, yes. But what else is he brewing behind closed doors?

If he has a weapon able to wipe out magic, nowhere in Eherea is safe. Where the borders to the fairylands used to be a natural barrier preventing humans from conquering territory in the north, Erina's inventions may lift that restriction, giving him access to new lands, new power.

My stomach sours all over again as I watch Clio unfold the cloth protecting today's attire.

"We need to get them out of the dungeon." I settle on the chair across from her, resting my head in my hands as I brace my elbows on my knees. "If they're free, they'll recover their magic, and Erina has no power over them." My voice comes out muffled, and I'm wondering if Herinor can pick up even those distorted words. Probably. It would be a novelty if anything were easy or would work in our favor.

Clio smooths her apron over her thighs, studying me with those vigilant jade eyes. They have more fire today than the color of her hair, their vibrancy partially restored as if by some magic of its own even when her fairy powers have been suppressed by the drug. "You know I've debated running over and over again—not that I could fight my way out of here with the guards following me everywhere but into your room. But I've debated it often enough to know the layout of the palace and the rotations of the guards. But with you about to be married to the Tavrasian king and Tori in the dungeon..." Her gaze grows distant as if she can see straight through the wood and stone of the floors separating us from our males, and a shiver runs through my body at the thought of how close Myron is. "I can't find it in my heart to leave without them."

Because the Princess of Askarea is a good female. If I hadn't already liked her during our training sessions at the Crow Palace, now I do for sure.

"He's your mate." I'm having a hard time wrapping my head around the concept of mates, even after Clio's lengthy explanation of the soul-bond existing between fated fairies. She couldn't leave him behind even if she wanted to.

"He's my everything." The pride shining in her eyes tells me what a creature that male has to be—one of the best. Because Clio deserves nothing but the best.

Clio didn't tell me details about how they got together or how long they've been a mated pair—a story for another time, she'd said—and I didn't dare ask when my head was spinning from seeing Myron fast asleep in the dungeons. At least, that's what I tell myself, that he was asleep from the effect of the drug they keep giving us rather than from a punch to the head.

That sour taste is back in my mouth, and my shoulder aches where Myron has a matching one. I haven't given it much thought with everything going on, but now that the sensation is back, I can't help obsessing about the fact that we have the same tattoo.

"When Erina took me to see Myron…" I pause, waiting for Clio's attention to make it back to this room. Only when her gaze meets mine do I continue. "I noticed a tattoo on Myron's shoulder." With sweaty fingers, I pull my nightgown aside to expose my own inked bird and turn so she can take a closer look. "The same crow on the same shoulder."

Clio's head tilts, expression neutral as she examines the black curves and lines making up the mark I can't remember ever receiving. "How long have you had this?"

"It was there when I woke at the Flame estate." The memories of those first days of vomiting my guts up are nothing I like to recall.

"And before?"

We both know the answer even when she's never seen my naked shoulder before she was assigned as my lady's maid.

"The only tattoo I had before is this." I hold up my right hand where I was given the mark all prisoners at Fort Perenis get inked into their skin. A thin chain identifying them as criminals sentenced to rot in a fortress at the edge of the world.

At least, I used to think the island in the northeast of Eherea was the end of our world. Then Myron mentioned he was from a different continent in the east, and everything changed.

Neredyn. Where the gods curse their creations, and generations suffer for the wrongdoing of their ancestors.

"If Erina truly intends to marry you, he'd better cover that up. No one will be pleased to have a criminal as a queen." The way she says it tells me that she approves of the thought of defying all traditions and advertising that a so-called traitor is wearing a crown, and a part of me agrees. A part of me is rebellious and ready to fight with all I have to make this an impossible endeavor for Erina.

Then I think of his threat—*You will marry me, Wolayna. If you refuse, I will destroy him*—and all that was hopeful inside of me crumbles back into a heap.

"As for the crow tattoo—I doubt Ephegos put that on you." Leaning forward, she traces a fingertip along the smooth image in expert assessment. "This wasn't put there by ink and needle."

"What do you mean?" I run my fingers across the edge of the mark where the crow's wing winds around my biceps. "How can you tell?"

She gives me a knowing look. "Even if I don't have access to my powers right now, I can tell when magic is at work. Trust me."

And I do. I do trust Princess Cliophera of Askarea.

"If Myron has a matching one, this might be something connected to you breaking the curse," she muses. "Perhaps the goddess herself put it there."

A shudder rakes along my spine at the thought of Vala marking me. But with a flying crow, not with an image of water the way one would expect from a goddess of the element?

"There might even be an underlying connection. Does it ever hurt? Tingle?" Sitting back on the sofa, she tugs on the buttons of her apron. "Gods, I hate this uniform. I want my leathers back."

A smile creeps onto my features at the disgruntled expression on hers. "You wear it like the princess you are," I tell her, taking in her posture, the elegance and grace of even her smallest movements. "But you're badass in your leathers."

"I'm badass in anything." She flashes a predatory grin, reminding me of the powerful fairy slumbering beneath the composed servant she's playing.

"You are." Because she is.

"Now, does it tingle every now and then?"

I didn't miss her question earlier, but an actual connection established between Myron and me through the tattoos on our shoulders… Now that's something taking me a few heartbeats to digest. "It has hurt before." The moments of searing pain come back to me, the tingling sensation… "It definitely has a life of its own."

"Or you can feel *him* through it." Her head tilts as she ponders. "It's rare—not unheard of. But rare that a pair is connected through such a bond."

My pulse picks up pace. "What *bond* are we talking about?"

Clio turns to unfold the cloth bag, casually extracting the fabrics inside before she spreads them out on the backrest of the sofa. "A bond gifted by the deities. I know someone the Guardians bonded to a fairy. A human who now possesses magic." Her expression softens, her hands gliding over the golden silk of the dress she laid out.

"The Guardians bonded a human to a fairy?" My mouth won't close.

"Long story. The quintessence is that they are mated now."

I'm glad I'm already sitting down, or my knees would give out at the news. "Does the other human have a tattoo like this?" And more importantly... "You believe I'm bonded to the King of Crows?"

"I don't know if you're ready for an answer." She raises a brow as she picks up a long golden sleeve and lets it plop back onto the sofa. "If anyone can tell, it's you—and him, of course, but he's a little inaccessible at the moment."

"That's one way to put it."

I try not to have an opinion on what this means—if it's even true.

You didn't think breaking a goddess's curse wouldn't leave a mark on you. Ephegos mentioned it weeks ago at the Flame estate. Did he know? Did he know Myron was alive? And if he knew, who else knew?

I suddenly wish Kaira was here. If anyone, she could tell me what was going on in that house during the days I was imprisoned there. Not having seen her since my arrival in Meer makes me uneasy. Especially knowing how unpredictable Ephegos is.

"Clio, have you seen a Flame woman around the palace? A few years older than me. Brown, long hair, brown eyes. She has very little Flame blood, so you could mistake her for a human, I guess."

"There are so many humans around here that it's near-impossible to notice them all—or remember every face."

I don't know why I'm disappointed. She's only a servant in this palace after all, unable to wander the halls freely and take note of every single individual coming and going.

"But if you mean the feisty warrior who wouldn't stop coming to the servants' entrance of the palace every morning, demanding to be allowed to see you, then yes."

That sounds remarkably like something Kaira would do. After all, she took herself on a journey to follow the carriage taking me to Meer. Her showing up at the palace every day would be a logical consequence if she was serious about not letting me go alone.

Then, I need to ask myself what interest she has in my survival other than learning about the love that broke a millennia-old curse.

A groan works its way up my throat, and I'm tempted to let it escape.

"Until now, they haven't let her in farther than the kitchens." Clio eyes the empty breakfast tray on my table as if the answers to all our problems lie in the breadcrumbs.

The kitchens… "What is she doing in the kitchens?"

"Apparently, Ephegos ordered her to prepare your food specifically."

The information settles in my stomach like a heavy boulder. "So she's the one administering the drug to my meals?" It wouldn't be a first. So much for trusting anyone.

"That's my guess. She could be making it extra delicious, though." The attempted joke doesn't remotely stir a laugh out of me. Not even a smile.

"She doesn't strike me as the type with the patience to cook." Imagining Kaira behind a stove is enough to bring that grin forward after all. "Poor ingredients." She'd chop them with the spirit of waging war on them.

"So, what about her?" Picking up the dress, Clio rises. Apparently, the time for sitting and musing is over.

I drain the glass of water I filled in the bathing chamber. "She came to Meer with us… Kind of."

"Kind of?" Clio raises a thin, copper brow.

So, I tell her the story of how I met Kaira and how I don't trust her not to lace my food with the drug Erina developed with Ephegos's help.

While I'm talking, Clio helps me out of my nightgown and into the golden dress that seems to be made for a queen rather than a prisoner, and I can't help but think back on the black, feathery gowns Myron provided for my attire at the Crow Palace. I hated them back then, but now that soft, smooth golden silk slides along my skin, the room illuminated with late summer light, I wish for the darkness of Myron's realm. I yearn for the cold emptiness and the dire shadows. That darkness, I knew how to handle. It's such an innate part of me that it now misses the grayscale of my time there. But the gold and airy light of the Tavrasian palace? It's intimidating on a level that has me quivering at the mere thought of stepping back into Erina's throne room. No shadows provide a reprieve from eager eyes in these halls. And I have too many things to hide.

TWENTY-FOUR

AYNA

An hour later, I'm walking down the now familiar stairs to the main level where too many people are already collecting in front of the throne room. Herinor hasn't left his place at my side since the moment I stepped out of my room. The small nod he exchanges with Clio every time he takes over on the threshold has become a routine as much as the dreaded walks past the Tavrasian courtiers. He ushers me through the corridor forming where the lords and ladies part to make way for the stranger who's supposed to become their new queen. I try not to think about what's awaiting me today. If I'll be executed or if there are more evil plans prepared that Erina hasn't deigned to share, I don't even want to know. It's enough to be paraded around court at every opportunity without regard for the state of my stomach or my constant fatigue as side effects of the drug.

Today is no different. Erina's guards stand at attention as we pass them, and the courtiers steal eager glances at my dress, whispering behind my back as I cross the threshold into the throne room. My hand itches to check for the thick, golden bracelet Clio put on my right wrist to cover the chain tattoo where the long sleeve might slip and expose it.

No one told me what today's occasion is. Another lunch or a banquet, or merely an opportunity to humiliate me.

Erina is sitting on his throne, sepia uniform and crown perfectly in place, and smiles at me with that false curve of his lips most people mistake for kindness. Beside him, Ephegos stands in the position of honor right of the throne, and from Erina's other side, Katrijanov smirks at me like he's been gifted a particularly entertaining present.

The whispers of the audience ebb into silence as I drop into a curtsey hurting my pride more than my tired legs. My back is weak, and my arms lack their usual strength, and the seams of the dress itch across my shoulder. I resist the urge to scratch, focusing on straightening with enough grace to hide my otherwise obvious weakness. If I had my magic, I'd flood this room and wash away the white flowers decorating the small tables scattered along the edge of the room, the golden plates and crystal goblets. I'd shove the water down Ephegos's throat before pulling it back out and doing the same with Erina and Katrijanov for their hand in my fate.

For their capturing Myron and Royad and the third Crow whose name I yet need to learn. Not to forget Astorian.

It's only when I lift my head again that I realize Erina's gaze has drifted to the table closest to the dais. A table with three chairs, one of them occupied. My breath catches, and my heart stutters.

He's sitting on the chair closest to the wall, dressed in sepia finery, hair brushed and tied at the nape of his neck. His skin is even paler than I remember, except for the purple and black bruises on his jaw and cheek. But his eyes—

Myron. I mouth his name, voice failing as I meet his gaze.

It's impossible to make out their color across the thirty paces separating us, but they are clearly no longer all-black.

The itch in my shoulder has returned—no, not itch. It tingles right from the edge of my biceps to the base of my neck where the bird is inked onto my skin by Vala's magic, if Clio is to be believed.

The corner of his mouth lifts in a pained half-smile before he smooths his expression into the mask of the Crow King, and all emotion is gone. If it wasn't for the way his hands clench in front of him on the edge of the table, I could have been fooled into believing he's here out of his own free will.

But it's Ephegos's magic holding him in his seat. I recognize the way the Crow flexes his fingers in an obvious use of power and the way Myron goes rigid as the force of it binds him more tightly. There is no way for him to get to me if Ephegos doesn't allow it.

I'm about to yell at him to release my husband and get to his knees before his king, but the fucking traitor grins and lifts his other hand a heartbeat before my breath leaves my mouth, an onslaught of magic sealing my lips so I couldn't get a word out even if I screamed at the top of my lungs.

Katrijanov places a hand on the pommel of his sword as he steps down from the dais, marching to stand behind Myron, his smirk intensifying as he glances from Myron's neck to his sword, then to me. A clear warning that he could slit Myron's throat with one quick move and there's nothing I could do about it.

While I ponder the merits of dragging the small knife that goes everywhere with me from my skirts, Erina summons me with a gesture of his hand. "Sit with me, Wolayna."

Instead of pointing to the chair a foot next to the throne, right behind where Katrijanov was standing a moment ago, Erina gets to his feet and stalks down from the dais like his general isn't threatening the love of my life and his traitor friend isn't binding the King of Crows to a chair like a common criminal. The tirades of hatred I have for all three of them are ready to erupt the moment Ephegos releases his magic on me, and I refuse to take as much as a step while they are threatening Myron—not that I can articulate my intentions.

"Move," Herinor orders in a low growl. The menace in his voice isn't directed at me, though. I've known him long enough to tell when his frustration is with me. His anger is with the King of Tavras and the traitor Crow he made a bargain with. And now, he's unable to help his true king, even when Myron is right there within reach.

Guardians, I want to run to him so badly. Want to touch him, just to reassure myself I'm not hallucinating, that he's real and alive, and that the sensation in my shoulder isn't only in my imagination.

Bonded, Clio's diagnosis comes back to me. We are *bonded*. Whatever that means, I hope we'll get the time to find out. Right now, all I can do is try to keep air flowing in and out through my nose as I keep myself from doing anything rash that could mean Myron's end.

I don't even try to calm my racing heart as I take one unsteady step after the other with Herinor's blade at my back, my gaze never drifting from Myron's. With every pace forward, the tingling in my shoulder heightens, becoming a pulsing, an ache matching the one in my chest at the proof of violence on my Crow's skin.

Erina reaches the table first, seating himself in the chair closer to Myron, leaving the one across for me. The throne room feels like an endless tunnel of sepia and gold, the resuming whispers of the courtiers reminding me that this is all a show. They cleaned Myron up and put him in finery fit to dine with a king. To a human who's never seen magic at work, he must look like he's the king's dear guest, receiving the extra protection of General Katrijanov. Erina even smiles at him as he whispers something I can't make out with my human ears.

Just like he does to the rest of the court, I must appear like Erina's guest of honor with the way he's been parading me at such events. Little do they know that, in a different world, it would have been my father on this throne instead of Erina. In a different world, I would have been the Princess of Tavras. But in this world, I'm someone whose claim to the throne is about to be annihilated. I won't be a threat if Erina gets his will. I will be a pretty breeding tool to pop out heirs that will secure the continuation of his own line. And the way he's putting Myron on display to show me his cruelty has no bounds, I'm inclined to say he'll get his wish.

But what will happen once he has what he wants? What will he do to Myron? To Royad and Astorian and the nameless Crow down in the cell? Are they still alive? Or has he gotten rid of them because he believes Myron is all he needs to keep me in line? Or is there something more he wants that I yet need to figure out?

Ten more steps and I'll be sitting at the table with the male I'm married to and the man who believes it's all right to steal someone else's bride. I can only imagine Myron's rage equals my own as I finally reach the table and slide into the chair Erina pulls out for me like a caring partner would. The gesture is disturbing and disgusting in equal parts.

Yet, I can't bring myself to look away from Myron now that I finally have him in front of me, and his eyes...

His eyes are blue like the ocean.

My breath catches for an entirely different reason, and my voice dies even as Ephegos's magic releases me.

Beautiful. His eyes are beautiful. Like the waters of the Quiet Sea. The same shade of turquoise-laced blue reminding me of gentle waves and caressing breezes.

He must see it in my gaze, for the mask he so carefully crafted slips, and for a moment, it's all there: the love, the despair, the hope... It's the hope that kills me as I try not to crumble at the sight of him.

Alive.

Ignoring my throbbing shoulder, I lean back in my chair, awareness prickling along my skin wherever Myron's gaze wanders as if in search of something. His posture hasn't changed, but his eyes are burning like the sun itself, and within those blue irises lies freedom. I can almost taste it as I keep staring at him like a complete fool. Freedom, and the call of the ocean.

I don't know how many minutes have passed when Herinor clears his throat and Myron's gaze ices over, as does his face.

"Herinor." His voice... Like silk sliding over the edge of a blade... Goosebumps rise on my arms beneath the fabric of my gown, and my heart thunders in my chest in response to the most significant sound in the world.

But it's not my name he spoke. *Herinor.* He recognized his kin behind me, and whatever warmth lingered in those eyes retreated beyond the mask.

"Good to see you alive, Myron." I can tell Herinor means it, and judging by the glare Ephegos throws in Herinor's direction, the Crow traitor knows it, too. A dangerous game Ephegos is playing. And I still don't know what he gets out of it.

"Myron." Erina inclines his head in fake politeness, his hand drifting across the table to catch mine where it's resting beside the golden plate. "May I introduce to you my fiancée, Wolayna."

I could swear the ice in Myron's eyes turns to death. There is nothing of the male left of him, only the monster, yet, he can't shift into his Crow form with his magic sedated with the same drug they are giving me.

"Pleasure." As if trying to hide the slip of emotion, Myron doesn't look at me, but the muscles in his jaw flick beneath his bruised skin, and I know he's ready to sink his teeth into the King of Tavras.

"Oh, I'm sure it is." Erina puts on his regal smile as he stands from the table, addressing the entire room. "Make it known in the entire realm that King Erina Latroy Jeldnedyn has found a bride."

The audience explodes with cheers and claps, Odja shuffling over to congratulate His Majesty on his *excellent* choice. It's embarrassing and awkward and so utterly wrong that I still don't have words when servants enter from the side doors, carrying platters of little cakes and bottles of bubbly wine. It's the traditional meal for an engagement party, which, I realize, this is.

And Myron is here as Erina's secret weapon. One threat at the Crow King, and he knows I won't refuse.

TWENTY-FIVE

MYRON

My shoulder is killing me more than the bruises on my stomach and sides where Katrijanov made sure to land a few hard punches before dragging me into a sparse bathing chamber and ordering three guards to scrub me down and put fresh clothes on me.

The first moment, I hadn't understood what he wanted with those other than to potentially drag me to the King of Tavras in the upper levels of the palace. But Erina had visited the dungeon before when he wanted to gloat, so that option soon became irrelevant.

Now I know.

Ayna's steel blue gaze hasn't strayed from me since the moment she spotted me at the king's table. How I wish I had my magic so I could lay waste to this palace as I grab Ayna and run.

I can't. I won't even try with my powers securely incapacitated by the drug they gave me. Enough to keep my mind slow and my body weak—and my magic out of order. But the real reason I haven't moved from the uncomfortable chair they assigned me is the words Katrijanov whispered to me before leading me into the throne room.

Try to escape, she dies. Try to attack King Erina, she dies. Try anything at all. She. Dies.

I'm not risking Ayna's life even if it means I need to remain prisoner to a human king for the rest of my existence. Probably not as long. Their drugs will run out at some point if they keep increasing the number of fairies they need to subdue. Four grown males are a lot to keep in check, especially powerful ones such as Astorian and Royad. Silas isn't a magical weakling either, but his power derives more from his physical prowess.

I'm not even going to think about the amount of the substance they need to keep my own magic at bay. Probably double the dosage Royad gets.

However, the drug isn't enough to silence the power of the mark on my shoulder. It's led me before when I was looking for Ayna, but whatever is happening now is a whole new dimension of anguish. Like a presence of its own, the tattoo keeps pulsing on my shoulder.

It doesn't matter that Ayna is sitting right in front of me. This, I believe, is an ache that can only be soothed if I pull her into my arms in affirmation that she's real and alive.

She looks worse than the last time I saw her, even if she's wearing a golden gown that doesn't fail to highlight her curves with its tight bodice and low neckline. Her hair cascades down her back in loose waves, only strands pulled back so they stay out of her face. Her face...

Her cheeks are flushed, her lips pink like berries reminding me of how incredible she tastes when I claim her mouth with mine. I want to sink my fingers into those ash-blonde strands framing her delicate features and feel the heat of her breath on my tongue. Ayna's eyes shutter as she tries to read mine, so close that all I need to do is reach across the table and touch her soft skin and I'll be a happy male. A ghost of a smile flashes across her mouth... That mouth. I remember vividly what it's like to have it on mine, the bliss of every time her lips part for me. The way my entire body reacts to just the thought of kissing her. But the moment is fleeting with Katrijanov standing guard, hand within casual reach of his sword, and Erina informing the entire court that he intends to marry. *My. Wife.*

That fuck of a king is dead.

Rage is a breathing beast inside of me, not unfamiliar after being trapped in my half-Crow form for all of my life. But this sort of rage is sweeter. My blood boils beneath my skin, ready to spill as I exact vengeance. I scan her starved body to determine just how much I need to hurt the three creatures who have a hand in her torment. For every meal she's missed, I'll tear a gash into their bodies. For every time

251

they've hurt her, I'll make them suffer a month. For taking her from me, they will die.

Ephegos's bonds are the only thing holding me back. Or are they?

Behind Ayna, Herinor shifts his weight, exposing the blade he holds hidden so the rest of this pathetic court can't see that the king's new *fiancée* isn't here out of her own free will. He's ready to kill her. Shaelak be damned. The very Crow who used to guard Ayna's door is now ready to kill her.

I couldn't care less about the apologetic look in his eyes. I've known he's ruthless. That's the entire reason I chose him as a backup for Royad when it came to guarding Ayna. But he made his choice. And he chose wrong.

"Aren't you excited for us, Myron?" If Erina keeps pushing me, I might forget myself and call him for the monster he is. And I know what it means to be a monster, so I may judge.

The cheers and claps of the crowd swallow up our conversation as the rest of the court settles into their assigned places and starts devouring the butter-yellow cake servants are placing in front of us. Under different circumstances, I might have laughed at the colorful dish, so at odds with everything my life used to be. When I'd yearned for lightness, for color, all I had was a dark palace and black feathers. Now that I'm surrounded by a dizzying kaleidoscope of extravagant textiles and ridiculous pastel butterflies on half-spherical cakelets, all I can think of are the shadows that used to surround me— and how, between those shadows, I kept Ayna safe.

Here, I'm as helpless as the sugar butterflies sticking to the icing. With one bite, Erina could have my head. And I can't lose my head when the rest of myself isn't up to speed. A clear mind might be the only thing that could save us in here.

Ayna sits like a doll, frozen with her hand in Erina's, a gesture, I'm certain, he chose to land another punch. Smart king. The magic-leveling drug is proof that he is a thinker and strategist—something even more dangerous than a man blindly grasping for power. Then, why does this surprise me? I remember the days when the Tavrasian brides were delivered at his father's order, and he chose well, delivering political opponents or their daughters to my doorstep.

And before him, the old line of kings who didn't quite agree with the idea of giving up women.

Something touches my boots, and I hit the bonds holding me in place as I instinctively want to lift my palm to ready a magical blow—or at least get my shield in place. Katrijanov's fingers wrap around the hilt of his sword, but he doesn't draw it—yet.

And I…

I hold my breath as I realize this isn't an attack. Quite the opposite. I might be restrained, but Ayna isn't, and that gentle nudge is her toes brushing over the leather of my boots right above my ankle.

I'm suddenly too hot and too cold, all pain forgotten. All but the searing sensation in my shoulder that threatens to break me apart if I don't reach over the table, grab Ayna, and pull her into my lap right now. My gaze finds hers, and the defiance shimmering in the depths of fog and endless rivers gives me hope. She hasn't spoken a word—be it because she doesn't want to, isn't allowed to, or magic keeps her from it—but I can see in her eyes that she is ready to fight. She might not pull her hand from Erina's, playing along to protect me. But she is ready to fight when the time comes. And so am I.

If only I weren't the one thing Erina knows to use to force her hand…

"When's the wedding?" I ask her, schooling my features into cool disinterest while I savor the glide of her toes along my calf. Were we alone, I'd moan, allowing myself to acknowledge what this simple touch does to both my heart and my groin.

Something primal awakens inside of me at the sight of her—her lids fluttering as she fights to keep her expression as empty as mine, her mouth parting as she holds back words I'm sure are meant for no one in this room but me—and suddenly, there is only one thought reverberating through my body, my mind.

Mine.

Ayna is mine. Not Erina's. Not anyone's. But *mine*.

I'm fucked.

I have no idea how this happened, but I'm so fucked watching my mate's hand clutched in the fingers of another man. And all I can think of is the hundreds of ways I want to worship her.

But first, we need to get out of here.

As I scan the room for potential exit routes for the hundredth time, my mind barely complies, too occupied with the well of emotions threatening to burst through the mask I've forced onto my features. I remember loving Ayna, remember wanting her. But this is a depth of feelings I wasn't prepared for. I have no idea if Crows have mates. There haven't been any female Crows since the curse, and the females who were forced into our claws were never around long enough for any bond to occur.

This is different.

There's something in the way my entire body lights up at the sensation that screams of a connection going beyond attraction, affection, or even love. This is a bond that will, if not recognized, drive me insane because, deep in my black Crow soul, I know there is no escaping a mating bond.

And I don't want to escape.

"I assume you're attending, my dear guest?" Erina's voice pierces through the cloud in my head as I stare at the open balcony doors flanked by guards in blue and black uniforms.

Blue and black. Not sepia like the palace guards. Those are military like Katrijanov.

"I'd be offended if I wasn't invited." Thank the centuries of keeping control over my Crow urges that I manage a response—and one that makes King Erina's smile falter for a beat.

"And what do you think about my bride? Isn't she the sweetest thing Tavras has to offer?"

Ayna's lips twitch in a grimace while my own curve upward in the first real smile since I woke from the dead as I direct it at Ayna, taking in every detail of her features, the soft, silvery blonde of her hair, the way her breasts strain against her dress with every shallow breath she takes. How it hitches when she notices where my gaze has drifted.

"The very sweetest indeed, Your Majesty." Before Erina can put on a self-satisfied grin, I amend, "And I would know. I've tasted her."

Herinor's mouth presses into a tight line as if he's having a hard time keeping his face straight while Ephegos throws me a deadly glare from where he is chatting with Odja near the dais. Katrijanov's hand tightens on his sword, and Erina... Well, Erina's face has gone blank, every false smile wiped with one little line.

I must admit, it's a dangerous game—even more dangerous than Ayna's foot drifting higher toward my knee or the frenzy raging in my chest, threatening to take out all reason. But it's a game I will enjoy until Erina lets someone drive a blade into my chest. Because now that I've learned that the King of Tavras's weak point is his pride, I will do whatever is in my power to take him down piece by piece.

TWENTY-SIX

AYNA

Erina's hand clutches mine like a vise, his gaze on Myron turning cold as ice while my heart threatens to beat out of my chest.

He didn't just say that in front of everyone. Myron didn't just tell the King of Tavras, whose prisoner he is and who is using him to make me pliant, that he's put his mouth on me.

There's no point in hiding the blush rising from my neckline all the way to my cheeks. No one but the people at this table heard him, and they all know how close Myron and I are—were. We are no longer if Erina has anything to say about it.

My mouth went dry a while ago when I decided that, if I can't reach for Myron with my hands, I'll at least touch him with some part of my body. My toes are the only option I'm able to hide beneath the long white tablecloth as I sweep them along his boot. I wish I could reach high enough to touch the fabric of his pants. The heat in his gaze is almost overwhelming, like a physical touch, only more intense, piercing through my skin, my flesh, to the very core of me.

A small voice in my head—probably what's left of my reason—keeps reminding me there's something massively wrong with being turned on by that small, forbidden touch, by the effect it seems to have on the male bound in his chair. The majority of me, however, doesn't care. The pain in my shoulder has turned into a hum, and the warmth spreading through my body originates in the inked outline of the crow.

"You will watch your tongue," Erina hisses at Myron, keeping his posture straight and composing his features into those of the King of Tavras when I can tell he is struggling to keep ahold of his temper.

Myron inclines his head at Erina, his gaze never leaving mine. "I'd rather our Ayna here would *watch* my tongue."

I don't know if it's the best idea to push the King of Tavras when he has a soldier ready to stab Myron at a wave of his hand, but I can't help it. My eyes are glued to Myron's lips as his tongue flicks across his lower lip as if to remind me of all the things he can do with it.

Pressing my thighs together, I drop my foot and keep my fingers from tracing my own mouth as the memory of his kisses makes my heart race.

More than one of the guests is staring, but I don't care. I care about nothing as long as Myron is here.

I *should* care. Making a spectacle out of myself won't help either of us.

"About time you understood that." The voice enters my mind so unexpectedly that I drop the fork I picked up to keep my hand busy.

"Over here," the voice directs my gaze across the room, *"by the servant entrance."*

It takes me a moment to spot a familiar face in the line of servants standing in front of the hidden door at the side, but when I do, I know it's her.

Kaira's uniform is sepia and white like that of the other servants, but unlike the men and women who are actually part of the palace staff, the part-Flame sticks out like a sore thumb. Her posture is too straight, too proud, her gaze defiant and directed right at me instead of scanning the tables for plates they can pick up and deliver back to the kitchens. Where the others are clearly making sure they don't miss the moment they are needed, Kaira is merely waiting for me to catch onto what's happening.

As if in answer, her voice climbs into my head. *"Exactly."*

Well, fuck the Guardians—how is this even possible?

Kaira's brows lift. *"I didn't know Crow queens could curse like sailors."*

"That's probably because you didn't know I used to be a sailor of sorts," I shoot back in my head, testing out if I can communicate the same way she can.

In response, she dips her chin. *"Trust me, I only figured it out a few days ago. With you sleeping all the time, it's quite difficult to get into your head."*

259

Not that I appreciate anyone being in my head but—
"How does this work?"

Beside me, Erina is saying something, his features pinned into an expressionless mask, but I barely notice him, what's left of my distracted attention directed at Myron while I'm trying to wrap my head around Kaira speaking to me in my *head*.

Myron is keeping his calm like the millennia-old fairy he is, following Erina's lead as the king eats his engagement cake while mine remains untouched on the ornate plate before me.

"Magic, I assume." There is a humor to Kaira's voice that eases the tension in my chest. Whatever heat had collected in my body has left my limbs and core like water draining from a cracked jar. *"Even though you don't have any magic right now, my minuscule magic seems to be enough to speak to a random human in the middle of a foreign throne room."*

Wait… *"So, you don't speak to anyone you want in your mind? Just me?"*

"Just you, dear Wolayna." Her lips quirk as if in an apology even when I can tell an apology is the last thing on her mind. *"Were you going to climb Myron like a tree right in front of everyone, or do you have some common sense?"*

I wish the floor would open up and swallow me. It's embarrassing enough to have the whole room witness the looks Myron and I exchanged, but having someone front row in my mind as I fantasize about all the ways he used his tongue to—

I cut off my thoughts right here before private memories can replay in my mind.

"Interesting." Kaira shifts from foot to foot as if standing there for another minute is too much to bear, but her face has smoothed over, no longer hinting at our silent exchange as she lets her gaze drift across the room, lingering on Ephegos for a long moment before continuing to Erina, then Katrijanov. *"This is the general who visited Jeseida's estate a few times."*

"He's the one Ephegos made the deal with to sell me to Tavras." The fact no longer hurts. I've accepted that I so wildly misjudged someone's character. It's time to stop dwelling on that and focus on solutions instead. *"Since Erina is using the drug to suppress magic, I assume Katrijanov has been involved in this process as well."*

Kaira doesn't seem surprised as she responds, *"I've been spending the past days sneaking around the servant levels of the palace to map escape routes. There will be a moment when we need to run, and I want to be prepared."*

Uncertain of whether I should be touched or skeptical of Kaira's interest in my freedom, I set my fork to the cake on my plate.

"You're still spiking my food every day in the kitchen for all that I know. And now you're in my head without any reasonable explanation. Give me one reason I should trust you." Because that's the only question I should be asking.

My fingers find the golden fork once more as I force myself to act normal while I have a fucking Flame in my head. If only that was Myron. *That* would be helpful.

"Hey, I heard that." The hurt in Kaira's tone is brief, and I don't turn my head to check if her face mirrors it. *"And before you continue accusing me of being untrustworthy."*

I lead the fork to the cake and slice into the icing, severing a butterfly's wings in the process. How symbolic. *"I have been sensing your presence since the day you were brought to the estate. It took me a while though to figure out what was going on, and since I don't trust anyone there, I kept it to myself that I could perceive some stream of consciousness from the most recent prisoner. It wouldn't have ended well for me to advertise it."*

I barely taste the sweet and creamy bite I shoved into my mouth.

"Ephegos and Jeseida would have found a way to use it to their advantage, and as I mentioned before, I'm not happy with the way he is accumulating power and trying to take the place as Jeseida's heir. A Crow ruling the Flames…"

Her voice drifts away, and I swallow the piece of cake as if I am going to use my corporeal voice when I merely need my thoughts. *"You've been* hearing *me since Ephegos brought me in?"* It's one thing to have a Flame chatter in my head. It's an entirely different one to find out she's been listening to my thoughts for *weeks.*

"Not like now. It was more of a"—she searches for words—*"presence. You were an ever-present cloud of being in my mind. Does that sound weird?"*

"It would be a lie to say no.*"* And that's the politest answer I muster. *"You could have told me a bit sooner, don't you think? With everything going on…"*

"With everything going on, it was safest not to tell anyone. I didn't hear any clear thoughts until the day I found out Ephegos sold you to King Erina. So, I decided to follow you to Meer." It

sounds more like an apology than I care for, and the fact that she kept me in the dark—

"Since you're the only one I could hear, I needed to find out what's going on. I went where you went. I got Ephegos to allow me to see you and bring you the tea with the magic suppressant so I could lay eyes on the woman whose thoughts kept pushing at the edge of my consciousness." When I glance at her between bites, she amends, *"It's not as if I chose to listen in on you. You are the one projecting your thoughts into my mind."*

"Not that I know how to even do that, I am not projecting anything." And I'm not sure if this strange connection is a blessing or a curse.

"I'm not sure either. But one thing I know. I've been an outcast in the Flame Court for too long. Not enough magical blood to truly count as a Flame, not even to be considered breeding material." I can feel her cringe at the thought. *"If there is someone I'm connected to on such a deep level—unbidden or not—I'm going to follow that person wherever they go, be it right to the grave."*

The determination in her tone takes me more by surprise than the fact that she's willing to abandon her people for a human prisoner. My gaze falls on Myron, on his smooth features now that he has stopped pissing Erina off on purpose, the bruises marring his beautiful face and a pang of something unfamiliar, yet so powerful it nearly takes my breath away, makes itself known in my chest.

"If you can truly read all my thoughts, you know exactly how much I love Myron." If she's ready to leave her people

behind to follow me into doom, she should at least know I will never have any romantic interest in her.

The thought earns me a startling laugh which I'm not certain is in my head or drifting through the murmurs and chatter of courtiers. When I shoot a glance at Kaira, she smiles at me. *"Don't worry about that, Ayna. I have no such interest in females."* Her tone grows somber as she amends, *"I have loved deeply before, but the male died."* And that's all I'm going to get for now. Enough to put me at ease that she's not following me for the wrong reasons.

It's a different bond. One that I'd love to understand, but Erina's voice demanding my attention is more pressing than exploring the *whys* and *hows* of the part-Flame in my head.

"The wedding is set for the end of the month," he repeats, his eyes trained on Myron, whose face has hardened to granite, tendons in his neck standing out as he fights the magical bonds Ephegos is keeping in place.

End of the month. Six days.

Suddenly, it doesn't matter who is following me or forced to be my lady's maid, or even my guard with good intentions and bad affiliations. It's only Myron and me, and the endless canyon opening up between us in those few days left to make my escape. Erina has Herinor and Ephegos, he has Myron, and Royad, the nameless Crow, and Astorian in the dungeon, and even a drug to make us all pliant.

And I have nothing to pit against his cruelty.

TWENTY-SEVEN

AYNA

"He can't do this," I fling at Herinor, who has joined Clio and me in my room for a change. "He can't force me to marry him when I'm already married to Myron."

I try not to panic at the memory of Katrijanov escorting him back to the dungeon after the party, of the shiver running through my body when Myron's ocean-blue eyes met mine over his shoulder before crossing the threshold. Magic or no, those eyes hold the power to silence the world around me, to make me drown in everything that he is.

I can't allow myself to even think of him, or I won't be able to form a clear thought.

"He can do whatever he wants. That's the problem." Clio is lounging on my bed, gesturing at Herinor whose vigilant gaze follows my pacing around the room. "He's a fucking king with no regard for the laws of the fairylands."

"What *are* the laws of the fairylands?" It's not like anyone ever explained to me. All I know of the fairylands is the Seeing Forest, a very limited perspective of a much larger realm where a variety of other fairies live in peace under the rule of Clio's brother.

"Mating bond over marriage." Clio shrugs when I stare at her, trying not to read into the meaning of her words.

"There is nothing more sacred than a mating bond," Herinor agrees.

"I didn't strike you as the romantic type," Clio quips, fiddling with the maid's cap until it comes loose from her head. Massaging her scalp with one hand, she tucks the cap into the apron. "What?" She observes Herinor's glare with as little respect for the warrior as any creature could hold—she's the Fairy Princess after all—and crosses her ankles, her feet dangling over the edge of the bed.

"Just because I never had the chance to *find* a mate doesn't mean I'm a barbarian." Herinor holds Clio's gaze, and I could swear the two of them will tear each other to shreds if I don't get one of them out of the room.

"You *are* a barbarian." Clio gestures at his overall appearance. "The nice armor and tidy hair don't change anything."

Watching Herinor grind his teeth, I ponder who of the two I need more at this moment and who I'll kick out.

"Can we please stay on topic?" I decide I need them both to work on the matters at hand. "I can't marry Erina, married or mated. I can't marry him."

"Because you want to overthrow him and take the crown of Tavras for yourself, Lady Milevishja?" The scars on Herinor's forehead scrunch as he raises his brows at me. "Because if that's what you want, you might be better off marrying him and poisoning him once you've been crowned queen."

"He has a point there," Clio reluctantly agrees, fingers still in her hair as she undoes her braid with a frown on her features.

It's been a while since I shared the news with Clio, but Herinor knew from the day Erina filled me in since he was standing guard during that fateful conversation. This is the first time he's brought it up, though.

"Not happening." I stop by the window, eyeing the darkening gardens in search of a solution. "He is a monster."

"You thought Myron was a monster when you met him," Herinor reminds me, and he's not wrong.

"He never tortured someone I love to force me." On the contrary. The day of our wedding, he handed me a knife to protect myself from him if need be.

"Truth," Herinor admits, sitting back in the chair that seems too small for him. "He'd never have done such a despicable thing."

My gaze drifts to Clio, who is rebraiding her hair. "Don't forget Erina is holding *my* mate prisoner, too." Despite her calm exterior, the fire of vengeance burns hot in her jade eyes. "And the other two Crows, of course."

She'd happily sacrifice Royad and the other male if that meant Astorian got out alive, I have no doubt.

"The wedding is in six days. How do we get them out so Erina loses his leverage?" It's the only question I should be asking, but there are so many swirling in my mind, like how did Kaira get into my head. Can she hear me now? When will I see her again? I haven't told Clio and Herinor about what happened with the part-Flame in the throne room. For now, it feels too intimate to share with anyone.

"I shouldn't be in here when you're planning. If I know, my deal with Ephegos might force me to inform him."

Clio stops him with a sharp look. "If you as much as think of telling him anything we speak about in here, I will end you, with or without my magic." Her hand drifts to her hip where a sword would usually be hanging, and the menace in her expression is convincing enough to make me quiver.

I've seen this female fight, and I don't want to be on the receiving end of her wrath.

Apparently, Herinor doesn't either since he stands from his chair and marches for the door. "Find a way around my bargain, and I'll help you." He glances between Clio and me. "Both of you."

Without another word, he walks out, the door creaking as he closes it behind him.

"Weird fairy," Clio comments, standing from the bed and joining me by the window.

Wondering if Herinor heard that, I listen for footsteps or voices from the hallway. Everything is quiet like any other night when Clio joins me in my room to perform her lady's maid duties. And like every other night, I know that there is no such thing as a conversation Herinor isn't privy to.

Him leaving is a gesture, a show of his goodwill. If there's anything he could do, he'd have already done it. He has done plenty to help me even with the many things he did to hurt me.

My mind travels back to the first day I met him when he cut my skin open.

"I have a plan. One where I don't need to break my bargain and where the pain will benefit you."

His words before he's sliced into the tattoo on my back. I didn't understand then, was too blinded by my fear to acknowledge something I should have realized a long time ago.

He knew. Herinor knew Myron was alive. He knew about the connection the tattoo formed between us. He knew that Myron would feel it and know I was alive, too.

Uncertain of whether that counts as betrayal or as actual help, I turn to the door. "You knew he was alive, and you didn't tell me."

Clio understands without explanation that the words are meant for Herinor. Her arm wraps around my shoulders. "Come on, Ayna. We need to get you out of this dress and into your nightgown."

I don't object, merely let her guide me into the bathing chamber where she opens the faucet to fill the bathtub. Once the water is running, she shoots me a victorious grin. "Now he can't hear a thing."

Hot water thunders into the tub, filling it angrily and with enough noise to drown out all other sounds.

By the Guardians, she's right.

"One of the many reasons I believe there is value in being your lady's maid." She helps me out of my dress and gestures for me to slip into the tub. "This might be the only time in the day where we don't have an audience and our conversations remain fully private." Before I can ask any questions, she settles on the rim of the tub and adds, "We both don't have access to our magic, so we're dependent on Herinor as the muscle of our operations. How do we find a way around his bargain?"

Determination shines in her eyes as they meet mine when I sink into the filling tub.

"I have no idea. But we have about five minutes until the tub is full and we become transparent again, so let's figure it out."

The golden dress abandoned on the bathroom floor, we tuck our heads together in hopes of finding a way to make it happen.

Dinner arrives late that night, brought in on a wide wooden tray in the hands of the same servant who carries it in every night. Clio left shortly after my bath, a frown on her features and her cap back on her hair. The main worry, for now, is that, even if we could find a way to sneak down to the dungeon, we don't know what condition the males will be in when we find them. Without Clio's full fairy strength, she can't carry them out of their cells if they are unconscious like the last time I was down there. Even if Herinor was able to help us, he still could carry only one at a time. It might take too long to get them out, and if we're discovered, I wouldn't put it past Erina to torture the males as a punishment for us. Not to mention what Ephegos would do to Herinor.

The woman wordlessly sets the tray on the table and leaves with a bobbed curtsey, allowing me some privacy to eat—or wallow in self-pity about my fate.

Every other young Tavrasian woman would probably kill to be in my position, engaged to the handsome King of Tavras, but all I can think about is my husband in the dungeon, the bruises marring his face, the heat in his gaze when my foot slid up his boot, the sensation in my shoulder that seems to ease only when we touch.

I've long stopped paying attention to the constant throb in my flesh where the inked bird covers my skin, but what Clio said about *bonds* makes a weird kind of sense when my mind can't seem to stray from the topic of Myron of Whinghaven. My heart flutters as if those dark feathered wings were beating between my ribs instead.

I will free you, Myron. I will find a way. I don't expect him to respond, but the sensation in my shoulder intensifies as if my tattoo provided a direct channel to him—as if the separation is equally painful to him.

The silver covers clink against the teacup as I slide the tray closer, the scent of peppers and meat climbing into my nose. My stomach grumbles violently. Apparently, the sugary cake wasn't enough to make up for the missed meals and lack of strength, and I could devour several of the steaks I used to be served in Myron's court.

I lift the cover, taking in the appealing draping of vegetables around slices of pheasant, but that's not what catches my attention. It's the barely visible piece of parchment stuck under the piece of rye bread at the edge of the plate where the sauce doesn't reach.

With shaking fingers, I pick up the bread and extract the paper, shooting a glance around the room as if Ephegos or Erina might appear out of the walls to witness the secret message someone is apparently trying to pass me.

As I unfold it, a narrow scribble challenges my ability to decipher letters. It's so unreadable it takes me several attempts to realize it's a language I know, but once I do, my heart beats faster, adrenaline coursing through my veins at one simple sentence: *Don't eat the bread.*

Gaze darting to the thick slice of fresh bread I placed beside the plate on the wooden tray, I wonder if that's where the drug is hidden. I hope that's what the message implies and it isn't some ploy to lead me on a wrong track to consume only the parts of the foods that are laced with the drug.

It's not like I know anyone's handwriting, which leads me to the decision of trusting whoever smuggled this message in with my dinner—or not.

I go with trust. Not because my most recent experiences have led me to believe this world is a trustworthy place where people mean no harm, but because how much worse can it get? Usually, my evening meals knock me out, so if I do ingest the drug, it will be just another night out cold and a morning of hurling up my guts.

But if the message is real and I get to eat actual food that will strengthen me instead of weakening me, I might have a chance of recovering some of my powers. And if I manage to do so over a few days, maybe I'll get strong enough to stand a chance against the guards outside my door.

Not against Herinor, though. Even if his magic wasn't in the game, he'd easily outmatch me with his physical strength and his skill with a weapon.

I swallow the lump forming in my throat. He isn't supposed to aid me. His bargain won't allow it. But what if he turns his eye when I make my escape? Would that kill him, too?

Before I can come to a conclusion, a knock sounds on the door, making me jump in my chair as I crumple the note between my fingers and shove it into the décolletage of my nightdress before ripping a large piece of bread off, hiding it in the vase at the center of the table, and rearranging the white and pink flowers so there are no traces left.

"Come in." Bread still in hand, I turn to the door without standing from my seat and pretend to chew. One never knows who's coming to check on me.

A moment later, my whole body chills as Ephegos steps into the room, led by General Katrijanov, who hasn't bothered to wipe the blood from his face where a thin streak graces his cheekbone. He flashes me a cold smile that I don't return. I do, however, notice that his gaze wanders to my hands—either to determine whether I armed myself with the dull knife they provided with my meal or because he is interested in whether I've started eating.

His lips twitch before he packs away that smile and turns to Ephegos, who is studying me, head cocked as if expecting me to stand and curtsey or simply fall to my knees in front of him.

I don't bother to stand at all. Before their magic and strength, it doesn't matter if I even attempt to defend myself. I'll lose. I'll always lose—unless I get my powers back, which, judging by the quick glance Ephegos sends toward the tray on the table before spotting the bread in my hand, I'm on the best way to achieving.

Whoever wrote that note might truly want me to live.

"To what do I owe the pleasure," I ask after laying the bread back in its place and pretending to swallow the bite I never took.

Ephegos's features turn into that fake friendliness I remember from his time at Myron's court. *Traitor. Monster.*

Katrijanov steps forward first, lowering his head so he looks straight into my eyes. I refuse to shrink away, steeling my spine even when I've used up most of my strength for the day and my emotions are all over the place, swirling like a hurricane of terror and hope fueled by that sizzling connection originating in my shoulder and ending in the dungeons where Myron is being held captive.

The blood on Katrijanov's cheek is fresh, but the missing gash in his skin informs me it isn't his.

"Got into a fight, General?" I ask him with less fire than I feel while he straightens and stalks around the room as if in a military inspection.

Ephegos laughs a melodious laugh I want to shove back down his throat. "The brave general faced a particular brand of monster just a minute ago. Fortunately, Crows with an establishing mating bond are easy to control... Something I'd like to be able to say about humans as well. But you, dear Ayna... You are a piece of work. You have always been, from the day you set foot in Myron's court."

"At least you still acknowledge it's *his* court." I try not to spit at him and quietly thank whoever sent the note that my head isn't spinning yet the way it likes to do during dinners when the drug's effect is kicking in.

"His court." Ephegos muses at the ornate ceiling as if the little curves and swirls will respond. "It was. Now it's mine." His grin widens as he steps up to the table, sitting down across from me. Katrijanov stops his tour by the window, eyeing me like an eagle does his prey, and a shiver spreads along my body. A sort of expectation is surfacing in his eyes, and I know he's waiting for something to happen.

His chin dips as if in agreement.

Wait... "What do you mean, *Crows with an establishing mating bond?*"

Guardians, he knows. He knows about the connection. He's probably seen Myron's tattoo when he's tortured him in the dungeon.

Anger so profound it makes bile rise in my throat and wash through me. I flap my hand across my mouth so I don't throw up all over my dinner. I still need to eat the meat and the vegetables even if I feel like my appetite will never return. I need my strength to free Myron.

To free the male Vala bonded me with.

I can't yet handle the thought of him being my mate, but what happened during the banquet is proof that they are all onto something.

Ephegos's chuckle is soft, his gaze pitiful as if I'm a little puppy he intends to save from the streets. How I hate him. More even than when I found out he betrayed all of us.

"Mating bonds are a beautiful invention of the gods to keep immortal creatures loyal." He cocks his head so bird-like I can see his Crow features even when he doesn't shift. "Useful, don't you think? Especially when vengeance comes into play."

The dark glint in his eyes promises nothing good.

Mating bonds. Clio was right. Deep in my core, I know that she was, that they all are, but it hurts too much to allow myself to hope this will lead to anything other than pain.

"Why didn't you tell me he was alive?" I bite out the words, keeping a leash on my temper so I don't do something stupid like outright attack him with my bare hands.

"And take away the pain that comes with losing a loved one? I don't think so." He leans over, gesturing at the plate. "Eat."

I pick up the fork and spear the first slice of meat with so much force the prongs bend, earning a raised brow from Ephegos.

"The bread first." He picks it up and hands it to me. It's then that I know the note was from someone who intends to help me. It's the look on Ephegos's face as he watches me set down the fork and reluctantly lead the bread to my lips. "Faster."

His eyes flick to the fork, to the curved metal piercing through the tender meat at an odd angle where it should be straight. This is different. It's not the magic in my chest rallying to aid me; that's still silent as the deep waters of the Gulf of Tears, but a new strength that I have never experienced.

"Eat, Wolayna," Katrijanov warns, stepping closer and drawing his sword. "Now."

The nausea lifts from my stomach as I realize that, while my powers might have been subdued, my body has changed under the blanket of the drug. It is only beginning to lift, and I already feel strength humming in my muscles where they have been weak for weeks, small changes that I yet need to learn to interpret, but the effects are clear. I bent a fork with my bare hands, and it wasn't even intentional. What if I channel that new sort of power, put it to use? Could I stand a chance against the general at least? I'm not hoping to defeat a creature capable of magic, and Ephegos proves me right as his power snaps around me like iron bonds, immobilizing me, and he plucks the bread from my hand and shoves it into my mouth while Katrijanov holds his blade to my throat.

"Swallow," he orders, and I do because Ephegos's magic is now cutting off the air supply through my nose, and I need my mouth free to be able to breathe. It's the oldest trick in the world, yet it works. The bread slides down my throat, scratching and pushing at the tissues as I swallow the half-chewed bite.

"Good girl." Ephegos's smile makes me want to puke into his face, but my head is swimming—from lack of air or the drug taking effect without delay the way I'm used to—and I sway in my seat.

Ephegos's magic holds me upright, but I don't manage to keep conscious long enough to know if he eventually drops me—or does something worse.

TWENTY-EIGHT

MYRON

Unlike the last times, the torture chamber is illuminated enough to see every last splatter of dried blood on the stone floor. It would be easy to rinse it away, but leaving the traces of pain is such an effective way of intimidating the wits out of a victim. I would know; I've used that tactic on the Crows who dared hunt Ayna in the woods before she became my wife.

Wife... I shake my head at a word so weak, so pathetic in comparison to what she truly is to me while, from my shoulder, the sensation of the bond is ripping through my chest, my limbs, my entire body until all I can do is pant and gasp.

"A bit early to pass out," the guard whose name I really don't care to learn comments. "Usually, he at least pierces you with a tool a few times before you start hyperventilating."

It's true. I've used the controlled over-oxygenation to escape Katrijanov's expert skills on the table I'm strapped to. A strategy I learned early in life when my father had deemed cutting me open with a burning knife over and over again the best way to prepare me for stepping into his legacy one day. *You need to understand pain in order to learn what it takes to be a King of Crows,* he used to say when he excused his cruelty.

I wasn't the only one he hurt. As my cousin and direct heir, Royad shared my fate. The days when we were tied to my father's table side by side, Royad's eyes filled with fear, and my heart beat out of my chest when I couldn't free myself to help him... Those days still haunt my sleep. Those and the moment when I found Ayna in the forest at the feet of the Crows, her human body breaking.

"I wouldn't miss the fun for the world," I spit at the guard, baring my bloodied teeth where he hit me in the face, just to show him that, no matter how hard he strikes, I won't break. I'll take my time-outs, sneaking into oblivion every now and then, but when I return to consciousness, I'll grin at them while they try to rip me apart.

Nothing can. Not anymore. Because Ayna is alive and beautiful and needs me. I can feel her very essence in my bones, can hear the echo of her heartbeat in every thump of mine. Even if they shatter this shell, a part of me will remain untouched—and that's the part that belongs to her.

My soul.

"Spoken like a true fool." The guard adjusts the strap at my wrist until it cuts into my skin, waiting for a wince I'm not willing to give him. "You should know better than to provoke your tormenter."

"As if you care." I spit my blood on his black-and-blue uniform. One of Katrijanov's men from the Tavrasian military, not a palace guard. I noticed that early on, in this dungeon, guards answer to Katrijanov. The highest Tavrasian general walks in and out of here like it's his second home. This isn't a place to make the king's enemies disappear or to store criminals until their trial or execution. This prison is a place of war.

The guard shrugs and heads for the door, leaving me to my fate the way he always does after securing me to the table so hard I can't feel my hands and feet after a few moments. Maybe that's his way of showing mercy. At least, I'll barely feel the knife on those parts of my body until a lot later, when they toss me back into my cell and I wake up from the unavoidable unconsciousness I drift into when they push beyond my limits.

Thank Shaelak, all those injuries were well hidden when Ayna saw me in the throne room. I couldn't bear the look on her face if she saw me like this. It was bad enough to witness the pain in her eyes as she assessed the visible injuries, the bruises on my jaw and cheek that are a joke compared to the real injuries.

I close my eyes, readying myself to face Katrijanov with the same cold nonchalance I usually muster, and focus on the sensation of Ayna's presence through the bond.

It was more potent after she touched her toes to my shin, almost as if that brief physical proximity triggered something in me that I can no longer lock down, but the resonating response I seemed to receive earlier has dulled once more. Whether that's because she is at the other end of the palace, levels above my cell, or because they gave her the same damned drug that keeps my own powers in check, I can't tell. I wish I could. That would stop me from musing about the worst possible scenarios—like that they found a way to nullify the bond just like they managed with the magic.

Before I can work myself into a blind panic, footsteps sound far down the corridor. Two pairs—one heavy, one relatively light. And a third pair—

I blink my eyes as I recognize those footfalls, the measured cadence, the power in each step, the familiar lightness.

"My friend," Ephegos says as he enters the stone chamber with his signature smile, and I can't help but feel like a missing part of me has returned. Until I recognize the hatred so well concealed in his gaze and remember all the things he's done to take his revenge on me for his half-sister's death. He will stop at nothing to see me suffer.

I know I'm right a moment later when Herinor crosses the threshold, an unconscious Ayna draped over his arms and an apology in his eyes.

Fuck the Guardians. Fuck my father and all the Crows of his generation who angered Vala enough to curse us and drive us from our homelands. If we'd never set foot on Eherean soil, we'd never have ended up in a place where what few Crows I trusted would turn against me because of that curse.

And he wouldn't carry my mate into this godsdamned torture chamber and set her down on the second table. A table I have never given a thought to since I've always been alone in here with whatever cruel masters of pain were working my body to shreds. But in this reality, Herinor puts Ayna's wrists and ankles in leather straps, her silver-blonde hair spilling over the edge of the metal table as he ties her up. She is in her nightgown, a long, sepia dressing robe tied at the waist covering most of her body. Gods, she looks like they pulled her straight from her bed.

The tattoo on my shoulder is ablaze with awareness even when she's out cold, her chest rising and falling with slow breaths. Herinor has his hands on *my* mate, and the urge to rip his throat out is second only to the need to tear the bonds holding me in place and pick her up from that table to carry her to safety.

"Don't worry, Myron. She's all right … for now." Ephegos traces his finger over the rack of tools by the wall, his smile widening.

"Worry? About a human woman?" It's the only defensive mechanism I can come up with, pretending I don't care when everyone in this room already knows what she is to me.

Ephegos isn't stupid. He saw the tattoo on my shoulder, and judging by the way he uses Ayna against me, he must know this is something more than a plain inked mark I got to memorize our curse. He has realized what is going on. Plus, he has Herinor, and Herinor is one of the oldest Crows alive. If anyone knows what Crow bonds look like, it's him.

My tattoo is a fucking mate Mark, and I can't wait to see what Ayna's looks like.

Katrijanov? He's the outsider when it comes to magical relationships one doesn't get to choose yet can't live without, but even he knows what's going on.

"About your mate," he corrects, stalking past my table, not sparing me a glance as he heads straight for Ayna, the sword in his hand ready to spear me if I should ever make it out of my leather shackles. That he might be readying it to hurt Ayna is an option I can't allow myself to consider.

"Tell me, Myron." Ephegos pulls a handkerchief from his sepia finery—the traitor—wiping the blood from the edge of the table and pockets it before he perches beside my hip. "What is it like to die for love? Must be a redeeming end."

I spit at him.

"I see you still haven't forgiven me. Good." He flashes his teeth, that hint of insanity shining through. "Because I haven't forgiven you either. But even more important than that…" He wipes my spit from his sleeve on my bare arm. "You are one of the strongest magical creatures out there and a great measure against the effectiveness of the serum we developed."

I try to follow him, but he pulls a syringe from the pocket of his jacket and holds it needle-up in front of his face.

"Is that the drug you keep giving us?" I wish Royad, Silas, and Astorian were here. Together, we might be strong enough to take on the traitor Crow and the general. Even Herinor, who doesn't look like he intends to fight if I manage to free myself. He doesn't look like he is ready to help me either.

"This is a new one." Pride shines in Ephegos's eyes as he makes the transparent liquid swirl in the body of the syringe. "I call it the *deep sleep* … for your magic, of course, not for you. I want *you* wide awake while we test your mate's limits."

Every fiber in my body rears up, straining against the weak leather restraining me. Weak—but I'm weaker. Weeks of being drugged and tortured haven't helped my general condition.

With a curse, I slump on the table, seething at Ephegos if there is nothing else I can do.

"I don't know how much more your body can take, My- ron." He looks me over with that fake pity he's perfected, and I know that, this time, there is no escape. I can hyperventi- late as much as I want. This time, I need to stay alert because, much as I'd love to tell myself that there's a way out of this, Ayna is right there, and I can't close my eyes when they are setting my mate up to suffer.

Ephegos has come to see me break. He has brought the only weapon that might actually be able to accomplish the task. And she's more beautiful than I even remember—beau- tiful and oblivious.

"Touch her and I'll rip your fucking head off."

Katrijanov has the nerve to laugh while Ephegos lowers the needle to my forearm and pricks my skin. His smile wid- ens into a manic grimace as he injects me with the *deep sleep*.

This time, I don't pass out from the drug. I am wide awake, my magic retreating even farther behind the cur- tain that keeps it concealed, and I'm powerless as Katrijan- ov sheathes his sword and pulls the thin blade from the tool rack.

He doesn't heat it up the way he does before he cuts into my skin but pulls up Ayna's sleeve and sets the tip to her bare forearm.

"No." My voice is faster than my thoughts, but I don't care. The leather bites into my skin as I fight against my restraints. "Don't touch her."

Herinor has stepped back, his gaze meeting mine with the same helplessness I feel. He isn't here because he enjoys seeing me suffer. I don't have the capacity to figure out what else would make him turn against me; the single drop of blood welling up on Ayna's pale skin is enough to drown out all other thoughts.

Crimson and perfectly round like a polished crystal, it sits as Katrijanov pulls back the knife. He flashes me a challenging look, an invitation to try to stop him.

I'm fucking aware that, as long as I'm strapped to the table, there's nothing I can do. At least, Ayna isn't awake to feel the prick. But I am. I am fully awake, my blood pounding through my veins as I pick up the scent of hers—iron and salt and the wind of the ocean. Suddenly, it's all I can smell. My senses rush back to me as if the curtain has been lifted, and I can hear Ayna's slow heartbeat, her shallow breathing, can make out the floral scent of her soap like a thread of life in this chamber of pain and death.

I only notice that Ephegos injected me with another serum when he pulls the needle out and steps away from the table. "Now you have all your fae senses and none of the options to act on them. Let's see how you enjoy that." He turns to Katrijanov with a nod, letting his words sink in.

All my fae senses—

The bright room is suddenly brighter, the colors more facetted. I can hear the footsteps in the hallways above, the low chatter of voices outside the dungeon. Royad and Astorian are talking to Silas about their suspicion that I might not return this time—they heard the guards talk…

I need to close my eyes as every detail hits me at once, but none of them are as hypnotizing as the scent of Ayna's blood. It lures me like the flame does the moth, tearing my focus back toward her—not that it ever truly left.

I can taste her on my tongue, feel her in my chest. Her skin is warm, radiating through the room with that same magnetic pull as her blood. I need to touch her. Gods, do I need to touch her.

"It's working." Katrijanov's voice is a hum in the background even when I can hear everything in clearest detail. Ayna's presence drowns out everything else—so does the Syringe Ephegos lowers over the crook of her elbow, shooting me a cruel smile.

"Let's see how he does when she's awake." He injects her with the second serum and waves Katrijanov over.

The general lowers the blade to her skin just as Ayna's eyes fly open.

TWENTY-NINE

AYNA

I 'm in a cage. *I'm-in-a-cage-I'm-in-a-cage-I'm-in-a-cage,* and I can't breathe. I-can't-breathe-and-I-can't-see. Can't see and can't hear. Can't hear because I feel everything at once. The cool humidity settling on my skin, the scratch of something hard against my arm, the fabric sliding over my body like a shroud, the leather cutting into my wrists and ankles.

My wrist. My mangled wrist.

I try to yank it free, but the bonds won't give.

Then I smell him. Like a gust of warm wind, his presence envelops me. Wind and pine. Not only pine but an entire forest of evergreens and blossoms. Earth and moss and the salty tang of a coastal brine.

Myron, I form his name with my lips, but my voice won't respond. Or I don't hear myself speak as my senses fail me.

"Ayna." I hear him, though. Recognize his velvet voice even through the strain making it sound like it's been dragged across glass shards.

My head snaps in his direction on instinct, and my eyes open. No … they have been open for a while, but I couldn't see because I'm on sensory overload. It's all there, yet I can't process it the way I'm used to.

"*Myron*," I try again. This time, he hears me. His ocean-blue gaze is on me, his pale features drawn and tired.

And there is blood on his face. It's smeared around his mouth, dripping from the corner of his lips.

"I'm here, Ayna."

I can't tell if he's whispering or shouting, everything is revolting inside my body at the sight of Myron injured. The bruises I'd already seen earlier fade from my perception at the sight of fresh blood.

I will kill whoever did this to him. I will rip out their hearts and feast on them.

The thought is as startling as it is satisfying.

"Who—" I don't get to finish asking him who hurt him so I can make my list of people to eviscerate, for a sharp pain shoots up my arm as something etches into my skin, and I scream, the sound reverberating through the stone chamber. Ephegos's face appears, blocking out the view of Myron as he leans in, his champagne-scented breath assaulting my nose.

"Welcome back, Ayna. Or should I say, welcome to the world of fae?"

"Breathe, Ayna." Myron's voice anchors my soul as the rest of me seems to become unraveled. Like a spool of rope on a ship, I come apart. Like a cloud tossed into the wild storms above the ocean. My heart is a pounding, painful lump in my chest, reminding me that I'm alive, that I can't escape the agony of the blade slicing into my arm.

I smell my own blood now, little tendrils of rust and salt that aren't strong enough to tune out the song of Myron's scent.

"In and out. You're strong. You're capable. You are a survivor." Myron's words carry me through the blurring world even when they are glazed with the bone-grating texture of fear.

The knife reaches my shoulder, cutting away the fabric of my dressing robe.

"I have a theory I'd like to test, Ayna," Ephegos murmurs as he leans over me again. I haven't had a chance to process the meaning of his words from before, what he meant with the *world of the fae.*

"What are you doing to me?" My voice sounds off. Too smooth for the agony in my body, too rich for the way my dry throat is tormenting me.

The blade pauses, lifts from my skin, and I wait for the pulling agony that a knife wound is—I've experienced enough of them to know, and this one runs along my entire arm. Nothing happens. Where I expect blood to gush from my severed skin, my arm remains unusually dry where a pair of hands runs over it like a cat over a carpet, careful not to hook claws into the torn tissue.

"Let's see how fast you heal." Ephegos lowers himself a few inches until his face is level with mine, then lifts one hand from my arm to wave behind me. "Adrian?"

I have less than a breath to comprehend that he signaled to Katrijanov to step forward, which he does. There is no warning other than the gleam of malice in the general's eyes before he strikes me in the face.

Pain explodes in my cheek, leaving something wet trickling along my jaw. Blood. He split my skin with that punch. From the corner of my eye, I notice the spiky, silver ring on his middle finger.

"Take your hands off her." Myron's roar fills the stone chamber like a strike of thunder.

"Or you will kill us," Ephegos finishes for him in a sing-song voice. "I've heard it all before. And guess what." He whirls on Myron, turning his back to me, which allows me a moment to breathe while his attention isn't lingering on me with the promise of more pain, but it's on Myron. And I can't bear the thought of Myron taking the next blow just because he doesn't want to see me suffer. "You're bound by magical shackles and injected with a serum that suppresses your magic. Your strength won't help you here, King of Crows. Your tantrum will only cause her more pain." Ignoring Myron's horrified expression, the fury in those beautiful eyes, Ephegos turns back to me, examining my cheek with a probing finger. I try not to wince at the searing sensation running through my bones.

It might be broken.

"Perhaps I've pushed her too far with the drug," he says to Katrijanov as if I'm not even here. "I should have waited a day or two to let her recover so the serum kicks in faster."

Katrijanov inspects my face with a shrug. "She's breakable as any human prisoner for now. Perhaps we should give her more."

I don't even want to know what that means—what they do to their prisoners—but the bruises on Myron's face—Guardians, the red lines crisscrossing along his bare torso and arms—

The pain in my cheek is forgotten as my vision finally manages to focus on something other than Myron's features.

They tortured him. They cut him open over and over again on different occasions. The various degrees of scabbing and healing tell a whole tale of violence and misery that I'm not ready to know.

There is no unknowing what is obviously the map of torment during his captivity in this dungeon. If I thought I'd been bad off with the drugging and being forced to marry a cruel man because of my father's crimes and his last name, Myron has had it a million times worse.

"What serum?" I demand. If I can get him to leave Myron alone, I will be able to breathe more easily.

Fragments of memories come back to me... The table, the tray, the note. The note. I manage to tear my gaze off Myron to whip it to Herinor, who's been suspiciously quiet. He wasn't there when Ephegos and Katrijanov came to pick me up for torture. But was he the one who sent the note? *Don't eat the bread.*

His face yields nothing as he stares back at me with unreadable green eyes.

Whatever was in the bread, I ingested at least parts of it when they forced me to eat.

"An antidote to the original drug." Ephegos's smug expression is the last thing I want to see right now, but he forces himself between Herinor and me with a graceful step. "You've been drugged since I collected you at the palace in the Seeing Forest. Theories say that the effect can last quite a while when a magical creature is being sedated with it for longer periods of time and in high dosages." He gives me a pointed look. "And you, dear Ayna, have been requiring unusual portions of the drug. I would say I'm impressed if you weren't such a nuisance."

Antidote. They gave me an antidote. Grimacing at Ephegos, I reach into myself, but there is no hint of my powers.

"Excuse me for raining on your little plan, whatever that is." Every word hurts like fuck, and I don't care if I can keep him engaged enough to forget Myron even exists. Who knows how long until the serum he gave Myron wears off and he regains access to his magic? There is hope—

And hope is foolish and the only thing that can truly break us. I know it when Katrijanov takes his place next to Myron's table, wiping my blood on the thigh of Myron's pants. At least, they didn't strip him down completely to carve him up. Again with that hope... I bite down on my tongue to keep myself from shouting out all the curses I have in store for the general as he grins down at my Crow.

"Oh, Ayna..." Ephegos shakes his head, stepping closer to my side, revealing the view of Herinor once more.

The male shakes his head infinitesimally as if in warning. I have no idea what he's trying to tell me. He can't help; he's made that clear hundreds of times, and I don't expect his help, even though it would have been nice if *one* thing in life was easy.

"Ayna, Ayna. You're too smart to be a pawn in this game, but you're a pawn all the same." False pity drips in every word Ephegos speaks. He doesn't seem to be having any regrets though as he lifts another syringe to my arm.

On the table across the room, only a few paces away, Myron is thrashing as he tries to get to me without success.

"King Erina made a clever move, sending you to the Seeing Forest at last Ret Relah. He saw an opening to make his enemy bloodline disappear for good. But you survived. You, clever girl, survived and won the heart of the Crow King." He seems to be musing more than explaining, and it has nothing to do with the syringe—at least nothing I can fathom, yet. "When both Myron and you survived, he saw an even better plan form before him." He gives me that look I used to find endearing when I still believed he was a decent male who had my best interest at heart. The look that reminds me of a concerned friend. "Erina has been experimenting for a while, and with my help, he made great progress with his collection of anti-magical substances. Tavras is thriving, but Erina wants to expand his reach. The Southern Continent isn't interesting enough to conquer, and trade has been good, so that would weaken rather than strengthen Tavras's position. In the West, Cezux has been stronger than ever with Dimar II on the throne in Jezuin and the ties to the Askarean rule."

I try not to let my mind wander to the many questions threatening to pop to the surface. I need him to speak, need him to spill all those secrets he's been hiding. Even Myron has gone still now that Katrijanov has sheathed his blade, his pointed ears listening, his ocean eyes finding mine across the room like he could touch me with a gaze.

"That leaves Askarea itself. The wealthiest realm in all of Eherea, or so they say. I wouldn't know. I was never invited to King Recienne's palace in Aceleau." Bitterness laces every word as Ephegos pauses with the syringe right above my arm. One more inch and he'll prick my skin. "Askarea has never been an option for conquest. But the serum changes things."

Clio's words come back to me from our conversation after Erina informed me Myron is alive. Erina had used her… *To create a weapon. Something that will take out fairies the way a punch to the nose can take out humans.*

And he wants to use that weapon to conquer the fairy realm. Guardians above. Erina is even more devious than I'd thought.

"And what role do I play?" It's all I can think of to ask to keep him talking as he starts moving the needle closer to my skin.

I can't escape. No matter how hard I pull on the leather, it holds fast. Besides, if I start thrashing now, I might accidentally touch the needle and speed up the process.

"You?" Ephegos asks as if he's forgotten I'm here, his gaze finding mine with loathing and malice. "You are my means to keep Myron in check while I watch him go insane with the yearning for his mate." His eyes cut to Myron, and I want to scream just so he returns them to me.

"And the others?" I prompt, the only way now to divert his focus from my Crow—I don't dare repeat in my mind what he said, what they've all indicated: my mate.

Ephegos's laugh cackles like a caw as his features start shifting into bird form the way they used to when the curse was still active, but his arms remain tucked into his sepia finery. Only his hands turn into claws, the syringe nearly slipping from his grasp. "Royad and Silas will find their end before long. As for the Askarean general… He'll be quite useful in the months to come."

He leaves it at that, not elaborating, but it's not difficult to put two and two together even when my face is still hurting like Eroth himself struck me with his wrath.

"You are intending to use him as a bargaining chip," I conclude with all the horror my body is capable of.

On the table across the room, Myron shakes his head an inch, his eyes hard as if steeling himself against the truth Ephegos shared with us.

Katrijanov flashes a cruel grin from behind Myron. "A bargaining chip and a tool to keep our real bargaining chip in line."

"Clio." It's a whisper, but the Crows in the room pick it up while Katrijanov reads it from my mouth.

"I assume the King of Askarea will be willing to negotiate faster when he learns who we hold captive, and said captive will not set a toe out of line when we keep her mate for torture." Ephegos tilts his head, bird-like mouth opening as the rough hiss of his Crow voice escapes. "Just like you won't try anything foolish, Ayna, because you know I could end your mate at any moment. I could strap him to this very table." With a few slow strides, he crosses the room until he stands behind the metal Myron is strapped to, and traces a claw along his prisoner's muscled arm. A thin, crimson line follows in its wake, but smart as he is, Myron isn't moving for the same reason I didn't try to wriggle out of my bonds while the syringe had been hovering over my arm—avoiding worse damage—but the rapid rising and falling of his chest is proof of the agony he's so expertly hiding behind the mask of his unreadable face. Unreadable, except for those eyes locking on mine, filled with fear not for him, but for me.

"You will marry Erina, Ayna. You will bear his children—yes, multiple. A king can never have enough heirs, just in case—and then you'll live out your days at his side, knowing that one wrong word is enough to put your mate on this very table and have him carved open. Over. And over. Again." He enunciates each word. "The new serum allows for the fast fae healing and the vivid perception of all sensations—including pain." His features shift back to his human face, and the cruel smile turns even more pronounced as he exchanges a look with Katrijanov, who's drawn his blade once more, setting it to Myron's shoulder and stabbing him without warning.

The searing pain in my tattoo tears a scream from my throat, and I could swear Herinor takes a step forward, hands lifted as if he's ready to pull me off the table and carry me away, but he lowers them and turns back into a statue. The room blurs as tears shoot to my eyes while the rest of the room remains silent.

Why isn't Myron screaming? Why isn't he fighting?

The panic his silence evokes makes me manage a deep breath, allowing me to pack away the pain for a heartbeat or two, just long enough to see Myron lie still on his table, eyes shuttering as he fights a toneless war against the agony. No tears run down the side of his face where his blood is pooling under his hair, dripping over the edge of the table.

They won't let him bleed out. They won't. They need him alive in order to control me.

Ire replaces the despair constricting my chest, bursting through my veins like molten steel—no, like water, boiling, raging waves ready to eat up the world.

My Crow. They hurt *my* Crow. And they will all die for it.

What was a cacophony of images and sounds before has turned into a crystal clear scene, no blurriness, no haze. The world is a precise array of colors and textures, of tastes and scents, of emotions and ... wrath. Endless wrath.

Whatever Ephegos injected me with, it lifted the damper on a part of me I hadn't been aware of. What did he say? *Welcome to the world of fae.*

Just as I'd felt my magic when Vala gifted it, I feel my entire body light up with a new sort of strength. It's not magic, that's still fast asleep, but something different. Something *more*. I'm no longer human.

The sensation prickles across my skin like a dark melody, rushing along my bones like an echo of purple-glazed night. My fingers tingle, ache, break. One by one, they crack, and I cry out—but not in pain but in delight at what I realize is happening.

One after the other, my fingernails expand, lengthening in both directions, eating up my bones, my skin as they turn into talons, my hands into claws, my arms shrinking and shrinking as my body implodes into an unfamiliar form. A small, powerful form with beating wings and shiny black feathers.

I'm out of my shackles, and the world has turned into a kaleidoscope of possibilities as I flutter off my table right at Ephegos's face.

THIRTY

MYRON

I need to control my shallow breathing in order to slow my heart rate long enough to heal the deep hole Katrijanov pierced into my shoulder. The pain is secondary. It's nothing compared to the terror of Ayna's screams as our bond transfers part of my suffering to her. What a cruel mercy Vala chose for me. Gifted me a mate to lift my curse just to let me suffer as my agony becomes hers.

"I will never get enough of this," Ephegos whispers at me, his breath brushing my hair.

Monster. He's a worse monster than all those Crows who caused the curse. He betrayed all his values for a meek vendetta.

"Torturing us won't bring her back," I utter as Ayna's screams turn hoarse.

I need to get my wounds to heal faster, damn it, so I spare her the agony.

"It won't bring Sariell back, you're right. But it's justice to watch you writhe in pain, Myron. It's justice to watch Ayna's will being sucked out of her as she becomes my puppet. It's justice to take your crown and your people and reestablish the Crow Kingdom."

I don't bother pointing out that I'm not writhing. I'm lying as still as the pain will allow so I can focus all my energy on healing so I can free Ayna of her agony.

"There is no Crow Kingdom left," I hiss through clenched teeth, praying to Shaelak that Ayna's screams sound worse than what she feels. They are so rough now I'm led to believe her voice will fail any moment. "And nowhere to establish a court of monsters." Because that's what the Crow Court would become under his rule.

"I'm ready to test my luck, Myron. Are you?"

I'm about to snap my teeth at him just because it's the only part of me that's currently close enough to hurt him, but Ayna's golden form disappears from the corner of my eye, and her scream turns into a caw. Thank Shaelak for the shock locking me in place, or I'd have given away the graceful, powerful bird fluttering straight for Ephegos's head.

Katrijanov croaks a warning, but it's a feeble sound, his fingers clutching at his throat as the tang of magic fills the air and I notice Herinor's flexed fingers at his side. Damn him and his bad choices, but he's made a good one just now.

Ephegos manages to turn his head in time to meet Ayna's claws, talons ripping into his face. His scream turns into a caw as he shifts so fast he's a blur of feathers and skin. Skin, where his feathers were singed in the Flame attack, when he'd faked his death.

He's taller than Ayna's bird, but his wings don't work, keeping him bound to the ground while Ayna flutters above him, claws coming down again and again. Often enough to force him to shift once more while her talons hit his shield in violent attempts to break through.

My shoulder has almost healed, thanks to the serum Ephegos gave me—one that makes me a better torture victim that can be broken more frequently while it patches itself up in an endless cycle—but my magic ends there. My ability to shift is blocked just like my Crow magic. All I can do is stare in astonishment as my mate beats her elegant wings, feathers shimmering in the torchlight, and brings down her wrath on the male who caused all this misery.

"Grab her," Ephegos hisses, back in his humanoid form, his cheek bleeding from a cut right beneath his eye. I hope it becomes a thick scar. Since Crow talons are the only thing leaving scars on Crows, the odds are it will.

I don't know if he spoke to Katrijanov or Herinor, but he whips his magic out, not to capture her. Instead, it lands a blow to my stomach, making pain explode in my abdomen where I'd tried to relax as much as possible while the wound in my shoulder heals. My breath is stolen as every muscle locks up in response, too late to protect itself from the impact.

The bird whimper-caws, and I know she either feels through the bond what happened or watched it happening. Herinor is on his way to her, his fingers reaching high toward the ceiling where Ayna is circling in assessment of the scene, her black eyes piercing Ephegos with the bloodlust of a Crow temper. I know the feeling all too well; it defined most of my life, even when I was able to control my body enough to remain in my almost human form during the times of the curse.

"Watch out!" My shout dies as Ephegos hits me again, with his fist this time, landing a punch to my jaw where the old bruise has been retreating under my healing magic.

Blood coats my tongue, originating from the place my teeth cut into my cheek at the impact. My vision blurs.

Ayna is a dark form flickering in and out of the fading light as I fight to keep my eyes open.

No matter how I tear on my shackles, there is no escaping this, no way for me to save her as Herinor plucks her from the air with a rope of his magic and tucks her under his arm like a bound chicken.

"Let her ... go." My voice is weak, breathless, as I still struggle with the aftereffects of the punch to the stomach, but at least, my healing powers are catching up as if the serum's effect is still unfolding to its full capacity. If only it would free all of my powers the way the antidote Ephegos gave Ayna does.

A few more heartbeats and my shoulder will be fine, then my jaw will catch up and my stomach... Perhaps then, I'll be strong enough to free myself.

Katrijanov has other ideas, though. Free of Herinor's magic once more, he surges forward, slamming his knife into my chest deep enough to pierce my lung, and leaves it there.

"Just so you don't get any ideas while we take care of your little female," he says as he shoves at the hilt one last time before turning and heading for Herinor, who does his best impression of a loyal soldier while both Katrijanov and Ephegos inspect Ayna's thrashing bird's body with enough caution to know they believe it was her who attacked both of them with a magic she isn't even aware of. But I'm not quite as certain with Herinor involved in the scene, with the way he meets my gaze across the other's heads.

"What happened? How did she turn?" Ephegos demands, his voice disappearing between my labored breaths as I keep up my own fight to remain conscious. My body can only heal if the knife is removed. Katrijanov is a particular bastard for knowing that and using it for torture.

"She isn't supposed to turn," Herinor says in that measured tone I'm used to, no sign of emotion or remorse for incapacitating the female he just made an obvious attempt at helping. I try to wrap my head around what role he plays in all of this and why, for fuck's sake, he hasn't gotten her out of here before Ephegos and Katrijanov kill her. Sure as we all end in Hel's realm at some point, the Crow has murder in his eyes.

"I'll be back for you later," Katrijanov says to me over his shoulder before he leads the party from the room, and all the pain I've managed to control in my panic of seeing Ayna hurt bursts through my body with a vengeance.

THIRTY-ONE

AYNA

I'm trapped in a feathered body, all strength I believed I had sucked from my limbs as Herinor carries me up the stairs between his large hands like a pigeon for slaughter. Guardians, I've never noticed how enormous his hands are, his fingers reaching around my chest while his magic keeps the rest of me bound.

My scrawny legs ache from uselessly kicking at my restraints, my wings pulse with exhaustion, my tiny heart pumps so fast it might work itself into a standstill. My voice has reduced to meaningless caws, my thoughts to the image of Myron's eyes as they locked on mine for a brief moment while I was up in the air. Shock and petrification. He hadn't known I was capable of shifting, just as I hadn't known—or any of the males currently walking with me.

"The antidote was supposed to lift the effects of the drug slowly. She didn't have much magic before. Only the water wielding, but that I could have easily controlled if it hadn't happened so fast." Ephegos turns to Katrijanov. "You saw her eat the bread, too. She'd eaten at least half of it when we entered her room, and she took another big bite when we were there. That should have been enough to keep her under control for a day if not longer."

"Something went wrong," Katrijanov agrees, his gaze flying to Herinor, whose hands are gentle around my body even when his magic holds like steel. He isn't hurting me now that I've stopped fighting. It's more important for me to hear every word they speak. If I'm not strong enough to escape, I need to be smart enough. And for that, I need all the information I can get.

"Don't look at me like that," Herinor grumbles at the general. "I didn't help her. I caught her for you when you messed up with the drugs."

He sounds almost convincing to me, but the tiny, reassuring brush of his finger over the side of my tucked wing tells me he has a plan. I also don't miss Ephegos's probing glance in Herinor's direction. He'd know if the male broke his bargain. He'd be dead, not carrying me through the palace.

"Take her to her room," he orders, already turning into another hallway with Katrijanov. "She needs to shift back before we can do anything else."

It's the best motivation I can think of to make me want to stay in this bird form forever, though I don't doubt they will stop at nothing to force me back into my human body if I don't cooperate.

Herinor doesn't change his grim expression as he walks past the few guards spaced out along the main hallway leading up to the residential level, ignoring when they study us with curious interest.

"Never seen a stray bird?" he barks at one of them, who cringes against the golden ornamentations on the wall like he slapped his face.

It would have been comical, if not for the panic coiling my stomach into a tight knot at the thought of Myron down in the dungeon. Herinor didn't allow me a glimpse at my husband before he carried me out of the chamber, effectively blocking the view with his massive torso. As he does now.

All I can see is the dark floor ahead, the gold and sepia walls, the ceiling full of filigree, and the large window at the end of the hallway—until he turns left and walks up the stairs and my gaze falls on the female form approaching at a busy pace.

I recognize the servant's uniform before I recognize her face.

"Kaira—"

I realize I called out to her in my mind when her head snaps to the side, searching the space for any sign of me.

"Ayna? Where are you?" She slows her pace. Stops, gaze finding Herinor cradling me in his hands. Her face twists as if in an effort to keep any sign of distress tucked away behind a mask of confidence. *"I can't see you, Ayna. Where. Are. You?"*

Behind me, Herinor seems to grow an inch as he throws back his shoulders, gait turning more energetic at the sight of the part-Flame.

"Find me in her room," he whispers at her as he casually strolls past her, not bothering to look at her twice, but I can sense the heat rolling off the female as we pass by, the way Herinor's muscles quiver as if in self-restraint.

There is something going on here, and it has nothing to do with the fact that Kaira isn't supposed to be anywhere but the kitchens and servant areas.

Kaira's chin drops an inch as she steps aside as if clearing the warrior's path. For every other person, it must have appeared like a fae guard almost walking over a human servant, but for me... For me, it seemed those two have been spending more time together than just those few days in the carriage on our way to Meer.

"Ayna?" Kaira's voice fills my small bird-head, and I wonder how it fits in there. I've stopped wondering how I've turned into this form, though. Musing about the *whys* won't change anything.

"I'm the bird." It sounds so ridiculous that I want to take it back because I'm human, not fairy or fae or Flame, or any other creature. Yet, I've shifted.

"Fuck—" Kaira's footsteps click down the hallway so fast I am certain she's running. A door creaks, and I can hear her turn. *"How did that happen?"* The distress in her voice makes my heart race even harder. *"Did they put a spell on you?"*

"Crows don't put spells on people."

"How do you know? I've seen them do all sorts of horrible things." She sounds farther away, as do her footsteps as they fall along a set of stairs I can't locate. My new senses are incredible, but that is beyond their capability.

"So have I," I remind her, because I have. *"They can't put spells on people."* Another reason I am so certain is that I feel it in my bird bones like a truth I was born with.

"Almost there," Herinor murmurs as we round the final corner into the hallway leading to my room.

I want to ask him why he tries to make it sound like a reassurance when there is nothing he can do other than execute Ephegos's orders. All he can do is take me to my room and leave me to my fate the way he's always done—even before I broke the curse, at the Crow Palace.

"Hold on, Ayna," Kaira calls before her voice fades entirely. *"I'll be there soon."*

Another reassurance that has no meaning. Even hearing her voice in my head hasn't made her an ally I can fully rely on, no matter how much I want to.

Herinor ignores the guard at my door saluting him like an officer and kicks the door open, not deigning to explain why he's carrying a bird around.

"Make sure the stairs are clear," he hisses over his shoulder before he slams the door in the man's face.

He doesn't stop to set me down until he reaches the window, which he closes with his magic before placing me on the table and sitting in the chair in front of me, bringing his face level with mine.

"I know you're afraid, Ayna. It's scary to shift for the first time, even for a born Crow." His voice is gentle, soothing

311

as he keeps his hands on either side of my body, bracing me or keeping me from hopping off the table and trying to fly away, I don't know.

"Can you change back?" He strokes his thumb over my back.

I need to talk to him if I want to understand what's going on, so I'd better try.

I have no idea how, but I visualize myself in my human body, hoping it would be that easy.

Apparently, it is. Because a moment later, I sit on the polished wood of the table, my legs tucked under my naked body and pushing Herinor aside with an expanding shoulder.

He leaps off the chair, blindly grabbing for the blanket resting at the foot of the bed and throwing it over my form before turning his eyes back on me. "Good, now let's figure out how to get you out of here."

"I thought you couldn't help me." My voice is dry and every word hurts like the Guardians scraped my vocal cords from my throat.

"I'm not helping you." His brows knit together as he helps me step off the table while I clasp the blanket around my shivering form. "I'm helping Myron."

My mouth opens, but no words come out.

"Did you send the note?" I manage after a few moments of speechlessness. "Because I'm sure telling me not to eat the poisoned piece of food counts as help…"

"I'd be dead if I'd helped you," he reminds me, his scars stark on his tan face as we reach the sofa where he sits me down before opening the armoire, rummaging through its contents. "Only finery in here," he grumbles. "You need practical clothes. Kaira will bring something…"

"Kaira, or me." The door closes, and Clio walks in with a stack of linen in her hands that could be beddings or a set of peasant clothes. I pray it's the latter.

"We have about five minutes to get out of here." She kicks the door shut with her boot and drops the stack on the sofa next to me. "And before you ask, yes, I stole them, and no, I don't feel the least bit guilty about it." Her gaze wanders to Herinor, who has stopped his digging to stare at her instead. "No, I don't have my magic back. I'm just that awesome without it." She flashes a brief grin that doesn't touch her eyes. "Now get the fuck out of here before the bargain kills you, Crow. I won't forget what you did for me."

I have no clue what's going on, wild shivers still raking through my body as I try to pick up a piece of linen—a shirt—while also not exposing myself.

Clio sighs, shoving at Herinor's back as she directs him toward the door, ignoring the reluctance in his steps.

"What did you do, Herinor?" I think it's the first time I called him by his name, but it doesn't taste bitter despite our history.

He shakes his head. "I can't help you, Ayna, and I'll forever regret that I can't. But I can help everyone else. So I do." My heart clenches at the look he gives me, full of devastation and fear. Who would have thought a big, ruthless male like him could fear anything? "Ephegos ordered me to take you to your room, but he never said anything about making sure you stay here. Disappearing for now is the best I can do. You don't need my help. You have Clio and Kaira. Trust Kaira." His voice wraps around her name, and I know he has more to lose in this palace than I could have ever imagined. "And never forget you have the gods on your side. Vala gave you a mate to fight for. Shaelak gave you wings to match his. Now go and fly, little bird."

I only notice my heart is breaking for him as he's crossing the threshold, closing the door behind him to disappear to the Guardians know where.

"Enigmatic like the rest of them, isn't he?" Ever pragmatic, Clio picks the shirt from my hands and pulls it over my head, moving down the blanket. My breasts bob as she gently pushes me back to tug the shirt in place, and I instinctively reach for my chest.

"I'm sorry I didn't bring you fancy underthings to keep everything in place, but this is a rescue mission, and I couldn't care less what your breasts do while you run."

I'm inclined to laugh. Instead, a tear shoots to my eye, lingering on my lashes as I try to shake the shock of the past hours.

"I don't know what happened, but it can't be anything good, judging by your looks." Skimming me head to toe, she hands me a pair of brown linen pants that remind me of Tavrasian peasant attire. "And I don't know what Herinor has been up to, but you don't think I've been sitting around, twiddling thumbs while they have both our mates in the dungeons."

There, she said it. mates. Both our mates.

"He really is my mate," I admit in a whisper, a numbness spreading where pain was dictating minutes ago. The panic hasn't ebbed, though, my heart still pounding mercilessly.

"Can we push the epiphany back until we're out of here?" She picks a pair of sturdy slippers from the armoire while I fill her in about what happened in the dungeon, monitoring her every move with my new spectrum of senses.

"He gave me that serum before to wake up my fairy senses, and he gave me the drug that nullifies my powers. I still have none of them at my disposal, thanks to said serum." Grimacing, she helps me into my slippers. "Not what I'd call combat gear, but we're not going into battle." The *yet* is a silent addition we both know she doesn't need to speak. Soon enough, we'll face a war Ephegos has been helping Erina prepare. Humans attacking Askarea with magic-binding weapons… My stomach turns, and I retch on my shoes, barely missing Clio's hands as she hops aside at the last moment.

"Whatever of the drug is left in your system will purge fast since you ingested it through food, and he gave you the serum to wake your senses, so you should be fine within a day or two." Her eyes snag on the bruise on my face, which I've mercifully been able to ignore—or have I been.

"What's wrong?" I wipe my mouth on a corner of the blanket, realizing my face isn't throbbing the way it was in the dungeons.

"The bruise is almost gone. You are healing yourself." She brushes back my hair and ties it with a strip of fabric she rips off the hem of my shirt. "Ephegos is a fool to experiment on you with his potions. Whatever he gave you triggered your powers to wake up. He probably wasn't expecting that you'd turn into a Crow yourself."

I try not to think about the implications of her assessment. A Crow. The first female Crow in millennia.

"He certainly made a mistake he'll regret once we're all out of here and have our powers at our disposal." The conviction in her tone is almost convincing.

"You're coming with me? We're all getting out?" It's a vain hope, and I try not to cling to the thought of seeing Myron again, free of shackles or anguish. The real Myron with all his vast fae powers and his ocean-blue eyes.

"*You and I* are getting out." Clio tucks my hair in place, hiding the lengths in the collar of my shirt to make me less recognizable. "We need to leave the males behind for now until we are both at our full strength and we can rescue them."

I try not to let the panic take me over again at the thought of Myron in chains, Myron in pain, Myron unconscious and bruised and bleeding. Apparently, my mind is dead-set on showing me exactly those images I fear so much because all I can see now is his gorgeous body strung up on the metal table, his blood pooling beneath his head as pain sears both our shoulders.

I make a mental note to ask Clio exactly how mating bonds work and force myself to stand. "I thought you wouldn't leave without Astorian." I understand now why she said it back then. I feel the same about Myron. The thought of abandoning him is almost unbearable.

"If we stay, none of us gets out. Plus, you'll be married to Erina within a week. It's not like we have a lot of options to work with or excessive time to make better plans." She guides me to stand, and I let her. "Herinor found a way around his bargain. Help Myron because Ephegos hasn't explicitly forbidden that. Too full of himself to believe he could be outmatched by a drugged and shackled male. Now it's time for us to act before Ephegos binds Herinor with another order."

A soft knock on the door has both of us holding our breath. Clio pulls a knife from the skirts of her uniform, stepping in front of me like she is ready to kill. Knowing her, she is.

"Just me, Ayna," Kaira announces herself through the door before it swings open. I instantly relax.

"Come in." Placing my finger on Clio's arm, I indicate for her to lower her weapon as Kaira joins us, a satchel slung over her shoulder and a skirt draped over her arm.

"Herinor told me what happened," she informs us as she closes the door behind her. "The guard is gone for now, but he'll return soon. If you want to run, now's the time." She doesn't spare Clio a glance. "And you should wear this instead." The skirts she pulls from her arm unfold into a servant uniform, white apron and all. "It will be easier to smuggle you out if you blend in. Nothing against you, Princess," she says sweetly to Clio, who glares daggers at her. "The pants are perfect for running once we're out of the palace, but until we're past the gates, you'd better put on these."

Thankfully, Clio's pride is second only to her need to get her mate out of the dungeon. And that makes her pragmatic more than ever. With a few efficient movements, the two females have me in the uniform, adding the white cap to my head to cover most of my hair.

"You got my note, then?" Kaira asks as she pulls her satchel to the front, digging up a piece of bread. *"This one is clean."*

Out loud, she says, "You're probably hungry if you missed another meal."

My stomach grumbles, but I still have the taste of bile on my tongue. "Later. Let's get out of here first."

THIRTY-TWO

AYNA

"I'd say I'll fly out of here, but I have no idea how to shift." I follow Clio along the dim servant corridor running parallel to the main hallway. I'd known the royal palace was huge and a complicated construction with secret passageways, but I'm learning only now just how many side corridors and hidden pathways were integrated into this building.

Clio shoots me a warning look. "You'd better not. I need you coherent and able to communicate when we make our way out."

"Besides, a bird fluttering through the palace draws more attention than another servant," Kaira adds, for once not arguing with Clio.

Since we've left my room, they haven't agreed on a thing, Kaira reluctantly letting Clio take the lead since the female has been staying at the palace a lot longer than her. But occasionally, they need to consolidate their knowledge when the approach of servants or guards forces us to divert from the original route Clio chose. At least my face is more or less concealed by the low light as long as I keep my head down, allowing Kaira to navigate me by directions spoken into my mind. I'm surprised Clio hasn't caught onto our silent conversation.

"Here," Clio pulls me around another corner, her hand surprisingly sweaty, like a normal human's. Between Kaira, the part-Flame, and Clio, the subdued fairy, I am the one with the best senses at this particular moment, so I do my best to warn them about approaching boots and voices. Most of them are on the other side of the wall in the main hallways, though I learn quickly, tuning out that portion as best I can so I don't give the others a heart attack every time I hear something.

"We're almost at the side entrance," Kaira narrates in a murmur this time. "If we're lucky, no one has noticed you're gone yet, and the guards there won't heed us any notice when we stroll out the door."

"So much for that theory." Clio glares over her shoulder, apparently not satisfied with Kaira's hopeful nature. "I've lived long enough to know practice is never quite what you plan for."

The wisdom in her jade eyes tells me it's not solely to get on Kaira's nerves, even when half of her comments might have been.

"How did you even shake your own guards?" Kaira demands. "I thought you were escorted everywhere."

"I was." Clio leaves it at that, but her hand tightens on the knife she's hiding in the folds of her skirts. I'm surprised not to find any blood on her.

"You could have disposed of them earlier," I whisper, my own voice thundering through the narrowing stone path like thunder—at least, that's what it sounds like to me. Clio needs to strain to hear me.

"Who said *I* disposed of them? I left them at your door when I entered."

When we both glance at Kaira, she wildly shakes her head. "I didn't kill them."

"Herinor—" I don't know how I feel about him risking so much to help everyone else so they can help me.

"I would assume it was him," Clio agrees. "Smart male. If he weren't so fucking stubborn, we could have gotten out long ago."

"He's not stubborn," Kaira interjects, and I nearly smile as her affections for the male surface so casually it almost feels like we're on an evening stroll... Then we reach the end of the tunnel, and two guards are eyeing us with expert assessment, their hands on their swords as one of them demands to know where we're going.

"We are on an errand for Lord Ephegos," Kaira lies without hesitation, and I've never been more grateful Eherean fairies can lie like thieves. "He is indisposed at this moment, but he needs a few things from his estate in the city for his … guest."

The guard cocks his head while the other one's young features soften. "Good to see you, Kaira." His gaze lowers to her mouth then to her chest as if he's recently seen more of her than just her face. His long, braided hair and trim beard are in stark contrast to the short gray hair and shaved jaw of the older guard whose grumpy expression hasn't changed.

"And you Julj." The way Kaira's lashes flutter at Julj makes me dizzy.

The small gesture is apparently enough to take Julj's mind off why we're here to begin with, and I'm not certain I like the way he's appraising Kaira like she's his favorite pastime.

"I've been hoping to…" His eyes dart sideways, skipping over me as he notices Clio's curved form. "See you later tonight."

"Stop flirting, and let the women do their job," the older guard scolds the younger one, his stern face landing on Kaira while Clio casually shifts in front of me, looping her arm through Kaira's.

"We really need to go, or Lord Ephegos will be very disappointed and not give any of us leave." She says it to the older guard, but it's the younger one who seems disappointed as he gets the message.

"We wouldn't want that." His gaze hops back and forth between Kaira and her as if he's planning not only tonight but his entire week's evening activities starring the two servant women in front of me, who mercifully have managed to keep the guards' attention off me.

"Definitely not," Kaira agrees and winks at Julj as he opens the door for us.

My stomach tightens as they walk out the door and I follow, setting one foot after the other on my path between the two men, their eyes alert and ready to discard any danger from outside—or from within.

I've almost made it when a hand lands on my shoulder and the older guard stops me. "Wait."

"Kaira," I reach for her through our connection when every spoken word would give away that something is wrong.

The part-Flame slows, her hand slipping from Clio's arm, who turns, her whole body tense for a fight.

I don't face the man as he steps to my side, studying me from a head above.

Shit. If he recognizes me, this is over. Between the three of us, we might defeat two palace guards, but the noise would alert more guards, and even if we managed to escape, Ephegos and Erina would hear about it, and they would make Myron and the others pay for it.

"Keep your calm, Ayna," Kaira orders. *"Breathe."* Out loud, she says, "Anything wrong?" Her gaze darts past the older guard to Julj before returning to me.

The man hasn't lifted his fingers from my shoulder—the very same shoulder that hurt like mad earlier when Katrijanov stabbed Myron in the tattoo. I try not to cringe, try to stand tall while keeping my face slightly averted and in the shadows the palace walls throw over us.

His fingers slide to my neck, and I can hear the sound of spines snapping under the force of a hand. I've seen too much during my years on the Wild Ray and in the prison at Fort Perenis not to know what a deliberate hand can do to a neck like mine. My hairs stand at the back of my neck as fear floods my veins, pushing me to *run-run-run* like an animal.

"It's the Crow instincts, Ayna. Don't listen to them. Focus on your breathing, or you'll shift right here." Kaira's voice is a soothing anchor, keeping me from jolting into a run. If I run, he'll know. If I run, I'll damn Myron to more pain. If I run—

The hand reaches higher, grazing the nape of my neck, and I almost quake, my body tensing to fight in a mirror of Clio's readiness to slaughter. My gaze meets hers, signaling that I'm prepared.

She shakes her head ever so slightly, indicating for me to hold still.

The fingers curve around my bound hair and tug.

I flinch.

"Hold still, foolish woman," the guard grumbles. "I'm just fixing your hair. You know how much King Erina hates when his staff is perceived as sloppy. It reflects on the reputation of his court." He pulls hard enough to hurt, until the hidden lengths of my hair slide free of my clothes and flop down between my shoulder blades. I don't breathe. "There, better. "

He drops his hand, stepping back into position beside the door, and I don't hesitate when Clio waves me forward. Kaira walks to my other side as they frame me until we make it to the next corner.

I only manage a full breath when Kaira drags me into a narrow alley where the sparse light doesn't reach and the noises of the palace no longer follow.

Clio takes off her maid's cap then fiddles with mine until it comes loose. "That was close."

"Close enough to make me wish I'd packed fresh underwear," Kaira agrees.

I instinctively sniff, wondering if she is joking or if she really peed her pants.

"Joking," Kaira informs me through our mental connection. *"But I really don't have spare underwear in here."* She rummages through her satchel, pulling out a small canteen of water. "Drug-free. Promise."

Clio steps out of her servant uniform, revealing the same linen pants and shirt I'm wearing before she helps me take off my skirts and apron, while Kaira is changing into a set of leather pants I wish I knew where she got.

"Let's find a place to hide until the two of you have the drug out of your system."

THIRTY-THREE

AYNA

The city is alive with evening dwellers as we sneak from corner to corner, all dressed in inconspicuous attire, our hair braided and rolled up into buns the way many peasants wear for practicality. A cool breeze announces summer is coming to an end, and I shudder at the mingle of scents and smells wafting along the alleys.

We made it out of the noble district half an hour ago, our progress delayed by the many occasions we had to dodge a night patrol. Somewhere between passing out in my bedroom from whatever was in the bread and being tortured, I lost track of time, day and night blurring into one big mass.

Now that the oil lanterns are flickering to life and armed soldiers are making their rounds through the city in routine patrols, I have a clearer grasp on reality than I've had in weeks.

Gray clouds are shifting across the darkening sky, driven by the sluggish wind hitting from the east. From the ocean. My heart leaps in my chest at how close I am to the troubled waters that mean freedom, then slumps at the impossibility of bolting and disappearing without looking back the way I did when I joined the Wild Ray. Closing my eyes for a heartbeat, I inhale deeply, tasting the brine in the distance. I've barely escaped with my life, gambling with that of four others—five if I count Herinor, who has been risking his life to find a way around his bargain with Ephegos.

At least, I have two capable females at my side who are familiar with my current condition—which is mildly beside myself at the thought of my mate in the dungeon and a hidden pair of wings and feathers stuck in my body.

"Here, drink some more." Kaira hands me the canteen without waiting for my response. Despite all her bickering with Clio, she's made it her mission to keep the two of us fed and strong, and I can't help but admire that about her.

Gratefully, I take a sip before handing the canteen to Clio, who frowns but drinks.

"I'm tempted to stay right here and not move until that poison of a drug is out of my system." She gestures at the packed dirt road leading between the one-story buildings in this district. There's a small front garden with a vegetable patch where a few stalks of lettuce and what looks like an early-ripened pumpkin sit in the shadows.

I've never been to this part of Meer, but judging by what I've seen so far, we can't linger, or we'll be reported. Even when this isn't the district of estates and palaces, the houses are formidable, and poverty seems something nonexistent.

"Perhaps we should go near the docks and find a ship that will take all of us away when we get the males out," I suggest, forcing myself to mean the *when*. I can't live in a world where not succeeding is an option.

"You need to live with that option," Kaira says in my mind, reading every last of my thoughts. I can't tell if I'm relieved I'm not all alone in my head or if I'm annoyed by the lack of privacy.

"Relieved," Kaira answers for me, shooting me a smile as we round another corner.

"You know we can't simply run away once we have them back," Clio notes. "My brother will be eager to know I'm still alive and that his general is ready to lead his armies in the upcoming war."

My stomach folds into a knot—as if it hasn't been one tight cluster of knots since the moment I learned that Myron is still alive—and in Erina's and Ephegos's power. "I know. I just wish it were that easy."

"Running away isn't easy, Ayna." The wisdom in Clio's tone gives me pause, and I meet her gaze, falling into step beside her. "You need to live with the guilt of knowing who and what you sacrificed in order to save yourself."

"Sounds like you've tried that before," Kaira quips, and I wish the two of them wouldn't constantly challenge each other.

Clio doesn't strike back with a smart-mouthed comment this time, merely nods and sighs. "I wish I didn't."

"One of the many stories taking too long to tell?" I ask, squeezing her hand for a beat as we step into the next alley.

"One of those stories." She forces a smile, and even Kaira doesn't comment when the female has laid open a vulnerability that others would be ashamed of.

"If the two of you have another half-hour walk in you, I'm sure we'll find someplace we can stay for the night," Kaira eventually says, taking the lead as if she's mapped out the city in her mind. By now, I wouldn't be surprised if she has.

"How did you manage to be in the right place at the right time so often," I ask her, trudging on behind her while my senses reach far ahead, learning their limits and scouting our surroundings.

Kaira shrugs. "It comes with its benefits being unremarkable on all levels." She says it like she doesn't care, but I see her frustration, have witnessed it before when she told me she wasn't taken on hunts to the Seeing Forest because she's only part-Flame. Her average height and average looks and unremarkable hair color. There is an advantage to being able to blend into crowds because of being purely average, but it also is a stab to the gut to not stand out in any way.

"You are remarkable to me," I tell her through our connection, and I could swear a ghost of a smile crosses her face. It's hard to tell from this angle, but when she speaks again, her voice is lighter.

"Julj is the only one who seems to be attracted to unremarkable," she narrates, her gait more energetic and her tone almost humorous. "You wouldn't believe what sorts of information one can squeeze out of a man who thinks with his cock."

Clio's grin is the first genuine one I've seen since Kaira joined us in my room, and it's a good look on her. "Finally something we agree on."

"What's your status with him?" I ask the Flame while in my mind I add, *"I thought you had a thing for someone slightly ... more experienced."*

Kaira's gait falters briefly before she catches herself. "Julj? He knows what my breasts feel like through the fabric of my uniform, and that's about it." I can't help but grin, too. *"And the other one... He's..."*

"Intimidating," I supply as she continues the conversation through our mental connection.

"That, and I can't decide if I want him or am afraid of him."

"He does give off those 'dangerous Crow' vibes," I agree.

"Does he know who you are?" Clio wants to know, unaware that we've already moved on from the topic.

But Kaira is ready as if jumping between conversations has already become second nature to her. "Julj knows that I'm part of Ephegos's staff serving in Erina's court, but he has no idea I'm a part-Flame on a rescue mission to save—"

She stops herself by flapping her hand over her mouth, drawing a suspicious glance from both Clio and me.

"To save who?" Clio prompts, her tongue ready while mine is tied by a million thoughts.

"That's what I want to know, too," I agree when Kaira doesn't immediately speak.

She'd been the least trustworthy of all of my so-called allies until she started speaking into my mind. But if I'm honest with myself, even that doesn't make her my friend or someone I can trust, just someone who knows more of my secrets than anyone else.

"My sister." Kaira's words are a whisper, but in my head, they ring loud like the warning bells of the royal fleet under attack.

"What do you mean, *your sister*?" Again, Clio beats me to it, but this time, I remain silent as I hold Kaira's brown gaze, understanding dawning.

"How is that possible? You're part Flame." I search for anything that would resemble my father in her features, coming up blank. Her nose is too wide, her eyes too brown, and her jaw too square. Not even the smile she gives me resembles anything close to my father's.

Clio goes silent while Kaira and I stare at each other, reading into each other's features.

"We don't share a father," I realize as her lips twitch in a sad smile that I recognize instantly. Should have recognized the first day she visited my room at the Flame estate.

"When I was little, it was common for human partners of Flames to be shunned and forced to leave after they gave birth to a Flameling." I can't decipher whether that's shame in her eyes or sorrow. "Elenja Woltaya was allowed three months with her part-Flame male and her daughter before being kicked out of the Flame community. And had they known how little magic I'd have, they might have sent me with her back then. To this day, I can't rid myself of the memories of my father's disappointment when he realized how useless I was as a Flame."

My heart stops. Literally stops before chasing to catch up the lost beats. If what she says is true, I have a sister.

"Is your father still alive so I can kill him for being an elitist ass?" Clio grunts, the only comment she has for now, and I can't help the small smile stealing itself onto my lips.

Kaira's gaze doesn't stray from mine. "He didn't survive the battle in the Seeing Forest." Not a hint of grief. Not a single tear. Not even a tremble in her voice. "I had no family left and might have left the Flames had I not accidentally overheard Ephegos's discussion with Jeseida where he explained who you were: the daughter of Elenja Woltaya who became Elenja Milevishja, wife of Ivan Milevishja, the last of the royal Milevishja line." She reaches across the distance, placing her hand on my forearm, and I don't shy away, too stunned to even think of defending myself in case she is just another person lying to me, manipulating me, wanting me dead or trapped, or intending to use me as a tool for their revenge.

"I have family now. Someone worth running for and fighting for. And I chose to run from the Flames to join you here. I lied to Ephegos, pretending I don't care about you, that I believe you deserve your fate. I played the good little servant to gain his trust. And he trusted me enough to let me prepare you for the palace that first day. He trusted me enough to let me prepare your meals. So I took whatever chance I got to understand what's going on in the palace, to explore all possible routes for an exit. To acquaint myself with the hulk of a Crow that he appointed your guard."

"Herinor," Clio supplies, but Kaira and I are both aware Kaira knows exactly who Herinor is. I could swear her cheeks blush the slightest bit at the mention of his name.

"Herinor," Kaira repeats, clasping her fingers in front of her as she turns into another alley, this time not heading along but stopping at the splintered door of a shed in the backyard of what seems to be an abandoned home. "He told me your story, Ayna." She ignores the way Clio scans her with her jade eyes as if ready to stab her with one of the sharp ends of the loose wooden boards making up what's left of the door. "And when I learned what Ephegos had planned for you, I couldn't just sit by and watch you being taken away again."

"Why didn't you tell me?" It's the only question that matters—the only question that ever matters, I learned the hard way during my time at Myron's court. There is always a reason for someone's actions, no matter how despicable.

"Because I couldn't risk anyone finding out." There is genuine fear in her expression now. "My father kept my mother's last name a secret the way it's custom when Flames take human lovers. But when he died and I had to take care of his things, I found a hand-drawn picture of her in his nightstand. It said '*Elenja Woltaya on our first Ret Relah*'. I knew it then, that it was her. Elenja isn't a common name among Flames."

"It's a Tavrasian name," I insert as she pushes open the brittle door and leads the way into near darkness, ignoring Clio's skeptical glance.

But the female doesn't object when we make our way into the half-light of the shed and Kaira closes the door behind us.

"This is where we stay until the two of you lose the effects of the drug," she says matter-of-factly, as if she has been leading us toward this place all along.

"How do you know it's safe?" Clio interrogates, exploring the long, narrow space with her hands raised for combat as if expecting one of Erina's guards might step out of the shadows.

"It's not a trap if that's what you're asking."

"I'm not." Clio shakes her head. "I just…" She stops at the end of the single room, apparently deeming it safe enough because she sinks to the flipped-over crate in the far corner and rests her head in her hands. "You planned this. You knew where we were going." The accusation in her tone is obvious. "You could have told us—told *me*—that you had a plan."

Kaira guides me to join Clio, flipping over another crate for me before sitting down against the wall across from us. "As I said, I earned Ephegos's trust by continuing to drug you, Ayna, but he didn't give me much leniency. I was allowed to travel between his estate in Meer and the palace, but that didn't give me spare time to find a hideout for when we escaped."

Too exhausted from torture and being drugged, I simply wait for her to continue speaking. By now, nothing should shock me anymore, yet when she mentions how she knows about this place, my heart does something I hadn't believed it was still capable of: it flutters with excitement.

"Herinor found it for us."

I should have been surprised, should have wondered, but with the way she seems to have formed an attachment to the Crow and his little tells when it came to her that he'd help, I'm more surprised he managed to find a way to actually do so.

"How did that bastard do it?" Clio asks the question I can't seem to get to leave my tongue. "That little Crow shit kept telling both Ayna and me that he can't help her because of the bargain he made with Ephegos."

Kaira's face lights up, the rising starlight falling through the broken windows illuminating her soft expression. "He told me the same. He couldn't help you"—her gaze falls on me—"so he helped *me* instead."

The same way he helped Myron rather than me.

It makes sense. Total sense. Yet, there is one thing I still can't wrap my head around. "Why does Ephegos trust you? Why not put the same sort of bargain as a condition for you to work for him that he demanded from Herinor?"

Beside me, Clio nods her agreement, the skepticism never leaving her face.

Kaira's smile is broad and victorious this time as she glances between Clio and me. "You forget one thing when it comes to Ephegos."

"And that is?" Clio prompts while I try to figure it out on my own.

He wanted revenge on Myron more than anything and earned the position of a Flame prince in the process of betraying his best friend. He hates Myron, and so he hates everyone the Crow King loves, including me. He will stop at nothing to get what he wants, including working with a despicable king who extends his power to the fairy realm. The

Flames are his new people even when he wants to reestablish a Crow Court somewhere.

Before I can come to a conclusion, Kaira responds, "He needs allies, people in his own ranks he can trust. People who aren't part of a trade or partnership that will eventually fall apart like the one with Erina and Katrijanov. He needs those two to gain power and get his revenge, but they are both human and will eventually die while Ephegos will outlive them, and only the Guardians know what he'll do then."

I don't want to know either, but I should because, if there is anything I can do to stop him from waging war on the fairy realm... I don't know if I have it in me to think of saving another kingdom when all I want is to save the male I love and run. The male who is tied to me by the whims of a god—or two, if Herinor is right about Shaelak giving me Crow wings.

"Ephegos desperately needs supporters in his own ranks; that's why he might have been faster with trusting me at least not to kill you off or try to run. He has no idea of all the things I've been up to because guards are so wonderfully silent when they hope to get lucky with you." She shakes her head as if tossing the mass of hair back that's neatly braided and coiled into a bun, then bats her eyes the way she did at Julj. "It's not my favorite weapon, but when it comes to saving the only family I have left, I know no boundaries."

I believe her. For the first time since I met Kaira, I have no second thoughts about her motivations. She's on our side just as Herinor would like to be. And he found a way to help us by helping everyone but me.

Clio seems to be less convinced, so I do the one thing I know will put all cards on the table.

"Do you know anything about mind-readers, Clio?" Turning my head, I attempt a smile as I present the final secret Kaira holds to my friend—

And earn a panicked glance from the female that makes me wonder how bad her experience with that sort of magic could possibly be.

THIRTY-FOUR

MYRON

By the time footsteps sound in the hallway again, the room is dark, the torches having burned out and the smoke of their extinguishing lingering in the air. I wish it wouldn't overpower every last trace of Ayna's scent, but there is little I can do with my chest pinned to the table with a knife and my limbs restrained by leather bonds.

My healing power strains to get to work around the steel piercing my lungs, sealing the wound until it hits metal and every breath makes the blade tear deeper into my tissues again. It's a fucking mess.

Ephegos gave me back my senses, but not most of my magic. Yet, I feel stronger than I have in weeks. The vastness of my fae powers doesn't matter when I know Ayna is alive. At least she might have a chance to survive.

I stifle a groan, having long given up on trying to keep my focus with the constant pain, the shallow breaths that never provide enough air, and the smothering sensation of the *deep sleep* Ephegos injected me with. If Ephegos returned to finish me off, I don't know if I have any fight left in me.

"Wake up." A harsh whisper combined with a slap brings me back from the momentary merciful darkness in my head, and I stare at Herinor's familiar features behind a hand wiggling in front of my face. "How many fingers am I holding up?"

I try to count, but everything swims in the torchlight. He brought a torch—not an everlasting one like in the palace at the Seeing Forest. Those were convenient.

I wonder how my mind is capable of going there when I have more urgent matters right in front of me.

"Fuck off." It comes out weaker than I'd intended.

Herinor laughs. "The correct answer is *three*, but I'll let this one slide since you are obviously not your full self."

Without warning, he grabs the knife in my chest and yanks it out with a sloshy sound that makes me wonder if there'll be any blood left in me if my heart continues pumping it out so frantically.

"Don't faint. We have to get you out of here before they return."

I try to obey, but darkness is already tugging at the edge of my consciousness.

"Myron," Herinor hisses.

My eyes snap open as he presses his hands to my wound, applying his own power to speed up the healing process. He might not be as powerful as me, but he isn't as magically chained as I am right now either, so, for the moment, his healing power outmatches mine by far.

As if in response, my body gathers final resources to help knit my tissues back together.

The pain subsides little by little, but with the urgency of a life-threatening wound to keep me alert, I become even more drowsy.

"You're getting out of here, Myron. Do you hear me? I haven't given up my loyalty to you. Not in the way it counts," he amends because we both know he has made a bargain with Ephegos that won't allow for the same level of loyalty— not where it counts—no matter what his morals say.

"I've never taken you for the sentimental type," I croak, wasting my energy on a lost cause. "I'm not getting out of here, and we both know it."

"A little faith?" He pulls back his hands and tugs on the leather bindings at my wrists, opening them one after the other.

Gods, it feels good to be able to touch my blood-soaked chest—where my battered heart is calling for Ayna like a primal song I have no chance of escaping. It's that thought pushing me to grasp onto the flecks of light dancing along the walls as the torch flickers in the slight draft coming from the open door.

With a soft snapping sound, the leather gives at my ankles, and Herinor grasps my arm, sliding his hand under my shoulder to help me up.

"Can you walk?"

I can't even stand without my legs shaking so violently it feels like I'm weathering an earthquake.

"Guess not." Herinor assesses the situation and leans me back against the table.

Not the table, I try to say, but my mouth is so dry I barely get a sound out.

Herinor seems to understand anyway. With a few efficient movements, he has me slung over his shoulder, grunting under my weight, but never faltering as he marches for the door, torch abandoned by the table covered in my blood.

Ignoring the pain racing through my body as I'm jostled with every step, I close my eyes and pray to our Maker that he'll pave our way out—or gift me a swift end if I'm meant to never see the light of day again.

Ayna, the song inside my chest reminds me.

I keep my eyes open.

Ayna is not the only one I should be thinking of, even when she's all my body and mind want to make space for. I have a cousin and two other males I'm responsible for down there in the dungeon.

"We need to get Royad and Silas out, and Astorian," I remind both Herinor and myself.

"I need to get *you* out first." He doesn't slow when we pass the door leading to the cells where the others are locked up, oblivious. "Now, shut up so I can focus. If you do, I promise I will kneel to you when you're out and coherent and have your queen by your side once more."

There is no mocking in his words, no sarcasm. I think he means it.

My fae senses rush ahead to distract myself from the constant agony of being hauled around the uneven corridors of the royal Tavrasian dungeon. If this is supposed to be a normal prison, I don't want to know what Fort Perenis is like, where Ayna spent months awaiting her fate.

A shudder rakes through my body, and power rises in my blood, the first hint of it since the Flames captured us. Gods, how could I have been so naive? How could I not have seen that Ephegos would know I was alive? He used all the assets he could get his fingers on to trap me.

The corridor ends in a set of winding stairs. My head hits the rough stone wall. Herinor doesn't apologize. A head wound and a concussion are nothing compared to what I've been through.

"Not far," he mutters, breath labored as if my weight is actually affecting him. "Try your best not to draw attention to yourself."

A painful chuckle bubbles down my throat, and I swallow it. "Hard not to while draped over your Shaelak-damned shoulder," I retort, pulling myself slightly to the left so his bones stop digging into my barely healed wound.

"My Shaelak-damned shoulder will save your royal ass." Herinor was never one for court protocol and courtesies, but, gods, he's taking the whole *don't-give-a-shit* attitude to a whole new level, given the circumstances. "Now shut up and pretend you're dead."

While it's easy to just dangle down someone's back when you're physically intact, what people tend to forget is that fresh injuries will keep you from relaxing enough to pass for deceased. I do my best anyway, biting back the grunts of pain as I drop my arms, my shoulders protesting when they tug on the bruises spreading along my sides. And the knife wounds crisscrossing along my skin… I'm not even going to mention those because they are not Herinor's fault. No matter how he failed to remain loyal to me, he wasn't the one slicing into my skin over and over.

My healing powers will slowly take care of those.

A door blocks our path, and Herinor stops, unlocking it with one hand while he keeps the other one on my legs to keep me from sliding off. Then he's moving again, swiftly and with determination.

"Why?" I whisper as we get to the end of another hallway where he stops yet again to unlock a more elaborate door.

"Because I'm forbidden from helping her," he snaps in a hiss, adjusting me so I don't slide off his shoulders. "So I need to help you instead. Now shut up."

I do. I'm quiet as we make it through an empty hallway that leads us from the dungeon, Herinor's steps slower than I know what he's capable of without carrying an extra weight, then past a set of windows with a view of lush gardens. Herinor doesn't stop until he gets to a plain wooden door, where he fiddles with a lock while my heart races at the sound of footsteps approaching in the distance. Not so far distance… They are just around the corner, and we barely make it into the narrow pathway before they make it around the corner.

Herinor braces his hand against the wall, controlling his breathing as he patiently waits for them to pass.

Their voices are hushed, but my fae senses are alert, picking up every single word.

"Lord Ephegos ordered for an additional set of guards in the hallway on the third floor," one of them says. "I wonder if something happened with King Erina's betrothed."

"He wants to make sure no one steals her away in the night," the other guard responds, his tone annoyed enough to inform me of what he thinks of the King's choice.

My stomach tightens at the mere thought of anyone finding Ayna unworthy of anything, and I almost leap off Herinor's shoulder, but the sharp pain in my side reminds me why I'm up here.

"Did you hear what happened in the throne room?"

The guard with the deeper voice makes a noncommittal sound, so the other one explains. "Apparently, the king had an additional guest invited to his table. A stranger no one knows anything about. They say he needed Katrijanov to keep the guy in check."

"Why would he invite a dangerous man to his table?"

"Not just any man... A fairy."

"A fairy?" The shock is obvious in the man's voice.

"One of the prisoners, I assume. I heard rumors he has someone down there. Some fairies he's been experimenting on. Maybe it was his way of showing his new bride he has the power to defeat even a magical kingdom. What a king..."

I block out the rest of the conversation in order not to make a mistake and let my rage take over. If that's what people think, they are closer to the truth than they actually know. Erina is working on weapons to defeat fairies. He has managed the first steps, all he needs is to make the process faster so he can produce larger amounts. If he achieves that, Askarea is fucked.

I blow out a slow breath. At least, no one guessed who I am. Certainly, Erina didn't advertise Ayna is already married to the King of Crows. That would make it a lot harder to lay claim to her.

It takes me all I have not to growl at the thought of him even wanting to lay claim to her.

"Easy," Herinor whispers, shaming my primal fae side into silence while I stop myself from moving.

We weave through dark hallways, Herinor's steps steady while my strength is fading even when I'm free and the drugs should be wearing off with time. My body is at its limits.

But my mind is not. It's racing like a Crow mid-flight when we turn the corner and Herinor abruptly stops, almost letting me slip from his shoulder. His hands circle my leg as he holds me in place, and my head hits the wall all over again. I try not to notice the pain and remain as still as a corpse, the way Herinor told me to, not that I care for following anyone's orders—only when they make sense, and Herinor made a point.

"Where are you going?" a deep male voice demands. I don't recognize it.

Herinor shifts his weight to hide my torso from the man, moving me a bit higher on his shoulder, his bones digging into my ribs.

By the time he responds, my lower lip is bleeding from biting it to hold in a grunt. "Disposing of a prisoner who didn't make it," Herinor says matter-of-factly, probably featuring his signature grumpy face that will scare off anyone lesser than a powerful Crow. "You know how the general likes the dungeon clean of any traces of..." He pauses as if waiting for the other man to fill in the rest of the thought and, when he doesn't, continues, "Of what they do down there with them."

There is some mumbled agreement, then feet shuffle aside, and a door swings open. Herinor rolls me over so I'm draped over both shoulders instead of dangling down his back, and I swear I'll hurt him for how ungently he handles me, no matter if he's the one getting me out into the sweet, humid night air.

"Soon," Herinor grumbles. "Just a bit more patience. I'll set you down soon."

"I'll hold you to that promise," I murmur, words weak from pain and exhaustion.

Herinor musters a small chuckle. "I know you will. Trust me, I'm counting the heartbeats 'til I can set you down." He pauses, taking a long step across a segment of uneven ground, thoughtful and out of breath. "And you'll probably have my head for my betrayal. Perhaps that will be a mercy."

I'm not ready to respond to that. Even knowing how he's chosen Ephegos's side before, I'm not sure I have it in me to kill him for treason the way I would easily kill Ephegos if given the chance.

Not true... I have it in me to kill without remorse if the situation demands it. I did so for a hundred years, watching my brides die one after the other; even when I wasn't the one to kill them, I was still the reason for their death. I'm not any better than Herinor when it comes to the amount of blood on my hands.

For a while, he strides in silence, his heavy breaths the only tell he's struggling as we follow a gravel path toward a pit where I assume they dispose of real deceased prisoners. Instead of throwing me in, he ducks past the narrow wall shielding it from one side, and crouches, rolling me onto the cobbled ground on the other side of the wall.

I can't help the groan of pain as my shoulder hits the stone, and I sag in a heap of weak bones and shredded flesh.

"You've seen better days, Myron." Herinor studies from above, sweat beading his forehead and scar-flecked face unreadable the way I remember him.

"If you believe putting me out of my misery will save you, now would be your chance." I hold his gaze, ignoring the way my healing power strains to catch up with all the injuries, visible and hidden.

Herinor's chin dips, the light-brown scruff on his chin shimmering in the moonlight as he draws his blade—correction: one of his many, many blades—but instead of slitting my throat, he lays it down next to my head like an offering.

"I believed in your way, Myron. I truly did, or I wouldn't have guarded Ayna for you—in the Seeing Forest and now. But I wasn't patient enough to wait for you to succeed. I lost faith. With trusting Ephegos and following him, I lost all hope for a place in your court, I understand that." His features turn grim as, overhead, a cloud shifts in front of the silver moon. I try not to interrupt the male as he pours out his heart while I decide what to do with him—not that I can do anything much with the way my body still needs to recover. If I kill him, it will be because he allows it, not because I could possibly outmatch him in the state I'm in. "I understand if I'm too big a risk to take with the bargain I made with Ephegos. I understand if you need to dispose of me before I can cause actual damage."

"You don't call what you've already done damage?" I interject, my dark chuckle turning into a cough, and Herinor flinches.

"We need to get you to safety before they start looking for you." His eyes snap to the corner where the wall turns into a dark alley framed by run-down houses.

"We need to fucking get Ayna out of the palace. And Royad and Silas and Astorian," I bite out. My head is clearing up enough in the fresh breeze carrying in from the seaside to think straight. "If Ayna is still in the palace, there is no way I'm leaving."

"I know." Herinor shakes his head as if he doesn't, but I see in his eyes that he understands better than anyone why I can't leave without her. "She's with Clio and … a friend."

My heart thuds wildly, defying gravity as it forces me to roll to the side and push into a sitting position, ready to shove to my feet and run in whichever direction Herinor points me. I know it's stupid to trust anyone with the many betrayals that have led me to this point, but I can't help it. My shoulder tingles where the tattoo is etched into my skin, heat creeping through my arm, and the heaviness falls away long enough to grab the male's collar in an actual threat as my other hand grasps his knife and sets it to his throat.

Herinor doesn't flinch now. "Since I can't help her directly, I made sure she had all the help she could get." The look he gives me is nothing if not convincing. "If things went according to plan, she should be not far from here, recovering and safe."

My entire body is tensed to strike, fingers still like the dead as they keep the knife under his chin, ready to slice into his skin at the sign of the slightest lie. "I swear, if you're lying, I'll make sure they can't decipher which male's corpse they've found." The malice in my voice has nothing to do with the fear for my own safety. It's all for my mate. My fucking beautiful *mate*, who I will die to see free. And I will take down anyone in my path, friend or foe, to protect her.

"Put off killing me a little longer, and I'll take you to the meeting point." Herinor's gaze is full of acceptance for whatever choice I'll make. The tug in my shoulder might very well drag me across the entire city without his help to where she's hiding.

I shake my head. "It's not like there are many Crows left in this world—fewer even whom I can trust. You got me out of the palace. Now, take me to her, and prove that you got her out, too."

THIRTY-FIVE

AYNA

Wrapping my arms around my stomach, I retch into a corner for what feels like the hundredth time. Nothing is coming up anymore, but that doesn't keep my system from rebelling.

"Another few hours and you should be good," Kaira chirps from her place by the window where she has a clear view of the street and the yard. "If you only ate a few pieces of bread, your body should have processed most of it and will be clean by sunrise."

"Sunrise sounds like a year away," Clio croaks, yielding groans and grunts alongside her dinner in the other corner as the detoxification process sets in for her as well. "I don't know how anyone can develop an instrument of torture such as that drug. Not even a fairy wine hangover is that bad."

"That's because you're a fairy," Kaira points out. "I've vomited for hours because of that draught you call wine."

"Hey, you're a fairy, too." Clio buries her face in her hands as she waits for the next wave to hit her.

"Barely. I have but a spark of fire." Kaira glances at the darkening sky. I can see it from my place on the dirt floor, and it mirrors the way I feel.

"Don't forget the mind reading," Clio reminds us all, and Kaira shoots me a look that I can only interpret as punishing.

"You didn't need to tell her," she says into my mind, tone laced with a sort of hurt I hadn't believed the female capable of.

"I told her because she is my friend and our ally. You were already sharing all the personal details in front of her." I don't mean it to sound like an accusation, but with the constant nausea, it comes out that way. *"Sister. I would have preferred not to have that sprung on me on a flight from a hostile palace."*

Kaira's eyes flash in the silvery light glimpsing through the clouds. *"I always wondered what it would be like to have a sibling. Now I know everyone was right."*

"What did everyone say?" I shoot quietly, wondering how long it will take Clio this time to catch onto us having a mental conversation.

"That I'll know what it's like to hate someone and love them at the same time." She turns back to the window.

"And what is that like?" Because I don't love her right now. All I feel is frustration and the ache in my head that is becoming a throb.

"The best feeling in the world." I think Kaira's mouth curves into a smile, but I can't be certain with the next assault of nausea making me dry-heave, hand braced on the crate beside me so I don't slump into the puddle of vomit.

Aloud, she says, "If I understood what Ephegos and Erina are doing correctly, there are two types of drugs: The magic nullifying ones like the *deep sleep* and the basic one that I had to put in your food every day."

Clio moans at the mention of the *deep sleep*. "They injected me with that one so often I'm not sure my powers will ever return. But they gave me the basic one as well... The one that takes out our fairy senses, too."

Kaira nods. "You truly got the short end of the stick here."

I'm less surprised by Kaira's acknowledgement of Clio's pain than by Clio's acceptance of it, at the brief smile they share before Clio returns to spitting bile.

"Then there is the antidote that lifts the effects of the drug. The one they gave you, Ayna." Her face doesn't show a sign of our silent conversation from before as she meets my gaze, but her eyes do. The softness there has nothing to do with the warrior I met that first day at the Flame estate. "You really should be fine soon."

"Did that one turn me into a Crow?" I can't help asking even when it sounds ridiculous.

Clio shakes her head. "I don't think there is any substance capable of turning you into something you aren't already."

"Truth." Kaira is quick to agree. Too quick, and I groan in frustration as another surge of nausea hits.

"How do you know?" I demand after breathing through the assault, forcing my stomach to keep it in since there is nothing left to expel.

Kaira's cheeks turn darker—or it might have been the clouds pulling tighter. "Herinor and I have a theory."

"A theory?" I prompt, unable to muster the patience I'd usually have for someone who's already in the middle of explaining.

"Let the female speak," Clio interjects, and of course, she's right.

"So, the theory," she says with a sideways glance at the fairy, never pulling her attention from the streets for longer than a few breaths, "is that you've been a Crow for a while."

My mouth opens then closes, no words spilling from my tongue even when I have a million thoughts about how that's impossible.

Welcome to the world of the fae, Ephegos had said. Not as in, welcome to a new world, but welcome to a world I could finally see now that my senses are cleared of the drug. It makes a painful lot of sense.

"Think about it," she responds to all those thoughts at once, encompassing the main issue. "The antidote took the blanket off your powers and your senses. You started perceiving the world differently—like a fairy."

"Or a Crow," Clio chimes in, getting on board with that theory way faster than I could have imagined.

"Right." Kaira nods, gesturing at me. "The tattoo on your shoulder is a mark of Vala, a reminder of what you did and who you are."

"And who am I?" I'm no longer sure I know.

"The Queen of Crows, breaker of the curse, and chosen by the Crow King," Kaira recites as if she's been studying these lines for exactly this moment. "Or, in other words, Myron's mate."

"We already know that," Clio interrupts, her patience spread as thin as mine. "Get to the interesting part."

"Herinor believes Vala wasn't the only one involved in the mercy of bringing Myron back from the dead."

I don't breathe because it's easier not to get sick from the stench of my own vomit all over again if I don't. And I can't miss a word.

"He thinks, as their maker, Shaelak might have been involved in creating the marks on both your shoulders and gifting you more than just a mate."

Herinor's words come back to me in a flash. *Vala gave you a mate to fight for. Shaelak gave you wings to match his. Now go and fly, little bird.*

He didn't mean that metaphorically. He meant it literally.

"Herinor thinks Shaelak made me a Crow?" The disbelief is hard to hide.

"Herinor has been alive long enough to know the gods interfere rarely, but when they do, things are brutal and final. But if a deity deems you worthy, they will grant you something to mark you theirs as well."

"Water magic from Vala," Clio says with a nod as if it's the most logical thing in the world.

"And Crow wings from Shaelak," Kaira adds. "You redeemed his creatures and saved them from Vala's curse. It's his way of thanking you."

"By making me one of them?" I am suddenly cold, shaking like a little child waking from a nightmare. It might be the drug or the news or both.

"By making you Myron's equal," Kaira corrects, much to Clio's chagrin, because the female whirls around on her knees, baring her teeth at Kaira in the first real fairy move I've seen her make since the battle in the Seeing Forest.

"Don't for a second try to make her feel like she was ever any less than his equal. Ayna was *born* his equal. Survived hardship just like he has." Green fire flares in her eyes. "She fucking *saved* him. Saved his entire people by deeming him worthy of her love." Her fingers curl at her sides. "If anyone was made anyone's equal, it is *him*."

Not daring to speak, to even move at such a display of fierce loyalty, I hold my breath as I wait for Kaira to respond.

The part-Flame blows out a breath. "I wish I had friends like you, Clio. I'd never again feel like I'm worthless."

That takes Clio off guard, and her anger cracks, turning into something different—not pity but a warmth I haven't seen in her before. "Don't betray us, and you might."

Kaira smiles, and so does Clio. Nausea hits, and I vomit on the floor right between them.

So, I'm a Crow... Not that it matters. Nothing does as long as we get back our magic and retrieve the males before anyone can notice we're gone. Rather than bemoaning what seems to be a fact, I grab the canteen Kaira placed beside me and rinse my mouth before gulping down a few swallows.

By the time the first droplets of rain fall from the dense clouds covering the sky outside, I've curled up by the side of the stack of crates near the center of the room and closed my eyes. I don't wake until Clio's and Kaira's whispers drift into my consciousness.

"Where do you think you got your mind reading from? Mother or father?" Clio asks. Something rustles as if the female is sitting next to Kaira by the window.

"Since my mother wasn't magical, it has to be my father. He never said anything though."

"Sometimes it jumps generations." Clio's tone is wistful even when she's lowered her voice to nearly inaudible.

"Do you read minds?" It's bold of Kaira to ask, but by now, I'm used to her being straightforward and unafraid.

Clio's quiet laugh fills the room like a memory of better days. "No. But I know someone who does. It's an annoying power," she amends. "If I ever see him again, I'll ask him to help you learn to control it."

The pounding in my head, combined with exhaustion, drags me back to sleep before Kaira's whispered response fills the room, and I welcome the darkness. It's a place where worry and pain don't torment me. A place where I can summon images of a Myron without bruises and cuts covering his skin. A place where no magic is holding me back when I touch him. A place where Erina doesn't exist, or tomorrow. Just us.

His scent fills my nose, earth and moss and brine weaving together in a texture I want to use as a blanket as I nestle deeper into my dream where his form becomes near tangible. My shoulder tingles as I murmur his name, the sensation like a summoning, but I'm too exhausted to follow, so I hold onto it, relishing the sense of connection where pain and silence dominated for so long.

I'll get him out. A few hours of rest and I'll be ready to get him out.

Reality rushes back to me much faster than I'd hoped when a pair of hands pins me to the ground so hard the breath is stolen from my lungs. My eyes fly open, and I find myself staring at endless, fathomless wrath.

THIRTY-SIX

AYNA

A tapestry of rain and wind tunes out the whispers in the corner before it's swallowed by the ravaging pace of my drumming heart.

"Ayna—" His voice is breathless, his eyes wild, his lips pulled back in a snarl.

And my heart. Fucking. Shatters. As I realize I'm not about to die at the hand of the male hovering over me. At the look in his eyes as he assesses my face as if he can't believe I'm here, whole.

"Ayna," he repeats, softer this time. A whisper. A plea.

"Myr—"

His lips crash down on mine in a brutal kiss before I can finish his name, and the world around us vanishes—simply ceases to exist. Energy rushes from the place our mouths touch, thundering through my veins, my bones, until all I can feel is the warmth and the darkness coiling within me—his warmth, his darkness. Or my own. It's hard to tell when I no longer know what we are, where we are, who we are. All I know is that he's here and I can feel his breath on my skin and his heartbeat against mine. For a moment, there is no past and no future. There isn't even a present. It's him and me, and we're eternal, starting at the point where his fingers graze the bare skin at my collar and where his mouth tastes mine.

It's everything and nothing like I remember him because it's not just his touch that sets me ablaze; it's the sensation of him settling in my tissues. One single touch—one kiss—and I'll never be the same. I thought I was ruined before—from trauma and loss and pain—but it's this moment—this earth-shattering kiss that is my undoing.

I have the vague idea that there was someone else in this room with us, that we're not in my dream, but that's about as far as my mind gets when I'm about to drown in the sensation of his kiss, of his mouth molding over mine, his tongue flicking against my lower lip as his hand releases one shoulder to fist my hair.

Opening for him, I savor the slide of his tongue against mine, the heat of his body where he half-covers me on the floor.

"Ayna," he murmurs between kisses as they turn softer as if he's starting to believe I'm real, that he is truly kissing

me while I'm still unsure if I've ever left my dream. "Ayna
… Ayna."

"Fucking pull yourselves together," Herinor's harsh voice
sounds from nearby, kicking me out of the blissful moment
of surprise and instant, desperate want for the male whose
mouth won't leave mine. "I'd like to keep my dinner down,
thank you very much."

Myron ignores him, ignores Kaira and Clio, who are
shadows at the edges of my vision. In my shoulder, a zing-
ing sensation replaces the tingling, almost like it's aching
for skin contact.

It's that thought that brings me back to reality, making
me pull away an inch while groaning my frustration as cool
night air replaces the heat of his breath on my face.

"You're alive." I take in his face, bringing my hand up
to cup his cheek where a bruise was blooming the last time
I saw him.

On a table—he'd been strapped to a fucking torture table.

"As are you." His fingers skim my cheekbone as he slides
his arm under my shoulder and pulls me against him as he
kneels. "There are two options, and I'm only polite enough
to say this because Herinor saved my life." His voice is a
growl, his eyes darkening, tracing my mouth with a gaze so
intense I feel it like a touch. In response, my stomach tightens. "You all get out of here now, or I'll take my mate out
into the rain. I don't care as long as I get a minute with her
before we face the rest of this crisis."

I'm surprised he hasn't kicked them out with his
magic—then I remember his powers must still be deep

asleep from the effects of the drug Ephegos injected him with.

There's not one trace left of the panicked male from the dungeon, not one hint of weakness, only pure male rage contained behind those eyes as he seems to be counting to ten in his head, waiting for their response.

Rage, as his fingers brush the inside of my elbow where a needle pierced my skin, the sensitive inside of my wrist where leather straps locked me in place.

"Outside," I whisper before he gets a chance to explode and take out his fury on those who aided his escape instead of the monsters who deserve it. "Let's go outside."

Myron has me scooped up in his arms before I can finish speaking, his hard chest pressing into my side, and I don't even think to struggle. Safe. I'm safe with him. Safe with this terrifying version of him.

He doesn't stop until we're on the threshold where he shoots a warning over his shoulder. "I don't care who watches, but don't hold me accountable for what you see."

His nostrils flare as his gaze locks on mine, pupils blown out until the whole irises seem to be swallowed up by darkness.

A flicker of fear floods my system as we step into the rain, Myron's hair tangling around his head with every stride he takes into the small garden framing the yard. The wind whips wet strands in all directions, making him even more beautiful in an untamed way that promises I'm right to be afraid. Not afraid of him but that he'll let go of me and vanish the way a dream dissolves into the harsh reality of pain.

There is no pain now, only the pulsing need to be close to him, to breathe him in and taste him on my tongue. To drown in everything he is and ever will be. My body remembers too well what it's like to be with him, the way his kisses set me aflame and his touch has me moaning.

This is different. More intense in a way that makes my world narrow to the primal need pulsing in my veins. I hardly recognize myself. Every breath is a yearning, every heartbeat incomplete until it matches his.

As if summoned by a silent call, my hand slides up his arm to his shoulder where the tattoo lies bare and washed clean by the pouring sky.

This is Myron. This is my mate. And touching him feels. So. Good. As my fingers graze the inked lines at the edge of his biceps. He stops in his tracks, every muscle in his body going taut as his eyes snap to mine.

"If you do that, I won't be able to tell you how much I missed you, how much I loathed every moment we were separated. I won't be able to kiss you gently and confess my love for you, my need to tie my soul to yours. I won't be able to tell you how sorry I am that I wasn't there to save you."

My fingers stop right where the first line of night-black ink swirls across his skin. "What will you do instead?" I can't get a breath down my throat as I try to read the wrath in his eyes—not for me but for Erina and Ephegos and Katrijanov. For everyone who hurt me.

His lids lower until all I can see are two silken half-moons of black lashes, and he blows out a breath, arms tightening around my shoulders and under my knees.

"I'll lay you down on that patch of grass and fuck you mindless, Ayna."

My heart leaps into my throat, heat melting my core while he holds himself in place, giving me the option— talk or…

"We can always talk later." I bite my lip, keeping myself from licking a trail of rain from the side of his throat. Guardians—that scent mixed with fresh rain, all signs of blood and pain washed away from his flawless skin…

Relief floods me like a drug of its own, and want—

I press my knees together, already mindless at the mere look of him resisting the primal calling that is the bond between us.

Inhaling him, I drag my finger over the curve of the tattooed bird … and nearly scream at the surge of heat flooding my body. Not the burning kind that makes you cringe but the pleasurable one that makes you arch into the sensation. Myron groans low in his throat, his body quivering against mine.

"Talk later," he agrees, already marching for the corner of the yard farthest away from the shed, where a wall blocks the view of the street and small trees and bushes promise a modicum of privacy. My shirt gets caught on a branch as he squeezes past a bush and lowers himself to his knees on the wet grass. His eyes hold mine captive for a long, breathless moment as my hand glides up the curve of his neck, spearing into his hair, wet silk, smooth and soft.

I don't know if all of the drug has left his system, but I can sense my own magic trickling back in as if it's been waiting for this moment to make an appearance.

Myron sets down my legs, brushing back strands of my hair, and I take the opportunity to straddle him, wrapping both arms around him as he brings his mouth to mine in a brandishing kiss. The taste of him—I moan against his lips, greedy for more, for all of him. Rain drenches our clothes, our hair, trickling down our faces, but the heat between us turns it into steam. I reach for his bare chest, tracing the edges and grooves of his muscles, and he moans my name like a prayer, like speaking it will save him. The sound turns me to liquid, making me arch into him until my breasts are pressed against his chest, our bodies flush, and he splays his fingers on the small of my back, pulling me tighter against him.

Sweet pressure builds in my core at the feel of his strength, at the hardness of his body against my curves. The buttons of his pants rub along my core, but they aren't what makes me squirm with delight. It's the steel length of him contained beneath that makes the friction so delicious.

"Gods, I've been dreaming of this moment." His tone is gravelly, proof of how hard he's fighting to not just tear my clothes off and bury his cock inside of me.

I want him to. I want every inch of him inside of me, want to feel the pulsing heat of him straining against my tightening core.

His hands slide to my ass, rocking my hips against him. It's not enough. It's never enough.

As if sensing my desperation for more, he removes one hand, running it up my side to my breast where my soaked shirt clings to my skin.

"So beautiful," he whispers, kissing his way down the side of my neck, following the line to the base of my throat, and my body sings at each touch like it's been ignited by something hotter than fire. Something more eternal than those torches lighting the palace in the Seeing Forest.

His fingers circle my nipple, teasing and swirling over the coarse linen of the wet fabric covering it, each touch too intense and not intense enough all at once. I'm going to combust if I can't get my hands on him.

Leaning into his arm, I give him better access, savoring each graze of his lips as I reach between our hips to unbutton his pants and moan with delight when his teeth scrape over my shoulder right above the tattoo.

"I need to see it." His voice catches as he glances up and our gazes lock, my hands stilling where they were starting to tug on the buttons of his pants.

My mind is so thoroughly blank I can't fathom what he's talking about, but his eyes lower to my shoulder where my shirt covering me is near transparent with rain.

"The mark," he explains, fingers sliding to the collar of my shirt as if in question. "Herinor told me you have one in the exact same spot as I do." His hand releases me to reach for his own shoulder, and I instantly bemoan the loss of his touch.

"Turn around." His grasp is gentle as he places his hands on my hips, lifting me from his lap and placing me in front of him on the grass. The wall beside me is made of roundish rocks and held together with mortar and moss; the bushes to the side block the view of the abandoned house, and behind us, the shed is far enough away for the rain to drown our conversation with its relentless fall.

Myron waits for me to do as he requested or deny him, his gaze burning like the best possible fire as he scans every inch of me, the outline of my curves where my shirt sticks to my body, the wet hair sliding over my shoulder as I pull it aside to tug my shirt down before I turn to the side, exposing my shoulder.

His soft gasp runs through me like a delicate touch, like the brine coasting along the deck of a ship, teasing the sails before catching on and pulling them into motion. I can feel his eyes scanning the black lines running from below my neck to the side of my shoulder, feel his hunger through our connection like it's my own.

"More," he says, tone near reverent, and I know the shirt needs to go, or neither of us will find peace.

He needs to see all of it, all of me, just like I need to see all of him. See every inch of skin to assess the degree of violence I want to rain down on every last creature who hurt him.

I'm far from graceful as I pull up my shirt, trying to convince it to slide up my torso in an attempt to remove it, my fingers clumsy and my patience nonexistent. Myron's hands catch mine in a gentle grasp, arms circling my waist as he stops me mid-motion, fingers sliding around mine as he carefully, painstakingly slowly pulls the fabric up, up, up. Until my head slides free, then my arms, my hands.

My hair flops down between my shoulder blades with a smack, sending rivers of rain down the small of my back, and my breath catches as he follows the trail down the length of my spine all the way to the waistband of my pants and back up again, veering to the side. To the shoulder with the inked bird.

The first touch of his finger to the swirling lines that are the tattooed feathers sends a shiver through my entire body. A tremble that doesn't seem to want to stop.

"Ayna—" Myron's breath warms the skin at the base of my neck as he slides my hair aside, kissing his way along the column of my spine, careful not to touch the black lines. At first. Then, his mouth brushes the side of the bird, and I could swear the wings flutter—or it's my heart that foolishly speeds in my chest like there is no tomorrow. His tongue swirls over the center of the mark, and I cry out, bowing my head to give him better access. Myron's growl reverberates through my body, setting my core aflame with desperate need.

I can't wait-can't wait-can't wait another moment to touch him, so I reach behind me, finding the side of his stomach first, then dropping my hand to his knee where his leather pants cling to his form. He hisses as I slide higher on the inside of his thigh, right along the seam of his pants until I'm back to the buttons. Myron catches my hand for a moment of frustration during which he makes up for it by licking the rain off my skin along the outline of the inked bird, and Guardians be damned, it's nearly enough to make me forget I was reaching for his cock. But I remember... Oh, I remember the moment the sound of metal sliding through leather informs me he took it upon himself to open his pants, and he pushes up his hips a few inches as he sets my hand to the top of him.

My fingers tighten on instinct, eliciting a deep moan from Myron as his free hand circles my chest, skating my breast until he finds my peaked nipple, teasing and taunting while his mouth wanders back up the side of my neck.

His other hand frees mine, reaching between my thighs, and I spread them in response, desperate for any touch of his, even the slightest friction he can provide through my soaked pants.

And Guardians, does he know where to touch me. My core spasms as his fingers skim my center, brushing up so lightly I want to complain that he should stop teasing me, but before I get a word out, his hands find my hip and shoulder, and I'm spun around and put flat on my back. Myron hovers over me, one hand braced on each side of my shoulders, wet hair framing his face as he assesses me with predatory intent, gaze tracking my face, bare breasts, my stomach, down to my pants, which he somehow managed to untie. And my treacherous eyes linger on his lips only for a heartbeat before they wander down to where his knees rest between my thighs.

His mouth crashes down on mine, and this time, he doesn't intend to let me go the way he did in the shed; he doesn't give me a choice—because we both have made it already. We chose each other over everything else. This moment that belongs to us alone while the world may go to shit around us.

With one hand, he peels me out of my pants while his tongue expertly slides against mine, exploring my mouth. Sharp teeth graze my lower lip as he nips and sucks, devouring me in breathless, desperate kisses that I will never get enough of. But it's the push of his hard length against my entrance that has me losing control. I need him inside of me now—

Thank the Guardians, Myron truly meant what he said because he doesn't hesitate as he sheaths himself inside of me with one long thrust, filling me inch by glorious inch until I can't think, until the rain becomes a sensuous lick against my skin, the grass beneath me a million kisses, and as he starts moving… The way he stretches me with each slow, relentless thrust draws moan after moan from my throat, and he devours them all like that proof of what he's doing to me, of what he's capable of making me feel, belongs only to him. Like *I* belong only to him. And in this moment, I do. With body and soul. With everything I am and ever will be, I belong to him.

Pleasure coils low in my belly, spreading with every time he slams in to the hilt. He isn't cautious with me the way he was before the curse broke, and I don't want him to be. I want—I *need*—to feel his strength, his power, need to feel that he's alive. And that he's *mine.*

I buck my hips to take him deeper, and his growl of approval nearly sends me tumbling over the edge, but it wouldn't be Myron if he didn't have a modicum of control even in a life-changing moment like this. He slows the pace, drawing out my pleasure as I teeter along a cliff of unknown depth. I'm not afraid because he's here to catch me—or to fall and shatter with me.

"My Ayna," Myron murmurs between kisses, and his words spread through me like a gushing river, driving out the desperation as they sear the flesh beneath my tattoo.

His mouth covers mine as he thrusts into me, tongue meeting mine in a practiced dance. My legs tremble as he grabs my thighs, pulling them up for a deeper angle, and I splinter. It hits with the force of a tidal wave, turning me into a whimpering, quivering bundle as I climax around him, nails biting into his shoulder where his tattoo seems to come alive in swirling lines on the edge of his biceps. Spots of bright light dance at the edge of my vision, and I think I might black out from the onslaught of sensations, but Myron is right there, his arms gathering me up as he sits back on his haunches, driving even deeper as he prolongs my pleasure to what feels like an eternity.

"Myron—" I want to say I don't know what. Every last word has been wiped from my thoughts, leaving me exactly what he promised—mindless.

But it's enough to push him over the edge, his thrusts picking up pace as his control slips, and he finds his release with a primal groan that runs through me like a bolt of lightning from the sensitive flesh that are my peaked breasts to the apex of my thighs and deep into my core, almost making me climax all over again. His arms crash me against his chest as he shudders inside of me, burying his face at the base of my throat, every hot breath proof that he's real, that he's alive. That we both are.

"My Crow," I whisper as he lifts his head, gaze locking on mine with the intensity of a storm-tossed ocean, and a smile forms on his mouth, stealing my breath all over again.

THIRTY-SEVEN

MYRON

Forcing myself to let go of Ayna might be the hardest thing I've ever done.

Her rain-slick skin invites me to explore her, her scent beckoning like a flowerbed after breaking free from an eternal winter. And her eyes—

Her eyes might be the most beautiful thing in the universe as she gazes up at me, glazed with the aftereffects of pleasure. I don't dare look lower than her face because, if I do, I won't be able to stop myself from worshiping every inch of her until the world ends. On my shoulder, my tattoo resonates as if in agreement, and the way Ayna keeps eyeing me gives me ideas that she wouldn't object to.

From the distance, a faint grumble of thunder reminds me that even though I've finally claimed my mate, the world isn't waiting for us to be done. For now, the memories we just made have to be enough.

"You two done over there, or are you going a second round?" Herinor's shout tells me we weren't as quiet as I'd hoped. At least, the bushes block us from view. And even if they hadn't, I would have fucked Ayna in the middle of the throne room and not cared, just to ease that need to claim her. Of course, Ayna can never know how weak I am when it comes to her. I may defy my enemies, withstanding pain and torture, but one look from her and I'm on my knees.

"Shut up, and pray I won't tear your head off," I growl as I reluctantly lift Ayna off me and pick up my soaked pants and shirt.

The way her lips curve at my retort tells me she has ideas of her own, and they have little to do with anyone's head but that of my cock. Gods, I need to get my thoughts under control, or I'll go into battle hard like marble.

Taking a few deep breaths, I decide that I'd better get used to it and tug up my own pants, buttoning them with a grimace before helping Ayna into her shirt. Her tattoo is visible through the wet fabric, the outline darker than before.

"We should get back inside," she says, brushing back her hair as she leans closer as if pulled by gravity. My hand finds the side of her waist on instinct, guiding her to my left so my sword arm is free even when I don't have a blade to wield and no opponent to wield it on.

"We can't get any more soaked," I point out. Not that it matters.

She glances down her front then at my chest, and my breath catches as she leans in and places a single kiss right above my heart. "The others are waiting for us."

I'm not sure I imagine the blush darkening her cheeks as she starts walking—and my feet follow without a thought. I go where she goes. That's my new credo.

When we make it to the shed, Herinor is waiting by the door, eyebrows raised and his hand on his sword like he's expecting to find Ephegos on the other side of the splintered wood instead of his king and queen. My arm tightens around Ayna's waist, and I wish I had a shirt to offer her to layer atop hers so her curves would remain hidden from Herinor, whose gaze has dropped for a heartbeat before remembering that this is *my* mate he's staring at. But she doesn't flinch under his scrutiny. She owns her almost nakedness in a way that makes me adore her even more.

At my warning glare, Herinor steps aside, leading the way to the back corner where Clio and the Flame he called Kaira are sitting on turned-over wooden crates, heads tucked together in whispered conversation as if to distract themselves.

The Gods know, we gave them something to need distraction from.

At our approach, their gazes snap up, and I flash them a grin.

I'm not embarrassed—on the contrary, I'm the proudest male alive to call the Crow Queen my own.

"Can you feel your magic?" the Flame asks, shifting into business mode so fast I don't have time to level Herinor with a look as he raises his brows at me again, eyes wandering between Ayna and me. Her boldness instantly makes me like this Kaira. And the fact that she has the broody warrior wrapped around her little finger.

Ignoring the stench of vomit and damp earth that immediately reminds me of the dungeon, I pick up a crate and turn it over for Ayna before sitting down on a second one. "My fae senses are working, my healing power, too. But that's about it." I leave out the magic of the mating bond that keeps tingling as if in reassurance it's still there.

Ayna doesn't respond. Instead, she closes her eyes and takes a deep breath. Droplets of water collect on her skin where it drips and runs from her hair, her shirt, her pants. Opening her palms, she lets the water trickle through her fingers to the floor where it pools in front of her toes. "Some," she eventually answers. "Not enough to drown Ephegos with a spring tide yet, but it's coming back."

A smirk tugs at the corner of my mouth. This is my Ayna, ready to shove her water magic down the traitor's throat.

"We need a plan," Clio is the first to address the actual issue. "We can't just run back to the palace and hope they will not notice when we sneak into the dungeon, assuming you are still helping now that the two of you are reunited."

The fear darkening her eyes matches the urgency in her tone, and there is no doubt the Princess of Askarea will go back alone to rescue her mate if we don't want to.

"Of course, we'll help."

I don't correct Ayna when she speaks for both of us. Royad and Silas are still in captivity as well as Astorian, and we can't delay for a moment longer than absolutely necessary. As soon as Erina notices I'm gone, he'll kill at least the Crows. For Astorian, he has other uses, I've learned. Despicable use that's not so different from the plans he had for me.

"How long until they'll notice we're gone?" I direct the question at Herinor, but it's Kaira who answers.

"They won't realize Clio and I are gone for a while unless they question the guards who let us out of the palace…"

My throat closes up at the thought of them walking out of Erina's home right under the guards' noses. "Guards *let* you out?" Just to be clear I didn't mishear.

Kaira bobs her head. "Long story. We took a servant exit, disguising Ayna as one of us so they'd let her pass. Nothing happened. We're here."

Clamping my mouth shut, I hold in all the retorts I have for her recklessness. "Nothing happened," I grind out, more to convince myself.

Ayna shoots me a sideways glance that has my stomach easing, and her hand drifts into mine. "Nothing happened," she repeats in a whisper, but her heart is beating like she's reliving those moments, and the petrifying panic floating through the bond is enough to send fury charging through my veins all over again.

"Easy, Myron. Kaira was helping Ayna, not trying to get her caught." Herinor places a hand on my unmarked shoulder, squeezing as if with compassion. "You'll get used to seeing threats at every corner. Just remember which ones to attack and which ones to recognize as your allies."

It's his tone that gives me pause, the wistfulness in his green eyes as I glance up at him. There is a story to be told—one which he hasn't chosen to share, though I can sense the weight of it in every word.

"I'm ready to go back as soon as my magic kicks in," I say to Clio. "None of the males deserve to be left behind."

The Askarean princess nods her gratitude, flexing her fingers before her face. "I wish I could do more than form a snowflake or two. It's not enough to break through magic-nullifying cages or fight my way out against an onslaught of palace guards."

"Military," I correct. "The dungeons fall under Katrijanov's reign.

Clio cocks a copper brow in question, and Herinor rushes to explain. "Whatever Erina is up to, there are no palace guards in the dungeon. They all wear military blue and black just like Katrijanov."

Unimpressed by the news, Kaira snaps her fingers, sending tiny sparks to meet the single snowflake Clio has managed to produce. It melts on her fingertip just as she releases it.

"What was that for?" the female snaps with annoyance, earning a shrug from Kaira.

"Trying to see if emotions help bring your magic back faster."

I have to give it to her, it's a smart idea, but judging by the level of emotion I just went through while losing myself in Ayna without regaining even a little of my power, I doubt it has any effect. I don't mention that, though.

Herinor strides to the window, glancing out at the street, and once more, I'm glad this part of the city is mostly abandoned houses. The likelihood of us getting caught is minimal compared to the better quarters of Meer.

"I'll need to head back before Ephegos notices I'm gone," Herinor says, fiddling with the hilt of his knife. Herinor *never* fiddles. "He hasn't forbidden me from helping anyone else, but he might find ways to limit me even more once he notices both of you are gone." He gestures at Ayna and me. "And you—" Then at Kaira, where his eyes linger for a heartbeat longer than they'd normally do. "I'll be looking out for the signal," he adds, a frown forming on his forehead as he inclines his head at the Flame, at Clio, and then bowing at Ayna and me.

Without another word, he shifts into his bird form, inky black feathers eating up his leathers and weapons as he turns and flutters out the broken window.

"What signal?" Ayna asks, and I know with absolute certainty that, while Ayna and I were busy in the rain, the others used the time to make plans of their own.

ANGELINA J. STEFFORT

THIRTY-EIGHT

AYNA

K aira rubs her hands together as if hoping that would bring forth another spark. It's the most magic I've seen her use, that ice-melting flicker of fire, but it's nothing compared to Clio's full powers or mine—I'm not even thinking about what Myron is capable of now that the curse is broken.

The Crow King has been uncharacteristically silent by my side, his fingers twining with mine as he listens to Clio laying out the plan. It's a good one, I have to admit, but if Clio's and Myron's magic continues to recover at this rate, everyone we want to rescue might long be dead by the time we make it into the palace.

"I got the servant uniforms; I can get the military ones," Kaira says with conviction when I question her for the fourth time. "I got you out of the palace. Trust me to get you back in."

"Trust me to want to help," is what Kaira says through our mental connection, while Clio is debating the merits of merely cutting down a military patrol in the streets and stripping off their uniforms.

"I do trust you," I reassure her through that same connection. Aloud, I say, "If I could shift and fly in, would that help?"

Myron's hand tightens around mine. We haven't addressed my Crow form in his presence, so for him, this is the first time he has heard it from my mouth. It still feels like a lie to me.

"*Can* you shift at will?" he asks instead of telling me that I shouldn't, that it's too dangerous, that I'm too inexperienced. His eyes meet mine, ocean-blue shadowed by the rainy night. I spot every streak of light in his irises anyway, my fae senses enabling me to perceive the world in such detail it almost becomes overbearing.

"I haven't tried."

He nods in encouragement as if expecting me to do it then and there.

"Is it wise? What if I can't shift back?" The moments of confusion when I shifted for the first time come back to me, the surreal scope of the world from up high beneath the ceiling.

Bracing a forearm on a knee, he studies me intently. "Considering we're planning to break into the King of Tavras's dungeon to retrieve three males from captivity while neither of us is in top form, wisdom has long left this discussion."

Clio huffs a chuckle, which Myron pointedly ignores.

"We all know you for your lack of wisdom, King of Crows," she shoots at him as if he's an inconvenience on her path to free her mate when, in reality, he's the best asset she has.

"Is that so?" Myron's head cocks like in his bird form, muscles flexing down his bare back, and I could swear a shadow flickers along his arm.

"Wasn't it you who traded all hope of breaking a curse for the freedom of one female?" I don't recognize Clio's tone, and I don't appreciate it.

I understand she's worried about Astorian, ready to run to his aid right now, but insulting Myron will not lead anywhere. It won't free the males we've left behind.

"I've done exactly that and worse," he admits, not one hint of pride in his tone. No shame either. "And I'd do it again. For my mate's safety, I'd sacrifice my kingdom. For *my mate's* freedom, I'd sacrifice myself all over again."

"No sacrificing." I stand between them like a buffer absorbing the rising enmity. "It's not his fault Astorian ended up in captivity." It's the only reason I can imagine Clio behaving so openly hostile. She must be blaming him for Tori's misery. "It's not anyone's fault but Ephegos's and Erina's." Those scheming bastards.

"And the Flames," Kaira adds quietly, all heads turning to her as she saves me from having to physically restrain Clio as she hops to her feet, more graceful than a human should be capable of—because her fairy powers are returning. Slowly. But they are.

"Jeseida is the one who worked with Ephegos and Erina on the drug. She's the one who used the Crows the Flames captured to draw magic from their blood."

Her words land like rocks between us, knocking the air from my lungs.

"You knew? You knew what they were giving me all this time?" It's an accusation as much as it's a statement of relief. Knowledge is power, and we need every last bit of information we can get in order to defeat Ephegos because I'm certain that, once we enter the palace, he won't let us go without a fight.

"I'm sorry," Kaira says into my mind. Aloud she says, "I told you I'd been looking for a way to leave the Flames. When Jeseida started working with Ephegos, I realized that the world is bigger than just the Flame estate and the Seeing Forest and our ancient palace that our Matrone so desperately wanted back. Ephegos came with ideas of grandeur that Jeseida wouldn't let go of. A new Flame kingdom, a world where Fairies can no longer annihilate our whole species the way the Crows did when they took the Seeing Forest from us." There is no bitterness in her tone, but it's clear Jeseida would do anything to achieve that goal.

A goal so similar to Ephegos's: Reestablish the Crow Realm.

How those two goals work together without another war, I cannot fathom, and I don't need to. Somehow, Erina got involved, using that substance made of Crow blood to his own advantage—to expand his own realm.

"Exactly," Kaira responds to what she read from my mind, and I don't care, as long as we find a way to stop them.

"Jeseida was the one who captured us," Myron assumes, and Kaira bobs her head.

"If you mean an older Flame with fire-red hair, then yes, that's her."

"She trapped us. Poured that damn drug over us to break down our powers." The horror spreading in my stomach matches the expression on his face.

I sit back on the crate, lacing my fingers with his again to reassure myself he got out, but the thundering of my heart won't ease.

I say the one thing that keeps pushing to the foreground as we sit together, putting our plan together. "This is bigger than just Ephegos's revenge on Myron."

Clio nods then shakes her head. "I don't care how big this is before I have Tori back."

And I cannot blame her. I felt the same way less than an hour ago when I didn't know if Myron was being tortured or already dead. Or if Erina and Ephegos had even worse planned for him.

I reach across the puddle of water at my feet, wondering when my magic will be strong enough again to weave an armor of liquid and slit throats with strings of it again. It simmers beneath my skin now, there enough to give me hope, but not yet strong enough to give me confidence.

"We'll get him out. All of them." I turn to Myron, watching the guilt dipping his shoulders at the thought of Royad and Silas, before I turn to Kaira. "And Herinor."

Her lips tighten. "I wish that was possible. Ephegos will never release him from the bargain he made."

To my surprise, Kaira's pain pacifies Clio enough to give her a smile of support. "Then we kill Ephegos."

Morning light creeps in through the windows as we wait for something to happen. Myron's magic hasn't stirred, and Clio still hasn't summoned more than a snowflake.

My own power is increasing though. By the time we have some of the food Kaira brought, I've dried Myron's leather pants by pulling out the water with my power and sent the puddle into the vomit corner to wash away all traces of our detoxing.

To my surprise, Myron hasn't hurled up his guts yet, so the dosage they gave him must have been so strong it hasn't started wearing off. But once it does, he'll follow in our footsteps.

By the time the sun sets, he's on his knees, gracing the corner with his retching, and I sit beside him on a crate, brushing my hand over his back in slow, soothing strokes. Clio eyes us from the other side of the room, her impatience written on her features as she tries to make the rain freeze on the windowsill. Tiny streaks of ice are lacing the broken glass as night falls over the city of Meer, tinting the room once more in darkness and starlight.

The street is quiet, and the rain has subsided. Myron is sitting in a corner, breathing through his nose as I pull fresh rainwater in through the window to clean away the bile where he emptied himself out. Kaira's eyes are following my magic, lighting up with my increasing strength while I'm just glad I have something to keep myself busy as my mind is spinning with the countless ways our plan could possibly go wrong.

"It will be all right," she comments in my mind, the only one to truly see behind the collected facade I've put up.

"I've lost everyone before. My parents, my crew, my lover. I watched them die just as I watched Myron die." My stomach cramps in a fresh wave of nausea that has nothing to do with the drug that has long left my system, and I need to suppress the sob building in my throat. *"I can't lose anyone else."* Myron, Royad, Clio, Kaira, and even Herinor. I can't bear the thought of Clio losing her mate or to lose Silas, whom I yet need to meet. If he followed Myron all the way into the enemy's dungeon to free me, I can't allow him to die.

Kaira comes up to my side, wrapping her arms around me and pulling me into a tight embrace. "I know," she whispers. "But you're not alone. You won't lose me. We're blood."

"Sisters," I acknowledge, a shiver of warmth running through me.

"Sisters," she murmurs into my shoulder.

Myron's head lifts, gaze locking on mine. Of course, he hears every last word that isn't in our mind connection. He wasn't amused when I told him about my blood relation with Kaira, less even when I shared that the part-Flame has a direct path into my thoughts. The corner of his mouth lifts in a sad smile.

His last relative is still in the dungeon, and if we don't hurry, we might not make it in time to save him.

"We need to get them out." My hand finds Kaira's as I pull out of her arms.

She squeezes it. "We will. Herinor is doing whatever he can to help them."

"To help his court," Myron corrects, getting to his feet and strolling over, careful not to step onto the small trickle of water I'm sending out the gaps in the front door. At least, the shed no longer reeks of vomit.

Clio meets us at the center of the room, her arms wrapped around her torso. The expression she wears reminds me of a little girl hoping to convince fate with a glower. "As long as he believes helping Tori aids his court, he can do whatever he wants."

Kaira purses her lips, holding in a comment that would reignite the bickering that has been going on between the two females. Something about it puts me oddly at ease. So much unfiltered emotion is comforting in a way only families can be, and I haven't had a true family since I was little. The crew of the Wild Ray came close to a family. But this—

My hand finds Myron's as he stands behind my shoulder, brushing a kiss to my temple.

"Your magic has gotten stronger," he says to Clio, gesturing at the icicles on the windowsill.

Following his gaze, Clio notices what I do at the exact same moment. The ice has spread from the window all the way to her toes where trails of water crisscross through the room.

"Must be the urge to freeze Eroth's Veil over so Tori can't cross in case anyone decides he needs to die." Her eyes flash a dangerous shade of green, defying even the near darkness— or my new senses let me see colors in the dark now.

"Must be," Myron agrees, lifting his hand an inch.

Icicles crumble, filling the room with crystalline music as they rain to the ground. Myron's mouth twitches into a smirk. "Mine, too."

My stomach flutters. It's not much, but it's magic. His powers are returning to him faster than we'd hoped.

As if in answer to the smile spreading on my mouth, an invisible touch caresses my cheek as he leans down to whisper in my ear. "You bring me to life, Ayna. Your presence alone makes every last part of me be the best version it can be."

I don't know what it is about his words that makes me wonder if I like some of him best when he's at his worst—like the relentless lover.

A shudder rakes through my body at the mere thought, and Myron's nostrils flare as if he can scent the instant heat pooling in my core. The wicked grin he gives me makes me wish we could leave everything behind and live in a world where only the two of us exist.

At least for an hour. For a moment. A heartbeat, so I could kiss him breathless.

"That's disgusting," Clio narrates, her gaze flying between Myron and me, and for once, Kaira agrees.

"Only because it's not you and your mate," Myron growls at her, and for a beat, I can feel the power rise in him the way it used to when I pushed him before the curse was broken. A ripple of energy runs through him, tinting his skin black along his forearms. I could swear the tips of feathers push through and retreat as the color fades back to pale.

That lifts the corner of Clio's lips, and she nods with satisfaction. "Works every time."

I'm still trying to understand what she's talking about when a gust of air swipes through the room, almost pushing me off my feet. My skin prickles as awareness of Myron's power floods me.

Shit—

Clio knows exactly what she's doing getting a rise out of Myron. His magic is returning in response as if to a threat.

"Well, that took long enough. I thought you'd break free from the drug when you... You know..." Her gaze bounces to me, one brow crooked, then to the window of the backyard. "I don't need to repeat what the two of you did out there, do I?" She grins and flips her fingers, ice crystals appearing above her palm where Myron's magic doesn't reach. "Can you shield, Crow King?"

Myron's forehead creases as he seems to be trying. "Emotion does seem to help with bringing the magic back faster, but not necessarily with regaining all the control needed to use it."

"It worked with Clio," Kaira chimes in, and suddenly, all her annoying of the fairy princess makes total sense. She did it on purpose to help the female regain her magic.

"My powers flooded in most whenever you brought up Tori, so I thought I'd return the favor." Clio shrugs, more back to her old self than I'd hoped for. It's not even a full day since we ran, and she's already freezing over the room. Myron is mere hours behind, so there is real hope we'll be setting out to the palace before the new day ends.

Rays of morning light pierce through the clouds, breaking up the night's terror and bringing back the hope that's so dangerous. I embrace it because, with Myron at my side, I feel braver and bolder than I have in years. He's the wind under my wings and the sun on my skin, and the wrath that will destroy my enemies—if I don't destroy them first.

THIRTY-NINE

MYRON

After the number of rounds Ayna has been pacing in the limited space, an oval trail should be appearing on the ground Clio has been freezing and unfreezing for the past hours while I've resorted to watching my mate. The lines of her body are too hard after weeks under the influence of the drug, of not keeping down her food. It painfully reminds me of the first day she arrived at the palace in the Seeing Forest, straight from prison.

Rubbing my hand across my sternum to ease the heaviness in my chest, I rest my head against the dusty wood making up the wall. The sun is declining, painting thin streaks of gold and orange along the packed earth floor. Under different circumstances, I'd have bemoaned my fate: home gone, power gone, what's left of my family locked up… But I have Ayna, and the tingling in my shoulder reminds me this isn't a dream.

"Any changes?" Kaira wants to know, rummaging through her satchel where all her food supplies have been used up.

I shake my head, the same response I've given her the last seven times she asked. My power hasn't stirred since Clio taunted me about my intermezzo with Ayna between the bushes. Thankfully, she hasn't tried again, or I might have accidentally torn the shed apart with an onslaught of the erratic magic I can't yet control.

"It will come," the Flame promises, and I choose to believe her. I've watched it happen for the fairy princess and Ayna, so it's only a matter of time until it happens for me. Time Royad and Silas don't have if Ephegos is to be believed. They don't have a purpose for the King of Tavras or for the Crow traitor. It's me on whom he wants to exact his vengeance. And I have to admit, it's a good plan. Using Erina to draw out my pain by sitting by as he marries Ayna.

Not going to happen.

Magic surges into my limbs so fast I need to clench my fists and push my feet into the ground so I don't allow it to burst out of me and accidentally harm one of the females waiting with me. If only I could create a shield, then what little power I already have control over would be useful to wrap it around Ayna so whatever assaults of my power may break down this place eventually won't harm her.

The thought alone is enough to make my hands shake all over again.

It's foolish to promise myself I'll never see her hurt again. Ayna will fight at my side when we free the others, and only a mad person would believe she won't find her path into harm's way.

So I wait, resorting to studying Ayna, learning her movements, her tells and shows when she's nervous, the way her hands rub over her stomach when it growls in demand of food we no longer have available, how her hand keeps drifting back to the side of her biceps when she finds my gaze every other moment and our bond tears at the center of my chest, tugging me toward her.

I stay on the floor, no matter how strong that pull. I will need to keep my hands off her during our rescue mission as well, so now feels like a good time to practice, even when all I want to do is rip her clothes off and take her right here on the dusty ground.

Ayna's eyebrows rise as she meets my gaze, heat shimmering in hers as if she can sense the direction my mind has taken me, and I press my mouth into a tight line so I don't tell her exactly all the things I want to do to her.

"For fuck's sake, Myron," Clio complains, stopping her own pacing in the path between Ayna and me, blocking my mate from view. "Could you be any more obvious?"

My growl is as involuntary as it is menacing.

"I know it's been a hot minute since you claimed her, but we have other problems right now, like mastering your fucking power." She waves her hand at me as if that's all the explanation I need.

"How much time did you have with your mate when it all started?" I don't want to ask, but it comes out anyway. There's so little I know about mating bonds that, even though I have a few centuries on Clio otherwise, I feel like a novice next to her.

Clio's gaze turns mock-deadly. "You don't ask a lady such unspeakable questions."

But both Ayna and Kaira are listening intently, probably eager for an answer as to when that initial frenzy will wear off.

Clio grinds her teeth, wiping away her mask with a sigh. "Never. It never wears off. You just learn how to balance things."

I blink. Because that's not the answer I'd hoped for.

"Deal with it, Crow King." She turns on her heels, flicking her fingers and releasing a flash of ice at me.

I dive out of its path at the last moment.

"Focus on your magic instead of on Ayna's curves, and you'll find that balance a lot faster."

Shaelak bless Astorian, who knows how to deal with this particular female. Then, on second thought, Astorian isn't so different. The two of them together must be explosive when turning on the same enemy.

Perhaps the gods have a bigger plan after all and this whole mating thing isn't just random in our magical world.

By the time the moon peeks in through the windows, I have mastered to shape the beam of my magic with my palms. It's harder than I care to admit, but it's progress. Perhaps Ayna's offer to stand in front of me so I'm forced to make my magic bend in order to avoid pushing her over and hurting her has something to do with it.

I'm far from satisfied with the semblance of control I have, but Royad and Silas are still in the dungeons, and I need to get them out alongside the fairy general who has proven more ally than the Crow I used to trust and is now setting the heavens and Hel's realm into motion to destroy me.

"We should go," I say to no one in particular, but my gaze is on Ayna. Always on Ayna, like she's the axis around which my universe spins.

Clio steps to Ayna's side as if that will tear my focus from her. "Can you pick up a blade and fight with it with your magic?" she challenges. "Because if you can't, you're not a help but a liability, and I can't risk needing to look after a Crow King when I have a fairy general to save." If I've learned anything about Cliophera de Pauvre of Askarea, it's that she will always put the ones she loves first. She doesn't need to refer to Astorian as her mate for me to remember what he is to her. Ayna is her friend; even Kaira has a weird connection to her. I am the only one she'd be willing to sacrifice if it comes to a choice of whom to leave behind.

Honing my focus on the sword sheathed at her hip, which Herinor left for her, I swipe it out of its sheath with a flick of my power—and blink in surprise when I hold it in my invisible grasp. Ayna grins at me, pride shining in her gray eyes as she draws up a string of water to block the blade from coming at Clio the moment I lose control.

I don't. Instead, I wink at my mate, smirk at the fairy princess, and twist the sword into position at her throat while Ayna's water wraps around it until the sharp edge is covered in a protective layer.

"Is that enough control?" I draw back the sword and shove it forward once more, allowing it to cut off a thin strand of her impossibly fiery hair, and Clio gasps with outrage.

"Be grateful your mate means something to me, or I'd freeze your heart over right now." She picks up the strand with a swift motion before turning to Kaira. "I think we're ready."

Personally, I don't think we are, but waiting will only get the prisoners killed, so it's now or never.

"The night will give us enough cover to sneak back to the palace." Without waiting for a group consensus, Kaira leaps right back into planning. She glances at Ayna with that slightly distant gaze I've noticed them exchange whenever they speak in their minds. It shouldn't bother me that someone else is privy to Ayna's thoughts when even I, as her mate, can't reach that far into her. I stifle a grunt. Maybe it's a connection between siblings that leads to blind understanding. Maybe it's a Flame ability I haven't yet heard about. Or maybe it's plain cruelty of fate that I will never know all the nuances of thoughts flaring behind those beautiful gray eyes.

I have to admit, I was shocked there is blood relation between the two of them. Between Clio and the Flame, Ayna's temper seems more similar to the princess's.

"If we're fast, we could make it in and out before sunrise," Kaira continues. "Herinor will help us get into the palace. Will let *me* into the palace, more specifically," she corrects. "Ephegos didn't forbid him from helping *me*. So, I'll be the one letting you into the palace right after he helps me get in."

"Sounds complicated," Ayna comments, and I couldn't agree more, but—"Herinor made a bad call bargaining with

Ephegos, but after everything he's done to protect you and get all of us out, I'd rather he remain alive so I can get him out as well. If thinking of his aid in a specific way will save his life, I'm inclined to do just that."

The three females nod, all of them aware of what it will cost Herinor if he helps Ayna directly. Shaelak help us if Ephegos figured out what's been going on and punished the male for it."

"Let's get out of here while we're still strong enough. If we wait any longer, we might become too weak from not eating or sleeping enough." Of course, Ayna is the practical one. She would never have survived this long if she hadn't learned to adapt fast and be pragmatic.

I hand Clio her blade, withdrawing my power as soon as she takes it from my grasp, and prowl to Ayna's side. "I'm ready." Or as ready as I'll get without a week's worth of rest.

Kaira claps her hands. "All right. Let's get to the eastern gate. I'll let Herinor know we're coming."

"How exactly does that work?" Clio prompts, sheathing her blade. "I'd like to be prepared in case your signal involves a dramatic uproar that will cause us to have to fight our way in rather than getting to the others in secret and only having to fight our way out."

She has a point.

"It won't cause anyone on our side to fight," the Flame promises. Somehow, I'm not convinced.

ANGELINA J. STEFFORT

FORTY

AYNA

The city is a vast ocean of star-sized lights as we make our way toward the palace, Kaira leading the way, Clio bringing up the rear, and in between, Myron and me. I can sense his gaze on the side of my face as he stalks beside me through the night like he has invented it. A true creature of darkness with unfathomable power. The way he snatched Clio's sword away was startling and brutal, and so fast even my new senses had a hard time following.

A part of me wonders if the colors and nuances I now perceive will wear off, if I'll return to human Ayna soon, but if anything Ephegos said is true, my human part isn't the one

I need to be worried about; it's the Crow buried deep within me that was set free in the torture chamber.

"Ready?" Clio asks, keeping to the shadows as we follow a wider street where a few people are packing up what seems to be the leftovers of a market, loading it onto a wagon.

"To face Ephegos?" I shake my head. I'm not even remotely ready to run into the Crow, but I'm pretty certain that by now he must have noticed my absence. That might explain the increased number of soldiers drifting through the streets this late at night.

I dive behind a barrel, pulling Myron with me as one of said patrols rounds the corner across the square, their heads turning as they scan the wide space between the houses. Apart from some forgotten vegetables that made it off a market stand and the occasional city dweller, they don't find much. We're too fast to get out of sight and too good at hiding. We need to be, or we'll never make it close to the palace. Once there, staying hidden will become an entirely different challenge.

Shifting into our Crow forms is off the table since I haven't managed to even pull on the power that made me turn in the dungeon, and Myron won't change without me, not that his ability has fully returned. All he can do is make a few feathers appear on his arm. The way he won't leave my side is both sweet and terrifying. If we get caught, I'll need him to leave me behind and run.

"So the plan remains the same?" Myron's tone is smooth like he's done this a thousand times. "Kaira gets us in and we use the servant corridors to get close to the dungeon entrance?"

"Unless you can magically get us in?" Clio drawls, her spirit back now that we're finally in motion. "Much as I'd love to offer, my site-hopping ability hasn't returned." And she wasn't willing to wait a moment longer once we were all strong enough to fight. I don't blame her. I'd do the same if it was Myron in the dungeon instead of Tori.

"That would have been convenient," Myron comments. "In and out in the blink of an eye. Would have solved all our problems."

"We can't afford to wait that long," I remind him. "The moment Ephegos realizes you're gone, Royad and Silas are in immediate danger of suffering his retaliation."

Myron flinches almost imperceptibly, but I notice the way I notice everything about him. Every breath, every blink of his eyes, every time his mouth presses into a thin line when we discuss the dangers of our mission all over again.

Plan or no, we're unprepared and weak. Thank the Guardians all but one of our opponents are human, or we'd be dead the moment we set foot into the palace.

Kaira leads us past a quiet street with mostly residential buildings before we step into the richer quarters where I recognize bits and pieces from my childhood years. A carved fountain here, an estate there, a statue...

It's beautiful and overwhelming, and with matters at hand, so utterly inconsequential that I find beauty in the architecture of this city. The thought is still a mouthful to swallow, but I force it down whenever it pops up. It doesn't matter what blood runs in my veins, only that I have a family to save before I get the hell out of what, in a different time, might have been my kingdom.

We keep our heads down as we march along the side streets, disguised as peasants. Myron is the hardest to disguise with his impossible height and build, but just like he's an expert at drawing attention when he enters a room with the authority of an unapologetic king, he has mastered avoiding gazes when he needs to. All but mine, which seems to be glued to his bare shoulder where his tattoo stands stark against his moonlit skin.

The palace looms ahead, onion-shaped roofs towering over the rest of the city as we approach from the east. I recognize the same narrow side gate we used when we left earlier, and my stomach tightens.

"Julj is on duty every night this week," Kaira says over her shoulder. If I knock a certain way, he'll open the door for me."

Myron pauses. "I thought Herinor would do that."

So did I.

"He'll open a different door." Kaira grins, so very fairy of her even when only a minuscule part of her is Fire Fairy. "Having Julj let me in will get Herinor's attention, though."

Well, that explains the frown when Herinor reminded her of the signal. It also explains Kaira's flirting with the guard.

"Hide there." She points at a wooden fence separating a carriage shed from a backyard, and we dive in, careful not to disturb the water trough at the corner. Myron's arm sweeps around me, pulling me into him as Clio crouches in front of us, keeping a close eye on Kaira, who's striding right for the gate, head high, braid swishing in the gentle breeze, and her maid's cap back on her head, like she doesn't have a care in the world.

My new senses struggle to keep focus on the female approaching our gate into the palace when my side is lined up with Myron's hard chest—his very bare hard chest—and his fingers are absently tracing the edge of my waist. I swallow the instinct to curl into him and ignore the rest of the world when we are so close to our goal—so close to danger.

"I expected you sooner," Julj says by way of greeting, opening the door for Kaira, and the female slips inside, her servant uniform disappearing behind the coarse wood.

"Will you be all right?" I ask Kaira through our mind connection, reading a laugh right back.

"I'm always all right with Julj. He can't tell left from right when it comes to a female's body."

I have no idea why that amuses me and scares me at the same time.

"Tell me you're not about to offer him left or right or any part of your body." I don't add that Herinor might not like the idea, but she picks the thought right from my mind.

"Herinor knows what I'm about to do. He doesn't like it, but he agrees it's necessary." Her tone isn't as light as her bodily voice before, when she waved goodbye and headed for doom.

"Lord Ephegos's tasks must have taken quite a while," the second guard's voice enters our conversation as her present situation leaks into her thoughts. I startle an inch into Myron, who secures his arm around me, his warmth the only reminder I'm not hallucinating all of this. It's the same voice

405

as when we left, and I can feel his hand on my hair like a phantom touch.

"I was looking forward to your visit yesterday," Julj says, ignoring the older guard's remark. I wouldn't be surprised if his gaze was glued to Kaira's chest.

"I was held up by other duties. But I'm here now. I actually have a few minutes right now," Kaira adds in a whisper. *"Why don't you show me what you were looking forward to exactly?"* In my mind, she says to me, *"I will be fine, Ayna. Promise. I'll let you hover in my mind though so you know when it's time to run for the gate."*

She could have warned me sooner about this particular part of the plan. I didn't like the way he sized her up when we fled the palace, and I like it even less how she's willingly returning to his arms now—for me. For Myron and Clio, and the males still stuck in the dungeons. Perhaps a little bit for Herinor because he can't help me. So she took on the burden for him.

Perhaps she took it on much sooner than I realized.

At the Flame estate, when she first brought me tea, she said she wanted to know me because I'm blood, but perhaps that was only part of the truth. She wanted to go with me to Meer—but she might as well have followed for the male. And here, at the palace … she already admitted that she has been helping him.

"You know I can hear every last part of your doubt, Ayna," she reminds me, a low moan slipping into her thoughts, and it's not her own. Julj must be enjoying the encounter already. *"He better be because I know exactly what I'm doing."*

"What are *you doing?"* Not that I really want to know. But now that she's mentioned it—

"Something you don't want to see your sister doing, so shut up, and let me focus."

I try to do exactly that while they seem to be moving through the corridors near the gate, leaving behind the older guard, and for a brief minute, it works. For a minute, I can ignore the groans and whispers Kaira channels my way to keep me informed about the progress of her mission. A mission I really wish she didn't need to take upon herself, and not just for her sake. Then, another voice mingles with the sounds, and I almost leap out of my skin. *"What the fuck do you think you're doing?"*

Myron shoots me a confused sideways glance, but I shake my head. I will tell him later about everything I just witnessed. For now, I need to fully focus so we don't miss the moment we need to sprint for the inconspicuous door, praying that none of the guards manning the many small towers will notice us.

"Move your naked ass and step away from her. Because if you touch this female again, I will cut more than just your hands off."

Oh, I know the voice. I know it too well, and I'm not ashamed to admit that the first time I heard it I was scared shitless.

"This shall be interesting," Kaira narrates as Herinor's growls sound through her mind into mine, and the soldier begs for mercy. I can only imagine what is going on by the grunts and swears waving through Kaira's thoughts. I have

the faintest sense of something wet spraying onto my shirt before Kaira's voice returns to my head.

"Is the gate clear?" she asks Herinor, who grunts his confirmation. *"All right, Ayna. Hurry. I'll open the door for you."*

I don't tell Myron and Clio how I know the gate is clear as I grab his hand and get to my feet, waving Clio along as we stumble from shadow to shadow to the steel-enforced rectangle in the wall that means safety for now—and a point of no return. Once we're in, we must continue to the dungeon. And this first door will have been the easiest.

Despite the rush and the stop-and-go of our progress, my feet are light on the cobbled ground, my breath even and my focus clear. There's something to say for those fae senses I have been gifted alongside a mate Mark, if that's what the tattoo on my shoulder is called. Whatever the gods did, they knew exactly what they were doing.

We dodge eyes as we slip from one corner to the next, easy as ghosts in the night, starlight never touching us longer than a few heartbeats between the ripping clouds above. Thank the Guardians for bad weather.

The gate draws nearer, my heart pounding in my throat as I want to sprint the final distance to make it inside safely. The door is opening, and it's not far enough away to risk another stop.

"Wait!" Kaira shouts in my mind the same moment Myron's arm snatches me around the waist, tugging me against the wall beneath a narrow roof so hard it knocks the breath from my lungs. Clio is gasping for air on his other side, wriggling her shoulder out of his grasp and ready to complain

when a male form steps through the gate, stalking toward the nearby bushes and—

Fuck me—"Is he…"

"Peeing on the royal bushes? He is," Myron confirms with that cold amused voice I remember from the early days we shared at the Crow Palace.

Clio laughs between deep breaths. "That was close."

"It's one single human guard," I point out, catching my breath while I relish Myron's touch, the way his fingers are splayed across my stomach. "Even I could have incapacitated him with my water magic."

The look Myron gives me drives a shiver deep through my bones. "You don't actually think I'll let anyone who sees you in this palace live?"

He's right. I know he's right. If word gets around that I've returned to the palace—and with an escaped prisoner—there's no way Erina won't mobilize his entire army to keep me there.

"I'd rather you not become a killer tonight." His gaze softens, and something like a blush creeps into his cheeks that makes him look utterly adorable while simultaneously horribly attractive—and the meaning of his words trickles through the haze his attention creates in my mind.

"You know I've killed before, on the Wild Ray. And at your own palace." I no longer care to try to correct myself that the palace in the Seeing Forest was never actually his. We don't have time for technicalities. The guard is done peeing and buttons up his pants before returning inside.

"I guess that particular one doesn't care about the reputation of Erina's court," Clio comments, ignoring our ongoing conversation.

Myron's gaze doesn't leave mine as he uncurls his arm from around me, inhaling deeply through his nose as if scenting whether the air is clear.

"Kaira?" I reach out in my mind, ready for anything, but she hums in response, opening her thoughts to me.

"I'm all right. Hiding in an alcove but all right. He didn't see the other guard's body, thank the Guardians, which means I'm cowering right next to a dead man." The image she sends makes me shiver, and I try not to show my distress in any other way.

"Is the air clear now?"

I wind my fingers through Myron's, ready to inform him about everything I just learned through the magical channel connecting me to my sister, but Kaira occupies my attention again. *"You need to hurry. The man poked around for a bit when he realized the gate was abandoned. It'll be a matter of minutes until he reports and new guards fill in for the ones Herinor disposed of."*

So, he killed them both. I'm glad I didn't have more to eat.

"Let's go." This time, it's Myron who takes the lead, his senses stronger than mine perhaps and picking up more from the palace than me, or he just has an infallible instinct for danger. Does it matter when it gets us to the gate and the door opens, led by Kaira's calloused hand, and she waves us inside?

FORTY-ONE

AYNA

We follow Kaira to the right—the opposite direction we'd come from when we fled the palace—and it takes about fifty steps for us to make it to a hidden room where half of Julj lays on one side of the rough, narrow space while the other half is dripping off the walls across the room.

I swallow.

"Herinor was thorough." Myron bends down to pick two knives and a sword from Julj's belt, which has magically remained intact. He wipes them down on his pants and hands me the longer of the two knives while he offers the smaller one to Kaira, who shakes her head, pointing at the weapons belt on her hips.

"Herinor brought me this from the other guard." I can't tell if there is some fuzzy warmth weaving into her voice at the memory of the male handing her the weapons of a freshly killed soldier or if it's just my imagination.

From behind her, Clio reaches over Kaira's shoulder, smoothing the collar of her uniform into place where it hangs sideways off her shoulder. "I'd fix this if I were you, or Herinor will disembowel any other male who lays eyes on you," she notes with a smirk that doesn't fit the horror on Kaira's face as she realizes the front of her uniform is still un-buttoned, exposing creamy skin and the swell of her breasts hidden under a wide band of fabric. "The hair, too." Clio gestures at the disheveled braid, studying Kaira redoing her buttons with surprising clumsiness.

Something about the way she just used her body to dis-tract a guard while Herinor disposed of the first one makes me believe her horror isn't from embarrassment for her nakedness but from the thought of Herinor killing on her behalf.

"You're thinking too much," she narrates in my head, and perhaps she's right. We have other matters at hand.

"Don't read my thoughts," I complain. Even when it's a tool to help us navigate our break-in, her mind reading is becoming annoying.

"I promise I'll learn how to block you out once we get out of here alive." She shoots me a quick glance before she gestures at Myron. "You'll find your way to the right cells once we're in the dungeon?"

Myron's expression changes to outright offended. "How about you focus on your task, I focus on mine, and we all stay alive?" It's not a suggestion, and we all sense that power of his rising in his blood. He's as terrifying as he was that first day at the Crow Palace, but instead of cringing from him, I'm proud to call him mine. He might be a menace, but he's *my* menace.

Clio steps into the space between them, ignoring the splatter of blood at her feet like the warrior she is, and raises a finger at Myron. "You, keep your temper under control, or you'll be the reason we're detected, and you"—she wheels on Kaira, brows raised and eyes stern in a way I've never seen her, but it works like almost any look works on Clio—"lead the way before the new guards show up and we all need to do more killing than we care for. I've got a mate to free, and the Crow King has some friends to save, and I'd really like to do so before breakfast."

"I'd hate to miss breakfast," I agree, trying to ignore the nausea rising in my stomach at the thought of food in combination with the bloodbath Herinor created in this chamber.

Myron's lips twitch, eyes narrowing on the female then flicking to me. "Breakfast sounds like something all of us could use."

A minute later, Kaira is guiding us through the narrow corridors leading away from the gate toward the lower levels of the palace. I didn't know just how many hidden passageways existed in this palace, and at every new turn, I'm surprised they are abandoned.

"No one ever comes this way," Kaira whispers as she stops at a corner, glancing left and right just in case the routine of spatial abandonment has changed while we were gone. "Herinor found me this passage and opened it."

Because he can help anyone but me. Or because he'd do anything for her—the state we found Julj in suggests it's the latter.

"Let's hope that hasn't changed." Clio grabs her sword harder, eyes sparkling as she turns left as if she's walked these hallways hundreds of times.

When Kaira doesn't object, I know she's chosen the right direction. "Not far now," the Flame huffs, her breath stirring the dust on the walls, and for a moment, I marvel at the shimmering orange particles tinted by firelight intruding in the space through small cracks and tiny holes in the walls. My eyes work just fine in the near darkness, and I've never been more grateful for how the Gods turned my fate.

Our feet are near soundless on the packed dirt floor, leaving our hearing undisturbed to pay attention to the light ruffles of guards' boots when they shift their posture along the hallway running parallel to ours. Every other turn, voices carry through the walls, echoing along the stone and precious metal the space out there is made of, and every time, my heart nearly stops as I listen for a familiar voice or a caw, I'm no longer sure, but it's never Erina or Ephegos, or even Katrijanov talking on their way through the palace. Somehow, their absence makes me more anxious than their presence would have. At least, then I'd know where they are.

All the way, Myron's fingers linger on the small of my back as he walks in silence beside me, gaze ahead and magic at his fingertips. The crackling sensation of his power wraps around us as he tries to form a shield that will take the brunt of any surprise attack should we run into guards after all, but it isn't more than a second skin. It won't hold off anything magical or something sharp like a blade. His powers are recovering slowly, and hopes are that, by the time we make it to the dungeon, he'll be able to produce something stronger than this. As if in response, his magic crackles along my skin, intensifying as it weaves another layer, and another.

"There—" Clio's voice is so low only our superior senses can pick it out of the twilight of the stairwell she's diving into, braid swishing behind her like a streak of fire.

The entrance to the dungeon. How do I know? The door at the bottom of the stairs opens, and Herinor steps aside, inclining his head at the princess before looking Kaira over. His gaze skips over me as he nods at Myron. "Silas and Astorian are in their cells."

He doesn't need to mention what that means for Royad.

"How long?" Myron's tone is dry, emotionless, an assessing king readying for a decision neither of us wants to make.

"The guards picked him up two hours ago. I overheard them from the side corridor. They mocked him it was going to be his last time in the torture chamber." Herinor's words hit right in the chest, and I grab for Myron's hand in silent support.

"We'd better hurry." It's all he says as he takes the lead into the narrow space between the iron bars framing empty cells.

This is a different part of the dungeon than where Erina brought me to see Myron. Abandoned and reeking not even half as much as the active regions of this Guardians-forsaken place.

"Change of plans," Myron says with that lethal calm informing me he's gone into fighting mode. "We free Silas and Astorian first. Clio and Ayna make sure they get out alive. Kaira knows the way out and will guide you."

That leaves Myron and Herinor to retrieve Royad.

My stomach ties into a knot. "I'm not leaving you behind." It's a fact he'll need to accept.

Myron doesn't disagree—or agree. He simply marches into the dungeon, followed by Herinor and me, Kaira and Clio bringing up the rear.

After a few minutes' walk in silence, we turn a corner where torches line the walls and the stench of mold and vomit fills the air the way I remember. What I don't remember is the odor of blood—iron and salt and a sweetness that makes my head swim.

"I leave you here," Herinor says, sheathing his sword and bowing to Myron, still ignoring me.

I try not to take it personally. Considering his deal with Ephegos and the risk he takes if he accidentally intentionally aids me, his life would be forfeit in a heartbeat.

"Ephegos has been waiting for you to return. Be careful. And don't get caught," he advises before he strolls off down the larger one of the two corridors the main path splits into. "Especially don't get caught by me. Ephegos might order me to kill you all, and I don't know if I can defy a direct order."

His gaze swings to Kaira last, and my heart breaks at the way his mouth tightens when their gazes collide.

Only when his footsteps fade into the distance does Myron nod and start down the smaller corridor, blade in his hand and magic at his fingertips, his shield tightening as I pull on my own power to ready myself for whatever might come our way.

It comes our way exactly half a minute later when we turn the corner and a pair of guards step into our path out of seemingly nowhere.

Myron's invisible power flies out in a surprising blast to cover their mouths and muffle their screams as Clio freezes the blood in their veins with one heart-stilling touch. Apparently, his magic is recovering faster now that his focus is on his target and it's about life and death—not only his own. My breath only returns to normal once Kaira and I grab the two iced-over corpses and drag them a few feet back into the direction we came from and hide them behind a sharp corner.

"That was almost too easy."

I can't help but agree when Clio wipes her hands in her tunic, frost disappearing from her fingers like she didn't just annihilate two lives with a mere touch. I don't know whether to be in awe or be slightly unsettled.

Awe wins as the female shoots me a grin and waves me closer to her side so I'm wedged between her and Myron, leaving Kaira to follow as we continue our path, eyes and ears open for more guards.

We're luckier than we deserve. Not one single soldier patrols this part of the dungeon as we move silently along the rows of empty cells. My heart is lighter than it's supposed to be. Perhaps we'll get to the cells fast and get at least Silas and Astorian out before we are detected and someone raises an alarm.

"Careful with the bars," Clio warns, letting Myron take the lead again as the corridor narrows and the ceiling drops into a low, looming structure that will give me nightmares. This is a cage just as bad as my cell at Fort Perenis, and my breath can't move past my clogged throat. "They might be painted with the magic-nullifying drug."

We all keep our arms close to our bodies, careful not to touch the iron framing our path.

"Breathe," Kaira instructs the same moment Myron glances over his shoulder, face drawn with concern.

"I'm fine," I tell him, directing my attention to the details my human eyes were never able to see: hues of green where moss grows between the rocks making up the structure above, fragments of quartz so tiny I'd usually overlook them sticking out of the smooth rocks. The whisper of Clio's braid against her shirt. My own hair getting caught on the rough-spun linen of my shirt.

And footsteps. Heavy, arrhythmical footsteps.

Myron picks up pace, leaving the rest of us to scramble after him as he turns into a mostly open space where the smell of blood and infestation dominates that of all others.

"Silas." He stops in front of the closest cell, staring at the still form in the corner.

And, damn if they didn't punch the male into a pulp. Blood is oozing from his nose like he just passed out a moment ago after a heavy beating. His back is scattered with cuts and burns, and his arm—

My stomach turns as I notice the iron needle sticking out of his flesh as if forgotten by his tormentors—or left in there on purpose.

"Silas," Myron whisper-shouts again, doing his best to rouse the male from his oblivion while at the same time cautious not to draw the attention of potential guards lingering nearby.

"You haven't forgotten us after all, Crow King," a husky, mocking voice prompts from a few feet away, and I realize who the footsteps belonged to.

"Tori—" Clio storms past me, stopping a mere inch from the bars that would mean losing her magic all over again. Thank the Guardians, her rational mind is still in place at the sight of her bruised and battered mate limping up to face her through the iron fence.

"If I'm far enough gone to hallucinate you, Cliophera, I might be beyond saving." His voice breaks as he reaches through the bars with one shaking hand, stopping a breath from Clio's face as if anxious she might disappear at a touch.

True to herself, Clio swallows her sob before it can wrestle up her throat. "Stop the serenades and tell me how to get you out instead." She wraps her fingers around his, a shiver visibly running through both of them as they connect, and pulls him a step farther toward her so his face is mere inches from the bars. "You stupid male got yourself trapped and caught searching for me."

He's so still I don't believe he's breathing, and neither am I—neither are any of us as Clio's panic and frustration break out of her in the only way she seems to allow herself to let them.

"I couldn't sit by and wait while you were the Guardians knew where."

"You could have trusted me to get myself out. I wouldn't have to sneak back into this fucking shithole had you not gotten yourself trapped." She's speaking to both Astorian and Myron now, even when her eyes never stray from her mate. "Erina could have never bullied Ayna had you not gotten yourself caught and imprisoned and strung up on a fucking torture table." There are tears in her voice—tears of anger—but she wipes them away with the back of Astorian's palm as she leans her face against his hand.

"You'd have done the same." It's a weak defense, but I've known Clio long enough to be convinced he's right.

"I wouldn't have gotten myself caught."

Astorian raises a brow. "Then why did I have to come looking for you in a foreign realm and find you in a servant's uniform."

Clio kisses his hands over and over again like that alone will set him free, will heal him and un-break him where he's obviously broken in so many places he struggles to keep upright.

"Your brother would have had my head if I'd let anything happen to you."

"Just as he would have mine if anything happened to you," Clio retorts with a smile, tears streaming down her face."

"Much as I hate to break up the reunion," Kaira interrupts, "we need to get out of here before anyone can have anyone's head."

"You completely missed the point, Kaira." Myron stalks closer, eyes darting back to Silas every other step until he stands right next to Clio.

"Find one, find both," he says to Astorian, who inclines his head at him, deep respect shining in his unusually reddish-brown eyes. I can't see much else of his features other than that; beneath layers of blood and grime, they must be as flawless as any other fairy's. His longish hair is tangled and knotted, caked with blood, and shaped into stiff tresses that could be of any color beneath the dirt. The cuts and bruises on his bare chest seem older than those on Silas's skin, and thank the Guardians that at least one of them is awake and coherent.

"Find one, find both," Astorian echoes, and a deep understanding seems to pass between the two males that only those who've shared a lifetime—or deep trauma—can ever achieve.

I promise myself that I'll ask Myron to tell me the whole story once we're out of here and safe, but first we need to get the others out and actually survive.

I wish, for once, things were easy.

FORTY-TWO

MYRON

Every muscle in my body is stretched taut as I hold myself in place while Astorian and Clio have their moment. A few breaths—I can grant them that before I lose my patience. We need to get him and Silas to safety before figuring out if there is anything left of Royad to save.

My chest hurts at the thought of being too late. Two hours of torture is a lifetime of pain. Two hours without intending to let the person survive is what I imagine Hel's realm to look like if he decides to toss you into his punishing fires.

"The bars are still painted in that bitch of a drug." Astorian nods at the steel separating him from his mate, his hands firmly wrapping hers despite the sword in her grasp. Even in this most heart-wrenching of moments, she hasn't let go of her weapon, that's how much of a warrior she is.

I bite back a curse, debating the options we have. "So, we can't rip them out with our hands."

"Not that you'd ever be strong enough, Crow," Astorian retorts, but there's no contempt in his eyes now. All I see is the gratitude of a male not to be forgotten and left to die. "But I'd suggest you not give up that magic of yours in a feeble attempt at breaking those bars."

I search the cell for a weakness as I notice Ayna scan the room and draw a string of water from the bucket in the corner of my empty cell where it sits just out of reach for Astorian as if to taunt him. They never gave me a full bucket like that—not to drink or to wash. Just the bare minimum to survive and that was laced with the drug. Damn those humans.

It's almost too late when I realize what Ayna intends to do by slinging the water around a bar, and my hand lands on her shoulder, my magic flinging out to cut off the water from her reach a beat before it touches the bars. "You don't know if the touch of your magic might have the same results as your physical touch." Who knows what unholy ways Ephegos and Erina invented to render our powers useless? We haven't learned nearly enough about it and have too much to lose to simply risk it.

Ayna's wide eyes inform me she didn't think through the potential consequences of throwing our magic at bars treated with a drug that takes said magic away.

"We can't afford to lose our magic." It's Kaira who agrees first, even when her own powers are minuscule compared to the vastness of Clio's and my own untested ocean of power that I have yet to fully get under control. And definitely not Ayna's. It's all that stands between her and freedom once I send her out of here with Silas and Astorian.

"You need to focus on what surrounds the bars." Astorian drags his hands back through the fence, reluctantly stepping away from his mate and knocking on the wall at the edge of his cell.

By Shaelak, he is about to fall over if he doesn't get healed. But first, we need to get him out.

"I could melt the rocks around the bars if I had my powers. Wouldn't be the first time." He exchanges a look with Clio that's so full of history that my chest aches all over again.

"Maybe I could wash them out with water," Ayna offers, her magic grasping the water that's now a puddle on the floor and forming it into a string once more.

Or I could simply blast the wall out altogether, but I don't say that since it won't help our secrecy, and if that's gone, they might not prolong Royad's suffering and shove him right to Hel's doorstep instead. My hands are shaking as I watch Ayna pit her magic against the side of the stone, etching little grooves into the surface with the water she wields, but it's too slow, and every time the water comes close to touching a bar, my heart stops all over again.

"Let me help." It's the most diplomatic way I can manage to break it to her that she's not strong enough to get him out—not yet. She will once she figures out what she can do

425

with those Crow powers that should set in at some point if Shaelak was truly gracious to her.

My mate isn't too proud to acknowledge that she's not making enough progress, and she drops her magic, saving her strength for now while I send out my senses to feel the stone and every last bit of energy in it.

When I find a place that feels more hollow than the rest, I direct a single blow of my power right there, praying that I wasn't too bold and it will hit the side of the bars.

I don't. The stone crumbles where my power connected, opening a hole big enough for Astorian to squeeze through.

"Don't come in," the male hisses as Clio dives for the gap. "I can make it on my own. We need your magic."

The nervous fidgeting Clio performs should get its own name, for I've never seen tension shift a person as much as it does when Clio watches her mate brace his back against the sharp rocks and push himself through the narrow opening without loosing the scream of pain I know is building in his throat.

He's barely made it to our side of the fence when Clio darts for his hand, pulling him the last few inches and catching him as he collapses into her arms.

"Fucking Erina," she hisses as she notices the rivers of blood gushing from the freshly opened wounds on his back. "I will freeze his eyes last so he can watch every bit of his body turn lifeless before he dies."

"I've always loved you for your thirst for blood," Astorian jokes, but I'm certain part of him means it. And I can understand. I've spent enough time with Cliophera by now to see nothing less than the relentless female she is. Loving, fierce, and relentless for the ones she wants to protect. Thank Shaelak, I'm on her good side—for now.

It's Ayna's fierceness that pushed past my defenses long before I ever fell in love with her, and it's the part of her that probably saved her when I'd long given up.

"Save the cheesiness for later," Kaira chimes, her tone slipping as she lays proper eyes on Astorian's state, the way his flesh is peeling back from his shoulder blade. "Is anyone going to heal him, or do I need to pull out the bandages first?"

"No bandages." Astorian coughs. "They will mess with my badass reputation."

"Nothing messes with your badass reputation, Tori." Clio kisses his brow, the only part of his face that isn't bruised or swollen. Gods, I don't want to think of what the three males have been going through since Herinor so heroically pulled me out of Ephegos's torture chamber.

Which reminds me…

"Here—" I step closer, placing my fingers on the edge of Astorian's biggest wound on his back and letting some of my power siphon into him. The result is instant. Flesh and skin layer back into place, smoothing into angry, red swells rather than open cuts and tears. Astorian sighs with relief as I repeat the procedure on the next cut, and the next, seeing to it that his back is mostly patched up before I move on to his arm and his chest, shoving a disgruntled Clio aside to gain better access to the crisscross of scabbed lines that is his torso.

Ayna's soft gasp as she monitors every movement and every little wound close is like a balm to my soul. She's alive. Healed. And more powerful than ever.

"You shouldn't waste your magic on an old fairy like me," Astorian grumbles, but his voice sounds so much better now that the strain of constant pain is relieved. "You still need to get Silas out."

"And Royad," Ayna reminds him, her face falling when Astorian shakes his head.

"I wouldn't keep my hopes up for the polite one. He was already half dead when Katrijanov had him dragged to the chamber."

My stomach fucking plummets to the blood-soaked ground. "Not an option. We won't leave him behind. Not unless he's a splatter on the wall."

I don't allow myself to think how close Silas is to being exactly that. How close Astorian had come.

How close *I* had come before Herinor got me out.

Gods. Silas was right. We're fucked.

As is Astorian. Instead of continuing to heal his bruises, I turn and lead the way back to the cell where Silas still hasn't moved.

"I'll get you out of here," I whisper before I search the wall for the best place to punch a hole with my magic.

It's some sort of mercy that Royad isn't in his cell because his is wedged between the ones bordering the walls, and there wouldn't have been any rock to blast out of the way, just magic-draining bars. I heave a breath, focusing on the weakest piece of stone, and release my power in a well-focused blow.

Rubble flies, hitting the metal in an ear-splitting rain, and I duck, grabbing Ayna with my magic and yanking her into me as I drop to the ground, careful not to touch the bars and risk either of our magic.

"Fucking Crows," Astorian notes. "Your magic is the worst."

He's observed my power since the day we teamed up in the forest, but he's never commented before.

Ayna groans something unintelligible, the sound running through my body and putting my entire system on alert. When I slide off her, an apology on my lips, I notice that the rubble might not have hurt her, but I did. On her forehead, a fresh crimson streak runs straight to her brow, the scent of her blood overpowering everything else for a painstaking moment.

And I've never hated myself more.

FORTY-THREE

AYNA

In the twilight between the throbbing in my skull and the sounds that could be someone calling my name or simply a side effect of hitting my head, Myron's ocean eyes appear in my field of vision.

"Remind me never to let you save me again," Astorian retorts from somewhere nearby, Kaira humming her agreement from the other direction.

"I'll heal her," Clio offers, but Myron's hand is already cradling my cheek, familiar, tingling warmth seeping into my tissues from where his skin brushes mine. "Or not..."

She appears behind Myron's shoulder, concern edged into her young forehead.

"Can you stand up?" Myron's hand winds beneath my shoulder as he gently offers his support, and I nod, head clearing as his magic seals my wounds and what could have been a light concussion.

"Thanks to your powers." I let him guide me into an upright position simply because I'm too selfish to pull away from him just yet and he's about to send me out of the dungeon with Silas and Astorian. I'm not ready to leave. Not when he's staying to get Royad out.

"Thanks to my powers, you were just injured." The frown on his beautiful face hurts more than the guilt in his eyes.

"You can fight about whether or not he's useful later. Now, let's grab the Crow and go." Clio claps her hand, gesturing at Astorian to slide through the wide opening Myron's magic broke into the wall. I feel the stream of cool fresh air a heartbeat before I realize the reason everything is tinted in starlight is because the hole reaches all the way to the outer wall, opening a view of earth and rocks—and the open sky behind the dust rising from a pile of rubble where thick stone used to block out the world.

"Shit—"

"You could say so," Kaira echoes my sentiment, already climbing through the opening behind the bars where Astorian is carefully lifting Silas into his arms. The male is still unstable on his legs, but he's ready to carry one of his former enemies to safety.

I don't know what happened between the Crows and the fairy, but it has to be more than just the days of sharing the same fate down here in the dungeon.

Clio is at his side in an instant, arguing that she can carry Silas instead, but Astorian is either too proud or too stubborn to let her help. When he nods at the sword on her hip, I realize he is too smart.

"We need you to fight if we're stopped. I can carry a hulk like Silas, but I sure don't have any magic at my disposal to fend off an attack, and you're as good with a sword as me."

The look they share pierces through my heart. The silent understanding in Clio's eyes informs me this is not the first time they have escaped danger and death together.

Myron's hand glides down my arm in a soothing gesture. "Time to go, Ayna."

That takes all the heartfelt sympathy and wonder right out of me, and I spin around to face him, his ocean eyes full of conflict as he glances between the escape he created for us, the door on the other side of the room, and me.

"I'm not leaving without you."

His teeth cut into his lower lip as he sorts through his thoughts. "We don't have much time. There is no way no one noticed the tremble my magic just caused, and it's a matter of moments before someone will come to check on the prisoners."

Who will be gone by then. But he will stay to save Royad, and hopefully, Herinor will be there to help.

"If we all go, that leaves only Herinor and you to fight Ephegos, Katrijanov, and however many soldiers they send your way." I swallow. "That's two against an unknown number, and even if you have parts of your magic back, it doesn't mean Herinor will be allowed to fight at your side. Ephegos could order him to do anything."

Myron's eyes close for a brief moment as he inhales through his nose. His throat bobs, his fingers lacing with mine. "That's not how bargains work. He can't help *you* because it is part of the bargain. But he still has a mind of his own. Ephegos can order him plenty of things, and he doesn't need to obey as long as it doesn't touch the original bargain."

His explanation is not even half satisfying.

"I'm coming with you."

Eyes flaring like tossing waves, Myron pins me with a look. "Please, Ayna. For your own sake and for mine, leave. I can't live with myself if something happens to you."

And if I stay, it will. He doesn't need to add that.

"Can you please make up your mind over there? Because I'd like to set down this colossus sometime soon, somewhere safe." Astorian's strained grumble reaches us through the dust-filled air as he nearly staggers under the Crow's weight. It's hard to breathe, but that has more to do with the thought of the dangers Myron is willing to shoulder to save his cousin.

"Leave without me," I say to the others, eager for them to make it out and get Silas to safety.

Myron sighs, but he doesn't object.

"See you at the shed," Kaira calls over her shoulder before stalking through the rubble toward the hole. They'll need to climb up the seven feet of earth and rock before they can slip through the gap, but they'll make it.

"If we don't join you by dawn, leave without us." Myron's words encompass every last one of my fears.

I swallow them down. If I allow myself to think about the potential consequences, I might try to talk Myron into leaving Royad behind just to make sure my mate gets out alive. Myron wouldn't forgive me, and I wouldn't forgive myself.

"Be careful," Clio hisses, already halfway up the earthen wall. "I'd hate to start all over again with making an almost human friend." Her tone is light, but the fear is written on her face as she glances back at me.

"We'll be fine." I wave toward the faint stars above her. "You can tell me how much you love me later. Now get out of here."

Astorian huffs a chuckle then grunts as she lifts Silas into Clio's arms when she reaches the top. I don't ask him what's so funny, simply wave at the small group and head after Myron, who's already waiting halfway down the corridor.

"Don't die," Kaira calls after me in her mind, but I don't reassure her I won't. We all know this could be our last goodbye.

"Take care of them," I tell her instead. Because if anything happens to Astorian, Clio will shatter, and I can't live with that. And if anything happens to Clio or Silas... I try not to let my mind wander to all the myriad possible ways this could go wrong. How they could get caught on their way out or through the city. Instead, I focus on the tall, dark form in the half-light of the corridor, setting one foot after the other toward doom.

Myron doesn't comment when I take his hand, following him as he leads the way down the rows of cells. So far, no one has come to check on this part of the dungeon, but it won't be long.

Not long is exactly one turn later where two guards step into our path, their eyes wide as they take in the menace in Myron's eyes and the long knife in my hand. My heart leaps into my throat at the sight of their sharp blades and the definite recognition in their eyes as they take in Myron's massive form.

"You—"

"Me?" Myron cocks his head, a gesture so birdlike I can almost see the feathers spilling down his neck and back, but his appearance remains distinctly human despite the predatory demeanor. If I didn't trust him with my life, I'd be scared shitless right now.

As are the guards. One of them opens his mouth to shout for reinforcements, but Myron's power has already wrapped around his neck, snapping it with ease while he lifts his own sword to stab the second one in the heart. Blood pours from the wound when he pulls the blade out, letting the guard drop on top of his companion, soaking the ground crimson while all I can do is stare.

"Let's go." This time, Myron doesn't take my hand, keeping both his sword and his magic at the ready, and so do I. Knife in hand and magic grazing the space for any water I can use while staying clear of the bars, I run at his side down the torchlit corridor, following the rough stone walls as we leave the cell area and continue toward a wooden door that has seen better days.

There, Myron stops, waiting for me to come to a halt beside him, and holds his finger to his lips as we both listen intently.

Silence encompasses the space, thick and looming like a predator, and that's what scares me even more than the sound of Ephegos's voice would have, or Royad's screams. It's the absolute silence of a shielded room, I realize, and there could be anything waiting behind it.

I try not to imagine Royad's dead body or a small army assembled to welcome us. An assault of Ephegos's magic might be enough to take both of us out with our power barely recovered and not nearly enough control to wield it like the weapon it could be.

"I don't know what we'll find behind this door," Myron whispers, his focus snapping from the tortured wood of the door to my face, the utter devastation in his eyes hitting me in the stomach like a physical blow. "I can't promise we'll get out alive. You can still go back and run. You'll catch up with the others before they make it to the shed."

Lifting to my toes, I cup his cheek with my free hand and pull his mouth to mine for a whisper of a kiss. "We both live or we both die. I won't leave without you."

Myron's lips mold over mine in a fierce, desperate kiss that tells me better than any words could that he feels the same way. "I love you, Wolayna Milevishja. I love you with everything I am. My dark Crow heart is yours until my last breath, be it moments from now when we walk through this door, or millennia from now when the gods get bored with my presence in this world. I'm yours."

I trace his cheekbone with my thumb, sweeping a strand of dark hair aside as I allow his words to settle inside of me.

"As I am yours." Those simple words are all it takes to drive a tear to my eyes—a tear I cannot afford but lift from my eye with my magic and tuck away.

Myron watches it float from my cheek into my open palm with wonder.

"Let's save your cousin." There is no time for big good-byes and extensive embraces. Royad is dying behind this door, and we can't be too late. We simply can't. Herinor will be there to help us or not, but we can't rely on anything other than our own strength, our own magic, to free him and make it out alive.

Myron inclines his head, face hardening into that of the relentless king I used to fear, and he draws upon his power, releasing it onto the door in one earthshaking blow.

FORTY-FOUR

AYNA

Debris rains down from where Myron blasted half of the wall around the door, and where forbidding silence was dominating, coughs and curses now penetrate the space. My knife weighs nothing in my hand as I hold it ready to stab whoever comes at us through the settling haze.

Myron is already sneaking to the side of the opening, gesturing for me to follow. It's clear he wants me out of harm's way should anyone attack without seeing who actually tore down the wall. Not that I don't appreciate his concern for my safety, but I have magic and a blade. And if one of us dies, I'd rather it be me.

"I've been wondering when you'd show up," Ephegos's voice snakes through the settling dust like a viper, making my pulse speed with fear and wrath.

He's the one responsible for all this misery. He's the one who kidnapped me and brought me to this palace, the one who captured Myron and Clio and Royad and Kaira. The one who didn't care whom he damaged on his path to revenge.

Slowly, he stalks closer, dark eyes like pits of night as they assess my disheveled state, the dirty clothes, the blade in my hand, and a smile tugs on his lips.

"You came alone? Where is the weakling king you love so much?"

Myron stays at the side of the hole, hidden while he gathers his power. I can feel it rising beneath my own skin as he readies to strike.

"You mean the fabulous male who saved his own people—including *your* sorry ass—and came back from the dead because the gods willed it so?" I put on my best smirk, praying to Shaelak and Vala to give me strength. If there is anything I've learned, it's that the Guardians didn't bother to do shit when I was drowning in despair, when I was fighting for my freedom, for my life. But Vala did. Vala guided me, gave me her power, gave me back Myron. And Shaelak bestowed upon me the power of the Crows. I only wish I could use it at will. So far, nothing stirs beneath my skin when I draw upon the energy that gave me feathers and made me shift. "Because if you're talking about him, I can assure you it'd be better for you if you never saw him again." I lift my knife, listening hard for every single tell of presences in the room where I can't see behind the gap framing Ephegos. With horror, I recognize the walls though. This is the room where I was strapped to a metal table, pierced with needles, and forced to watch Myron fight pain and helplessness. If I never see this room again, it's soon enough, but there is no way around it. Royad is still here, and I won't shy away from my fears.

Ephegos shifts, his fine sepia shirt crinkling as he adjusts his stance into a defensive one. A shadow moves behind the wall, tall and broad in a way that makes me believe I found Herinor. And the slow, rattling breaths—

Royad is still alive. I know on instinct that these are the failing lungs of my friend, and if we don't hurry, this sound will haunt me forever.

Myron is ready to strike, hand lifted at his side and focus on me. I incline my head an inch and step aside, making way for Myron to lunge, which he does. With powerful grace only a Crow can master, he lands in the opening, magic ripping free from his palm and soaring through the air. Swirling streaks like hot and cold air meeting in a visible glimmer brighten the air as I see his power for the first time.

A scream tears from Ephegos' throat as the blow hits its mark, but it's not Ephegos's skin and flesh the power pierces, it's the shield Ephegos conjured in front of him rattling with the impact. Sparks fly like when a hammer hits an anvil, and the sound is thunder and lightning cracking the sky.

Shit—

"You think I didn't see you there?" Ephegos shoots him a wide grin, that of a friend—and a traitor disguising himself with ease.

Myron comes to a halt in front of me, the muscles in his back flexing as he lifts his hand, and a glimmering, translucent layer wraps around both of us when he conjures a thicker shield of his own.

"I think it doesn't matter what you think." Myron's growl fills the room, and Herinor appears behind Ephegos, his gaze trained to the side where an edge of the torture table is visible, and hanging limply over it, Royad's tan arm—or what's left of the skin is tan. Most of it is raw flesh dripping blood.

My stomach twists as I try not to allow nausea to steal my focus. Inhaling through my nose, I take a step forward so I see better past Myron's shoulder and father into the room.

Katrijanov is there, and so are three guards, each of them grasping a sword and wearing various expressions of horror as they take in the Crow King on the loose. And by his side, their own king's betrothed. Separating us is the long, steel table covered in Royad's blood draining from his limp form. Tangles of brown hair stick to the side of his face as if someone turned him over from where his cheek had been pressing into his own blood and couldn't be bothered to smooth the strands away. The scar running upward from the corner of his mouth is bleeding, and on his other cheek, a mirror of it has been carved into his skin as if to mock the sign of weakness. His bare, bruised, and blood-streaked chest is still rising and falling but barely. I don't even want to think what cruel torture has created the pattern of wounds and bruises, or I'll forget every caution. If we don't get him out of here soon and heal him, he won't stand a chance. I've seen enough people die to know.

Myron knows too, for his head has turned to Royad as well, taking in his cousin with the ire of the gods on his features.

"You've come to take back your friend?" Ephegos asks even when we all know that's the only reason we're still here.

Myron doesn't deign to respond. Instead, he sends another blast of his power at Ephegos's shield, and I watch sparks spread all the way to the other side of the room. Ephegos has enclosed them all with a barrier of magic, and there is no way for us to get past unless we bring it down.

Fear and frustration fight for the upper hand as I draw upon the sources of water I've noted along the path, pulling the liquid toward me with silent concentration. If I manage to wash a hole into his power, I might get to do what I swore I'd do if I ever laid eyes on Ephegos again.

The thought of murdering another creature shouldn't excite me all that much, but this is Ephegos, and he deserves every last moment of suffering. It's the determination that keeps me going when the amounts of water feel like too much and my arm is tiring from the effort as I force the water to stay out of sight so I can spring it on him in a surprise attack while Myron does the debating. He's better at it anyway. I'd just provoke Ephegos, and he'd slit our throats instead of letting himself be sidetracked.

The strategy worked in the Seeing Forest after all.

Until Ephegos nearly killed me and Myron killed himself by saving me.

The panic clogging my throat is real, as is the pounding of my heart that drowns out all other sounds.

"It doesn't matter why I came as long as I get to rip out your throat before I leave."

It seems Myron isn't one for diplomacy today either.

Unfortunately, there is little we can do without risking Royad, whose throat is now at the tip of Katrijanov's blade. The Tavrasian general has used the moment of our regrouping to make the three strides toward the table and show us exactly how powerless we are. This won't be a big battle—or even a small one. This will be a test of willpower and patience, of wits and strength of magic. One wrong step and Royad is dead, it's implied in the way Katrijanov is glaring at me past Myron's shoulder with too much of that vicious glee I've seen flare there before when he sold me to the Crows, then when he came to see me at the Flame estate. He has something up his sleeve that we can't anticipate.

I wish I could speak to Myron mind to mind so I could tell him to watch out for the general, but the Crow is a master of battle. He knows how to keep an overview of a situation.

The three guards have inched closer to the door as if ready to bolt any moment, but Herinor is blocking their path, his mere presence inducing dread.

He's your ally, I remind myself even when I know that there is nothing he can do for me.

"You brought your little Crow woman, Myron." Ephegos appraises me as I step to Myron's side. I won't hide. I won't run. I won't balk from the danger. This is about all of us and I'd rather make myself useful before it's too late.

Besides, I can aim much better from here than from behind Myron's muscled body.

"She has a bone to pick with you just as much as I do."

That's putting it mildly.

I draw the water farther and farther in, moisture kissing my fingertips as I pull on the humidity in the air, the trickles of fluid from buckets in cells, and even the spill of Royad's blood on the floor where it seeps through the barrier Ephegos has put up. I don't care where it comes from as long as it hits Ephegos in the face.

"Is that so?" Ephegos cocks his head, features shifting into those of a bird, sharp beak and all, and hands turning into claws. His voice becomes a hiss, all black eyes tracking my movements as I shift on my legs for better balance.

Using the knife in my hand to distract his focus from my magic-wielding, mangled one, I take a slow step toward him. Myron follows, putting his shoulder between the Crow and me, and Katrijanov's hand twitches closer to Royad's throat.

"And there I thought I'd given it all to you. A kingdom, a king, a throne." Ephegos pauses, unsheathing his own sword as he studies the ire in my eyes.

"I already have a king." I stand beside Myron, my shoulder brushing his arm as I remind both of us who and what we are. Crow King and Queen. We are the Crow Court, the Crow Kingdom, the future of the Crows. If we fall—if Royad falls—everything Myron fought for will be in vain.

"Oh, but Myron is the past, Ayna. His court is dying. His people despise him, allying with the Flames his father once ordered killed. You're wasting your time with him. While Erina is the future. He might be only a human king, but his reign will expand to the magical lands in no time." There is more to this than what he's saying, but those few words are enough to put my self-control to the test.

"Erina is a monster, just like you." It's a challenge in itself to keep my voice level, but I manage that cold calculated tone I'm going for. If Myron can handle standing rooted to the spot, I can handle keeping my emotions off my face.

Letting my gaze drift across the room, I collect myself, but only for a brief moment until my eyes meet Herinor's, and the apprehension there speaks deep to my soul. He looks away, widening his stance as he takes in the guards in front of him instead. It would be easy for him to cut them down with one, powerful swipe of his sword. Easier even to knock them out with his magic. But would that count as aiding me? Would such a gesture cost him his life?

"Erina is a fool to believe he could ever take Askarea." Myron's tone is completely devoid of emotion. "You have lived through the Crow Wars. You know how powerful they are even in smaller numbers.

"Erina has found a way to speed up the production of the nullifying drug." The smirk on Ephegos's face makes my stomach turn. Why is the water taking so long to collect? Why isn't there more? At least, no one has noticed the thin trickle splitting from the pool of Royad's blood where crimson powder remains on our side of Ephegos's shield.

But if what he says is true... I don't want to think about what that means for the fairylands, for Clio and her family. For all of Eherea—because, once he has Askarea, who says he'll stop there. Cezux is human territory, as is the Southern

Continent. Easy targets once he commands an army of fairies by controlling their powers.

My stomach is full of lead, but I keep my head high and my magic flowing. The water is nearly there. I can feel it in my veins like a tide.

"Unfortunately, we're at an impasse here." *Don't look at Myron or at Royad. Don't look at Herinor. Keep your focus on Ephegos.* "I have no interest in a new husband—see, since I'm already married." To my mate. But I don't add that.

As if in response, the tattoo tingles with power. Myron is raising his own defenses once more. His defenses and the sort of power that can blow up walls. A memory of explosions in the Crow Palace floats into my mind, and I wonder if this is something all Crows can do and it has nothing to do with the Flames. Perhaps it was the breaking of the curse that gave the Crows back their full powers and they simply weren't able to handle them properly.

That would mean Ephegos wields that same magic.

It's a little late to worry if it was a good idea to come here at all. There's no running now. We need to push through the barrier and grab Royad before his life is forfeit. That will leave only one of us to fight with our full attention and both hands free on our way out. A part of me wishes he'd thought it through better.

"Not yet." Ephegos is still smirking, the bastard. "But you will feel a dramatic urge to marry him once Myron is back on this table"—Ephegos taps the empty metal surface beside him where Myron's blood is still crusted below layers of that of Silas and Astorian. What kind of sick person does that—"and your only way to spare him the pain will be to say *yes* to Erina of Tavras."

I shudder at the mere thought of it. Of course, Myron dives right through the threat, demanding answers rather than cowering with fear. "What do you get out of it, Ephegos?"

That's the one question I've been dying to get an answer to. It can't be merely the reestablishing of the Crow Court as their king. Ephegos is too power-hungry to be satisfied with whatever few Crows are left to rule.

Claws bending into fishlike gestures, Ephegos steps closer to the magical barrier. I swear I can see the air shift, a sign that his power isn't impenetrable everywhere. There are weaknesses, and I need to use them—after I take down Katrijanov. Because I can't touch Ephegos as long as Katrijanov holds a blade to Royad's throat. My friend will be dead before the water reaches the Crow. It has to be the general first.

"You are too short-sighted for a king, Myron." Ephegos lifts his fists at his sides. "That's always been your problem, or the Crows would have followed you until the end. But they didn't. They followed *me*. Even your friend Herinor followed *me*."

I try not to pay attention to the way Herinor shrinks an inch or how Myron's muscles bulge in his arm. It's only a matter of moments until this situation blows up—literally, if Ephegos doesn't hold his beak.

A shudder runs down my spine at the sight of his feathered face, his sharp claws, his featherless arms where burn marks mar his skin. His jacket has disappeared the way all their clothes disappear when the Crows shift into their bird forms—a trick I yet need to master or I'll end up naked every single time I shift. If I ever shift again.

"Whoever followed you is doomed." Myron's tone is dead ice in a colorless desert, and I believe Herinor's eyes are widening, but I don't allow myself to take a closer look.

"So here is my proposal for the two of you. You give yourselves up. Royad goes free. I don't track down the Askarean general and won't kill Silas purposefully. How does that sound?" With a twitch of his claw, he has the barrier withdrawing a few inches toward him, as if tightening the shield when he knows he'll need his strength for offensive magic, the glimmering dimming into a visual hum. Royad and the table he's strapped to are still behind the wards though.

The wards…

Our magic started unweaving the wards on our kingdom, and Crows started roaming the fairylands again.

It's been a while since I was told about how the Crows managed to escape the Seeing Forest first, even when wards had been placed around it to lock them in by the Askarean fairies, but now that it sprang to my mind, I can't ignore the urge to test the theory quickly forming in my mind.

If Herinor is right and Shaelak made me something resembling a Crow—the first female Crow since the curse—that sort of magic might apply to me as well as to the rest of the Crows in this room. The shield is thin enough where Royad's blood is leaking through. If only I could break it a few inches wide and sneak the water kissing my fingertips into the enemy part of the chamber, I could tear Katrijanov's knife from his hands.

I don't wait for Myron to continue his debating. Instead, I pray to Shaelak that he gifts me quick mastery of those powers he bestowed upon me and shove my magic against the weakest point in Ephegos's shield.

The wall of energy thrums at my invisible touch, pushing back and sizzling, the glimmer intensifying, but Ephegos doesn't seem to notice what I'm trying to do, and I call that a win. The longer my efforts remain undetected, the better the chance I have of taking down at least one of them before they openly attack.

A sideways glance from Myron informs me *he* noticed, though, and he twirls his fingers, sending a wave of power at Ephegos regardless of the chances of simply blasting through. "Never."

It's a distraction, though. While his brute power flares in front of the traitor's face, a thinner, more subtle thread of his magic twines with mine, guiding and stroking it until it reaches the spot in front of the table where the wards are thinning. Like a delicate blade, his power peels back layer after layer of the shield while simultaneously keeping Ephegos engaged in a conversation I've stopped paying attention to. What use is it listening to someone whose sole goal is to undermine you until he can trap you again?

The string of water tickles my palm, straining to be released, but I don't allow it past my shadow. It's too soon, and I don't want to risk Royad.

Soon, I tell it, stroking it into submission.

The glimmer fades right beneath the torture table,

forming an opening for my magic, and I almost stumble at the strain of keeping control while simultaneously pushing a magic I am only beginning to familiarize myself with. I don't wait for Myron to pull back his power but lunge. A streak of water rushes in a straight line like fire blazing along a trail of oil to the hole we've peeled into the shield. Myron strikes at the same time, but he chooses to attack with his sword, shoving his straight against the barrier right where Ephegos's heart is waiting to be silenced. It buys me a moment for the water to reach Katrijanov before my attack is noticed, but not enough to make it to the general's hands.

Ephegos blocks Myron's blow with an earsplitting crack, and I almost stumble as Myron shakes with the strain of pushing against the traitor's force. Katrijanov's eyes are on the wet trail on the ground, and he shifts his knife even closer to Royad's throat in a warning, a trickle of blood running from the tan, grime-covered skin right beneath the male's stubbled jaw. One wrong breath—

Focus. I need to *focus,* or we will all soon be strapped to a table and sliced open.

The image of that potential outcome infuses me with more courage than I thought I was capable of, and I go for Katrijanov's calves instead, wrapping my water around the back of his knees and tugging hard enough to bring an exclamation of surprise from his throat as he sways—sways but doesn't fall. The blade slides down Royad's throat, cutting along the front.

Shit. *Shit-shit-shit.*

Blood gurgles from the Crow's throat, and I could swear, his lids flutter once from the pain. He has moments like this. If I don't get to him in time, his life is over.

With all I have, I tear at the general's legs, but this time, he's prepared.

"Herinor," he shouts for the warrior, and Guardians be damned, he follows the order, coming up to the general's side, still avoiding my eyes as he stares down at the male bleeding out on the table.

He doesn't lift a finger to fight me, though. All he does is place a firm hand under the general's shoulder to stabilize him. What I notice a mere moment later is Herinor's other hand drifting to Royad's arm closest to his side of the table and placing the back of his sword-clutching fist against it.

Before I can see if he's trying to heal his fellow Crow or simply comfort him during this hour of death, power explodes on Ephegos's side of the chamber, and debris rains from the ceiling where Myron's power blasted through the magical barrier.

"Grab him and run," Myron orders—not me, I realize as I clutch the edge of the wall in hopes of catching my balance.

My water is still working to bring down the general, but at least, his blade is out of reach from Royad's throat. If Herinor would let go, he'd fall easily, but the Crow is standing there with war in his eyes as he makes his choice about whether to risk his life by allowing my efforts to come to fruition or to follow Myron's order. Letting Katrijanov drop could be interpreted as aiding me, and that…

I don't look as he hesitantly slides his hand away from the general then presses his mouth into a thin line of resolve, darting to cut the binds at Royad's wrists and ankles before lifting him into his arms and bolting to our side of the room.

"If you set one foot out that door, I'll make sure you don't live to enjoy the freedom you seek so desperately," Ephegos shouts his warning, but Herinor's steps don't falter as he brushes past me in the blasted doorway, taking Royad hopefully far, far away from here and healing him.

"Coward!" Ephegos's voice echoes through the room, but I quietly think that Herinor is braver than any of us to risk his life for us and that—if his bargain doesn't take him down on his way out—I need to thank him if we ever make it out of here.

Before I can finish the thought, Katrijanov struggles free from my grasp, reaching not for the blade he dropped but for the small syringe on the sideboard behind him. "What are you waiting for," he yells at the three guards by the door who look like they are about to piss their neat uniform pants any moment. "Grab the king's fiancée."

FORTY-FIVE

AYNA

They spring into motion like they've been slapped in the face. It's not their brutal swords I'm afraid of, though, but the serum in Katrijanov's syringe. If this is the magic nullifying drug, I can't let him come anywhere near me, or I won't stand a chance if he injects me, and I can tell by the glint in his eyes as he approaches me that he intends to do exactly that.

Beside me, Myron is fighting, his power whipping through the room, keeping Ephegos busy. Sparks glimmer in the air where magic hits magic, raining down like falling stars. I'd marvel at the sight were there not four armed men approaching me with murder in their eyes.

Without a second thought, I tug on my water, sending the string like a lasso around the first guard's neck and tugging hard enough to bring him down. The second man stumbles over in an almost comical manner that binds my attention a moment too long. The third guard is almost upon me, and his blade is much longer than the knife I wield, giving him more reach and an unmistakable advantage. I'm a heartbeat too slow, reeling in my power to slap him off trajectory, and his blade hits mine with too much force for me to be able to block it. Steel slides against steel as he pushes back, and the sword reaches my shoulder, piercing with ease through the linen shirt covering my skin.

Pain explodes where he shoves deeper into my flesh, and I bite back a scream. I can't draw Myron's attention, or I'll get him killed. Ephegos seems to have better control over his powers than Myron, even if he isn't as strong as my Crow.

I struggle against the man's force, drawing upon my Crow senses and the strength buried deep within me if Shaelak gave me all of a Crow's power.

The man grunts as I push him off, slinging my water around his neck and pulling taut as he lashes out with his sword again.

Guardians, it hurts. Blood streams down my arm in a river of crimson, but I don't let go of the water I direct to snap the man's neck. I drop the corpse and send my water toward Katrijanov, who has come within reach with his unholy syringe.

"We need to get out," I call to Myron, who's engaged in a battle of his own now, throwing blast after blast at Ephegos. There is no shame in running if it means we'll get out alive.

"Run." Myron's voice is strained from the effort of holding onto his power when he's so clearly still recovering from the nullifying drug. His power is draining fast, and if I leave him to fight on his own, he might not walk away.

"Not without you." I don't dare look his way as I sling the string of water around Katrijanov's neck once, twice, and pull hard enough to break bone. A sickening crunch tells me something broke in his spine, but the victory is short-lived. Just as I want to sigh a breath of relief, Katrijanov tilts forward, grabbing for me as he falls out of my magic's grasp. I see the needle coming toward me in an inevitable path. All I can do is duck away, but I'm not fast enough.

Myron is, though, his massive form sliding between the general and me, and a grunt tells me he took the impact. The man isn't the problem, he could lift him easily, but Katrijanov's needle made it into Myron's biceps as he clutches onto the male, legs failing.

"Fuck—"

I couldn't say it any better. In reflex, I step around Myron, ramming my knife into Katrijanov's neck, but it's too late. Half of the drug has made it into Myron's arm.

Shoving the man off Myron, who's suddenly unstable on his legs, I rip the syringe from Katrijanov's dead hand, careful not to squeeze in more of the liquid.

457

Of course, they have the serum down here if they are handling fairies. After what happened with me, Ephegos would never risk allowing his prisoners to go undrugged.

"Can you walk?" Discarding the syringe, I drape Myron's arm over my shoulder.

He staggers back toward the gap in the wall, eyes never leaving Ephegos, who's preparing to strike again, magic glimmering at his fingertips.

"Don't run, Ayna," Ephegos shouts from between a broken shelf and a split metal table, dust settling where Myron's power last hit. He is still on his feet, ready to wield his magic.

I don't even try to wonder what will happen if I don't get Myron out of here right now.

"Erina will be disappointed not to have a Milevishja wife… You know, just in case another Milevishja pops up who claims to be of the royal bloodline."

I ignore him, setting one tired foot in front of the other as I drag Myron into the corridor. If only I knew how to build one of those shields, I could ward off Ephegos's next strike.

Silver flashes through the room as he sends his magic flying, and I barely manage to yank Myron out of the way. My injured shoulder screams as I take his weight with it. Myron tries to keep his balance, but the drug is fast-working, and he's already swaying. Not long and he'll black out.

"Come on…" I pull him along, fighting to keep him moving while simultaneously searching for the water string I dropped alongside Katrijanov—may he never rise again—but can barely sense my own magic.

Ephegos is on our heels, slower than expected with all the strength he's used fighting Myron or simply reluctant to injure us in earnest. If he truly means what he said, he'll keep both of us alive—me to marry Erina for breeding little royals, and Myron to make sure I play along. Perhaps dying is the better option.

A groan of pain escapes Myron as Ephegos's next blast sears his shoulder right where his inked mark spreads on his skin, and I almost drop him as heat singes me in the same place like the mark connects us physically rather than just our souls.

We need to fucking run. But my feet are sluggish, and Myron's are failing.

"If you get us out of here, I promise I'll consider converting to the Neredynian faith," I whisper to Vala, or Shaelak, or any Neredynian god who'd hear me.

A glance over my aching shoulder informs me that Ephegos has made it across rubble and debris. Blood runs down his forehead where rocks hit when they rained from the ceiling, but he is in control of his limbs, and that's more than Myron and I can say for ourselves.

Not far... I can see the steel bars of the cells ahead, yet the exit is a lifetime away, and if Ephegos chases us at that speed, he'll catch up long before we can ever dream of climbing out the hole Myron tore into the outer wall, let alone escape into the city.

The corridor is swarming with guards—and they are wearing sepia.

Erina knows what's going on down here, or he wouldn't have sent his palace guards.

"There is nowhere for you to run, Ayna," Ephegos hisses.

I don't deign him with a look. Cleary, there isn't. He's blocking our way back, and in front of us, rows of guards are closing in.

We're fucked.

"We need to make it to the cells," Myron whispers, head lolling as he stumbles one step after the other. He doesn't have long. "Get him to the cells."

It takes me a moment to understand, but as I do, hope flares in my chest.

Steeling myself with a deep breath, I call upon my magic, dragging the thin rope of water toward me.

It's a hassle, costing me more than I have left to give, but I hold on, snapping the water like a whip along the corridor.

Horror in their faces, guards leap out of its way, crashing into the iron bars fencing the corridor. I don't stop to count how many. Too many for sure. It's an impossibility for me to fight them all and win, but I keep pushing, alternating with the lashes toward the front and the back, keeping both the guards and Ephegos at bay—for now. As long as I have a breath in me, I'll fight to defend Myron, even if it means I'll burn out. I won't lose him again.

The wound in my shoulder makes it difficult to wield the water, and I've long given up on my knife. It's up to me and my strength now.

Unless a miracle happens.

We inch forward, Ephegos on our heels and the guards trying to cage us in, but the only cage is my fear of losing Myron, and that's the strongest driver pushing me past my breaking point.

I break, and I break, and I break, power draining from me as I aggregate every last drop of water in this Godsforsaken dungeon. From the cells and from the guards' blood, it creeps to me, weaving into a stronger rope, threading itself around me as I call it to my aid. My skin tingles and heats, the pain originating in the tattoo no longer punishing but a reward, reminding me what I am fighting for.

I count the bars instead of the dead guards dropping where my magic severs their necks, and I wonder if this is Shaelak's power or that of Vala—water or Crow magic— or both. My legs are unstable as I take more and more of Myron's weight. He's about to pass out, and I'm not strong enough to carry him. I won't leave him behind either, and we're outnumbered.

"I love you, Ayna." Myron's voice kisses my cheek where his head rests against mine, his hair dangling into my field of vision.

"Don't you dare say goodbye." The anger in my voice surprises me more than anyone. "We're getting out of here." I push forward, one agonizing step after the other, Myron nearly dead weight. "Stay awake. Do you hear me? Fucking. Stay. Awake." Because the moment he closes his eyes, we've lost. "I'm not going back to prison because you need a nap."

It's a weak attempt at humor, and the smile hurts, turning into a grimace as one of the guards I'm about to cut down reaches for a knife instead of his sword—and hurls it right at my mangled wrist.

I've never known pain like this. Not even when they broke my arm on the way to Fort Perenis—not when they let it heal

461

without setting the bones. Not when I was about to die in the Seeing Forest. The blade slices clean through tendons and bone, and I nearly drop Myron with my other arm. My scream tears through the dungeon. If Erina hadn't known I was here, he would know now.

But he doesn't need to come down to this dark, filthy part of his palace. He has his loyal Crow friend to make sure I won't escape.

Myron grunts his protest as I try to tug him forward, ignoring the agony as best I can as I tuck my hand to my side. My magic is gone, snapped like my bones and ligaments, and retreated into that dormant place inside of me. I doubt I have the strength to call it back.

"Stop!" Ephegos bellows, and the guards freeze immediately. "King Erina wants her alive."

The guard who hit me lowers the second knife he is now pinching between his fingers, and I heave a breath. A few feet ahead, I can make out the silver light where Myron tore a hole in Silas's cell. So close. If I can push a little farther…

My knees buckle, and I catch myself against the nearest bars, Myron sliding off my shoulder. He's still awake, but his eyelids are drooping. "Don't fall asleep." It isn't more than a whisper. I've got nothing left. Not even a voice.

Myron's head rests against my side, his ocean eyes speaking of a freedom that isn't meant for us. My heart aches for him, for the king who came to save me, and whom I couldn't save, and a tear wets my cheek as I realize we're not getting out.

The air reeks of blood and dirt and my own failure as I hold Myron's gaze for just one moment. One moment longer before they'll put us back into cells.

"I'm sorry." Because there's nothing else I can say.

The forgiveness in Myron's eyes almost steals what's left of my composure, and I focus on him and nothing else. This final moment where my blood-caked fingers can tangle in his hair. Where his warmth seeps through my clothes. Where I can feel his heartbeat beneath my palm. Myron's lids flutter, blocking the view of those beautiful eyes, and my heart shatters.

It takes about three painful breaths until Ephegos's feathered face appears before me, a gleeful expression so different from the loathing in his eyes shaping his again-human features.

"It's over, Ayna." His magic snakes around me as he weaves another one of those barriers, locking us in, and I would have missed the soft cracks and thuds had movement not caught my attention over Ephegos's shoulder. One by one, the guards drop dead, their necks snapping at Herinor's silent hand. My heart stutters, eyes shuttering as I try to figure out if I'm seeing things from the blood loss and pain. It wouldn't be the first time my mind checked out because reality is simply too much to handle.

Ephegos reaches into his tattered jacket, extracting a set of manacles. "Myron isn't going anywhere, but let's make sure *you* don't get any ideas, Ayna, shall we?"

My spit lands right beneath his eye, and I laugh in his face. It's more a croak and sounds the slightest bit unhinged, but what do I have to lose?

Wiping his sleeve over his cheek, Ephegos studies me with hatred. I don't think I've ever seen his mask slip so entirely, but it fits. I prefer the honest detestation to the false grins and sugary words. Let's call things by their name.

"We shall nothing." I kick out as he grabs my hand, trying to close one manacle around my wrist, and my heel connects with his shoulder, making him drop my hand, which I ball into a fist and throw at his nose in a healthy punch.

My knuckles protest as I keep my hand curled tightly, ready to throw another one, but Ephegos is cursing and spitting blood. He hasn't noticed Herinor, and that's the only hope I have—bind his focus on me so the male can kill off the guards one by one. How he keeps them from screaming, I wish I knew. If I live to tell the tale, I'll ask him to teach me how to do that because the panic in the guards' eyes as they notice the trail of bodies Herinor is leaving in his wake tells me they didn't hear him coming either.

He's two thirds up the corridor, the silver light promising freedom crowning his head and shoulders, and had I not known exactly who he was, I could have believed one of the Guardians has joined us in this humble setting. But Herinor's growl makes its way through the space, eventually drawing all attention—including Ephegos's.

Crimson spittle runs down Ephegos's chin as he whirls around, weighing his options between pinning me down and fighting Herinor.

"See who's returned," he hisses over his shoulder, grabbing my punch-ready fist with an iron hold, and doesn't let go, no matter how hard I tug—which is no longer much.

What's left of my magic is a cool pond in the depths of my being, unreachable, similar to the way the drug made it disappear; only the awareness lingers. And my senses—

I can smell the freedom waving from Herinor's direction as he marches up, slicing through skin and bone, flesh and sinew. It doesn't matter how many guards stand in his way; he wipes them out like a male on a mission.

He's a few steps away now, his gaze hard on Ephegos as he marches up to us, throwing up a shield behind him to block out the remaining guards.

"You know you can't kill me—not in this world. You'll die if you lay a hand on me. And you most certainly can't save her." Ephegos reminds Herinor of the terms of his bargain. I hadn't known a no-killing-Ephegos deal was included, but I should have guessed, or Herinor would have long slit the fucking traitor's throat in his sleep. I can see it now—the ruthless brutality he warned me of that first day in the torture chamber at the Flame estate, the menace pounding in his veins.

"I might just try my luck." Herinor stops behind Ephegos, sword aiming at Ephegos's shoulder and his magic ready at his fingertips glimmering in silver sparks.

"No—" We didn't go through all of this just to have another person sacrifice himself.

Herinor's eyes fully meet mine for the first time since we entered the dungeon, and the resolve I find there almost brings me to tears. He means it. He'd give his life to get both of us out—his king and queen.

"Royad?" It's all I need to say for him to understand what I'm asking.

He curtly dips his chin.

Royad is alive and safe. At least, the best ones among us got out. Clio and Kaira and Royad…

All but Myron. He's the last of the good ones.

A trickle of magic wraps around my injured wrist, leading it to Ephegos's waiting one, and the steel manacle falls into place regardless of my injury. Trying not to black out at the fresh assault of agony, I grit my teeth.

"Don't fucking touch her." Herinor's gaze is that of a male ready to murder—again—and I don't need to think one beat to know there is only one outcome to this if he is dead-set on saving us: we'll all be dead. And Herinor will pave the way straight through Eroth's Veil.

"It's all right." Every word hurts, but I force them out anyway. I turn to Herinor, ignoring the way Ephegos forces the manacles even tighter. "Just get Myron out. I'll be all right." Because helping Myron won't break his bargain. He's done it before.

Whether it's the plea in my voice or the panic in my eyes, I can't tell, but he blows out a breath, ignoring the guards hacking at his invisible shield with their meek swords. He sheaths his own blade and side steps Ephegos, reaching for Myron's limp form, and my chest tightens at the sight of him, defenseless and pale. The light tingling in the inked mark on my shoulder is the only thing reassuring me that he's still alive.

"Don't you dare." Ephegos throws a blast of magic at the male, but Herinor takes it with grace, grunting at the impact of power on his shield, not more than swaying. "I'm the King of Crows. You have sworn loyalty to *me*."

Herinor sweeps Myron up in his strong arms, careful not to jostle him too much in the process, and I bemoan the warmth seeping into my skin where Myron's face rested against me. "I might have sworn loyalty to you; that doesn't keep me from saving my friend." His eyes find mine one last time, and I manage to force myself to turn away from Myron's face to meet his gaze. "I can't save you, Ayna. You're on your own."

Sweat beads Herinor's forehead, and his chest is heaving labored breaths. Something is definitely at work as he finds his way around the constraints of his bargain. It pains me to watch, and yet, I can't look away as Herinor takes a careful step toward the back of the dungeon where starlight beckons.

Nothing happens. He doesn't stumble, doesn't fall, doesn't disintegrate or dissipate into crimson mist.

Ephegos curses as another one of his blows scrapes against Herinor's mighty shield, and there is nothing he can do—nothing except shout after the male walking away. "You will regret this, Herinor. You'll regret you ever even considered betraying me."

Herinor stops and turns, Myron's head rolling against his shoulder as he lifts it in a casual shrug. "I wouldn't expect any less from a traitor." He inclines his head in a mock bow to Ephegos before turning to me. "It's been an honor, my queen."

The last word comes out half-choked, and I imagine I see a trail of blood trickling from the side of his mouth, but he spins around and continues down the corridor, not even bothering to lash out at the remaining guards with his magic when his shield is keeping them at bay.

I can't stop staring. I don't blink the entire time until he reaches the very end of the dungeon where he slips through the hole in Silas's cell and melts into the shadows. The starlight flickers for a moment, but I only know they truly made it out when the guards stumble like the wall they've been leaning against melts away, and they charge after the two males with their blades ready.

A part of me thanks Shaelak that those guards weren't equipped with the magic-dampening weapon that was used to capture Myron in the first place, but before I can wonder how far the two males will make it—if they will find Royad and the others—a fist connects with my jaw, and the world turns into a black pit where not even my Crow senses can help me.

FORTY-SIX

AYNA

S oft light filters into the room in hues of buttery yellow and whipped cream when I open my eyes. It's nothing compared to the clarity of my senses when I woke after being infused with the antidote to Ephegos's drug, but it's better than my pure human senses used to be. The smell of flowers, earth, and rich, expensive wood blends with the odor of sweat, blood, and fear, and my body is heavy like rock—just not as durable. The pain in my shoulder where Katrijanov stabbed me has reduced to a dull throb, a reminder of what happened, and the ache in my chest sets in instantly when I realize where I am.

Hardwood supports my weight, and fresh air fills my lungs, enhancing the soreness in every last muscle and the gaping hole where my heart has been ripped out—because, no matter that I begged Herinor to take Myron and run, I'm still here. I'm back in my room at Erina's palace, my dirty, blood-caked shirt and pants proof of the battle we fought—and lost.

I'm here, discarded on the floor like an item to be used later. And my magic is gone. Not one flicker of power responds when I reach into the depths of myself to draw upon Vala's water magic or the Crow powers Shaelak gifted me. An unnecessary glance at my arm confirms that my shirt has been shoved up and I've been injected with the drug once more—as does the nausea rising in my stomach. It hits like a wave, and I don't make it to the bathing room in time, so I dry-heave onto the polished wood, braced on my hands and knees—and curse when the wound on my wrist breaks open with a stinging pain. I sink back on my haunches, waiting for my body to stop revolting before I scramble to my feet and sway toward the door.

If I'm lucky, the guards will have mercy on me in my state and let me go.

I place my good hand on the door. Who am I kidding? If any of them had a heart, they'd have helped me flee long before. They'd have let me go when I tried to sneak past them in my early days at this palace.

Retrieving my hand, I stagger to the window. There is no room for tears when I need to find escape. A blurred vision would only make it more difficult to aim at their hearts when I eventually face them on my way out. Because I will. Find. A. Way.

I'm not staying in this palace to be used. I'm not staying to pop out little royals for Erina and most definitely not to be a tool for Ephegos's vengeance.

I'm the Queen of Crows, and what's left of my people needs me—as does my mate.

"I'll find you, Myron. I'll get out of here, and then I'll find you."

The door creaks open as I reach the window just to find guards with bows and arrows stationed beneath it—and around the gardens as if they expect me to hop onto the windowsill and fly away.

If I had access to my magic, I just might.

"She's awake," the man in a sepia palace guard uniform who enters the room reports through the open door, stepping aside to make room for three more guards ... and Erina.

I'm sick all over again, hands flying to my sides for weapons that aren't there, and that new sense of panic floods me at the sight of King Erina of Tavras, an expression of deepest dismay on his features. He runs a hand across his short-cropped hair then along his perfectly shaved jaw as if searching for imperfection.

His polished boots are too loud, his theatrical sigh too deep, his stare... His stare is that of a man with vengeance on his mind. He pulls up a bland smile so fast I almost believe I imagined the rest.

"Welcome back, Wolayna." He inclines his head in a mockery of respect, and it costs me not to spit at him. I grab the edge of the windowsill with my good hand instead, ignoring the blood trickling from my injured one.

I'm back at the beginning—one hand useless, locked in a room with a man who believes I deserve worse than death, and this time, there is no getting out.

Not unless I heal and get off the drug they injected me with.

I settle for sneering, unsure if I would get out a single word if I tried to speak.

"Ephegos informed me of your … lovely company last night. I must say I regret losing our other prisoners, though." He makes a dramatic pause as if waiting for me to ask, but I don't need to. I know exactly who he's talking about. Myron got out. Royad, Silas, and Astorian got out. They all got out, and there is nothing he can do to hurt them. "I hate for them to miss the wedding."

"I won't marry you." The words are out before I can make a conscious decision to speak them, and they sound exactly as scratchy and hoarse as I feel. He no longer has leverage over me.

Pulling his smile wider, Erina stalks toward me, assessing my state with the distaste of a king born with a golden spoon in his mouth. "See, this is where you're wrong, Wolayna. I may no longer have your mate to control you—yes, I know everything about who he is to you." His smile turns into a smirk, into something more evil. "But I have something better."

He lifts a hand, and one of the guards makes way, allowing Odja to enter the room. The man meets my gaze with a mixture of pity and disgust and starts reading from the piece of parchment in his hands.

"*To the people of Tavras. I, King Erina Latroy Jelnedyn, am delighted to inform you that I have found and retrieved the lost heir to the royal Milevishja line. After the unspeakable acts of violence of past generations, I have decided to pardon Wolayna Milevishja and take her as my bride instead.*"

Odja lowers the parchment, glancing at the king, who nods then paces even closer until he's mere steps away.

"I don't care if the people of Tavras know who I am. If anything, it will hurt you if they support me." I mean it.

Erina merely shakes his head. "I thought you should know… The pamphlet was sent to every last corner of my kingdom. There is no place you can seek refuge without people recognizing you now that I've distributed your por-trait"—he gestures to Odja, who holds up the page so I can see, and I find myself staring at my own face—"and when your mate hears that I'm still going through with the plan, he'll rush right back to save you."

"He won't." Because Herinor and Royad will make sure he stays alive and safe. And he isn't safe trying to peel me from the claws of a man who owns a weapon that can send his powers to sleep. He'd need an army to get me out.

My stomach folds into a knot.

"Oh the things fairy males will do to save their mates…" A knowing smile on Erina's lips that seems to be actual amusement. He meets my eyes, expression going cold. "No one escapes my dungeon and lives, Wolayna. I'll make sure the same applies to your friends and your mate." He tilts his head, scanning my appearance once more. "The wedding's tomorrow, dove. I'm sure we can patch you up enough to fit you into a wedding gown. And to make sure you say *yes*, we don't need Myron the Valiant." He nods at the guard closest to him. "She'll do."

The man signals out the door, and a tall, slender figure in servant clothes and a blindfold stumbles into the room.

I gasp, but her name I think only in my head. *"Kaira."*

Before she can turn toward the direction of my mental call, the guard pulls her back out the door by her bound hands until not even my physical shouts can reach her.

He turns on his heels, retreating from the room with the guards following suit, while I stare with horror, unable to produce one single word.

The door closes, a lock clicks, and the chasm in my chest tears open so wide I think I might fall apart.

The scream I loose rips through the room like a sharp blade through a curtain. Birds flee from nearby branches, and on the chandelier, a single crystal shatters.

The story continues in Claws of Death.
Coming November 2024...

MORE BOOKS IN THE ALCUNAIRE

THE WINGS OF INK SERIES
Fall of the Wild Ray: A Wings of Ink Prequel
Wings of Ink
Heart of Night
Claws of Death

THE QUARTER MAGE SERIES
The Quarter Mage
The Hour Mage
The Never Mage
The Ever Mage

THE SHATTERED KINGDOM SERIES
Shattered Kingdom
Wicked Crown
Shadow Rule
Lost Towers
Secret Court
Dark Refuge
Reborn Throne
Fatespun

ACKNOWLEDGEMENTS

I have to admit that even after writing over thirty books, every new first in a series is daunting. No matter how exciting it is to begin something new, the fear of getting lost on that journey is real.

Writing a story like this wouldn't be possible without the support of my family. Thank you Mark and Rafael for being understanding and patient when my head is stuck in Eherea all over again.

Every writer needs a team behind them. Mine is incredible and tireless when it comes to diving into my stories and finding all the little things I'd usually miss. Thank you Kath for being there basically 24/7 for my writing emergencies. Emily, you know I appreciate your perspective on the worlds I'm building. I know I wrote the right plot twists once you start yelling at me. Thank you for finding those little details where things don't line up, Beba. You're like a bloodhound ploughing through my manuscript. Margot, for always asking the right questions, and for those little gifs representing your reactions while reading. Thank you all for coming along on this new journey long before anyone else ever read a word of it. Dawn, you're a source of inspiration when it comes to my comma drama. Belle, for the countless times I message you to quickly ask which version a sentence sounds better.

Thank you Barbara for our regular working breakfasts. Your persistence during the most difficult of times has been an inspiration to me. I want to be like you when I grow up.

Kathi, for voice memos and coffees in bookshops while we relish the presence of the written word.

To the amazing Royals Guards. Thank you for being on my team. You are the core of lovelies that are my readers. When I write, you are in my thoughts. Your enthusiasm and support is what keeps me going when I'm exhausted or can't see the end of the tunnel. I can't thank you enough for making my book releases something to celebrate.

There are so many people I should be thanking at this point that it would take another four hundred pages, so in order to keep it simple: Thank you everyone who ever touched my life with a good word, a kind gesture, or a moment of peace when everything turned into a cacophony.

Last but not least, to my readers: My work is nothing without your imagination. With your amazing minds, you bring my stories to life. Thank you for taking a chance on me and my books.

Can't get enough of Angelina's worlds?

Scan this code to find more books by Angelina J. Steffort:

About the Author

"Chocolate fanatic, milk-foam enthusiast and huge friend of the southern sting-ray. Writing is an unexpected career-path for me."

Angelina J. Steffort is a bestselling, award-winning Austrian novelist, best known for her Wings of Ink series and her Shattered Kingdom series. With over twenty YA and adult fantasy and paranormal romance books under her belt, Angelina is far from done with inventing and exploring new worlds. That might have something to do with her passion for following the narrative of new characters and getting surprised by the twists they spin on her stories. Angelina has multiple educational backgrounds including engineering, business, music, and acting.

Currently, Angelina lives in Vienna, Austria, with her husband and her son.

Find Angelina on social media as @ajsteffort.

Scan this code to subscribe to Angelina's newsletter:

PRONUNCIATION GUIDE
Character Names

Adrian Katrijanov: A-dree-an KAH-tree-yah-nov

Astorian: Us-TOH-ree-an

Cliophera Clarette Tarie Amaryll Saphalea de Pauvre (Clio): Clee-oh-phee-rah Clah-rett Tah-rie Ah-mah-ryll Sah-PHAH-lee-ah deh POH-vreh (Clee-oh)

Ephegos: Eh-phee-gus

Erina Latroy Jelnedyn: EH-ree-nah LA-troy Yel-neh-dyn

Harian Aleji: Ha-ree-an Ah-jey-djee

Herinor: HEH-ree-nor

Jeseida: Dje-say-dah

Julj: Yoolsh

Kaira: Kay-ruh

Myron: My-ron

Royad: Roy-ad

Recienne Oilvier Gustine Univer Emestradassus de Pauvre: Reh-Syen Ol-liv-yeh Gü-Stin Oo-Nee-Vehr Eh-Mehs-trah-Dahs-sus deh POH-vreh

Odja: Oh-dya

Sariell: Sah-ree-ell

Sejen: See-jen

Wolayna (Ayna) Milevishja: Woh-LI-nah (I-nah) Mee-leh-veesh-jah

WORLD

Aceleau: Ah-Seh-Loh
Ansoli: Un-soh-lee
Askarea: Us-KAH-reh-ah
Brolli: Brol-ly
Cezux: Dje-Zush
Cliffs of Ansoli: Cliffs of Un-soh-lee
Dunai: Doo-NAY
Eherea: Ee-HEE-ree-ah
Eroth: Eh-roth
Fort Perenis: Fort Peh-reh-niss
Horn of Eroth: Horn of Eh-roth
Jezuin: Jeh-Zoo-in ("J" as in "jelly")
Ledrynx: Led-rynx
Leeneae: Lee-nee-ae
Meer: Meer
Plithian Plains: Pli-thee-un Plains
Ret Relah: Reht Reh-luh
Shaelak: SHAE-lak
Tavras: TUH-vrahs
Vala: Vah-la

Made in the USA
Las Vegas, NV
26 March 2025

20155102R00288